The Darkest Shade of Honor

The Honor Series
By Robert N. Macomber

At the Edge of Honor
Point of Honor
Honorable Mention
A Dishonorable Few
An Affair of Honor
A Different Kind of Honor
The Honored Dead

The Darkest Shade of Honor

A Novel of
Cmdr. Peter Wake, U.S.N.
(eighth in the Honor Series)

Robert N. Macomber

Pineapple Press, Inc.
Sarasota, Florida

Inquiries should be addressed to:

Pineapple Press, Inc.
P.O. Box 3889
Sarasota, Florida 34230

www.pineapplepress.com

Library of Congress Cataloging-in-Publication Data

Macomber, Robert N., 1953-
The darkest shade of honor : a novel of Cmdr. Peter Wake, U.S.N. / Robert N. Macomber. -- 1st ed.
   p. cm. -- (The honor series ; 8)
ISBN 978-1-56164-465-0 (alk. paper)
1. Wake, Peter (Fictitious character)--Fiction. 2. United States. Navy--Officers--Fiction. 3. United States--History, Naval--19th century--Fiction. 4. Cuba--History--1878-1895--Fiction. 5. Key West (Fla.)--History--19th century--Fiction. I. Title.
PS3613.A28D37 2010
813'.6--dc22
                                        2009043560

First Edition
10 9 8 7 6 5 4 3 2 1

Design by Shé Hicks

This novel is dedicated to

Nancy Ann Glickman

who taught me about the stars in the Heavens above
the creatures of the skies around
and most importantly—
how to live gently

from RNM
Space Cadet & Junior Birdman

"A people's voice is dangerous when charged with wrath."
Aechylus, Agamemnon, 458 B.C.

An opening word with the reader about this novel

After the first six novels in the Honor Series won literary awards, critical acclaim, and readership around the world, fans of Peter Wake got a surprise in the seventh book, *The Honored Dead*. It, and the rest of the series, is a first-person narrative by Wake himself, the manuscripts having been found several years ago in an attic in Key West. For the details of that discovery, read *The Honored Dead*.

By 1886, Peter Wake's forty-seven years of life, and various wounds received on three continents, were catching up with him physically, but he dared not slack off or rest for too long. His position at the Office of Naval Intelligence (ONI) was not secure in the least. Politics, an anathema to Wake, was rampant in the Navy and in Washington, and ONI was no exception. Within the Navy's officer corps, some misunderstood Wake's intelligence duties; many derided his lack of formal naval academy education; and quite a few were jealous of those exotic foreign medals on his chest. Among the capital's politicians, he was known for honesty and a tendency toward innovation in the field—dangerous qualities, to say the least.

In addition to these liabilities, at this point in the story our man still has a long way to go in his profession, for nineteenth-century naval officers expected to serve forty or fifty years before collecting enough pension to live decently in retirement. So Peter Wake, and his old friend Sean Rork, are still doing their best and facing whatever comes their way, but it's not getting any easier.

I have edited Wake's more egregious grammatical errors but kept his cultural observations, even though some may be considered politically incorrect to us in the twenty-first century. I strongly suggest that after reading each chapter, you peruse the endnotes for that chapter, for I've discovered some interesting background on the people, places, and events Wake encountered during this mission.

So, dear reader, welcome to the world of 1886 revolutionary Cuba, and her neighbor, Florida, as seen by a veteran intelligence agent who *thought* he knew his way around Havana, Key West, and Tampa. Perhaps you, too, will be surprised by whom you meet and what you learn in this book.

Onward and upward,
Bob Macomber
Serenity Bungalow
Matlacha Island
Florida

Lieutenant (J. G.) Sean Wake, U.S.N.
Assistant Gunnery Officer
U.S.S. *Chicago*
North Atlantic Squadron
21 May 1895

Dear Son,

For years, I've been reluctant to write down what exactly happened in the mission that evolved out of my visit to New York City in January of '86. The story is at odds with certain commonly held notions of our modern day regarding Cuba. And even now, nine years later, this account may well anger influential people in Washington, Madrid, and Havana. They have the ability to wreak retribution upon me and, by extension, upon you. However, the truth of what really occurred needs to be told. Parts of it may shock you, but I want you to learn from it. Someday, you may face the kind of decisions I faced.

Curiously, it all began with the confluence of three random and benign incidents.

First, a record-defying blizzard raced into New York that January weekend. The very air froze men's beards in minutes. Treacherous weather often forces dissimilar people closer to the fireplace, and each other. It heightens a propensity for conspiracy.

Next, that Saturday evening I dined with the political elite in Manhattan, where a strident young achiever named Theodore Roosevelt entered my life. Lastly, stopping for lunch at a Brooklyn tavern on Sunday, by chance I encountered a thoughtful Cuban writer, José Martí. The brash American politico, a quiet Cuban intellectual, and this jaded naval intelligence officer—we were an unlikely trio, thrown together by fate. You've known for years that we are all friends. Now you will know how and why.

The most immediate result of those frigid New York hours was my subsequent journey to tropical Key West and Havana. There I met some very sinister fellows trying to eliminate a new threat to the status quo. Unfortunately, that turned out to be *me*.

I soon realized that death would be the least of my problems, however, for the dark forces at work had targeted something far more precious to me than my life. That cold-blooded menace is still out there, waiting for its moment of revenge for what I did nine years ago. To be clear, I do not regret doing it, for it needed to be done. But I have no pride in the deed, either. And so, as this narrative unfolds, I think you will understand my hesitation to make any of it known. That hesitation vanished an hour ago.

Today is the twenty-first day of May, 1895. The entire equation has changed, for I just received a devastating message. José Martí was killed two days ago, leading patriots in battle at Dos Ríos, in eastern Cuba.

My dear friend, the poetic voice of Cuba, and of liberty everywhere, is gone forever.

Now, this tale of the beginning of my friendship with José *will* be told. It must be told. It is sometimes said that the truth is the highest form of honor. We shall see.

> With love from your father,
> Peter Wake
> Commander, U.S.N.
> Special Assignments Section
> Office of Naval Intelligence
> Bureau of Navigation
> United States Naval Headquarters
> Washington, D.C.

Lobster à la Newberg

Saturday, 9 January 1886
Charles Delmonico's Restaurant
Twenty-sixth Street & Fifth Avenue
New York City

When that Saturday evening began, my nerves were already in a state of irritation. I was expected to be in the presence of slick-tongued politicos in, of all places, New York City in winter. My disposition was even more out of sorts from the further expectation that I was actually supposed to *befriend* them, a prospect I found revolting. Like most military and naval officers, I felt politicians were but one short step up from the criminal shysters of the alleys. More than a few were far worse.

Nevertheless, I was requested to go—that means *ordered* if you're in the naval service—by none other than the senior admiral commanding the United States Navy, the venerable David Dixon Porter. In 1886 he was seventy-three, displaying a flowing gray and white beard Moses would envy, but he hadn't slowed down, not one bit. D. D. Porter still ruled the navy with an iron hand. One did not argue with Admiral Porter.

"Commander Wake, you are in charge of this effort. Millions in congressionally approved budgets are at stake, just as the navy is finally modernizing, and it is extremely important," Porter informed Commander Bowman McCalla and me, "to show the gentlemen in New York City that the navy is not only worth the expenditure, but that such a commitment is vital to the nation's foreign policy and relations."

Porter glanced over at my immediate boss, bureau chief Commodore John G. Walker, and the intelligence division's hard-working coordinator-in-chief, Lieutenant Raymond P. Rodgers, then continued his lecture. "The chairman of the House Committee on Naval Affairs, Congressman Herbert of Alabama, is on our side, due to the particular efforts of Lieutenant Rodgers here. But we need others with influence, especially those men in the northeast, to join the cause."

Porter's pale eyes bored into mine. "I think you, Peter, and you, Bowman, are the men for the job. Thus, gentlemen, you get to go and be friendly and informative."

Even as we chorused, "Aye, aye, sir," Bo and I thought that pretty speech all bilge water, to put it mildly. In the passageway after leaving Porter's office, I quietly grumbled that this was just one more damned burden for overworked naval officers to bear, and wondered why the great admiral didn't do the deed himself, or get one of the society types in the navy to do it. There were several who came to mind, none pleasantly.

After years of survival at naval headquarters in Washington, I know that sometimes it's not what men of power say that is important. It's what they don't say. The admiral didn't mention that the folks we were to meet in New York were Republicans, though I figured it out instantly. In New York and New England, the Republicans had enormous sway, especially the young up-and-coming types.

I also knew that Lieutenant Rodgers was a master at dealing with politicos. It came naturally, for it appeared that he had no other choice but to be a naval officer, well-attuned to the egos of the capital. Son of a famous admiral, grandson of a commodore, nephew of two other famous commodores, with naval officer cousins and younger brother, Ray had been brought up in Washington, D.C., immersed in the political culture of the navy and that city. Even with all of that on his side, I understood that Rodgers, whom I liked for his enthusiasm and respected for his ability, couldn't go to New York for that dinner.

No, there were some who thought he'd already burned bridges with the Republicans by supplying damaging information about them to Chairman of the House Committee on Naval Affairs Hilary Abner Herbert, a former Confederate general and devout Democrat, who had no love lost for anyone of the Grand Old Party. Rodgers' information detailed mismanagement of the navy during the previous Republican administrations. But what was young Rodgers to do? He was merely honest, and told Herbert the facts. Thus, it was I who was sent, with my friend McCalla, to New York to converse with the Republicans.

Bo and I, huddled in our boat cloaks against the arctic air blasting down Fifth Avenue, entered the most legendary eatery in the city, Charles Delmonico's high-society place by Madison Square. January ninth was the date, the third day of that bone-freezing blizzard.

We passed through the first-floor public dining room, where upper-class swells and their bejeweled ladies mingled amidst a décor of simplified elegance. The perfumed air, agreeably enhanced by a string quartet in the corner, was blessedly warm. As we tramped through, faces displayed open curiosity. Naval officers with less gold braid than a commodore seldom dined there, so why the presence of mere mid-level commanders? I could see them asking each other, "How can those sailors afford these prices?" Well, the simple answer was that we couldn't. We were guests of the gentlemen dining upstairs, out of the public eye and ear.

Several diners were eyeing my decorations. I felt my cheeks heat up in embarrassment as I caught whispered inquiries: "Isn't that the French Legion of Honor?" "What's that gaudy purple one?"

I don't mind explaining them in military company, but the genteel clientele of Delmonico's wouldn't understand, couldn't understand, the stories of how I came to have those medals. Most would get physically sick if they heard the details.

Porter had told us to wear our full dress rig, portray confidence, and be sociable, but not too familiar. I've never looked forward to full dress affairs. The uniform is bulky, hot, and itchy. I have to contend with people staring at my awards, which, since they come from foreign countries, are a bit unusual for an American naval officer. There is a further complication. I can answer in detail questions about the medals from France and Morocco, but have been admonished to be vague about the ones from Peru and Cambodia.

It seems those particular stories have political implications it would be best not to stir up. I would've forgone the two troublesome medals all together, but then thought about the possibility of running into the consuls of those countries in New York City—it is considered a grave insult not to wear the national awards a country has bestowed upon you. So my trinkets from Peru and Cambodia dangled with the others.

Bo McCalla, a handsome fellow who enjoyed considerable admiration from ladies, though he was committed to his wife and children, had it luckier that night. Like many naval officers, he had no medals, despite the fact that his career had been far more action-filled during the War Between the States than mine. At the moment, I envied his relative anonymity. No one stared at his chest. He was just another navy man passing through. I looked back at them and silently laughed—if those refined people only knew what Bo had done to keep the peace in Panama nine months before . . .

After ascending to the third floor, we bypassed an empty banquet room and proceeded down a carpeted passageway, moving toward the sound of male voices. Finding the appropriate private dining room, Bo and I were confronted in the doorway by a tall elderly man in black tie and tails. He stood with a sergeant-major's ramrod countenance, straightening even further when he saw the silver oak leaves on our epaulettes. Evidently expecting us, the doorman bid us good evening, flourished a gesture to enter, then called out to those inside the room, "Commander Peter Wake and Commander Bowman McCalla, United States Navy."

With that stentorian announcement, we passed into the *sanctum sanctorum,* a place at which the well-to-do down below would've dearly loved to dine, or be seen to dine. But evidently they, the merely well-to-do, weren't invited here.

For this was the lair of the chosen few.

Surveying the room and its occupants, I saw what a most comfortable lair it truly was. Intimate, quietly refined. No vulgar displays of new money in that room. No gold-gilded statues, no European art. It was a quiet, businesslike, thoroughly American place. A place for decision-making, and decision-influencing, not idle chatter about arcane topics.

Interspaced by red satin–draped windows overlooking the oak-treed square named for our fourth president, the walls were paneled mahogany with cherry wood wainscoting. Accented by brass oil lamps and reflectors were portraits of famous people I knew I should've recognized. The crystal gasolier above us shed a subdued glow, enough to read by but not enough to glare. Two marble fireplaces at either end of the room crackled with burning wood—oak, by the smell, no timid coal for this place—radiating merciful heat for my tropically thinned blood. The eastern fireplace had a mantel topped by a model of the *Constitution;* its western counterpart exhibited *Kearsarge.* Scrimshawed whale bones lay atop the furniture, and a display of knotwork adorned a wall display. Obviously, this was a crowd interested in, and probably very well informed on, maritime affairs.

But the room was merely the backdrop of the drama, for it was the actors within who were the most interesting. Ancient Negro men in red and black livery padded around on the thick carpeting, serving the latest gin cocktail and dispensing substantial hors d'oeuvres. In a manner implying long association, the servants respectfully referred to each of the milling gentlemen by Christian name: "Mr. Richard," "Mr. Jonathan," and so on. For their part, the dinner guests showed a dull paternalism toward the dark-skinned servants who were twice their age: "Why, thank you so much, Henry."

Among themselves, the gentlemen attendees were less reserved, exhibiting the standard theatrics of politicians— familiar gesticulation, occasionally accompanied by thoughtful contemplative poses, deep chuckles, sadly shaking heads, and sympathetic nods.

I observed with regret that there were no women present, a sad but not unexpected loss. Ladies were considered—or perhaps hoped to be—just too delicate for such an evening of political gamesmanship. I always thought that a silly notion, for I have known several women—my lovely wife and precocious daughter most conspicuously among them—who were keen observers of national policies and trends. I've found that most women can see through a man's façade like one of Edison's new lights through a fog. And a few women in the room, I thought, would lower the pontificating and increase the sincerity. But alas, 'twas not in the cards that evening. We were boringly stag. My displeasure at being there increased.

One thing that immediately imprinted itself upon my mind was the atmosphere in the room. I'd been in the palaces of Oriental potentates, but had never before been in a room full of such nonchalantly assumed authority. An air of *noblesse oblige* wafted through the place, tinged with preordained destiny and the responsibility that goes with it. "The National Situation" dominated the conversation of the fifty men around me, not a single one over forty or a veteran of our national fratricide twenty years earlier. All of them were Republicans. Rich Republicans. Abraham Lincoln would've felt like a hick pauper in that crowd. Laughter in the room was of the restrained kind, as befitting men shouldering the weighty roles of those with a bluer shade of blood.

In fact, my hosts were plainly worried and their dialogue showed it—the Democrats were in charge in Washington, with a president these men knew well. Grover Cleveland had been their state's governor until his inauguration the previous March. Yes, these twenty-five and thirty year olds had serious things to talk about.

After surveying the place for no more than twenty seconds, my friend Bo, being Bo, shaped a direct course for the table with drinks and food. "Reprovisioning . . ." I heard him mutter, which sounded like an eminently solid idea to me. I was just about to follow astern when grim-faced Commodore Ralph Chandler, commandant of the Brooklyn Navy Yard and the only other man present in uniform, entered the soiree and approached me. He was accompanied by a smaller fellow, several decades his junior, who looked disturbed—whether happy or angry, I could not tell.

"So *this* is the man who knows Panama, eh, Commodore?" said the spectacled young man as he stared quizzically at my Lion of the Atlas medal from Morocco. The accent was a combination of busy New York and cultured New England; the tone was pure energy. His eyes shifted to my Legion of Honor.

I caught a glimpse of Bo over at the bar trying unsuccessfully not to smirk at my capture so early in the game. He raised a glass mockingly toward me as Commodore Chandler patiently replied to his companion, "Yes, sir. This is Commander Peter Wake. He'll be happy to tell you about Panama and the French canal."

The fellow got even more agitated. "Well then, he's *pree*-cisely the man I need to talk to!"

I had not a clue who this possibly deranged person was, so I glanced expectantly at Chandler, who obliged me by explaining, "Commander Wake, this young man is the author of that naval history book that's going the rounds, Mr. Theodore Roosevelt."

Theodore Roosevelt? The naval historian, acclaimed author of *The Naval War of 1812,* lecturer at the Naval War College, blue-blood New Yorker, and deputy sheriff someplace out West? Was this boy the same firebrand who had not only just written about ranching, hunting buffalo, and living a manly life to the fullest; but had also published an essay on what the government really ought to be doing? Then I recalled that on top of everything else, Roosevelt was a former state legislator for New York—an influential politician on the way up. The figure in front of me looked far too young to have done any, much less all, of that.

But he had. And at twenty-seven years old, Roosevelt was already a force to be reckoned with in that great metropolis filled with legendary men who owned twice his number of years. Intense eyes goggled at me from behind nose-clip lenses as a right hand quickly gripped mine in what seemed the precursor to a wrestling hold. For a fleeting second, I had the strange thought that he was about to flip me across his back.

He didn't, however, and through the most dazzling smile I'd ever seen, Roosevelt exclaimed, "By golly! *Dee*-lighted to meet you, Commander!" Then he added, "We absolutely *must* talk later."

I couldn't help smiling in return; he had that contagious effect. I was old enough to be this man's father, and here he was, getting me excited about our coming conversation. I felt honored and stupid at the same time.

"Yes, sir," was all I managed to say before Roosevelt gave an acknowledging nod and spun around to greet somebody else. It was a tall, well-dressed man I later learned was Henry Lodge, a Massachusetts legislator who was being groomed to run again for Congress. He'd lost the year before, but not in the eyes of the men in that room. There was a crush around Lodge and for a moment I stood to the side, quite alone and a bit lost.

McCalla came up and softly whistled at the stern array of wealth and power around us. "Peter, old son, you were right. We're in dangerous water here. I say we get under way as soon as possible right after dinner."

"Good idea, Bo, but it looks like I'll have to stay afterward to talk. I've been set up by the commodore."

Bo was conjuring up a reply when Harry Tilghman, the manager of Delmonico's, came into the room and announced that dinner was ready, whereupon we all wandered into the room next door. There were nameplates at each place setting around the tee-shaped table. Old Commodore Chandler was seated at the head table, looking decidedly unhappy among his companions. I circulated the junior end of the long table and found Bo's spot, but not mine. That's when the doorman, sly smile barely showing, beckoned me to a place near the upper end of the long table. I was more than a little aghast to find myself seated between Mr. Lodge and Mr. Roosevelt.

"Ah, Commander Wake. Please sit down," Roosevelt insisted, pounding the chair back next to him. "Right *here* with Lodge and me! Good to have a *naval* man with us tonight."

I answered, probably a bit too uncertainly, "Thank you, sir," and sat down. He showed no notice of my hesitance, however, having engaged Lodge in a discussion about lobster, of all subjects. It seemed that Roosevelt was in favor of steaming the things in their shell and serving them thus, while Lodge countered with a preference for boiled lobster meat lying on the plate *sans* its armor.

Roosevelt suddenly turned to me for support. "And what say *you* about the best preparation of lobster, Commander? Steamed, right? You're from Henry's state and you've been around the world . . ."

9

That surprised me. He knew about my background? Most people thought of me as a Floridian, since my home was there. Few knew I was born and raised on the south coast of Massachusetts near Mattapoisett, east of New Bedford. In actuality, I hadn't lived there for any length of time since the age of sixteen, when I first went to sea on my father's lumber schooners. I wondered what else Roosevelt knew about me, and why he would even bother. My unease escalated into extreme wariness.

"I enjoy them both, gentlemen," I said, remembering Porter's orders and trying to be sensitive to personalities.

"Not good enough," decided my interrogator, white enamel flashing. "Too diplomatic! Which way would you want your lobster—right here and now?"

I didn't appreciate his tone, but said, "Tonight? The *hottest* way. That would be in a chowder."

"Aha! Hear *that*, Henry?"

Roosevelt quickly lowered his voice for the first time and leaned across me toward Lodge. "He told us we're *both* wrong—and *right* he is!"

Then he laughed. It was a genuine hold-on-to-your-belly laugh that attracted the attention of all hands around us. He said to me, "You answer well to your description, Commander. Admiral Porter told me you'd be candid. By the by, we're having lobster tonight, in one of the special concoctions of Charley Delmonico's chef, splendid fellow. Tilghman found him a couple years ago."

Lodge softly groaned. "Oh, no. Not that one again, Theodore." To me he confided, "I feel a tale coming on—the one about Wenberg's lobster that we've all heard *ad nauseam*."

Roosevelt stabbed a finger into the air. "*Pree*-cisely, Henry! And I tell it *ad libitum* because I can, and because I like to, *and* because it's a funny story, one our naval friend here will appreciate."

I swear I felt an electrical impulse when he next put a hand on my shoulder. "It seems the chef learned the pro-*cee*-dure for this lobster concoction from a merchant marine sea captain named Ben Wenberg. The captain said *he* got the recipe from the West Indies—a place you know your way around, I'm told, Commander."

He paused, but not for my answer, which failed to make it out in time. In two seconds he was on target again. "Well, sir, that lobster was an immediate *smash* with the patrons here and Charley Delmonico dedicated its name to the captain: 'Lobster *à la* Wenberg.' Great dish, everybody loved it. Wenberg became a culinary hero. People would applaud when he entered a room. Imagine that, Commander—people applauding with excitement for *lobster!* Ah, but then, dear Captain Wenberg managed to reverse his fortune. He became *persona non grata* here by somehow angering Charley."

Roosevelt leaned over and said *en sotto voce,* eyes wide in excitement, "Some say that . . . *rum* . . . was involved. But, of course, I cannot confirm that."

Not missing a beat, he continued the tale, "And therefore my friend Charley had a great dilemma. How does one continue to serve a dish everyone *loves,* which is named for man you now *dislike?* Well, sir, the answer was simple: keep the dish and alter the moniker. Charley reversed the name in an anagram from Wenberg to Newberg. Nice pun with the 'new,' also. Oh, it all must *irk* Wenberg something terrible, don't you think? Of course, we don't know, for he hasn't been seen here since. Good for Charley Delmonico!"

Around us a dozen men were listening to him. It was difficult not to—the man could effortlessly get attention and keep it. But people were doing more than listening; they were nodding and laughing, agreeing with Roosevelt, watching his every move and listening to every sound. The man was a natural orator, or perhaps a natural actor, even with a simple tale about seafood. I found myself wondering about his ability when campaigning on serious matters of state.

And then it dawned on me—Roosevelt was who Admiral

Porter wanted me to meet at the gathering, though he'd never specified him by name. Porter wanted to use and spread Roosevelt's influence among the Republican side. Plus, the old admiral shared a common bond with the young Roosevelt, for Porter was a writer too, having published no fewer than four naval books.

I knew the admiral was close to finishing his newest effort, the *Naval History of the Civil War*. It was widely known that D. D. Porter liked Roosevelt's *Naval History of the War of 1812*—he'd ordered every wardroom in the fleet a copy. I surmised that the two must at least be acquaintances and possibly friends. Porter, that wily old goat and veteran of a thousand political wars, was setting me up to be the unofficial naval liaison with Roosevelt, a New York Republican, during a Democratic national administration.

Just then the celebrated lobster arrived. It was neither boiled nor stewed, nor even chowdered. Instead, it was beautifully done up with slices of the meat laid on a pastry with a piping-hot thick crème sauce drowning the whole, something I'd never seen. Different and delicious, it has ever since been my favorite sea dish—not the least because of the story of how, and with whom, I first tasted it.

The lobster got the best of Roosevelt, silencing him as no human had that evening. No longer under his gaze, I had some time to relax. As I dug into my own dinner, I studied the man to my left, whom I suspected was another that Porter had in mind for me to meet.

From the preceding conversations in the room, I deduced that Henry Cabot Lodge was the scion of a wealthy Boston clan, a professor of something ridiculous called "political science" at Harvard—a cushy billet if I've ever heard of one—and a relatively senior member of the Massachusetts House of Representatives. Only in his mid-thirties, he appeared to me to be mighty starchy, with a pointed beard, stiff movements, and nose stuck firmly up in the air. I couldn't tell if his silence was arrogance or indifference, but I was pretty sure it wasn't from a lack of intellectual skills. After my cursory perusal, I decided that if he really was heading for congressional splendor in D.C., he'd fit right in, a junior minion to the smug power-dispensers over on the Hill. I couldn't help not liking the man.

Lodge caught me evaluating him and said, "My wife's father was an admiral—Charles Henry Davis. Perhaps you knew of him?"

Now *that* was interesting. I did indeed know of the man. Davis, who had fought in several actions at the beginning of the Southern rebellion, also had a reputation as a bit of an ocean scientist, specializing in hydrographic and celestial work. Worked at the Naval Observatory, where I had friends, and was known for having quite a sharp mind. His son was a serving naval officer, whom I now knew was Lodge's brother-in-law. Another connection in the tangled web that was Washington.

"I met Admiral Davis at the observatory years ago, but did not have the honor of serving under him. He was well respected, sir."

Between mouthfuls, Lodge looked at me deadpan. "He's been dead for nine years."

"Yes, sir, I thought it had been that long. I'm sorry for your loss."

He nodded and said, "Yes. It was considerable."

And that was the sum total of my conversation with Henry Cabot Lodge, one of the coldest fishes of a man I've ever met. Years later, Roosevelt, a great jokester himself, told me his friend Henry was one of the funniest men he'd ever known. That compliment was, and still is, a mystery to me.

To my right, Roosevelt's rapid annihilation of his dinner was soon completed, enabling him to converse with me once more, asking questions about my work. I had the distinct feeling he already knew the answers. His voice was subdued, without the high-toned inflections I heard before, but still quite intent.

"So, Commander, you work in the Bureau of Navigation at

naval headquarters?"

His inside knowledge cautioned me to be succinct. "Yes, sir."

"Work for a fellow named Rodgers, eh?"

"I work *with* him. He is a coordinator of information there, sir."

"Comes from an old navy family, I'm told."

"Yes, sir."

The conversation became a cross-examination. "But you're not, are you? Never went to the academy, came up as a volunteer during the war, I believe?"

I said, "Yes, sir."

"How unusual. Do you mind explaining?"

I did mind, but Porter's face flashed in my mind. "No problem, sir. I was a merchant marine officer, a first mate, on coastal schooners. I became a volunteer naval officer in sixty-three. Served in the East Gulf Blockade Squadron, out of Key West. They made my commission a regular one in sixty-five and kept me on."

"Ah yes, one hundred and thirty-three volunteers, out of six thousand, were allowed to stay in at the end of the war, if my memory serves correctly. And *you* were one of those chosen. How curious . . ."

Again he scrutinized my medals. "And you have seen service around the world?"

"Yes, sir. Most officers have."

"But they don't get those, Commander," indicating the medals.

He said no more on that topic, which I thought peculiar. Most people wanted to hear the stories.

"And I understand you live on an island in Florida, when on leave from your duties?"

I had no insight as to where this was heading. "Yes, sir. I own Patricio Island, on the southwestern coast."

"I've not been there. What is that coast like, Commander?" he asked.

"Beautiful in the winter and spring, hot in the summer, very wet in the early fall. Tranquil all year 'round. It's a frontier coast, Mr. Roosevelt—very few people there, yet."

"Hmm, well, I know something about frontier life out West, Commander," he said with a smile. "Your area sounds intriguing. Lots of opportunities for a vigorous man and family, I would think."

I thought of the islands. Yes, there were opportunities there, but also a lot of challenges. It was still pretty rough in many ways. Very rough in some ways.

"We do have some hard-working pioneers, sir."

Roosevelt's eyes lit up as he asked, "Say, do you *fish* there, Commander?"

I chuckled at the thought. I'm an unlucky fisherman, but enjoy eating seafood.

"We eat a lot of fish, but I'm no good at catching them."

His enthusiasm increased, along with that habit of accenting certain words. "I've heard of something called a *tarpine*-fish there. Supposed to be a *great* fight! Absolutely *capital* fight. Read an article about it in *Harper's*."

"It's a *tarpon,* sir. You can't eat them, too many bones, but they've become a famous game fish on that coast. Get pretty big— some up to six or seven feet long. Jump high out of the water and fight hard to avoid getting caught. It's all starting to attract northern pleasure fisherman to the area on excursions."

He slapped a hand on the table. "I see. Well, I like a bit of *sport* myself. Perhaps I'll visit and try *my* wits against one of these tarpon *fellows!* And I suppose you have a lot of commercial fishing there, for fish one can eat?"

"Yes, sir."

"And who fishes for *them?*"

"Most of those fishermen are local men, but quite a few are

Cuban. Come up from Cuba each winter and spring, camp on the islands, and periodically send the catch back. Been doing it for centuries. My island—Patricio—is named after one of them."

"Cubans, eh?" He said it like he was rolling the words over in his mind.

"Yes, sir. Seasonal fishermen. Their right to fish on that coast was written into the agreement selling Florida to the United States back in eighteen twenty."

"Yes, the Adams-Onís Treaty. Good politics, that treaty."

Roosevelt lowered his voice, his focus steady on me, paying close attention.

"And those Cuban fishermen? Any of them involved in the *politics* going on these days down in Havana? Or talking about it?"

I suddenly realized what he was getting at—the anti-Spanish revolutionaries, in Key West especially, were getting more and more press attention. I mustered up an innocent look and said, "Politics, sir?"

That grin came back. It was impossible to not smile when Theodore Roosevelt grinned at you. He lowered his tone even more. "Why yes, Commander. The smell of revolution, of *freedom* for the Cuban people from the Spanish tyrants, is in the air. Is it *not?*"

Lodge was straining to listen, as were our closest tablemates. So far no one had talked about the navy and our needs and plans, as I had been led to believe they would. And Roosevelt hadn't asked about Panama. I felt awkward talking about foreign affairs in that company, particularly since the official attitude of the United States toward Cuban freedom from Spain had changed with the new Democratic administration. The Republicans had always favored and supported it, some even pushing for U.S. annexation, but Grover Cleveland didn't want to get involved. Neither did I that evening, so I stammered out, "Don't know much about that sort of thing, Mr. Roosevelt."

He paused, clearly about to call me on my ambiguity, then let it go. "Why, yes, of course, Commander."

Roosevelt's voice went back up to its public volume, interrogation apparently over, and he asked cheerfully, "Say, do you have a *family*, Commander?"

I breathed easier. "Yes, sir, I do. My daughter Useppa is twenty-one and a Methodist missionary in Key West. Works with Negro children at a school. My son Sean entered the naval academy this last summer."

"A naval *academy* man! Congratulations on your son, Commander. I'm sure he'll make a *splendid* officer. And your daughter's name is Useppa? An unusual name, but very pretty."

"She's named after the island she was born on, just south of the one where I live now."

Evidently he'd only known about my career, courtesy of Admiral Porter, but not my private life. His head tilted to the right again and he smiled. "How wonderfully *romantic*. And Mrs. Wake? Is she on that *tropical* island of yours, waiting for her sailor to come home?"

"No, sir. I'm . . ." Even years afterward, it still physically hurt to say the words. "I'm a widower, Mr. Roosevelt. Linda died of cancer. It'll be five years ago this February fourteenth."

The color drained away from Roosevelt's face.

Within seconds, without a word of explanation, he was up and gone from the table. Others around us pretended not to notice, but Lodge's hand touched my left arm.

"Kindly forgive my friend, Commander. Theodore's beloved mother and his beautiful young wife Alice both passed away two years ago on the same day—February fourteenth." He sighed. "Saint Valentine's Day. He has a child himself, a little girl, born just two days before her mother died." Lodge shook his head slowly. "Tragic . . ."

I mumbled, "I'm so sorry, sir. I didn't know."

Lodge waved a hand. "Don't worry about it. He'll be back.

But don't expect him to talk about his wife, daughter, or mother. He doesn't. It's private."

"The daughter, is she well?"

"Yes. Theodore's sister Bamie is raising her." Lodge's eyes fell. "The little girl's name is Alice, after her mother."

Ten minutes later Roosevelt did return. He muttered a brief apology for having to excuse himself abruptly, one that contained no explanation of why. I thought his behavior tremendously sad, and possibly unhealthy, and searched his eyes for some glimmer of sentiment. None was there.

He quickly launched into a debate over tariffs with a man across the table, his dynamism radiating out through the room. I saw a pattern by that point—when Roosevelt spoke in public, he overwhelmed his listeners by force of personality, and no one argued an opposite view. Against his volume and emotion, an opponent would seem anemic, confused.

As for our severed conversation, it didn't resume. He wasn't ignoring me, I think. No, he was just completely occupied in discussions on a rapidly spreading variety of topics, from President Cleveland's illegitimate child, to the Chinese immigrant situation, to the recent army campaign against Geronimo. We didn't speak again until after dinner had ended.

Coffee, cognac, and cigars brought everyone into yet another room overlooking Madison Square. Most of them drifted out after one glass, some bound for the theater, others for convivial watering holes, a few for home. Roosevelt had disappeared somewhere by that point, so I hoped my social duty was done and I could disengage, with no regrets for leaving. That episode at dinner still bothered me.

The cigar smoke in the room was thick and acrid, like gun smoke. I've always hated that smell and wanted out of there, but our superior officer was still present, so direct flight was out of question. Bo and I faded into a corner and waited for Commodore Chandler to leave. He chatted with Lodge and some prosecutorial attorney for another twenty minutes, finally departing about ten o'clock.

McCalla right away suggested we go to Gilmore's Garden. It was close by, at Twenty-seventh Street and Park Avenue, and there was a late-night bout between an Irishman and a Dutchman. He said we could have some amusement watching the fight. I was moving toward the doorway when Roosevelt approached from behind me and called out, "*Glad* you're still *here*, Commander—now let's talk!"

I nearly jumped out of my skin. Glancing around for a table, I saw Tilghman's waiters were busy cleaning up, so I shrugged at Roosevelt, trying to conceal my disappointment at his finding me. "Yes, sir. I'm sure we can find a place to talk around here someplace."

"*Nonsense!*" came the jovial reply. "Still too *crowded.* We'll head for my place—just up the street. Let's walk. Oh, don't *worry,* your friend doesn't have to come. He can head off on the town. I know how you sailors like to go out on the town."

And with that said he was out the door.

With mock concern, Bo shook his head as we exited the restaurant behind Roosevelt. "Gee, I'd love to accompany you to your politician's home, Peter, but as you just heard the man say—"

"Just go, McCalla. Maybe I'll meet you later at Gilmore's. Or I'll see you in the morning for breakfast at the hotel."

"Right. Well, good luck to you then!" and Bo headed off downwind to the east, the wind flapping his coat around him. I turned north into the raw breeze, cursing my luck in general and Admiral Porter in fine detail, while trying to keep up with my new acquaintance marching on ahead.

And, of course, Roosevelt's version of "just up the street" didn't mesh with my understanding of that description. He lived in a town house on Madison Avenue near Forty-ninth Street—over a *mile* north of Delmonico's, against those winter gusts funneling down the avenue and hitting me like ice picks. It also turned out that Roosevelt traveled fast on foot. We got there in seventeen minutes, as he announced when we arrived at his stoop.

While he fumbled for his keys, I made light talk as I stamped my numb feet, saying hopefully, "Maybe talking about the jungles of Panama will help warm us up, sir!"

He swiveled his head around to me, sly grin stretching across his face, his white teeth not chattering one little bit, unlike mine.

"Jungles? Why Commander Wake, we're not here to talk about *Panama* at all. Oh no, my good man, I've got a far more in-*tree*-guing subject for *you*."

A Plea from Babylon

Saturday, 9 January 1886
Theodore Roosevelt's town house
422 Madison Avenue
New York City

It was mercifully warm inside, though the dimly lit entryway of the Roosevelt home was a strange sight, to say the least. Eyes from a dozen furry or feathered heads stared down at me from the walls, while below them an older Irish maid waddled out, all afluster for not being at the door when we arrived. As I pounded life back into my feet, Roosevelt informed her that he and I would be in the study, and suggested she make coffee.

His study had more musty carcasses—everything from a black bear to a beaver—scattered about the walls, above and betwixt the bookcases that lined every side. Quite a diverse collection of victims, I thought, but he didn't bother to introduce me to any of them. Instead, he gestured to a chair for me and hesitantly opened the door of a cabinet. It wasn't the strident Roosevelt public voice I heard when he spoke. His tone was calm, measured. His brow furrowed. Something was wrong.

"Some rum to go with the coffee, Commander? I hear all sailors like that. I have some from Barbados that I'm told is quite good. Called Mount Gay. A happy name."

That was, indeed, a very good rum, and I surely did want some to warm the insides of my own frozen body, but something told me not to say yes. I'd noticed during the cocktail party that Roosevelt hadn't had any hard spirits. His wineglass at dinner had remained untouched. And now the change in his demeanor was alarming me more than ever. Warning flags went up in my mind about the whole evening.

No, much as I wanted to have, and needed, a touch of rum right then, I decided to stay away from alcoholic drink for the rest of the night. "No, thank you, sir."

His eyes showed surprise for just a second, then he asked, "Would you do me the honor of using my first name, Commander? It's Theodore. It would make me feel less pretentious if you did so. I'm quite junior to you in age and in experience, sir."

I was tiring of this fast. "Yes, sir . . . I mean . . . Theodore. And please call me Peter. Now, what *exactly* can I do for you, sir? I mean, Theodore. I really thought we came here to talk about Panama."

Roosevelt sat down in the wingback opposite me and took in a breath, his face setting grimly. "We came here to talk alone, Peter, but not about Panama. That was a plausible conversation for others to hear back at Delmonico's. Everyone is talking about the French canal in Panama these days, so it was convenient. Please forgive me for the slight deception, but I am certain you'll understand in a moment."

I didn't know what to say, so I held my tongue. He went on, his head lowered. "Admiral Porter is a friend, so I asked him for help. He sent you."

I felt like yelling at him to get to the point. My patience is sorely lacking at times, a regrettable characteristic, and this was one of those times. I don't like word games. They take far too long and frequently lead to misunderstandings. So I was blunt, with more edge to my words than intended.

"Look, I was told to come up here and talk about the navy and our needs, Theodore. There was no mention of any private discussions with you, or even of your name, when I was ordered to attend the dinner."

"Yes, well, I'm afraid Admiral Porter was indulging my request for anonymity, Peter. I don't want anyone to know that I'm involved in what I'm about to tell you. In fact, I would like to be totally *uninvolved* from this night onward."

I tried to keep my vocabulary civil, but it was a losing struggle. "Theodore, I have no earthly idea what the hell's going on here and would appreciate a candid explanation right now. It's late. I'm tired. And I've got a long way back to the rooming house in Brooklyn in this damned storm."

Just then, with impeccable dramatic timing, the maid arrived with the coffee and set the tray on a side table, allowing my anger to linger in the air. Sensing our strained silence, she poured two cups, bid us good night, and quickly shuffled out, closing the door behind her. Roosevelt handed me a steaming cup, then turned to a map of the Caribbean that was spread out on the broad desk nearby.

"Fair enough. I've received a strange message, Peter. Not sure whom it's from or what it means, but I think it might have something to do with Cuba. But that's only conjecture on my part."

"So what's the problem? Just ignore it."

"It's not that simple, Peter. The message alludes to a person in the U.S. government that may be involved in things he shouldn't be. There are negative political implications of my getting involved, and possible national consequences of my ignoring it." He saw me about to repeat my admonition and held up a hand. "And the message is some sort of a complicated riddle. A secret code that I cannot, for the life of me, decipher."

Oh. Now I understood why I was there.

Everything leading to that moment came into focus. It was a planned event, courtesy of devious old Admiral Porter, who was playing some sort of Machiavellian game to which even his subordinate commanders, my bosses, weren't privy. Understanding that didn't make me feel any better.

"Theodore, do you know what I really do?"

"Yes, Peter," he replied somberly, then rattled off far more about my work than most in the navy knew. "You work for Commodore Walker at the Bureau of Navigation, ostensibly, but really for the Office of Naval Intelligence, located deep within the State, War, and Navy building next to the White House. I know that you are part of a group of seven men working in a small back room on the fourth floor on a secret-code-system project for use in naval telegraph communications. The need for that system became starkly apparent after messages from Commander McCalla's combatant forces in Panama were compromised in April of this last year.

"I also know that you've been in Cuba many times over the last twenty years, most recently while returning from Panama, and that you know much of what is going on there, and who is doing it. That is why you were picked to come here. Porter said you'd know what to do."

Hmm, so much for my secret work. I sipped the coffee to gain a few seconds, then asked, "So what *am* I supposed to do, Theodore?"

"Admiral Porter told me to let you have this message, decipher it, and act on it."

That didn't make sense. "Why didn't you just give the message to Admiral Porter so he could give it to me himself? That way you'd be kept clear."

"Because he knew you would want to talk with the recipient of the message—me. He figured that you might have questions for me, the answers to which could help in understanding the message. He also thought you might understand some of the hidden meanings. The admiral didn't tell you this ahead of time, so you'd be objective in evaluating it."

Roosevelt exhaled in exasperation. "Peter, I know this all looks odd."

"Odd? That's an understatement, Theodore. The oddest part is *why you?*"

"I don't know precisely why they picked me to be the recipient, but I don't need or want this right now. If it *is* about Cuba, I can't help those people, though I do sympathize with their cause for freedom—something that's known in this city."

"Very well, then, I suppose I should see the message. So let's take a look at it."

"It's not a written message. It was verbally transmitted to me and I've kept it," he pointed to his head, "in here. Memorized."

Incredible. This was reaching a level of drama I didn't like, but there was no other choice. Porter had sent me here for this, so I had to go through with the charade, wondering, even as I spoke, whether this Roosevelt character was some sort of fringe lunatic, albeit a rich one. New York and Washington are full of them.

"All right, Theodore, before you tell it to me I'll ask the basics—who gave it to you? When and where did they give it to you? Why didn't you write it down? If it's that complicated, how are you sure you've remembered it all correctly?"

He nodded acknowledgment of my inquiries. "Right. First question: a well-dressed older man, perhaps fifty or sixty, gave it to me. He appeared to be a somewhat dark-skinned Latin American, but he spoke English very well—that's why I think it's got something to do with Cuba. Many Cubans in New York are fluent in English."

I thought that conjecture a bit loose on the evidence, but said nothing as he continued. "Second question: the man came up to me on the train from Albany nine days ago, at approximately four P.M. on Thursday, the thirty-first of December, when I was returning to the city. We were both standing in the aisle of the first-class carriage, preparing to depart as the train pulled into Union Station. The fellow got my attention by leaning against me and smiling, then he whispered for me to memorize what he was about to say. Before I could say a thing, he told me the message. I was, as you would imagine, rather disconcerted and didn't think to follow him as he melted into the crowd when the door opened. That man's timing was excellent—he said the words, the doors opened, and he disappeared. I've never seen him before or since."

"Would you recognize him, if you saw him again?"

"Yes, definitely."

"So this happened on New Year's Eve day?"

"Yes, Peter."

"Before I hear the message, Theodore, let me ask this. Did he greet you by name? Did he say anything else? What was his accent?"

"He never used my name, never said anything else. He looked Latin American and his accent sounded Spanish to me. And no, I don't speak Spanish, though I'm not bad in Italian and Latin."

This *was* getting curious. "Theodore, why didn't you write it down?"

"I thought it too dangerous to have a transcript lying around, so I memorized it, as he told me. Besides, I didn't need to." He shrugged. "I was schooled at home—before I went to Yale—and learned to memorize things at an early age. Once you've done the Greek classics, Peter, everything else is easy. Do you want to hear the message now?"

Actually, no, I didn't *want* to hear it, or be ensnared in this little farce at all, but I dutifully said, "Yes, of course, Theodore, tell me the message—verbatim, please."

As the grandfather clock in the hall chimed eleven times,

Roosevelt stood and began to pace, hands behind his back. He waited until the last chime, then began reciting the message he'd heard from the man on the train.

"Memorize this message to you from the Isle of Bones: the green man's singing Hebrews are calling for *lex talionis* at *isla fidelis*. Their protesting father awaits you inside Babylon behind Lazarus's house in the garden of angels, at the second midnight with the light of day from now. You can save innocent lives. But beware, you have a Judas within the minions of your regime."

He ended, dropped into his chair, and fixed his peculiar gaze upon me. I wasn't impressed. I'd written down his "message" and thought it sophomorically melodramatic. Maybe the man in front of me really was mad, or had mad jesters as friends. What was I supposed to do then?

"Theodore, that's *it*? This nonsensical stuff is what you and Porter are upset about? Sounds to me as if somebody is playing a joke on you, a political joke, to get you to do or say something ridiculous that you'll regret later on in a campaign. Are you running for office?"

Roosevelt didn't like my comment or question. "No, not right now. And I never told Porter the message, so he only knows I'm concerned, which was enough for *him*. Yes, I too initially thought it might be a political ploy, but those are usually of another nature—women, money, power. This is different, Peter. The look in that man's eyes was extremely intense. He *believed* in his message. This was no joke or cheap ploy."

Studying my host, I saw no sign of psychosis or deception. No mal intent. Though he couldn't understand its contents, Roosevelt truly believed in the authenticity of the message. I decided that he was probably right. It probably *was* a valid communication and it did appear to be about Cuba. The first and second phrases told me that much. "Very well, I'll help."

"And you can decipher the riddle?"

"Maybe, Theodore. The first line refers to the old Spanish

name for Key West. Cayo Hueso. Island of bones."

"Aha! That phrase con*founded* me!"

"And *isla fidelis* refers to Cuba. It means—"

"Faithful isle. In Latin, of course. I know that much, Peter. But why does that mean *Cuba?*"

"It's the old Spanish motto for Cuba. Goes back centuries. Still used on their documents as the royal description of the island."

"Isn't that oxymoronic now? I thought there was rebellion in the air down there."

"It refers to their age-old fidelity to the Christian faith, Theodore. As far as the political situation goes, you're correct: the majority of islanders are no longer faithful to the Spanish crown. Many are no longer dedicated to the Church, either."

"By gad, now we're *getting* somewhere! We've identified Key West and Cuba in the riddle. I *knew* it was a good idea to have you come up here."

I heartily disagreed with that statement, but put my misgivings aside. "Theodore, were you able to deduce anything from the other parts of the message?"

Roosevelt was his usual excited self now, a man on the hunt. "Why yes, I *have*, Peter! *Lex talionis* is the Latin translation for the ominous Hebrew Law of Talions—an eye for an eye—from the Old Testament. Oh my, that Latin training *does* come in handy at times."

"And what does the 'green man' part mean, Theodore?"

"Not a *clue*, Peter. I was hoping *you* might know. Hmm. Green man's Hebrews sang for 'an eye for an eye.' Who are they? Are they in Cuba or Key West?"

I rubbed my temples, trying to think. For some reason, that phrase sounded familiar. "Green man's Hebrews were singing, eh? Well, Spanish for green is *verde*."

I mulled that over. "*Verde* . . . Hey, that's it—Giuseppe Verdi! *Verde* is the Italian word for green. The 'green man' is Verdi. Theodore, when I was stationed in the Med back in seventy-four,

I met Verdi, the famous Italian composer. Quite a strange duck if ever there was one, let me tell you."

He laughed and said he'd met the man too, while a young boy touring Europe with his parents. That reminded me of his pedigree. But there was more percolating in my mind about the riddle. Verdi's *singing Hebrews?* What *was* it about that? I thought aloud, to organize and possibly spur my memory. "I remember that he did an opera around then that had a double entendre in one of the songs. It had a reference that inflamed the patriotism of the northern Italians who were under the occupation of the Austrians then. Yes, it's coming to me now. It has to be Verdi. And the song was related to the Bible. To the Hebrews in the Bible."

Roosevelt walked over to a bookshelf and pulled out a massive volume. "Where *exactly* in the Bible, Peter? Hebrew people are all over it. We'll start with the Old Testament."

"I'm trying to remember, Theodore—don't rush me."

I needed to figure it out in sequence. "All right, the opera song referred to Hebrew slaves I think. Yes, that was it, slaves under occupation. Just like the Italians in the north. I remember that those Italians would cheer that song, yelling for encore after encore, flaunting the Austrian authorities, who finally outlawed encores of that song. I thought it silly at the time, but the Italians didn't."

"*Not* helpful, Peter. Give me something more. There's a lot in here about Hebrew slaves, too."

Roosevelt was far better educated and cultured than I was, so I asked him, a bit peeved, "Well, you tell me. What Verdi opera had a song about slaves? You understand opera and European culture and that sort of thing."

"Duced if I know, Peter Wake. Can't stand that caterwauling myself."

Hmm, well that was a shared trait between us. Opera was lost on my ears too. "Let me see, Theodore . . . oh, now I'm remembering something. Nacubo? Nasubo? No. But it was close to that. Nabuso? Nope. *Nabucco,* yes, I think it was *Nabucco.* That was the opera. And the song was . . ."

Roosevelt was next to me now, left hand holding the Bible, right hand gripping my chair. "Yes?"

"*Va* something. *Va? Pensiero!* It was "*Va Pensiero,*" the song of the Hebrew slaves."

"By Jove, Peter! Very good!"

I held up a finger for attention and, overly proud of myself, announced the *pièce de résistance* of my memory. "And I recall that song was based on one of the psalms of the Bible, which is why the Austrians couldn't outlaw the song itself, only the calls for encores of it."

He was already zipping through the pages. "*Excellent,* my good man! Now, which psalm was it?"

"I can't remember."

I think I heard him sigh, which perturbed me greatly at that moment. After all, I was the one without the fancy Ivy League education, yet I had worked out the opera connection. Roosevelt was busy, however. The Bible sounded like a factory machine as he turned page after page as quickly as he could.

"Hmm, there are one hundred and fifty psalms. I guess we'll start at the beginning and check them one by one."

Obviously, it was going to be a long night, so I poured us another round of coffee. My new coconspirator stopped perusing for a moment, went to the cabinet and poured a touch of rum in my coffee cup. "You earned it, Peter."

An hour later we found the right psalm. Number 137. Roosevelt read it aloud.

By the rivers of Babylon, there we sat down, yes, we wept, when we remembered Zion. We hanged our harps upon the willows in the midst thereof. For there they that carried us away captive required of us a song; and they that wasted us required of us mirth, saying, Sing us one of the songs of Zion. How shall we sing the Lord's song in a strange land? If I forget thee, O Jerusalem, let my right hand forget her cunning. If I do not remember thee, let my tongue cleave to the roof of my mouth; if I prefer not Jerusalem above my chief joy. Remember, O Lord, the children of Edom in the day of Jerusalem; who said, Raze it, raze it, even to the foundation thereof. O daughter of Babylon, who art to be destroyed; happy shall he be, that rewardeth thee as thou hast served us.

Roosevelt took a breath, then read the last line slowly, "Happy shall he be, that taketh and dasheth thy little ones against the stones . . ."

Neither of us spoke for a few seconds, the despair and visceral revenge of the psalm having impressed itself on our minds. It was unlike anything I'd ever heard from the Bible. He put down the great book and shook his head. "A bloody reprisal—an eye for an eye—on the Babylonian masters by their Hebrew slaves."

"And upon the Spanish occupiers by the Cuban people, where slavery is still legal. In fact, in the western hemisphere slavery is only legal in Cuba and Brazil."

I added, "Although, the Spanish authorities have given in and are transitioning the slaves in Cuba into free status. Supposed to happen sometime later this year."

"So Cuba is the modern Babylon?"

"It would appear *they* think so."

"And just who exactly might *they* be, Peter?"

Several names came immediately to mind, men I'd met in Cuba and other places over the last few years, but I merely said,

"Not sure, but hopefully time will tell."

"And they want me to go to Cuba and meet someone?"

I thought about that part of the message—*behind Lazarus's house in the garden of angels.* That would be in Havana. I knew the place, and the garden of angels behind it.

"Yes, Theodore, they want you to go to Havana and meet a man in a cemetery. A leper cemetery. That's pretty bizarre, and would indicate it might be a group on the periphery of the revolutionary forces."

He began pacing again, clearly nervous now that he was beginning to understand what he was potentially mixed up in. "Well, what is this malarkey about 'midnight with the light of day.' What the devil is the explanation for that?"

"A full moon, Theodore. They want you to meet them in the leper cemetery in Havana on the second full moon after receiving the message. That would be February's. For some reason, they think you can help them in their revolution, and in doing so, can prevent bloodshed. From this reference to psalm one thirty-seven, it looks like massive bloodshed." Then I speculated aloud again. "Something planned for a specific day in the future, a coordinated island-wide strike at the Spanish, perhaps. Where the delineation between Spanish soldier and civilian would be lost in the hatred and bloodlust?"

"Peter, you know the situation down there. How do they think I, of all people, can help?"

"I don't know, except maybe they think you could persuade the U.S. government into backing, and-or recognizing a revolutionary government on that day, or before that day, and therefore force the Spanish to leave the island and end the bloodshed early. But I'm only guessing at that, Theodore."

Roosevelt was listening to me, but at the same time he strode to the far bookshelf. Returning to me, he laid an almanac for 1886 in my lap. The book was open to the month of February. He stabbed a finger on the section at the bottom.

"Thursday, February eighteenth, is full moon here. Is it the same in Cuba?"

"Yes, it is. That's six weeks away. I recommend you don't do this, Theodore. Havana is dangerous these days and this sounds like a trap of some sort."

"*Me?* I have absolutely no intention of going, Peter. Remember? I'm not going to be involved in this, *can't* be due to my position, though I do admit I wish I could. Sounds like some exhilarating *action* to me. *History* is being made, and we are part of it!" He gazed out the window, but I could tell his focus wasn't on the snow piling up outside. Roosevelt's reverie was only interrupted to murmur, "Just think of it . . . *history* . . ."

I knew what he was going to say next and cringed inside, waiting for it.

"But I'll definitely recommend to Porter that *you* have a go at it, Commander. Certainly needs to be looked into, by the very best man we've got. So you go and have the excitement and see what's *what* with those locals down there. I'll get Porter to keep me apprised of the results, of course."

He shook my hand in one of his viselike holds, pumping it up and down, grinning from ear to ear, those teeth glinting in the lamplight, as he practically yelled, "By *gumphries*, Peter, I do *envy* you your profession! *Babylon.* Can you believe it, sir? Babylon is calling us!"

Hah. Babylon hadn't called *me*, but I knew that Porter would see it Roosevelt's way. He'd have me investigate the matter—all based on a superficial examination of a senseless riddle. It had been, all in all, a ridiculous evening, and one phrase repeated itself in my mind while this fiendish youngster kept my hand imprisoned in his passionate grip, without the slightest indication he'd let go.

God help me.

The Scribe

Sunday, 10 January 1886
Waterman's Tavern
Front Street & Hudson Avenue
Brooklyn, New York

Bo McCalla was waiting for me on the street corner outside the tavern when I arrived at seven minutes after noon the next day. The day was bright and cold and I was anticipating a hot meal. The snow had ended, but that icy wind was still blowing down the East River.

He had that bemused look I'd seen in Panama the April before, when I showed up at Colón dressed in rags, having just come out of the jungle. I'd been searching for a Haitian anarchist named Prestan, whose gang of thugs was causing problems for the French canal project. Neither the French, the Panamanian provincial authorities, nor the Colombian army had quelled the revolt.

At the time, Bo had been in command of six hundred bluejackets and Marines, and busy keeping some semblance of order and peace in Colón after days of riot and ruin at the hands of Prestan's men. He restored the peace. But that's another story.

Seeing him in Brooklyn, I knew I was about to hear some guff from Commander McCalla—there was that twinkle in his eye.

"All right Wake, what was she like?"

"Who?" I asked, knowing full well his insinuation.

"The pretty girl who took you in for the night after you left Roosevelt's place," he quipped lightly, then added with a leer, "Since you didn't make it to Gilmore's, or even come back to the hotel last night."

"Bo, please . . . show me a bit more respect than that. She was far more than merely pretty, she was *beautiful*," I retorted as we entered the tiny place and peered through the gloom for an empty seat. Foremen from the nearby Brooklyn navy yard occupied almost all the benches and stools. They were working on a Sunday, a true rarity, to get the ancient *Powhatan* repaired and back at sea. Ironically, she was to return on patrol near Cuba. No one gave us more than an annoyed glance as we barged our way through the throng. Naval officers at shipyards were considered a hindrance by dockworkers.

My reply silenced Bo's sarcasm for a moment. He grinned, then asked, "Really?"

"There're two seats over there," I said, ignoring his question and pointing toward a plank table in the dim back corner. A man was standing at the table, talking to a younger fellow seated there. As we approached, the older man, a great purple scar marring his jaw, walked out past us, leaving two empty stools on one side of the table. The remaining man was eating his lunch from a tin plate, a mug of coffee beside it. Not a dockie. Too clean. Maybe a clerk in the main office, by his suit and tie.

"Can we sit here, please?" I asked him.

"Yes," he answered, without glancing up from his stew. I

noted he had a Hispanic accent. There seemed to be a lot of that going around lately.

Bo crashed down on his stool and beamed at the fellow. "Thank you, sir. You working at the yard to get the old 'Pow Scow' back in shape?"

The man looked at us for the first time. "No, I do not work at the yard. And I do not know what a 'pow scow' is."

"It's the nickname for *Powhatan*," said Bo, but seeing still more incomprehension on the part of our tablemate, he explained, "She's an old ship. Always in for repairs. Oh, never mind."

The man's attention returned to his plate as I signaled the barmaid for two dishes of stew and two coffees. Bo got quiet. I could tell he was churning inside to ask about my night, so I relieved him of his misery.

"I spent the night in Roosevelt's guest room. It was too late to venture out in that storm last night."

"So?"

"There wasn't any girl, Bo."

He harrumphed, which I thought rather rude to my ego. "Well, that's sad, but not unexpected from you, Peter. Still the knight. So what happened with the young literary wizard and lion of the up-and-coming Republicans?"

"Oh, he asked me some questions and we talked until late. Then he offered me the guest room."

Since we had a stranger at the table, Bo tried to conceal the subject matter. "About where we were last year, eh? How much did he already know from Porter?"

"Not at liberty to say, Bo."

Occasionally I am compelled to lie to an enemy in my profession. But I have a rule that I never lie otherwise. Usually, in order not to lie, I say that I am not at liberty to speak on that topic. Most people accept that comment, but there are moments when that response to an inquiry aggravates the curiosity of the inquirer. Unfortunately, this was one of them.

"Oh, come on, Peter. Did he mention our work down there? *My* work down there?"

"No. That entire subject didn't come up. It was another subject."

Then I got to thinking. I wondered if Bo knew anything about the 137th psalm and its interpretations. That wasn't confidential, so I wasn't worried about the other man at the table.

"Hey, on another issue, Bo, let me ask you something. Know anything about the Bible?"

That took him aback. He answered warily, "Yes, a bit. Why?"

"Do you know anything about the one hundred thirty-seventh psalm? What it means? Any religious or political interpretations? I was never really exposed to it in the Episcopal Church growing up, and just wondered if you're familiar with it?"

Bo laughed. "A psalm, from the Bible? You are a strange one, Wake. Off the top of my head, I've not the vaguest notion as to what the one hundred thirty-seventh psalm even says, much less what it means. The twenty-third psalm I've got down pretty straight, but I'm not a Biblical scholar."

He chuckled again, then abruptly stopped, as a voice, low and steady, muttered, "It is a plea for divine help, for justice. The Jewish slaves of the Babylonians were calling for vengeance upon their tormentors."

That comment came from none other than our unsociable companion.

His serious eyes met mine as he continued, "The psalms of the Bible describe the perpetual human condition, which is the same today as it was three thousand years ago. That particular psalm is a parable illustrating the need for wrong to be reversed in the world. In both the Catholic Church, and that of the Protestant, it is a psalm not widely explained, since its vivid descriptions might lend itself to revolutionary ideas. Ideas considered dangerous to the authorities."

I sat there for several seconds, astonished. The man spoke matter-of-factly, like a professor to a student. He pushed his empty plate away, took a final gulp of coffee, and was preparing to stand when I recovered my wits.

"That was very insightful, sir. May I introduce myself? I'm Commander Peter Wake, obviously of the U.S. Navy. And this is Commander Bowman McCalla. Thank you for your viewpoint."

"My name is José Martí." He moved to leave.

"Excuse me, Mr. Martí. But your accent—are you from Cuba, sir?"

"Yes, I am."

"Cuba is an island that has seen more than its share of tormentors, yes?"

The ghost of a smile showed as he said, "Yes. But someday those slaves will be free."

"Of that, I have no doubt, sir. Cuba has a great people."

"You have been there?" He seemed surprised.

"Yes, sir. Back during our Civil War, and a few times since then when my ship visited port."

Bo, who sensed that I was on to something, asked, "Do you work here in New York, Mr. Marti? Or are you passing through, like us?"

Martí stopped moving toward the door. "I live nearby in Manhattan. I am a correspondent for newspapers in Latin America. In addition, I am diplomatic consul for Uruguay, Argentina, and Paraguay. Mostly, however, I send translations of American newspaper articles to the papers in South America."

Interesting. And possibly useful. I wanted to listen to him some more, to pick his mind. Here was no braggart, no drunk rabble-rouser. Martí was educated and articulate.

"Please, Señor Martí, perhaps you have time to spare and would allow us the honor of buying you a drink, so that we may learn the truth about Cuba from you. America is familiar with revolutionary ideas, sir. We were the example for the world, especially for the people of South and Central America in their struggle against the Spanish."

He stood there, apparently evaluating us and our potential value to him. "Very well, then, Commander Wake, another drink of coffee. Thank you for the offer. My skin and bones do not like this terrible weather. They miss Cuba's soft embrace. The coffee will help."

Bo slapped a hand on the table. "Some rum for that coffee, sir? It's after the meridian, so we're going to have a touch in ours. And please call us Bo and Peter."

Martí nodded and smiled widely for the first time. "Thank you again, but I do not drink rum. I prefer gin at those rare times I indulge in alcohol. And not in my coffee. Please call me José."

A Cuban who didn't drink rum? Who preferred *gin?* I studied him as he sat down. José Martí was a thin, almost delicate-looking man in his early thirties, his receding hair counterbalanced by a moustache that would do a walrus proud. He had the air of a brooding artist about him, a certain passion or intensity of thought. I instantly wondered if he'd been the one to pass the message to Roosevelt, but he didn't answer the description of the messenger. Neither did the man who left when we arrived.

"I've never met a man from Cuba who favored gin over rum."

Martí said, "It's true. My friends call me *ginebrito,* 'a little gin,' because I drink it sparingly. Gin and tonic water. You know about its medicinal value, yes?"

Medicinal value? Then I remembered. A Brit on a riverboat in the Mekong River had explained it to me. "Yes, the quinine helps fight malaria. An old Indian remedy."

"Very good, Peter. You must have experience of the tropical parts of the world."

"Yes, a bit."

Then I asked him, as innocently as I could, "Sounds like you've lived here in the United States for some time, José. How often do you get to return to Cuba to visit any family?"

"I have lived here since eighteen-eighty, Peter. And I have not been to my homeland since seventy-nine, when I was deported to Spain."

"Deported?"

"Yes. It would seem that the Spaniards do not appreciate my writing."

"You write against them?"

"I write the words of truth."

Bo asked, "Why deport you to Spain for mere words?"

"So that I am not in Cuba to cause trouble among the disaffected masses. In Spain they thought they could keep me under control more easily. They were wrong, of course. I am no longer there, am I?"

He took a sip of coffee after that, visibly relaxing. I asked, "What about the Cuban freedom fighters that we hear about in the press? Are they really strong enough to overthrow the Spanish?"

"No. But they are getting stronger everyday. Someday I will be able to return and see my wife and son."

"What do you mean, José? They're not with you here?"

Martí's tone darkened, those small eyes emotionless. "No, Peter. When the Spanish deported me, they kept my family in Cuba, as semi-hostages. The Spanish generals are very adept at crushing anyone in their way, using terror or shame or torture. I have felt physical torture, but that which is against the heart produces a pain far more severe. But I am not alone. For Cuba's people, it has been a cruel struggle to gain freedom."

"Like the Hebrews and the Babylonians in the psalm."

Martí slowly nodded. "The one hundred and thirty-seventh psalm is well known in Cuba, Peter. There will come a time for us also."

"Soon?"

"¿Quién sabe? Who knows, but God?"

"An eye for an eye? Now what was it they called that in the

Old Testament?"

"The Law of Talion. I hope it does not come to that, though the people are angry. I hope the Spanish just go home and the atrocities end."

Very instructive, I thought. But our conversation wasn't done. Over the next hour I heard Martí's story. He was indeed an artist, and as a youth had gone to school to be a painter, so good that by age fourteen, in 1868, he was accepted by the prestigious professional school of art in Havana. But then his public writing began with a sonnet titled, "The Tenth of October," about the patriots in 1868 who had declared Cuban independence from a village near the eastern end of the island called Yara, a Taino Indian word. The famous *Grito de Yara*.

A few months later, still sixteen years old, he was arrested by the Spanish authorities for anti-imperial and anti-slavery essays. Convicted of treason, he was sentenced to six years in prison and eventually sent to the Isle of Pines, south of the mainland of Cuba. Then they deported him to Spain, where he studied law and wrote more essays. In 1877, he slipped back into Cuba from France using an assumed name, but found no work and ended up teaching in Guatemala. In 1878, at age twenty-five, he could stand it no more and returned to Cuba, where his son was born. Six months later he was deported again to Spain, where he slipped away once more, eventually ending up in New York. Now he was writing without fear, but was a poet without a country, a man without his family.

José Martí was obviously a persistent man. But was he connected to Roosevelt's message? The more I heard, the more I wondered. The next question was whether our meeting was premeditated on his part. But how could it be?

"José, do you have a card? I find this discussion intriguing. We Americans are revolutionaries at heart, and always seem to cheer the underdog in these conflicts. I'd like to keep in touch. To learn about Cuba and the fight for independence. Here is my card."

I handed him my official *carte de visite,* an innocuous card which didn't say much about me and nothing about my work. He examined it cursorily—too cursorily, I thought—and slipped it in a pocket. His card simply had his name with the title of "Consul," above the three nations he represented. It was even more nondescript than my card. *So we both have innocuous cards, eh?* I said to myself. *Maybe we're in the same business after all.*

"Yes, Peter. We should stay in correspondence," Martí replied. I then proposed that, due to the delicacy of his past, I should use a pseudonym for him in our correspondence—Mondongo. That word meant "fish stew" in the Spanish Caribbean and was also the name of an island near mine in Florida. With a wily grin, my new Cuban friend agreed. Thereafter, the subject wandered to Cuban food and music, a pleasant dialogue, especially considering the weather outside.

We all parted ways an hour later; Bo to entrain for the Naval War College in Newport, where he was to brief newly promoted Rear Admiral Luce on our operations in Panama. Martí was bound for the offices of the *New York Herald* in Manhattan, to translate a story about the labor unrest in Chicago for a paper in Buenos Aires. I left for Washington.

After Martí departed, Bo said, "Pleasant sort, but more than just a writer, I'm thinking. Say, you never did tell me what that politico wanted last night."

"Next time, Bo. Have to go now. Good luck with Luce."

That was the last I saw of Bowman McCalla for a long time. He ended up getting assigned to the European Squadron for the next two years.

Politics on the Potomac

Monday, 11 January 1886
Office of the Secretary of the Navy
U.S. Naval Headquarters, 2nd floor
State, War, and Navy Building
Washington, D.C.

I stood along the far wall, behind my bureau head, Commodore Walker, who was beside Admiral Porter. The admiral stood before the desk of the civilian head of our service, Secretary of the Navy William Collins Whitney. Originally from Massachusetts, Whitney was of Puritan stock, a Yale graduate, successful lawyer, and most famously, a New York prosecutor of government corruption. His considerable forehead was creased in contemplation as he sat behind a massive desk, reading a report—my report, written hurriedly on the train down to Washington and typed just an hour earlier.

When he finally spoke, it was directed at Admiral Porter.

Having served many secretaries of the navy during his decades in the service, Porter was the only naval officer around cowed by no one in Washington.

"So let me understand this clearly, Admiral Porter. You're saying the impetuous Mr. Roosevelt believes that this silly missive is not a hoax, and that he feels that this government should investigate it, because not to would be a dereliction of duty. And therefore, by logical extension, should we decide *not* to devote time and effort to this, and something horrendous happens in Cuba or in Florida—then he will be only too glad to say 'I told you so' in the press. The patriotic Republican, who did his duty and warned the Democrats, but alas, to no avail."

Whitney didn't wait for a reply, he just shook his head and groaned. "Oh . . . I know young Theodore Roosevelt, gentlemen, and let me tell you, he's just the sort that would take great glee in doing just that."

Porter waited a few seconds, then answered patiently, "Yes, he is."

I noted the absence of the usual "sir." The admiral was perturbed, his discontent centered on the general hesitation shown by the Cleveland administration regarding Cuba. They were afraid of possibly antagonizing Spain. Porter couldn't have cared less about Spain in this matter. He wanted to know what was happening in Cuba and in Key West.

Whitney ignored Porter's lack of courtesy and pointed a finger at me.

"Commander Wake, obviously you think this should be investigated by sending a man into Havana. Do you think you should be the one to do it?"

In my heart, the answer was no. I was due some leave and had spent the previous two gray winter months in Washington, dreaming of Florida's sunshine. However, in my head I knew the answer was yes. I knew Havana well, and was best prepared for the job.

I tried not to show my reluctance. "Yes, sir."

Whitney shook his head again. "Very well, Commander. I don't like any of this, but you'll get your wish." The finger shot up again.

"But remember this well, Commander. Do *not* allow yourself to become entangled in any way, with *any* unsavory alliances, criminal actions, disreputable sorts, government corruption, or anything—I repeat, *anything*—that will embarrass the Spanish government, bring discredit to this U.S. administration, or embroil us in any more messes than we've already got on our plate. I can guarantee all of you," he swung his glare around to Porter and Walker, "that if anything like that ever got out in the press, our loud-mouthed nemesis Roosevelt would crucify us for even being down there, interfering with another country, etcetera, etcetera—conveniently forgetting that *he* was the one who started the whole damned thing."

Based on his monologue, it was obvious to me from his prohibitions that Whitney had never been to Latin America. Consorting with unsavory types and participating in suborning corruption within foreign governments was pretty much what I did when on assignment. The Office of Naval Intelligence was there to get intelligence and that was how it was done. I thought it unwise to bring that up, though.

Whitney's next words were in the tone of a judge about to sentence a defendant—the voice of doom, directed squarely at me.

"Is all that perfectly and indisputably clear to you, Commander?"

I glanced at Porter for some support, but he was busy admiring the ceiling molding around the ornate gas chandelier, a twinkle showing in his eyes. For his part, Walker was studying a solitary yellow bird hopping along the frozen windowsill, apparently lost and trying to peck his way inside to the warmth.

The symbolism of the whole scene was not lost on me, but

I said the only thing a naval officer was expected to say, when confronted by a superior with that question.

"Yes, sir."

⁓

Twenty minutes later we were all—*sans* Secretary Whitney—in Porter's office for another meeting. The admiral began immediately, his huge salt-and-pepper beard undulating as he spoke.

"Well, we have our orders from the secretary, gentlemen. Commodore Walker, please see that Rodgers gets briefed on this when he returns from Norfolk. This will be run out of his shop at ONI, but I want the details kept confidential among only the three of us."

Walker nodded. "Aye, aye, sir. I noticed that the secretary didn't mention that last part of the message—about a Judas."

"No, he didn't. I suppose he wants to ignore that right now. If it proves to be true, it'll probably be somebody over in Bayard's bailiwick at State. Let's hope it's not true."

"Aye on that, sir," offered Walker, adding, "There's some new people at State since the Democrats came in. The new ones aren't so keen on us engaging internationally, especially in somebody else's civil war."

I waited patiently to be brought into the discussion or dismissed. It always was—and still is, for that matter—infuriating to be ignored when superiors are gamming on about an operation in which *you* are the one about to risk life and limb. At last they got around to me.

Porter asked, "Peter, do you want Rork on this?"

"Yes, sir. He's on leave, but I can stop at the island in Florida and pick him up on the way."

"Very well, you can have him. Commodore, do you have a general plan for this assignment?"

"Yes, sir. The ostensible mission is a follow-up visit to Panama. En route, Peter heads down to Cuba, noses about in Havana. He'll be just another naval officer in transit, waiting for the weekly packet to Panama, where he will meet with de Lesseps and the French engineers to get a briefing on their progress. Nothing secret, let everyone know his plans. De Lesseps is due to arrive at Panama on February seventeenth, so that works out well. All very up-front and plausible."

Porter said nothing. Walker continued. "Meanwhile, Peter shows up at midnight on February eighteenth at the leper cemetery in Havana. If things start to unfold there, we delay his trip to Panama. If not, he'll depart aboard the packet on the nineteenth or twentieth. Either way, he'll eventually go into Panama to update Lieutenant Kimball's dismal report of last year, though I doubt the French will be doing any better these days. That's it, sir."

Porter's reply was even more abrupt than usual. Maybe nervous was a better word for it. I'd never seen him like that. "Very well. Peter, I think you got the secretary's message—don't embarrass the navy or the country. Stay away from our consulate in Havana after you first routinely check in. No uniform. Low-key. No trouble."

He flipped the pages of a calendar on a side table, jammed a finger on a date, then scribbled something on it. "I want a ciphered cable report of what you've found out by eight o'clock in the morning on Friday, the nineteenth of February. Send it to Commodore Walker—only Commodore Walker. You will receive instructions in return by four o'clock that same afternoon. Do *not* proceed beyond that point on the nineteenth without instructions from either me or Commodore Walker. Lieutenant Rodgers will be back by then, but he's just a coordinator of information and doesn't have the authority for decisions on this. He won't get your telegraphed report. That will be sent to the commodore's alias address. You will be directed in your actions only by me or Commodore Walker—understood?"

I understood only too well. The chief coordinator of ONI was being cut out of the knowledge on this mission. Porter could be crafty as hell.

I saw that he was waiting for my reply and blurted out, "Yes, sir."

The admiral swung around in his chair and faced a wall map of the United States behind him. A map of the world covered the opposite side of the office.

"Hmm. You going by train to Florida?"

"Yes, sir. Train to lower Florida on the Gulf coast, near where I live. Then I sail out to the island and get Rork. We'll take the schooner to Key West. From there, by steamer to Havana."

"How long will all that take?"

"Three days for the train, another three days by vessel. That would be six days to Havana, sir." The moment I said it, I knew I'd said too much.

"Thank you, Wake, but I can do the *simple* arithmetic myself." He looked at Walker. "When do you want him to leave?"

"Morning of Tuesday, February ninth, Admiral. I want Commander Wake in position in Havana by the sixteenth. That'll give him some leeway in case of transportation problems."

"Very well, gentlemen. Make it so, and good luck."

The commodore and I chorused, "Aye, aye, sir," and departed as Porter roared for his clerk to bring him some report on the disposition of ships in the European squadron. I pitied that clerk's afternoon. Outside the admiral's office, Walker quietly said, "Follow me."

When we got to Walker's office down the passageway, he wasted no time in pleasantries. He seldom did.

"The old man's way out on a political limb with this, Peter. Whitney is no fool, and knows Porter is a friend of Roosevelt, a brother author I suppose. He knows that the admiral pretty much set all this up. But remember this, Grover Cleveland and his cabinet, which includes Secretary Whitney, *intensely* dislike

Roosevelt. Cleveland and Roosevelt grudgingly worked together at the state capitol in Albany, but there was no love lost between them. And the Democrats are not forgetting some of Roosevelt's comments during the presidential election about Cleveland's love child and his morals. The president will probably be told of this assignment, but won't be enthused one bit by the manner in which it was initiated."

He paused, concern etched on his face. "So let's keep this thing under control and on plan, Peter."

His final comment referred, of course, to some previous assignments of mine. Specifically, the ones for which I got those medals from Peru and Cambodia—the same ones that were difficult to explain to the public or to Congress.

I feel compelled to explain a little background on that. You see, occasionally my actions on those assignments had deviated from the original plans formed by my superiors in Washington. Due to events changing on the ground, at times rather dramatically, I'd had to innovate out in the field.

Innovation. An interesting phenomenon. I've discovered over the years that plans that seem eminently logical while discussed in an office in Washington turn out to be not even remotely realistic when implemented inside another culture on the far side of the world. Thus, a little latitude is necessary—*crucial*, in my opinion—for the subordinate, though it is seldom granted in advance and must therefore be seized at the time of decision out there on the scene.

Innovation in the field is the sort of thing that frightens political people in Washington and is quite rare in this modern day of transoceanic telegraph cables and instant communications. Naval officers on distant assignment ashore are tethered to the highest desk-bound authorities back home and generally forbidden to use their own judgment. In my own defense, those earlier assignments all eventually turned out for the good, and the naval leadership, if not the political leadership above them, have always known that I'd do what was right.

Having explained all that to the reader, however, I must report Commodore Walker was looking as nervous as Porter at that moment, so I tried to reassure him with my reply. "Commodore, it'll turn out fine. Don't worry."

He groaned. "Oh Lord, Wake, you always say that—and I always worry when you say that. Just be careful down there on this one."

"Aye, aye, sir."

I sent a telegram shortly thereafter, advising Rork to be ready when I arrived at the island on the twelfth or thirteenth, and that the next day we'd be bound for Panama. My friend and shipmate for twenty-three years, Boatswain's Mate Sean Rork, United States Navy, was the one man in the world I trusted completely to get me out of whatever trouble I'd managed to get into. We both had the scars to prove it.

Next, I telegraphed my daughter Useppa in Key West. There was a chance I'd get to see her briefly as I passed through the island en route to Havana. I hadn't seen her for almost seven months. She was doing well, keeping busy at the Methodist missionary work she loved. I was very proud of her, but worried about her long-term happiness. She evidently had a beau, whom I'd not met, and like all fathers I was wary of him.

And Useppa was worried about me, particularly about my staying a widower too long. It had taken three sad years for me to come to terms with my heartache and resolve to go forward in life. Back in '83, Rork and I had survived a narrow—a very narrow—brush with starvation in the South China Sea off French Indo-China. That had been the spark for me to live life again. A short time later, an evening with a beautiful woman on a tropical island had been the flame—I knew I was still alive enough to feel love again.

Since then I had squired ladies about town in Washington, mainly to official functions where a sophisticated feminine companion was expected. And sometimes, when home in the islands on leave, I would take one of the island girls to vastly different social affairs—dances held in thatched huts on one of the various islands, where the settlers would gather by boat for an evening with homemade music and spirits.

But my daughter wanted more for me than the occasional social friend. She said I should—no, she said I had to—find a true mate. That was a tall order, in either Washington or Patricio Island, for someone like me. I was almost ready myself, but no appropriate prospects were on the horizon. Just couldn't picture myself with them, or them enduring me. Old sailors are set in their ways. Or maybe I'd lost my self-confidence. Or maybe I was gun-shy about commitment. In any event, it hadn't happened.

Useppa was also worried for me on another front. Since she'd become a missionary, she'd also become a temperance supporter. Because of that, I found myself in the unenjoyable position of being a large disappointment to my daughter because I drank spirits, of which she disapproved heartily. Our conversations on the issue were short. She bluntly objected to my drinking rum and bourbon and predicted a dire future of misery. I patiently told her to mind her own life.

I couldn't remember the name of Useppa's lad as I filled out the telegram form. Well, no matter. He wasn't the main reason to visit anyway—she was. I was looking forward to seeing my little girl again. Composing the message, my eyes misted. It had been far too long since I'd last seen her.

I left headquarters early, the better to get a good seat on the Alexandria & Washington train across the Long Bridge and out of the city to Virginia. When I wasn't at sea or on leave in Florida,

I lived at Boltz's Inn on Chain Bridge Road, just down from the new village of Vienna. It was less than an hour from the office, but the oak trees and pastures were a welcome respite from the smoke and stink of Washington City. Martha and Don Boltz, and their barkeeper Kathie, were longtime friends. In fact, I'd known Martha since she ran a place in Key West during the war.

After Linda died, I'd moved my children and myself to Boltz's Inn. Wanted to get them out of a cramped apartment down by the naval yard—not to mention away from the crime and bad influences of Washington. Without a wife to raise them, I needed all the help I could get with my children. Martha was wonderful with them, especially teenaged Useppa. We all had a few good years together at the Inn before my daughter, then my son, moved out. At eighteen, Useppa went to Key West. At seventeen, Sean headed to Annapolis. Now it was just me and a small room at Boltz's Inn.

Rork preferred to stay at the senior petty officer mess at the Washington Navy Yard. He said he enjoyed the city's night life, and it was free lodging.

The Refuge of Bachelors

Friday, 12 February 1886
Patricio Island
Southwest coast of Florida

Patricio Island lies a few miles inside Boca Grande Passage, on the southern fringe of the great bay called Charlotte Harbor, one of two large bays on the west coast of Florida. The other is Tampa Bay, 120 miles to the north. Charlotte Harbor has many dozens of islands, all of which are carpeted in a jungle verdure composed of mangroves, buttonwood, sabal palm, and gumbo-limbo.

Located about two miles west of the northern end of Pine Island, one mile east of Mondongo Island, and one mile northeast of Useppa Island, Patricio Island and the surrounding area is embedded in my soul. During the war, I commanded a small sloop gunboat, the *Rosalie*, which patrolled the coast and supplied pro-Union Floridians-turned-refugees who had assembled on Useppa

Island. When I married Linda in Key West in 1864, she was ostracized by the people there for marrying a Yankee, so I moved her to Useppa. She loved the islands and the lively people who inhabited them. The following year, when she gave birth to my precious daughter, Linda named our little girl Useppa after the island that had given her sanctuary. Our son, Sean, was born two years later at Pensacola, when I was stationed there.

Three months after Linda died during the winter of 1881, my children, Sean Rork (their *de facto* uncle), and I returned to Useppa Island, where we scattered Linda's ashes atop the high ridge overlooking the surrounding bay. That night, after the children were asleep, Rork and I talked about our future, and specifically about my professional prospects, which appeared grim indeed.

My career had always been hindered by the fact I never attended the naval academy, or even attended any college anywhere. Because of that, I would never be given a decent ship command. And now that I had two children to care for alone, what would I do? I'd been transferred to the newly formed Office of Naval Intelligence, but no one knew at that time whether ONI would last very long. Even if the unit did last long, no one knew what effect it would have on an officer's career. Most considered it a place for officers who couldn't be seagoing successes. In other words, "the failures."

I tried, however, to be philosophic about the assignment and approach it with enthusiasm. Besides, it was the only damn thing left for me in the navy. It turned out that I wasn't that bad at it. I produced results.

To Rork, who has a sense of these things, it didn't matter that ONI wasn't the pathway to flag rank for me. It was, he said, "still a navy job, an' a damned sight better than farmin' ashore o' skipperin' a lumber schooner. Aye, Uncle Sam's ever bleedin' navy, 'tis the only home for the likes o' us, me friend."

Rork's sister back in Ireland had died a few years earlier, so he had no family left. My children and I were his only family. That night on Useppa Island, we talked about both of us living in the Florida islands again someday, having a place to go to when we were on leave. A place to take our pensions when the navy finally said it was over. We talked about which island we'd pick and how we'd build our homes. But it was all a pipe dream, not a plan.

That pipe dream stayed with me, however, and in 1883, after that ridiculous assignment in Indo-China went awry, getting Rork severely wounded and me damned near killed, I went ahead and spent my life savings buying Patricio Island. Of course, I invited Rork to live there also. It's a horseshoe-shaped island with a large shallow bay inside, opening to the east. The bay is suitable only for the smallest of bateaus at the highest of tides.

There is a way onto shore, however. Along the west shore of Patricio, a deep-water swash channel sweeps up from near Useppa Island, able to float a four-foot draft at high tide. There, at the narrowest part of the island near the deepest water, Rork and I built our homes on a small ridge, perhaps thirty feet tall at the highest point, running along the centerline of the island.

The ridge on Patricio, like the hills and ridges of all the surrounding islands, was man-made. One basketful at a time, over hundreds of years, the original pre-Columbian inhabitants—the famous Calusa Empire—built up cities and towns on those islands. Thousands lived in that area.

When the Spanish arrived in 1513, they found a sophisticated culture. The Calusa were fully able to defend themselves, which they proceeded to do quite efficiently the second time the Spanish showed up, in 1519—wounding Juan Ponce de León mortally. It took the Spanish well over a century to subjugate the Calusa, mostly through treachery and disease. The last of the empire's pure descendants were gone a hundred years before my arrival during the war.

An old settler rainwater cistern was already there, probably built years before by some of the many seasonal Cuban fishermen. Rork, my son, and I, along with a few local friends, have slowly enlarged the cistern and strengthened it. The cistern was critical to survival, for there are no wells in those islands. In the summer, prodigious amounts of rain fell, but in the winter it was a prized commodity, the droughts sometimes going for six months.

Then we built our tropical bungalows. Rork and I have identical homes, both facing the sunset. They are plain affairs, but constructed like vessels—clinker-built, water-tight, and comfortable. Each has a wrap-around verandah, ten feet wide, that allows the sea breeze to rush through the house. Jasmine, Linda's favorite, grows wild around us, scenting the air better than any fancy perfume.

We kept the living quarters simple—more an indication of our building skills than an architectural statement. The inside of the house is a thirty-foot square box. The main parlor room stretches across the western half of the place, with a coral-stone fireplace in one corner and bookshelves lining the walls. Broad double doorways open onto the verandah on each side of the house, making the whole place open and airy. A plain galley with wood-fired stove occupies one back corner room, an unpretentious bedroom the other corner. The stove is my most expensive component, but I'm sadly deficient in its use. Rork does far better, though he's never had any training.

Our furniture is homemade, except for the sea chests that act as side tables. Containing our few permanent possessions, several of them have vivid memories for us. The most unusual is a huge, brightly painted trunk sent to me in appreciation by the emperor of Viet Nam, Hiep Hoa, only days before a coup and his subsequent execution. He should've listened to my advice—but I've told that tale in an earlier narration.

The walls are hung with trinkets brought home from around the world: a blow-dart weapon from the Cuna Indians of Panama, a Berber *ghanjar* fighting knife from North Africa, a chart of the Mediterranean, a silk painting from Cambodia, a bow with arrows from the Pacific. On a shelf is an ancient book from the Jesuit library in Peru. Both Rork and I read a lot. Our reading chairs are made from local buttonwood and gumbo-limbo, and cushioned by silk pillows sent by our friend Professor Petrusky in Saigon. Rork has no large table, but I have one made from a hatch cover, and on those few occasions when we have visitors, we entertain them at my place.

Our two bungalows are forty feet apart from each other, far enough for privacy—something a sailor craves as he gets older—but close enough for help or a friendly word. We usually stay apart during the day, busy on our individual projects. Improving our quarters, gardening, or working on our thirty-foot sloop, the *Nancy Ann*—there is always enough to keep us busy. In the late afternoon, all hands join for a sunset drink on my verandah.

Sunsets at Patricio are grand moments in time. On the western horizon, Lacosta Island is a line of dark green with coconut trees whisping up here and there, the lead-colored sea spreading out beyond. Closer in are dozens of small islets in the bay, their mangrove fringes discernibly lighter in color than the hardwood treed interior. Embracing them all is the bay. Dark green in the deep parts and paling to tan and white in the sandy shallows, it is our food garden and our link to the outside world.

The small keys like Patricio are home to swirls of shore birds that put on a spectacular show as the heavens darken. Clouds of them fly home to their island roosts as the sun turns to fire in the steel-blue sky. The trade-wind cumulus become tinted with gold and copper, lavender and peach. Silhouetted against that sky are blue herons, white pelicans, roseate spoonbills, brownish-white ospreys, and others I don't even know the names of, filling the air with graceful languid motion. With the surf pounding out the rhythm, the birds' different calls provide the melody for Mother Nature's daily evening dance of life. Every sunset at the island makes me feel humble, and very blessed.

There is a ritual, of course, for we are sailors, and sailors love rituals. At each day's sunset, Rork sounds the conch shell three times. He says its plaintive nature reminds him of Ireland's heartrending whistles and flutes. In response, we hear conchs from other scattered islanders acknowledging the same, indicating everyone is well, the day is done. A toast is then drunk, raising our glasses to the horizon and using the traditional naval toast for that day of the week. After dinner, perhaps a game of chess or checkers, a discussion of history or politics, or the retelling of a hundred sea stories that we each already know by heart.

Sometimes he hauls out the harmonica he's been practicing on and I'll hear a toe-tapping jig or a tearful ballad. Rork learned the instrument quickly, like it was hiding within him all those years. He breathes, and the music emerges. He can make me laugh or cry with that damned thing. Just another facet of that deep-souled friend who's twice the man of any president or potentate I've met—and I've met well over a dozen by now.

It is all so completely different from the chaos and conniving of Washington. Patricio Island allows a man to unwind and not worry what another man meant in deed or tongue. In the islands, a man means exactly what he says. For better or worse, there are no misunderstandings. There are no petty comments among frontier men.

The plants and animals surrounding us are intricate and delightful to observe. I sit for hours watching the dolphins hunting in the shallows, or the pelicans gliding within inches of the water. On our island we have wild boar, raccoon, armadillo, colorful snakes, and the occasional gator that wanders over from Pine Island, where they are plentiful. Fish fill the waters around us. Crab, clams, and scallops are everywhere. Fresh seafood is daily fare. Living on the island is an ongoing lesson in the beauty of God's gifts to man.

While working in Washington, I dream of Patricio. When on leave and down at the island, I forget Washington and the navy entirely. But the nights are the hardest time for me, naturally.

I am lonely, and for more than a woman's touch. I'm lonely for a woman's heart. The island home I love dearly is admittedly crude and awkward. A woman would soften it, and me. My outlook is jaded, and getting worse. I know I am missing a critical element of humanity—that I'm descending into a cranky middle-aged man far faster than chronology should allow. After years of grief for my loss and uncertainty about my private future, I'm ready for a woman to share the burdens of life and perhaps even cheer me up. But none I've met makes me feel at ease. So I've steamed onward in life, doing my job, worrying for my children, taking care of my old friend Rork.

And Patricio Island remains a refuge for old bachelors.

Rork met me as I jumped off Whidden's sloop to the dock. Old man Whidden was a friend in Trabue, near Punta Gorda, whom I'd known since the war, when he was on the other side. Since I took possession of the place in '83, I've paid Whidden to be a caretaker of sorts for Patricio Island when Rork and I are gone. I even bought the sloop we keep at the island—the *Nancy Ann*—from him. He explained, with a wink, that she was named after his girlfriend in Tampa from years earlier, in the good times before the war.

Whidden meets us at the train head at Fort Ogden on the Peace River, or the wagon road head at Punta Gorda, and gives us a ride out to the island. Whidden—he never used another name—grew up in the area, knows every mile of it, and periodically takes us fishing and hunting to places far away from human presence. A solid, quiet man of wiry frame and indeterminate age, Whidden is the best kind of friend or the worst sort of enemy, like so many men on that coast.

Waving our good-byes as Whidden shoved off, Rork and I made our way through the banana, papaya, and mango trees along the shoreline, then cut to the right and walked up the shell path to the houses on the ridge. Orange and lime trees, with some gumbo-limbo and myrtle, sprawled along the hilltop by the bungalows. A giant strangler fig tree dominated the area beside my bungalow, and I saw a boar pelt stretched out on a limb.

Rork shrugged, "Pork for dinner, Peter. Got the one that was raidin' the garden. Sneaky as a thievin' Irish bog-trotter, he was, but I'm sneakier."

The shadows were lengthening. It had been rather warm that afternoon on the sail down to the island; now it was delightful. I breathed in the jasmine and felt a smile spreading. I was home, if only for a night.

"By the by, Sean, little Kathie at Boltz's Inn says to say hello. I'm to give you a hug, but you'll just have to imagine it, you old dog."

That brightened him up. "Why Peter, me boyo—I don't have to *imagine* a hug from the lovely Kathie, I can just *remember* several from the lass. Aye, a true woman if e'er there was one."

I laughed. He was irrepressible. "I'm glad to be home, even if only for a night."

Rork's face stiffened. "So it's to be Panama?"

"Maybe later we'll go there, but not initially. I'll tell you after dinner."

We entered my verandah under the signboard that proclaimed *Tranquility Bungalow*—Rork's said *Fiddler's Green*. After dropping my sea bag, I sat at the table while Rork brought out the dinner, a fine mix of pork and grouper, surrounded by carrots and peas. The latest scuttlebutt on our friends was exchanged, but not a word said about our orders. That was for later. Dessert was bananas and carambola fruit, just in time for the sunset ritual.

All the other islands signaled their well-being, Rork did his wail on the conch shell, and before long it was dark. The day's light disappears fast in the tropics once the sun goes down. We lit the lamps, sat outside on the verandah, and took in the stars. My friend was quiet, contemplative. I wondered if his arm was hurting him, but didn't ask. He didn't want pity and didn't like to talk about the wounds of his life, emotional or physical.

Sean Rork's early years weren't that unusual for an Irishman. Born and raised in a poor family at Fethard, within County Wexford in the southeast of Ireland, his future was to work the land, as his family had for generations untold. But Rork departed from what was expected of him at age thirteen. Courtesy of the influence of Thomas Cloney, the owner of nearby Castle Dungulph, Rork exchanged his poverty on land for that at sea as a ship's boy in the packet service from Ireland to England and Wales.

In his early twenties he shipped as the bosun aboard a packet bound for Boston, where he jumped ship and signed the papers enlisting him in the United States Navy, just before the war of the Southern Rebellion. We first met in the middle of the war, right there near Patricio Island. I was newly in command of a sailing gunboat and he was the new replacement for a bosun's mate gone criminally insane. We've been together, on and off, ever since.

Sean didn't return to Ireland for twenty ears, until the spring of 1880, when he was aboard the frigate *Constitution* as part of the American famine relief effort. He told me later that what he saw then cemented his dislike for most of the British and his own decision to come to America. He's never been back.

By now, my friend was a senior bosun and I was a commander, both of us in ONI with only each other and the navy to care for us. Over the years we'd incurred some wounds, mostly minor in nature. There were a few that weren't minor, but we always recovered from them. During our time in Indo-China, however, Sean had been hit by a bullet intended for me while at the emperor's palace within the Forbidden Purple City. He lost his lower left arm due to the subsequent infection, and, I suspect, due to some incompetent Oriental witch-doctoring. French naval surgeons saved his life just before the famous Battle of Hué. Thank God for them.

Now he had an "appliance" that fit onto his stump, courtesy

of French Navy carpenters. It had various attachments—a lifelike, flesh-colored hand (complete with detailed false fingernails) made of India rubber; a marlinespike; and a hook. The false hand fitted nicely over the marlinespike, concealing it. His choice of appendage depended on the surroundings and his mood.

Sean had an intuitive sense of people. He could size up a man in seconds, or charm the silk off a woman in minutes. His long black hair, graying now, was in an old-fashioned tar's tail; what a landsman would call a ponytail. One undisciplined lock still would flop down on his face—a boyish effect women tell me they love. Even taller than my six feet, and lanky, he is still twice as strong as me despite his nine additional years of age. Recently, though he never complained, I saw that he was getting the ailment common to all sailors after thirty years at sea—rheumatic pains and swelling in the knuckles of his hand and feet. Cold, wet work at sea had done it to him and I worried about my friend's silent agony, a compilation of pains induced by nature and war.

He interrupted my reflection. "So what's it to be, then?"

The pleasant time of decompression was over. "Cuba, Sean. Apparently some revolutionaries have contacted a politician named Theodore Roosevelt up in New York City."

"The author?" Rork had read my copy of *Naval History of the War of 1812*. When on the island, he read quite a lot, preferring biographies and histories. I enjoyed novels.

"One and the same."

"Why him?"

"I suppose they think he has influence, since he's a bigwig Republican. Rising star."

Rork shook his head. "Them Dago lads're a little behind the times, aren't they? The Demo's are callin' the shots now."

"Yeah, but he still knows people. Anyway, they sent him a coded verbal message, saying it was sent from Key West. The gist of it was a summons to come down to a secret rendezvous in Havana, where I guess they'll probably plea for official, or unofficial, U.S.

help. We're going instead. Roosevelt's out of it now."

"Do you know which o' the rebel leaders it is in Cuba? Maceo? Or maybe Gómez?"

He referred to Antonio Maceo, the dark-skinned mulatto general in the resistance nicknamed "the Bronze Titan." Incredibly strong, he'd been wounded many times and was a legend in Cuba—one man the Spanish greatly feared. Máximo Gómez was the senior general of the resistance, and another legend.

"I don't think so, Sean. They're pretty well known. They wouldn't have to resort to theatrics." I showed him the contents of the message and explained the interpretation Roosevelt and I had come up with.

"Lots o' religion in that message. Latin phrases. A priest sent it."

"I don't think so. The priests down there are mostly from Spain and the Church is strongly in favor of the Spanish authorities. And the priests are paid by the imperial government, remember?"

"Aye, a good point, indeed. Still, the religious feelin' o' this is too strong. Got a feelin' in me bones on that. Me right foot's achin' an' you know what *that* means."

I did. I always pay attention to Rork's aching bones. His feet in particular. They frequently prove to be correct. "Well, I dunno, Sean, maybe there's some disgruntled priests down there that are ready to go against the Church."

"Mebbe. The Judas part is interestin' too."

"And a mystery to me."

"So what's the plan?"

"I figure we keep it simple. First off, we're officially bound to Panama to do an assessment follow up on Kimball's July report on the canal. Supposedly de Lesseps will be there now and I'm to try to talk with him."

"Oh, me boyo! That should be fun for ye. Remember the last time you two talked?"

Yes, I certainly remembered the evening. It was during

Ferdinand de Lesseps's first visit to Panama six years earlier, when the celebrated promoter of grand engineering projects arrived to great fanfare. He had convinced the world his sea level canal across Panama would be built with French efficiency, just like they'd done in Egypt on the Suez. He'd also convinced the world to invest in it, through him.

Because of my experience in Panama, and because I knew the proposed route of the canal well, he'd said he wanted to converse with me. We did, but I'm afraid the conversation did not go too well. What he really wanted was to do a monologue, garner my support, and not hear my unappreciated candor.

I predicted dire results if the French continued the way they'd started. Disease was the issue they didn't fully appreciate, and disease had dogged them since. It almost killed *me* back in '71 when we were only surveying the route. De Lesseps put on quite a show for me that night, insisting that French doctors would take care of any medical problems they *might* encounter. Then, tired of my spoiling his *grand entré,* he had walked out of our talk.

And now the canal project was in trouble. It was over budget, well behind schedule, and had to deal with more than eight thousand deaths. The estimated finishing point had been pushed back so many times that it was a running joke around the world.

More than a few people were saying de Lesseps and his canal were a giant fraud. There were calls by some in France for a police investigation of the funds spent. Others were calling for the French government to step in and officially take control completely, to have the French army officially control and complete the canal project. That kind of talk got the attention of the U.S. government, for it was a clear challenge to America's Monroe Doctrine.

In July 1885, ONI sent Lt. William Kimball to assess the situation. His report was dour, estimating it would take the French at least another twenty-six years to complete the canal at the present rate of work, and that he doubted they could even continue their present rate. The United States was watching it all closely, worried that France might go in, overwhelm the Colombian government's authority, and try to create a French colony—against the Monroe Doctrine—in order to salvage their project and their pride. They had already done that in Mexico, but regretted it after five years of war. Rork was right, de Lesseps would not be happy to see me, the harbinger of ugly predictions come true. However, I didn't care what the pompous French ass thought, and besides, it was a perfect cover for the Cuba mission.

"De Lesseps probably won't even see me, but I'll get in to meet the engineers I knew a few years back—if any of them are still alive." In the Panamanian summers, yellow fever was killing off young engineers just out of France's prestigious Polytechnique at frightful rates. "It's camouflage, anyway."

"Aye, an' time will tell. What route to Cuba? Regular o' quiet like?" Rork asked, returning us back on subject.

"Regular. Sail *Nancy Ann* to Punta Rassa in the morn and get on the schooner overnight to Key West. From there, we take a Mallory steamer down to Havana."

"An' once in Havana?"

"I figured we'd stay at one of the hotels on the harbor front, like other Americans do. Very quietly. Just naval personnel in transit. That fits in with our story."

Rork shrugged his agreement and I went on to the important part. "Then, at midnight of the eighteenth, we go to the cemetery. Remember that ancient one near the San Lazaro leper colony, behind the hospital?"

Rork rubbed his chin. "Aye. The one between the coast and the governor-general's palace up on that hill."

"That's the one. We loiter there and see what happens. Which'll be probably nothing. In any event, the following morning we send a cable report to Walker in Washington, via his cover address in New York, and wait for an answer by four in the afternoon. Only Porter and Walker have command authority on this. Lieutenant Rodgers knows some of it, but won't have decision-making power."

"An' then?"

"Either Porter or Walker'll tell us what to do next. After we're done in Havana, we transit south to Panama, do the assessment, and return home. Two months of leave in sunny Florida after that. Of course, since you've already had three weeks of leave, you get to go back up north three weeks earlier than me, *amigo.*"

Rork shivered. "Ooh, don't remind me . . ."

"Is *Nancy Ann* ready?"

"That she is, Peter."

"Under way an hour before dawn, then. And when we're in Key West, we'll have dinner with Useppa and her new boyfriend. I cabled her that we're coming. I want to meet this fellow, size him up, make sure he's a decent type. Between the two of us, you and I should be able to get him steering the straight and narrow. You can wear your hook for that, if you'd like."

Rork roared in laughter. He loved to show off that wicked-looking hook, especially to arrogant types. "The Great Motivator," he called it.

"Aye, we'll have a wee come-ta-Jesus meeting with the lad! An' afore we're through, that young worthy'll be inspired to be a right proper *gentle*-man around our little lass, that's for sure—o' we'll have his guts fer garters! So what do ye know o' this fellow?"

"Nothing really. Think he did some work on a church, or something, and that's how they met. Can't even remember his name from her letter. It's up north."

"Not to worry. We'll know 'im inside an' out by the time dinner's through. But really, Peter, if Useppa picked 'im, then he's probably a fine enough lad."

"Hmm, well, I guess you're maybe right on that, Sean. I suppose we should give him *some* slack."

Useppa's very intuitive about people, an inheritance from her mother. "All right, it's all set then. Early night for an early morn. We're returning to the island of Cuba, my friend."

"An' back in the game 'tis then, Commander. Methinks a wee bit o' adventure's just the thing ta stir up the blood a bit. So, a final toast then?"

We raised our glasses as he boomed out to the stars glittering across the sky above us, "To a willin' foe—an' the sea room to fight 'im!"

It was the old navy toast for Friday nights, originating in the Royal Navy, continued in ours. I didn't bother to tell Rork it was Saturday night. It's easy to lose track of time in the islands.

"And then we'll take his ship!" I offered in the expected bloodthirsty follow-up.

Later, watching the moon shadows filtering through the open doorways of my bungalow, I found myself reflecting on the difficult question of just who our foe would be in Havana. Then realized I was asking the wrong question. I knew Havana fairly well. The foes were apparent.

Who our *friends* might be, would be a far tougher thing to determine.

Nancy Ann was typical of the local boats—a centerboard sloop that drew only two and a half feet with the board up. We could sail through the back channels in her, crossing the grass banks and going places most larger vessels couldn't. By noon the next day, we'd rounded Chino and York islands and were close-reaching into a nor'east wind across San Carlos Bay, bound for the old cattle docks and hotel at Punta Rassa.

To the starboard, Sanibel Island's miles of lush fringe slid by and I caught a glimpse of old Captain Ellis' camp amidst the tangle of mangroves at Tarpon Bay. Ellis, an English ex–ship captain who was fond of rum, was married to Sofira, the half-Indian lady who befriended Linda on Useppa during the war and helped at the birth of our daughter. Her original husband, a sergeant in a pro-

Union Florida militia regiment, was killed by Whidden's outfit in an ambush on the Caloosahatchee River in the summer of '64.

Since then she'd married, then buried, another husband from disease over on Estero Island. In the mid-seventies, she took on Ellis as a husband and was still with him. Quite a woman, Sofira, but I felt sorry for her life with Ellis. I could see the old goat right then, standing in his sailing dinghy, yelling at someone ashore.

On our port side was the great San Carlos Hotel under construction at the new town of St. James on the southern end of Pine Island. Land speculators bestowed the grandiose title of St. James-on-the-Gulf upon this settlement, but it's really on the bay. The three-story structure with the huge verandah is still there, set well back from the shore, surrounded by palm and banana trees and a hemp plantation. Entrepreneurs built the hotel for visiting tarpon fisherman from the North, the thought of whom brought Roosevelt to mind. Someday he'll come down here, I predicted, to try his impatient hand at the sport. No doubt he'd use that new explosive, dynamite, I groaned to myself.

At Punta Rassa we had luck. The weekly packet schooner was in and, amazingly, right on schedule. She would leave for Key West in three hours. Rork and I loitered around the porch of George Schultz's Tarpon House Hotel for a while, listening to the excited conjecture among the fishing guides regarding Thomas Edison's new place up at Fort Myers. They debated whether it would be ready for the great inventor's expected visit with his new bride.

Prevailing opinion was that it would be, as everybody was in a lather to make a good impression on the Edisons, so they would stay in the area. Personally, I couldn't have cared less about him, but the locals could smell the money that a celebrity resident would bring in. Rork snorted disgustedly that the commotion reminded him of his hometown in Ireland, when an English swell would visit and all would bow low to curry favor.

Leaving *Nancy Ann* under the care of Mr. Schultz, we boarded the schooner and reclined in deck chairs, sailors aboard a ship who need not do anything except sit. It was an unnatural, disconcerting actually, mode for naval seamen.

By sunset that evening, we were out in the Gulf of Mexico, eight miles south of the docks and heading toward a distant horizon. Beyond us lay Key West, a place with many recollections for me. My blood was already pumping faster.

6

Key West

Sunday, 14 February 1886
Russell House Hotel
Duval Street, between Front & Greene streets
Key West, Florida

The Mallory steamer was due to get under way for Havana at sunrise the next morning, so we had enough time for a nice dinner. Russell House Hotel, a few blocks from the harbor on Duval Street, was the best hotel and restaurant in Key West. The haunt of naval officers during the war, it was still the place where naval and merchant marine officers dined.

In fact, Linda and I spent our wedding night at Russell House. That memory reminded me of the day's date. It'd been five years to the day since she died. I willed myself to concentrate on Useppa. The evening was about her.

Rork, upon further reflection on the subject, decided to wear his rubber hand instead of the hook. I again suggested the hook, but he wisely said that Useppa would immediately smell a rat and accuse them of intimidating her beau. Rork, as ferocious as he can act at times, is a sentimentalist at heart.

We were staying in a room on the third floor, and arrived downstairs at the reception parlor a little early. Charles Merrill, the owner and son-in-law of the original owner, greeted us. I'd known Charles for many years. He was in an unusual state of excitement.

"Useppa stopped by this afternoon and told me about your dinner, Peter," Merrill said pleasantly. "So we set up a special table for your dinner party."

"Ah, well, thank you, Charles, but we really don't need anything out of the ordinary," I replied, thinking of the bill. I could afford dinner for four on the standard fare, but nothing too extravagant. Naval officers don't make much money and that night's dinner wasn't on the mission's expense account.

Merrill smiled. "Peter, it's no problem. Besides, we have to put you in the special room overlooking Duval, because of the number of people in your party. Useppa said there'd be six, maybe seven. It seems that you'll have some very interesting dinner companions, my friend."

That was news to me. I was about to correct Merrill, when he looked over my shoulder and abruptly announced, "Why here's your lovely daughter now, Peter."

I turned and there was Useppa, clad in a green gingham dress at the front door. Around her was a rather diverse selection of people.

My daughter was the exact image of her mother at that age—petite, auburn haired, and fair skinned. Seeing her never fails to make my heart flutter. Literally, it's like seeing the past come back to life. The only difference from Linda was Useppa's slight limp, the product of a congenital ailment to her left leg. Years of compensating for it had reduced the disability to a nuisance, though it still occasionally caused her pain. Catching sight of her long-lost father, my little girl threw out her arms and reached up to embrace me.

"Oh, Daddy, it's been far too long—almost a year! And Uncle Sean, you look simply wonderful!"

After kissing me and hugging Rork, she pursed her lips and said, "But you look tired, Daddy. Are you eating well enough? They're not working you too hard, are they? I worry about that."

"Useppa, I'm fine."

"And my little brother, Sean? He doesn't write like he used to."

"He's fine too. Busy as a beaver at Annapolis." I gestured to the others standing around us. "Dear, I'd like to meet your friends."

"Oh, where are my manners? I'm sorry, Daddy. Mother would be aghast!"

She took the hand of the youngest man among them, and announced, "Daddy, this is Father Raul Leon, my special friend that I've written you about. He is junior pastor of the Church of St. Mark in Havana, the Episcopal church there. But he's on assignment helping Father Bautista at St. John's Episcopal, here in Key West."

What? This was her boyfriend? I stood there befuddled. I remembered her writing vaguely about a fellow named Leon who did work on or for a church. But a Hispanic Protestant minister? And what precisely did "special friend" mean? I scrutinized him closely.

He appeared around twenty-five, healthy, was decently attired, and had an apparently genuine smile and intelligent eyes. Not at all what I expected, but not what I'd feared either, which was a fast-talking ne'er-do-well who had somehow hoodwinked my daughter. I was still registering it—a Cuban *Protestant* minister?

Before I could formulate a response, Leon stepped forward and grasped my hand firmly. He said in fluent English, with very little accent, "It is an honor to meet you, Commander Wake. I've heard so many stories about your exploits."

Damn all, but I liked this boy, or man, rather. But I didn't want to think of Useppa with a man. I preferred her with a boy. Fortunately, Rork is quicker is such situations than I, and he covered my rudeness by barging in, extending his good right hand, and saying, "I'm Sean Rork, Father Leon. I'm Useppa's honorary uncle and godfather. Very nice to meet you—" he stepped on my right foot—"isn't it, Peter?"

Ready now, I took the cue. "Why yes, it certainly is . . . Father."

Let me explain right here that it is more than slightly disturbing to be a father of a pretty daughter and then have to call her beau "Father." One feels ridiculous.

Leon laughed. "Feels odd to say that, does it not?"

My God, this fellow could read minds! "Well, yes, actually, it certainly does . . . Father." Then I realized how dimwitted repeating myself sounded. "But let me say that it is also an honor for me to meet the man my daughter thinks is special. I'm afraid I didn't recall from her letter that you were a man of the cloth."

And probably a teetotaler who thinks I'm some sort of rummy from Useppa's stories, I figured, vowing that I'd truck no lectures from *him.*

"Please, call me Raul, Commander. I think it will be easier for both of us."

Rork, who can never resist a sardonic comment, chimed in quietly to me, "Glad I left the hook in me seabag, Peter. A bit out o' place here, don'tcha think?"

Useppa took all this in and lost her smile. "*Please,* you men . . . are we done with the barbaric references now? I've some more introductions."

She turned to the others. It dawned on me they'd been waiting for several minutes, watching this little family drama unfold. Quite a show, no doubt, and I was sure it would be all over the island by morning. I gave them my most sincere look.

"Daddy, Sean, this is Father Juan Bautista, of St. John's Episcopal here in Key West."

We shook hands. At first glance, Bautista didn't strike me as one of those prim and proper, fire-and-hell fellows, the kind I dislike intensely. I wondered what Useppa had told him about me, though, for he wore an expression mixed between respect and forgiveness.

Next there was a Negro couple, the gentleman of which also wore the white collar of faith. Evidently, it was to be a pious evening.

"Daddy and Sean, this is Reverend and Mrs. William Artell, of St. Peter's African Episcopal Church of Key West. Reverend Artell is also headmaster of the Frederick Douglass School, where I teach."

I knew from Useppa's letters that St. Peter's was the colored church in Key West. Fortunately, since the war, the racial situation on the island had been pretty much one of tolerance, though with the Republicans now displaced by Democrats in Florida and around the South, old hatreds were returning. Vengeance against blacks and Republicans across Florida was being reported in the press, with little sympathy for the victims. Reconstruction was over, and revenge had begun. Key West, however, had not seen much of that.

Mrs. Artell nodded and the good reverend shook my hand, looking at me strangely. When he spoke, it was in the slow baritone patois of a Bahamian, an accent I always enjoy hearing.

"I had the honor of knowing Reverend Pinder, who married you at the south beach many years ago, Commander. May I offer our condolences on your loss, and our confidence in dear Linda's passing into heaven to be with our Lord."

Well, that did it. I'd kept Linda's death from my mind until then. But his genuine empathy affected me deeply, bringing memories flooding to my mind. I focused on the pleasant ones from twenty-two years earlier—our wedding at the African cemetery on the south beach of the island, the only place available at the time. I could see Reverend Pinder, another black Bahamian, as he performed the ceremony no white preacher would sanction. The island and the navy were against such a culturally cursed union as a Confederate daughter of Key West marrying a Yankee naval officer.

Linda and I, with Rork as best man and my small crew around us, stood on that beach at sunset as Pinder blew the conch shell and solemnly intoned the vows and blessings. Walking away from the celebration later along that beach, we'd felt like the luckiest people under those tropical stars.

Now I thought my constitution would fail me, but I got out, "Thank you for your thoughts and words, Reverend Artell. Linda is gone, but I have two wonderful children still. And Reverend Pinder, how is he? I'd like to see him, if I could."

"He went home to the Lord four years ago, Commander. A good man, missed by all. On a more positive note, I must report that your daughter has done wonderful work with the children of the Douglass School. We are very fortunate to have her there. You must be so proud."

I was still recovering from the enormity of the previous six minutes and probably sounded overly maudlin as I said, nearly in tears, "Yes, I love her dearly."

Useppa squeezed my hand and changed the subject with, "Oh, Daddy, let's depart from memory lane and all go in for a nice dinner, shall we? There is so much to get caught up on."

She barely took a breath before leading the procession up the stairs to the special room overlooking Key West's main street, Duval, which famously went for a mile right across the island, from the Atlantic Ocean to the Gulf of Mexico.

My poor girl was nervous. This was a big moment for her and she was trying her best to be graceful and charming. "Uncle Sean, I want to tell you all about how the school is doing. And Daddy, Raul is working very hard in Havana. I bet you didn't even know there were Episcopalians there, did you? I've told them all that you were raised Episcopalian up north, but that mother turned you into a Methodist down south."

She was so grown up. I couldn't remember when I'd been prouder of her.

The evening was delightful, with light-hearted conversation about Key West, mutual acquaintances, and society's most recent inventions, which seemed to be coming at an ever faster rate. I found myself increasingly partial to the young pastor. However, three more surprises came my way that evening, courtesy of Raul Leon.

The first was during the dessert course, when Rork asked Raul Leon what his thoughts were about the anti-Spanish movements in Cuba. Raul, raised in Havana, had started life as a Catholic and converted to Episcopalian at seventeen. He amazed me when he replied that he didn't know much about that sort of thing, since he felt the clergy should stay out of politics. Well, even I was aware that *everyone* in Havana knew about what was going on—it was the main topic of conversation in all the taverns and businesses and homes—and I speculated that the lad was being a bit disingenuous. On a hunch, Rork asked if Raul had ever read José Martí's work, but the answer was, "Who is that?" My friend's eyebrows flickered, a sign of disbelief, but he didn't pursue the matter, apparently out of politeness.

The second surprise came when Raul paid the bill, the estimate of which had my innards in knots during the meal, explaining that he wanted to return the many kindnesses that everyone at the table had given him over the last couple of years. I instantly wondered how he had the money, when the charge would've been steep for *me*, and I was probably the best off financially at the table. He didn't explain, and out of respect for my daughter, I didn't ask.

The third surprise came when we were all departing from the dinner. Useppa lived in a back room at the Methodist rectory, by the church at Eaton and Simonton streets. Raul was staying at the Episcopal rectory, only two blocks east on Eaton, near Duval. As I watched them walk off it registered itself upon me that they were holding hands and strolling closely, in an altogether far too easy manner. Hmm . . .

My little girl had become a grown woman, in love with a grown man. I compelled myself to regard this as a normal, and even appropriate, state of affairs. But it also arrived in my mind right about then that the Methodist preacher and his wife were off island for several days. Thus the rectory house where Useppa lived would be unoccupied by others. I was tempted to follow the couple and ward off any temptation on Raul Leon's part for mischief, but Rork, as he often does, read my thoughts.

"She's a fine lady, Peter—taught an' raised by a fine mother. Don't worry. Let her go an' lead her life. She deserves it. Besides, 'tis Valentine's Day, remember?"

Rork is often infuriatingly correct on topics dealing with women and romance. He terms it "Gaelic empathy." I acknowledged his point with a nod, and forced myself to turn away from the street.

Before we retired for the evening, I asked Rork, "What did you think of him, Sean?"

"Well, methinks Raul's a good man, Peter. Aye, the lad has the scent o' a true believer. Yes, sir, that he does."

That made me feel much better, for it was similar to my impression. Then my friend added, "But havin' said all o' that, there's no doubt about it, Peter . . ."

Rork looked me square in the eye, his concern obvious.

"That young preacher man is a liar."

"Your revolutionary question?"

He nodded.

"I was hoping I misread that."

"Nay, you read him right, Peter. Methinks he's involved somehow, an' it makes sense. Anti-Spanish elements would be anti-old-line Catholic Church too, so they might try to involve Protestant lay people an' clergy. That lad's involved somehow."

I uttered the unthinkable extension to his opinion. "And therefore, so is Useppa?"

He shrugged. "Ooh, nay, probably not, Peter, 'cept maybe by bein' around that good young man."

In the back of my mind, I'd surmised as much, but didn't want to admit it openly. Useppa's life had been hard as the child of a naval officer, having an incurable ailment, and losing her mother so young. And Useppa's work was difficult and not always appreciated by society. Her needs were simple, and her heart gentle. I wanted so much for her to be happy.

But I dreaded what might be in store for my daughter if Raul was one of the revolutionaries. I grew anxious over what I should say to her. No, for now I'd wait.

"Too early to say anything to her yet, Sean. I'll need proof first."

"Aye, Peter. While we're down there, methinks we might nose a bit around Havana town askin' on the nature o' Father Leon. See what we hear about the lad. Might be enlightenin' for us."

"Yes," was all I could say. My mind was on how he paid that bill.

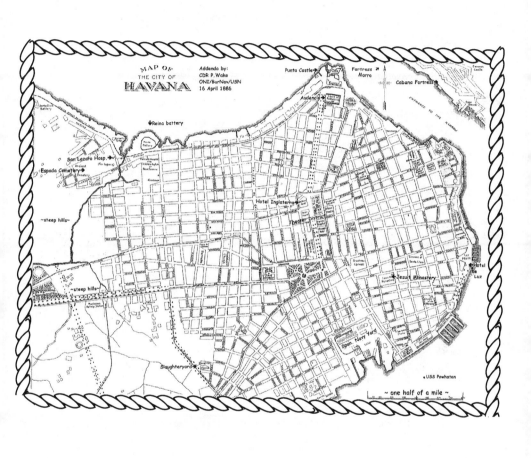

MAP OF
THE CITY OF
HAVANA

Addenda by:
CDR P. Wake
ONI/BurNav/USN
16 April 1886

Punta Castle

Fortress Morro

Cabana Fortress

Morro Castle

Entrance to the harbor

Audencia

Reina battery

San Lazaro Hosp.

Espada Cemetery

Ancient Cemetery

~steep hills~

~steep hills~

Hotel Inglaterra

Theater District

Jesuit Monastery

Hotel de Luz

Span. Navy Yard

Slaughteryard

USS Powhatan

~ one half of a mile ~

A Methodist Friend

Tuesday, 16 February 1886
Harbor front
Plaza de Luz
Havana, Cuba

Unlike several of my transits to Havana from Key West, the steamer ride was easy and over in ten hours. At four in the afternoon, we entered the fabled harbor under the ancient ramparts of Morro and Cabanas fortresses, impressive in their day but useless in modern warfare with high-explosive, rifled shells. Now the fortresses were used as prison cells for Cubans caught agitating against the authorities. The Spanish were quite creative in their use of techniques of interrogation and subjugation. Yes, to be sure, the methods of the ancient Inquisition were alive and well in modern Cuba.

In truth, the entire island was a relic of the past—the system of government, the culture, the trade. Everything, it seemed, was a holdover from the days of the great empire of Spain. Even slavery still existed in Cuba, over twenty years since the United States had bled itself dry to be rid of that abomination. The "Faithful Isle" was, and still is, nine years later, a giant living museum stuck in time. Jules Verne should write one of his novels about the place.

But as horrific and downtrodden as Cuba still was after twenty years of rebellion, the island continued to have a strong pull on my heart. The music, the food, the drink, the women, the laughter, the art—all were unique in Cuba, an island of dreamers who fantasized and argued about what could and should be. Rork, in one of his more cynical moments, once opined that this condition was all due to the "bloody damned heat" and "that exotic bloody rotgut they call rum." I remember reminding him that he loved Cuban rum. He retorted that he liked *decent* Cuban rum.

We disembarked after the consulate had closed for the day, so went right to our lodgings, a very short walk from the wharf. We'd stop by and report in to the consulate the next morning, a routine duty for transiting naval personnel. Our reserved room at the hotel was ready—a pleasant turn of events in Latin America—and we wasted no time in getting settled in our second-floor room. Filled with American businessmen, it overlooked the harbor, with the ferry docks to Regla, across the harbor, in the foreground.

On a whim, I had the desk clerk send a cablegram to Mr. Mondongo in New York, asking him if he had a contact in Havana who could socialize with us and show us the city. One never knows how these long-shot gambles pay off, but it took little time and I thought I might try it.

After that, we determined to scout out the city around the commercial waterfront of the northern docks. Industrial information is always useful at ONI as an indicator of strength and intent, so this was a good opportunity to assess that facet of the Cuban situation. Dressed as average businessmen, our brown suits a common sight in that area, we ambled along the wharfs from the hotel, studying the various types of shipping at the

Machina Wharf, San Francisco Wharf, and the Carpineti Wharf. They were all full, mostly of U.S.-flagged steamers, along with two Brits and three Spaniards. Whatever the political turmoil on the island, trade looked good.

Next was dinner at the Theater District, a twelve-block journey inland from the dock area, where we repaired to our favorite place, the corner dining room at Hotel Inglaterra. Despite the name, which meant "England" in Spanish, it had magnificent Spanish-Cuban cuisine supplementing the English dishes. It also had great potential for the type of gossip we were searching for about the Brit expatriate community, the social life of which centered around both the hotel and their church, St. Mark's Episcopal.

And gossip there was. It's been my experience across the world that the normally reticent British lose their cloak of restraint along about the third pint of ale or second gill of whisky. That's whisky without the "e"—the kind from Scotland. Havana proved that lesson too, and an hour after a sumptuous dinner of *paella* we were getting an earful of righteous British wrath about the persecution of the Protestants' mother Anglican church at the hands of the Spanish government and "their Catholic priest propagandists." According to our new friends, the Methodists in Havana were also less than appreciated by the authorities. Evidently they'd been spreading dangerous ideas too, things like human equality and democracy.

And all of this foment was by nonclergy, yet. Our bar companions were mercantile types engaged in the sugar trade to Europe. They were very angry on the subject of tariffs, especially on the importation of important British necessities of life, such as the whisky we were drinking. Rork, his Catholic soul no doubt rebelling, submerged any counter-comment to the growing tirade and looked on sympathetically while I primed the pump with another round of drinks, paid for by Uncle Sam via the navy's auditor general. Things were coming along quite well.

We were just entering the topic of Protestants' expanding

influence among the non-Anglos of Havana, when a face familiar to our hosts arrived. Ironically, it was the pastor of said Methodist church. Even more remarkable, he immediately shaped a course for our table, his eyes never leaving me, ignoring the scotch-enhanced grins of my new friends.

"Pardon my intrusion," he said to Rork and me with an eastern Cuban inflection. "I am Pastor Martín Lefavre, of the Methodist Church of Havana, and I am here at the request of my friend and brother pastor, Father Raul Leon, of St. Mark's Episcopal Church. You must be Commander Wake, of the American navy. How very happy I am to meet you, sir. I've met your daughter when visiting Key West."

The atmosphere instantly froze among the British. The pastor's little revelation about my profession threw a large wet rag on our tablemates' proclivity to gab. I'd neglected to tell them our profession, beyond a brief reference that we were seamen in transit, allowing them to believe we were cargo steamer third-mates. After staring at me for several seconds in near-horror, and before I could come up with a good explanation, our talkative friends made sudden excuses and departed the barroom—most likely to tell everyone in the place to shut up, that there were Yankee naval spies in the house.

Lefavre, a middle-aged man with heavy jowls, was the picture of innocence as he watched them disappear, then added, "Oh, I hope I didn't interrupt something, sir."

It was a struggle to stifle my exasperation. "Why, not at all, Pastor. So you know Raul Leon? Fine young man. By the way, this is my colleague Sean Rork."

Most officers disapprove of my close friendship with Rork, who is a bosun—an enlisted man—and not a commissioned officer. He's also twice the seaman of any naval officer I know. Enlisted men and officers aren't supposed to socialize together, but I should probably confess here that I have a certain aversion to rules applied stupidly without common sense. Therefore, I ignore that rule when with Rork and always introduce him as "my colleague," though that might make the stuffier of my fellow naval officers cringe.

"Mr. Rork, so honored to meet you, sir," offered the pastor.

Rork acknowledged the greeting with a nod, while I asked the question obvious to the moment. "How did you know I was here, sir?"

Again he produced a beatific smile, making me wonder if they practiced that in front of the mirror at the seminary. "Raul cabled me this morning, Commander, asking me to extend some Cuban hospitality and show you around the city. He thinks highly of you. Havana is a small town in many ways, so it wasn't difficult to find you."

I thought that over. Raul Leon had certainly wasted no time in buttering up his girl's father. Or was he alerting his revolutionary compatriots in Havana? "Please, Pastor Lefavre, call us Peter and Sean, it's easier."

What I really wanted was for him to stop using my rank, which he was stressing with volume. People were listening to us now.

"And you must then call me Martín, which is so much easier than Pastor Lefavre!"

He had us there. It was a confounded name to pronounce and I'd been wondering how the hell to spell it. He saw the confusion and explained, "French family—originally from St. Domingue, or Haiti, as it is called now. They fled to Cuba three generations ago during the slave troubles. Became Protestant years ago. So how can I help you, gentlemen? Is there anywhere you would wish to see while you are in our city?"

Rork shot me a glance. On intuition I asked, "Now that you've asked, Martín, do you know the leper colony? There is an ancient place near it. A beautiful garden, of angels . . ."

Lefavre hesitated just long enough for me to know we'd hit the mark. "Why yes, Peter. I know that place, but why would you want to go *there?*"

Was *he* involved in the Roosevelt message? Was his question *pro forma* as part of the code? Or was he truly astonished? I leaned forward, almost touching him, breaking the societal barriers against closeness, and said as nonchalantly as I could, "A friend in New York recommended we see that place, that it had a notable connotation to the people of Cuba. A connection with Babylon. Something to do with a psalm, I seem to recall."

"Ah, yes. Then . . . I shall be pleased to show it to you in the morning." The pastor abruptly stood. "But for now, I will excuse myself and not burden you further with my presence. I know it is a long day's journey over the sea from Key West. You must be tired and in need of rest." Was it worry or anger I saw in his eyes? He backed away from the table, waving goodbye. "Good night, gentlemen. I will call at your hotel at nine in the morning."

I got up to shake Lefavre's hand, but he had already turned and was heading out. Rork motioned for me to sit and quietly said, "That man had the look o' fear in his eyes. This is gettin' curiouser an' curiouser, Peter. You never told him where we were stayin' an' I don't recall you tellin' Raul either. So how does our suddenly arrived new friend Martín know where we're lodged? An' methinks he used your rank a bit too loudly in his greetin'—no doubt to warn others in this place."

"I think you're entirely correct, Sean. It would appear we are under surveillance—by the Methodists of Havana, no less."

"So the Roosevelt message was from the Protestants of Havana?"

"Well, Roosevelt's message did say 'their *protesting* father awaits you.' At the time, I didn't think it meant a Protestant."

"Well, most o' the revolutionaries we know in Cuba are Catholic, at least nominally. But now maybe the two have formed an alliance? Protestant clergy and Catholic rebels." He shook his head. "Heretics allied with people o' the true Church. Aye, the sainted Pope would keel o'er from apoplexy to know o' *that* little development."

"Yes, I imagine he would. But it does make sense though. An alliance of all the anti-Spanish groups, of everyone who feels they've been wronged by the royal authorities. And all of them have the Bible in common. Then, on some designated day, coordinated vengeance erupts. Babylon is overthrown and the slaves freed."

"So what do we do now?"

I wasn't sure. The admonition by Porter, et al, to keep an inconspicuous appearance was uppermost in my mind. And our idea was pure conjecture—we had no proof at all. "I think *mañana* I'll get close to the Methodist preacher and see what he knows, while you pay a visit to your spiritual brethren and see how much influence we might still have with the Catholic Church. Try the Jesuit monastery."

A sly grin spread across Rork's face. "Ooh, but aren't you a devious man, Peter Wake."

"These are dangerous times in Babylon, Sean. I'm thinking that a little deviousness is in order."

Just then the barman came over and asked, "Commander Wake, do you want another drink?"

Damn. So much for remaining discreet in Havana. The word was out, courtesy of a Methodist preacher who was warned by the boyfriend of my daughter. I wondered how long it would take to reach the U.S. consulate in Havana that a naval officer was snooping about the city.

The scene at naval headquarters flashed in my mind—along with my specific orders from David Dixon Porter: *Stay away from our consulate in Havana after you first routinely check in. No uniform. Low-key. No trouble.*

Well, things weren't evolving quite that way, and we'd only been in Havana for five hours. That fact that it really wasn't my fault would carry no weight.

Admiral Porter would *not* be amused.

Precisely at nine o'clock the following morning, February seventeenth, Martín Lefavre entered the lobby of the hotel. We headed off in a rough-springed buggy down Avenida de Luz. While I was being jostled around the old city, Rork would be checking in at the consulate, as casually as he could, so as to minimize their awareness of us. Diplomats have a tendency to whine about the navy interfering with their bailiwick—until they whine even louder for us to rescue them *from* their bailiwick—and I didn't need any more attention than we'd already managed to attract.

Lurching along on the buggy, Lefavre and I passed the ancient Jesuit monastery on Calle Compostella, a moldy graying monolith of forbidding appearance, the façade containing an inscription in Latin announcing its purpose. The pastor saw me studying the building and decided to explain, "That is a very old Catholic monastery, Peter. It is where the Society of Jesus priests live. Some of them are well known and accomplished academics from the observatory here."

I was glad he said that. It meant he didn't know of my amity with the Jesuits and that I'd already been to the monastery several times during past visits to the city. It also indicated that he didn't know the monastery was Rork's second destination that morning. We had both been there during earlier stays in Havana, as guests of a priest who knew a Jesuit friend of mine in Sevilla, Spain. Rork would see if our acquaintance was still there and, if not, try to make a new contact in case of emergency. It always pays to hedge one's bets, especially when the collateral is your life.

Rork's endeavor was possible because of my unusual relationship with the Jesuit order over the previous fifteen years. It started when that priest friend in Sevilla, Father Juan Muñosa, saved my life by helping me to escape a particularly disagreeable incident arising from a misunderstanding at the Alcázar. Ever since, the worthy men of that distinguished order have helped me in times of need. I have returned the favor, most notably in '81 at Peru—which helps elucidate the presence of one of those baubles on my dress uniform—and later at Hué in Viet Nam.

My correspondence with several Jesuit bishops around the world has been steady and productive. They know what I do for the navy. I am consistently impressed with the quality of information they gather from their far-flung areas and send to their leadership and, occasionally, to me. *Symbiotic,* is the word I believe scientist fellows would use for our relationship.

Based upon the events of the previous forty-eight hours, I was beginning to think this visit to Havana would be a good time to invoke that friendship. I was confident that Rork could come up with something, or someone, by the end of the day. He is a resourceful fellow.

Meanwhile, Martín and I steered the buggy through the theater area and stopped at the trolley station on the corner of Neptuno and Consulado, right by the Hotel Inglaterra. My host informed me the rest of the way would be by rail, and we disembarked. A boy showed up to drive the buggy away, the reason being given that the church needed it that morning. Somewhat skeptical, I boarded a trolley car with the pastor and we rode north along the Avenida Zulueta as more and more riders got on at each stop. The trolley took us down to the castle at the entrance to the harbor, then west along the seafront on Calzado de San Lazarus. Lefavre was quiet, saying little beyond a brief discussion of the weather, which was windy from the north and pleasant.

Twenty minutes later, we stepped down from the trolley and I was looking at the Espada Cemeterio. Pastor Martín Lefavre, I noticed, was looking rather pale. Around us were lepers from the San Lazaro Leprosy Hospital nearby. They were workers in the cemetery and, contrary to popular myths, they were neither grossly deformed nor melancholy. I could hear them laughing, with some jesting about the last grave they'd dug. I guessed that

Lefavre probably hadn't had much interaction with, or education about, lepers. The man was very nervous.

"Here it is, Peter. The cemetery of the lepers of Havana."

"I'd like to walk around, Martín. You can stay here if you'd like. I won't be long." I wanted to get the lay of the land in the daytime, in case things got dicey at the night rendezvous. He said—with obvious relief—that he'd wait for me by the road.

I walked around the perimeter, west along Calle Vapor and then down Calle Espada, and finally hiked across the cemetery itself. The cemetery was a miniature city of monuments and mausoleums set among a labyrinth of narrow alleys and pathways. Though most memorials were modest, some of them were quite ornate and large. Blacksmithing smoke drifted across from the Reina Fortress on the beach six hundred yards away, the acrid fumes settling among the whitewashed crypts. I tried to memorize the layout for later, but it was difficult—there were a thousand places to hide or run. Several apparent routes of escape ended in wrought-iron fences or coral-stoned walls.

At one point, I observed the lepers watching me intently. They weren't laughing now, plainly wondering what I was doing, wandering around in their cemetery. I shrugged and held my hands out, a common gesture in Latin America that is used for every situation. It didn't dispel their curiosity. They continued to watch me. I hurried my reconnaissance, edging back to my entry point, glad to be out when I approached Martín again.

The minister asked if I had found what I was looking for, to which I replied yes. Then he asked where else I'd like to see. When I said that was all, Lefavre didn't look surprised.

Rork was stretched out on his bed when I walked in. Once I got my coat off, I sat in the lone chair and briefed him. "I checked the cemetery and don't like what I saw, Sean. Never been inside before, just passed by. It's a true maze, with the burial chambers pretty high above ground. Good place for a secret meeting, or an ambush, even in the day. Worse at night."

"Is the minister still actin' strangely?"

"Yes. But I can't find out why. He's not talking much. First preacher I've ever met who stays quiet. Look, we'll just go do this tomorrow and get it over with."

"Got any ideas on how we handle it at the cemetery?" he asked.

"Only one—keep it simple. I go in and walk around until someone stops and talks to me. You stay back and watch for any evildoers forming an ambush. You're my reinforcement, but try to keep out of sight."

He looked askance at that and I said, "I know, Sean, but it's the only thing I could come up with. We'll go by a different route than mine today—by hack through the center of the city, west along Avenida Zanja, then walk the last seven blocks and approach from the south. Give it twenty minutes inside the cemetery, then leave, meet the hack again and come back here to the room. Next morning, I'll send the cable report to Walker. We leave the next day for Panama, once we receive orders to do so. So what did you find out?"

He chuckled. "First, the embassy lads acted their usual bored selves when I told 'em we were in town in transit an' due to be off to Panama in a day or two, so methinks we're doin' well on that account. At the monastery I discovered that our friend was transferred away in December—to some forsaken place in the Amazon, God help him. I inquired if the current archbishop o' the city was Jesuit and found he is most certainly not. Seems the Franciscans've got command hereabouts. Those boyos are everywhere."

Rork rubbed his temples. "Then I asked if the priests knew our old friend the bishop o' Panama, but no luck on that. An' then, I said I was lookin' for the head o' the order, thought mayhaps we'd have a mutual acquaintance, but was told he's out o' town. So I've no joy to share. They did say they'd pass along our names when he returns. Sorry, sir."

Not good news, but I tried not to show my disappointment. "So the Jesuit factor is out on this one? I was hoping we'd have our friend there in case things went foul. Well, we'll do it without them."

"I wouldn't count on them much anyway, Peter. My impression is that they're all cloistered academics here, with no political power like they have at other places. How'd you leave it with Pastor Lefavre?"

"I thanked him and said we were leaving soon for Panama. That we wouldn't see him again. I was wondering how he'd react. He seemed pleased."

"Aye, he's in this up to his neck, mark my words."

"Yes, I think so too. This has gotten interesting, hasn't it? At the cemetery rendezvous tomorrow tonight we might meet secular Catholic revolutionaries, or we might meet Protestant revolutionaries, or this all might be a large hoax and waste of time."

"I'm hopin' for the hoax. But time'll tell, sir."

It would indeed.

8
Midnight, with the Light of Day

Thursday, 18 February 1886
Espada Cemetery
Havana, Cuba

I've been in many eerie situations at various locales around the world, but none compares to my journey into the garden of angels that night in Havana. In addition to the normal apprehension one would expect, I couldn't help feeling a growing sense of dread, which I kept trying to dismiss as ridiculous superstition.

The Cuban moon was the main instigator of my paranoia. It lit up the diminutive white buildings of the dead around me in a stark grayish tableau, about the same color as a day-old corpse. From the sea came an increasingly strong wind out of the north, unusually cool, almost to the point of being cold. I shivered while trying to walk quietly out of respect for the departed, an absurd notion given the circumstances. Close by, a cat sounded off in either anguish or ecstasy, making my heart jump nearly out of my chest. To top it all off, I was convinced that the shadows were watching me, turning with me as I negotiated the snaking pathways, reaching out but not touching. Eerie is an understatement.

I saw and heard no one else, but had the fleeting ghoulish impression that lepers were rising from the graves and standing in those shadows. Psalm 137 went through my head. I hoped they knew the difference between me and their oppressors. I know it seems juvenile to anyone reading this, but I was as unnerved as ever in my life.

Until I heard Rork, that is.

According to plan, he was trailing me, a rear guard in case of ambush. But it was he that was ambushed—by a crypt. First I heard the thump, then the sound of a body falling hard.

Next came a loud monologue, accented in brogue: "Damn it all to *hell!* Sonovabitchin' little dago buggers can't even build a decent bloody grave without makin' the friggin' pavement buckle!" And that was followed by some very blue language that only veteran navy bosuns can string together without stopping to breathe.

Naval discipline eroded, I was unable to contain myself. Within seconds my laughter was as loud as his curses. Heading toward the sound of his oaths, I found him on the ground clutching his right foot. "Me bleedin' ankle's killin' me. Friggin' thing twisted."

I helped him sit up on the offending gravestone. "Stay here, my less-than-graceful friend," I told him. "Quietly, please."

He was still muttering, now in Gaelic, when I heard the scrape of a shoe on stone. We both went still, straining to see or hear the shoe's owner.

I had an idea and called out, "It is midnight, with the light of day. I am here to try to save innocent lives." Then I repeated it in my less-than-fluent Spanish.

That was a bad idea.

More footfalls, from different directions, getting closer. Rork's eyes met mine, then glanced back the way we'd come. From the opposite direction, I heard metal twisting on metal—the evil sound of a bayonet being fixed on a rifle's muzzle. He didn't need to say anything; I'd already said far too much. We were trapped. I helped Rork up, got him facing the direction of our entry, and had just begun to hobble away with him when a deep voice announced, "*¡Alto! ¡Manos arribas! Policia Tesoro Real.* Stop where you are and put your hands up. This is the Royal Treasury Police."

The muzzle of a carbine emerged from the shadow closest to us. We stopped, put our hands up, and half a dozen uniformed men showed themselves, their bayoneted rifles leveled at our torsos. A man in plain clothes stepped forward.

"I am Colonel Marrón, and you are under arrest for espionage and subversion of the Crowned Sovereign of Spain, His Most Catholic Majesty, Alfonso the Seventh."

I whispered to Rork, "Dump the Colts." Meaning, of course, to get rid of our Navy-issued Colt revolvers by dropping them behind the gravestone. Admittedly, it was a slim chance, but better to try.

They saw that feeble move, grabbed up our weapons, and took no chances from that point on, roughly searching us, even to the point of taking Rork's left-hand appliance apart—which they were intensely excited to see contained a marlinespike. All throughout, I protested we were there merely as sailors looking for the grave of a former friend, but that didn't slow them a bit. And to be candid, it sounded pretty thin to me, too, even as I said it.

Seconds later, Rork and I were shackled and tied—Rork most painfully. His good right hand was handcuffed to the back of his belt, and his left upper arm lashed to his right arm. Then they shoved us into separate box wagons for the drive to the dungeon at the Audencia, the Spanish government's prison located along the harbor entrance, one of those same antique castles we'd seen upon arrival at the city.

I spent the short journey trying to come up with a good

excuse I could tell Admiral Porter and Secretary Whitney. None came to mind.

"It's against the law to visit a cemetery?" I asked Colonel Marrón, my voice full of innocent indignation. His demeanor had become less dictatorial once he confirmed we were United States Navy personnel by our identification papers, a fact which clearly surprised him. Traditional trepidation of the *Yanqui* colossus to the north made him tread softer now, but he was no less persistent.

"Do not deny it. You are part of a plot to overthrow the imperial government of Spain in Cuba. We know about everything—about the secret message in New York, about you meeting with your co-conspirators in Key West, about visiting the cemetery this morning. You even repeated the message. And you were out of uniform and *armed* when captured. That makes the crime even more serious. Now is the time for truth, Peter Wake, to save yourself from a lengthy prison sentence—or worse—and your country from an embarrassing disclosure of its role in undermining the four-hundred-year-old sovereignty of Spanish Cuba."

He seemed to know a lot, and yet, he didn't know I was a naval officer when they first got us. Only afterward, when I produced identification, did they know that. I thought that a good point in our favor. The bad point was that we were in civilian clothes, which made us spies, and I knew what they did to spies. Especially armed spies.

I noted that Marrón's English was flawless, an important point since I wanted him to understand exactly what I was about to say. In view of that, I decided to continue my role of pompous anger, which of course was a total sham. The best defense is always an audacious offense. I didn't have many options. No, that isn't quite accurate—by that point, I didn't have *any* other options left.

"I am a United States naval officer in transit and decided to visit the ancient cemetery of Havana, to better know the history of this fabled city and look for the grave of a friend. As an officer and a gentleman, I am entitled to carry a personal sidearm, according to the internationally recognized laws of military conduct, particularly the Treaty of Paris of eighteen fifty-six. So is Mr. Rork, a noncommissioned officer of the United States Navy. It is a completely understandable precaution, given the lawless nature of your city, I might add."

I let that sink in for a brief moment. The bit about the Treaty of Paris was some inspired embellishment. I had no idea what the treaty really said, other than to outlaw piracy.

Then, using Secretary Whitney as my role model, I made my comments personal.

"And I have taken careful note of your identity and behavior, Colonel Marrón, and can assure you that *you*, sir, will be *personally* and *inescapably* held responsible for this egregious violation of international law and disregard for the traditional friendship of our two great nations—all just at a time when we are forging an even closer, *personal* relationship between Grover Cleveland, the president of the United States of America, and the prime minister of Spain."

That was all an even *more* spurious charade. I had no idea if we were trying to get closer to Spain; in fact, I thought the opposite was probably truer to fact. And at the moment, I couldn't even remember the prime minister's name. But I saw that the threat did get his attention. Now for the peace offering, a way to save face—vitally important in Latin American culture.

"Because I am, like you, a military man, I realize that sometimes subordinates get carried away. Apparently, your subordinates were trying to do their duty, so I am prepared to overlook their zealousness upon satisfaction of two things: first, Mr. Rork and I are immediately taken back to our hotel; and second, tomorrow night we are given the famous hospitality for which the Spanish are world-renowned. A nice dinner—but not too extravagant, of course. I made some naval friends here during the American Civil War, Vice Admiral Rodriguez being one, and I would very much enjoy seeing them again. I'm sure you can arrange that, and it would salve any misunderstandings caused by your subordinates tonight. And at the dinner, it would be my honor to drink to your health, and that of the sovereign of the Spanish Empire, the famous King Alfonso. I am sure that we can work together in the future to our mutual gain."

I doubt Colonel Marrón had been stunned by many prisoners during his interrogations in that dungeon, but I do lay claim to accomplishing just that. His dark eyes narrowed and his pointed goatee dropped a full inch as his mouth gapped open. I could see my salvo had given him pause while he tried to come up with an appropriate answer to me. When he did, it wasn't what I'd hoped.

"Your arrogant answer has been noted, Mr. Wake. By the way, Vice Admiral Rodriguez died ten years ago at Cádiz, in Spain. You will be taken to your cell now."

Oh, hell—I hadn't known old Rodriguez died. I thought he was retired in Havana. My mind blanked. I couldn't recall any other important personages in the government that might still be alive. Marrón stood as I was led out. His eyes were not confused anymore—they were angry. Initially, I thought Rork and I could talk our way out. Now I realized that the situation had progressed pretty far in the wrong direction. This would call for action on my part. Sadly, just what and how were unfortunately beyond me at that precise moment.

The only bright spot was that Rork and I were finally dumped into the same cell, a dank gloomy thing out of the Middle Ages. It was a scene from a Dumas novel—dripping walls, scurrying vermin, echoing groans from our neighbors. The only light came through the crack under the door, from a flickering torch in the passageway. I was certain that we were being listened to, for there were small holes set into the stone block walls that seemed to go through to the other side. Therefore, we kept our talk simple and spoke to the wall.

"Had one of the half-arsed idiots insinuate we was rebels, sir," said Rork to one of the holes. "What sort o' rubbish is that? Rebels in a cemetery? Why, 'tis gross disrespect for the dead on their part to even suggest such a thing, I say. An' I'm a good *Catholic!*"

Rork loves the theater and can go into it effortlessly. He really should've had a stage career.

"Yes, Rork, you're right. They seem to be very confused. They even accused me of being part of a plot to overthrow the government—can you imagine that? To propose that kind of accusation, when all we were doing was visiting the most famous cemetery of Havana. Don't they know that's a place steeped in history?" I said to another hole, adding, "and that Americans are well known for their reverence of the dead and for visiting cemeteries? Not to mention our poor dead friend Garcia, lying out there somewhere, waiting for us to come pay our respects. But I'm not worried; Colonel Marrón is a professional military man and will soon see that his subordinates made a mistake."

We carried on in that vein for a few minutes, whispering between us what we'd really seen and heard. Fortunately, Rork's interrogation had been the same manner as mine—nonviolent—and he'd replied in a like way to Colonel Marrón. Thus, so far in the episode the Spanish had nothing solid against us. Trespassing in a cemetery? At a time and place where a rebel rendezvous was supposed to happen? That's not a real charge—in an *American* court. Regrettably, that sort of logic didn't amount to anything in Cuba, given their history. It still doesn't today, in 1895.

A guard entered a while later and motioned for us to get up. Shackled in front, we were led down the passage through several locked doors, up some steps cut into the stone, and out to a portico, Rork still limping along with his left arm lashed down again. One of the guards was carrying an open satchel in which I could see Rork's attachments and my pocket watch. I could feel the ocean breeze, strangely comforting to a sailor, as both of us were put into another box wagon with no windows and taken away, without explanation. Things were looking grim indeed. Rork felt along the sides and door, looking for some way to escape, but found none.

"How's that ankle, Sean?"

"Fine as frog's hair, now, sir."

"With that limp I thought it was still bothering you."

"Aye, jus' what I want *them* ta see. Methinks a wee bit o' deception might come in handy. We're in a pretty tight pickle right about now."

And that, I thought, was more just than a wee bit of understatement.

Robin Hood

The wagon bounced along the cobblestoned streets for some distance, I estimated a mile or more, making Rork and me hit the sides with every tilt and jolt. We were traveling fast, which worried me even more. Trying to get rid of us before sunrise? After a harrowing turn, I heard voices outside and we stopped abruptly, slamming against the front of the box. Straining to catch brief bits of the conversation, difficult because my head was reverberating from the impact, I determined that someone in authority was taking control of the prisoners from the wagon guards. The guards sounded intimidated by the newcomers.

The door opened and we were taken out much more roughly than before, our cuffs unlocked and turned over to the wagon guards. New shackles were locked on our hands, and different guards shoved us into yet another, even more crudely built box wagon. It smelled of chickens and goats. Our new hosts were far more hostile toward us. Sadistic would be a better descriptor. They plainly took glee from shoving Rork on his ostensibly wounded leg and lashed arm. My last view of our previous guards showed them shaking their heads in sympathy.

It was not a sight to improve my outlook for our future. I immediately thought of the event back in '73, the infamous *Virginius* incident, when the Spanish government in Santiago de Cuba executed several American and British seamen from an American merchant ship named *Virginius*. They were suspected of assisting revolutionaries.

Were we being eliminated to cover Marrón's actions, as an easy way to end the whole affair? I could see the Spanish newspaper story now: *Two American sailors regrettably missing in Havana, probably victims of their own perversity in the fleshpots of the port.*

About ten minutes later, the wagon stopped. I whispered to Rork the time had come to make a break for it, come what may. The door opened, but the men who opened it weren't the new guards. These fellows were clad in filthy peasants' garb. One of them, evidently the leader, unlocked us. The others gently helped us down from the wagon. Rork was unlashed. I said nothing—better that they not know of my Spanish ability—and waited for some revelation concerning our status.

It came in broken English from the peasant who'd unlocked us. "Go . . . to . . . man." He pointed to another fellow who was walking away down an alley.

As we started to follow, the first man said, "Read." I was then handed a paper, which I couldn't read in the dark. The man shook his head, pointed up, and said, "Read in . . . sun." His gestures indicated a sunrise. Then he nudged us toward the man walking.

I took stock of where we were. Wherever we'd landed, it stank. Not the sewage smell of the old city, but worse, far worse. It was the smell of death, of rotting bodies, a smell I'd known before—on the second day after a major battle. And we weren't in the old city anymore. The streets weren't cobblestoned, they were dirt alleys. Where the cemetery had been a city of white and gray in the moonlight, this was a disorienting shanty-town jungle in shades of moonlit brown and black.

There were no large buildings, none of permanent construction, in fact. Around us were shacks composed of abandoned boards, cargo boxes, and palm thatch. The alley wound through more hovels, as black faces peered out of doorways to see what the commotion was, then jerked inside when they saw us. We certainly were not in the custody of Colonel Marrón anymore, or anyone in the government, but I had no idea of who our rescuers were, or how it had been accomplished. Were they revolutionaries? I assumed so, but no one had introduced themselves as yet.

The farther we walked, the worse the stench got—whatever it came from, we were getter closer. Our little parade paused, made a right turn, and entered a larger, more substantial hut. An armed black man stood at the door, pistol jammed in his belt. A lantern close by showed his yellowed eyes gazing coldly at us from under a large floppy hat. We stepped around him and went inside, where we were beckoned to sit on stools. Rork suggested to me that the people appeared predatory, as opposed to welcoming, and we should be on our guard for any opportunity to flee. That observation was validated the next moment, when an evil-looking fellow, no more than five feet tall and decked out in a greasy suit from the fashions of thirty years prior, came into the candlelit room.

He grinned a nasty set of teeth at us, two of them filed into points, and introduced himself in Spanish as Gallo Sosa, giving his occupation as *"El Robin Hood de Cuba."* I was not amused at all by this particular turn of events, for I had read and heard of Sosa over the years. He was the most notorious bandit of the Havana district, infamous for his train and bank robberies. And, unlike the legendary Robin Hood of England, Sosa wasn't much of a gentleman to his victims.

Somehow, we'd ended up in a possibly worse state of affairs. We needed to buy time, so I said, "*Buenos días, señoree.* Thanko you for your hospitaliteeo, but I do not speako Spanish beyond a few words of greeting."

He appeared somewhat annoyed by my bad grammar—it wasn't daytime—and that we didn't fully grasp what a magnificent character he was. In any event, he grumbled out in Spanish, "You will stay here until morning."

I again feigned ignorance, and by gestures he indicated we should stay where we were until dawn. Then, leering like a madman, Sosa presented Rork's stump appliance to him, the rubber hand affixed over the marlinespike. Presumably, they'd gotten that from the previous guards during the handover. Based on his reputation, I imagined that Sosa kept it during our walk to see if it would fit on *his* arm and, finding it not suitable, decided to give it back.

Rork said thank you and installed it quickly, tightening the straps until it was in working condition. Finally, the Robin Hood of Havana, slightly deflated by the ignorant *Yanquis'* lack of deference and language skills, threw me my pocket watch and stomped out in a huff, leaving us with two scar-faced *banditos* glaring from the corner by the door.

I must say that it is at times like this that Rork's talents come to the fore. We've been in some tight spots, and he always knows what to do when faced by armed brutes who are resistant to my more intellectual tactics. Cerebral foiling can only go so far. Then one has to get physical. Rork is good at that. The marlinespike helps immensely.

He once told me over rum that it was due to his Irish blood— an ingrained trait that can get an Eire man out of the scrapes he's gotten himself into, most of which involve violating some law. Then again, Rork blames almost everything on his Irish blood.

My friend's right forearm tensed as he said, "I don't fancy this a wee bit, an' 'tis time to do somethin' about it."

"I'll take the one on the left, you do the other one," he mumbled to me while maintaining a smile for our hosts' benefit.

On the face of it, I agreed—my target was smaller and older. Plus, Rork had that wicked spike. But then I thought a bit further. Where were we? Surrounded by hostile people, certainly. Which way was out of the slum maze we'd entered? I'd tried to keep track of our course but had lost all account of our path after the third turn off the second alley.

So before he attacked, I hurriedly asked him, "By the by, Sean, you wouldn't happen to know the way out of this hell-hole, would you?"

"*Me?* No, I thought you did. You're the bleedin' officer!"

That last part was said a bit too crossly, I thought. For the past twenty-three years, he's always brought up the fact that I'm the officer when he doesn't have a good answer to a crucial question.

"This is a hellova time to bring that up, Rork. Let's just stay here, at least until the sun rises and we can see our way around outside. Besides, maybe these boys will be tired by then and drop off for a nod. I could use some rest, myself. I'm not as young as I used to be."

He pondered that a second. "Good point, sir. We'll stay put with the bloody personality twins here. You looked like you knew this Sosa fellow when ya saw him."

"Only by reputation, and it's not good. Bandit, of the worst kind."

"Aye, spotted that straightaway. So why are we here? What happened back there in that first wagon?"

I'd been thinking about that. "As far as I can deduce, Sean, somehow Sosa bribed or connived or tricked the guards into giving us over to him. Maybe to get his own ransom payment from the U.S. Navy, or from Marrón. The other alternative is that Marrón intentionally had us given over to Sosa, in order for him to kill us and dump the bodies. To dispose of his problem, as it were. But

I'm beginning to doubt that possibility."

"How so?" he asked.

"We've been with them for some time now. If they were going to kill us, why wait? No, I think we're probably hostages. Let's stay put until we get a better idea of what's going on. They keep referring to morning, and by my watch sunrise is in an hour, at six-thirty."

That reminded me of our orders from Porter—I was to cable a report in a few hours. Oh well, put it on the list of things gone wrong. The admiral wouldn't like it, anyway.

"If we're hostages, why give back me spike?"

"Hmm, good point. I don't know. Maybe we're not hostages. Maybe the Methodists arranged this and we'll find out in the morning."

"Sosa, working for the Methodists?" Rork rubbed his chin.

That was when he suggested I read the paper given to me, which, in the stir of things, I'd put in my pocket and forgotten. By the light of a candle I read the crumpled paper. It was a message in English and, just my damned luck, the damned thing was in some sort of coded mumbo-jumbo. I was decidedly tired of codes and riddles by then, and groaned aloud at this new mental obstacle. Rork insisted on seeing it, had no comment, and handed it back with a hopeful look. Only a scientist or a navigator could figure it out. I wasn't the former, but could own up to the latter. I read it aloud again to mull it over.

"Greetings. You do not know me, but we have mutual friends in the Old World. You will be safe if you stay incommunicado for four more days. Do not venture out on your own, or the one who captured you will find you again. Then, on the fourth day, follow the instructions below and we will meet. All will be clear by then."

That part was easy. Now came the trial.

"When the castrator of Uranus reaches his zenith and meets with the great hunter, they will see below them the god of your calling reaching down to the one who vanquished the Titans. Follow the elliptic and meet me there one hour later."

Rubbing my temples I tried to concentrate. "Very well, let's start at the beginning. Friends in the Old World?"

We went over my friends in the Old World, which would be Europe. Rork suggested Jesuits, which I dismissed. They didn't operate this way and certainly not in a Catholic country—didn't need to. Royal Navy? No, this wasn't their style either. The French Navy? We both laughed. I struggled to think of any other friends in the Old World and realized I really didn't have that many.

I went on to the other parts. Four more days would make it the twenty-third when we were to meet whoever sent the message. February twenty-third wasn't anything to me. Rork shook his head.

I tackled the message itself, making an effort to remember my brief foray into classical mythology under Mr. Stonehead's incredibly dreary tutelage at Teignmouth Classical School, three long decades earlier.

"Uranus . . . ah, yes, was castrated—" I remembered the collective groan by the boys in the class when we found out what *that* meant, "—by Saturn. Very good, all right then, when Saturn reaches his zenith, his highest point in the sky, on the twenty-third, and meets with the great hunter, well that can only be Orion, then they will both see below them the god of my calling. What in tarnation is that?"

"The god of sailors? Or of war?" Rork proposed.

"Oh . . . of course, it's war. Too damned simple, that one. Thank you, Sean. It's got to be Mars, god of war. Now when Saturn and Orion meet, they'll look down on Mars and below that will be the one who vanquished the Titans. Damn, don't know that one."

"Wouldn't it be a big one, to have vanquished the Titans? Are there any big stars around those other ones?"

"Ah, thanks again, Sean! Not a star, but a planet, the brightest in the sky—Jupiter."

Rork puffed up his chest. "Glad to be of assistance, Commander."

Then he asked, "All of which means?"

"It's an unusual alignment of the celestial bodies in the sky. We follow the elliptic, the pathway of that alignment, and go to where it points, here on earth. And there we meet whoever arranged all of this."

"Now why the hell didn't they just put it into plain words?"

Valid question, with disturbing answers.

"Presumably to keep us, and them, hidden from the authorities in case this paper was found by the government. That means that somebody is trying to save us from Marrón. Which means that Marrón is searching for us. I would imagine he's not pleased with our disappearance."

Rork nodded pensively. "Aye. Quite friggin' angry, I've nary a doubt. So we wait? What about the cable to headquarters this morn?"

I looked around the room and felt the strength leaving me. My mind and muscles were just so tired, but I went over our options in a whisper to Rork. We could run for it, and either get taken into custody again by Marrón and his troops, or captured by some other bandit gang. Or we could stay and meet our enigmatic benefactor, which might shed considerable light on why we were in Cuba in the first place.

"We wait. It won't be the first time I've been late with a report to headquarters."

I didn't mention that when I'd been late reporting in during times past, it was because I'd been damned near killed while on distant assignment. With Rork usually right next to me.

So we sat there, in a slum filled with the stench of decomposing bodies, surrounded by the vacuous dregs of humanity, staring at hardened *banditos* staring back at us with dead eyes—for four very long days. One can imagine, by this stage in the tale, the disheartening suspicions, which were multiplying rapidly, that went though our minds.

Then I heard Sosa again, outside our door. He was laughing at something somebody said about what was going to happen to Rork and me. It involved pig excrement. I translated for Rork. Our morale deteriorated further.

Moments later we were lying on our stomachs on the bed of a two-wheeled cart, as Sosa's men piled manure-filled hay over us. Actually, to be more precise, it was hay-covered manure, compiled from an entire assortment of animals and humans, not just pigs. By catching snatches of the brigands' conversation—between their mirth at our fate—it seemed that government patrols were searching the area around the shack, and Sosa thought it best to spirit us out of the slum in the one vehicle Marrón's men wouldn't search too keenly. A dung cart.

Thus we were taken north and then west, away from the foul-smelling neighborhood, as part of an even more foul-smelling collection of barnyard sewage. One might ask how I could discern such details in the composition of the cargo. The answer comes from being in such close range to the subject matter. The stuff was in my nose.

As for my navigational observations, through a crack in the muck around my head, I could see that the sun was rising abaft the starboard quarter of the cart, which is how I knew we were bound northwest. Desperate to not think about what was covering my face, and where it came from, I concentrated on our course and speed, attempting to deduce our location and destination by infrequent glimpses out the crack.

Not more than an hour later, the cart stopped. The front tilted up and Rork and I sloped downward, headfirst toward the contraption's stern. Then we were dumped—literally—into a compost pile behind a barn. The cart clomped off, leaving us alone. There we lay, wondering whether we should rise up and run for it, when a goat came over to inspect the recent arrivals. It was a billy goat, who then proceeded to mark the new addition to the pile. I heard laughing nearby.

Seconds later, a peasant told us in Spanish to climb out and follow him. Walking through a banana thicket amongst some hovels, we ended up in a thatched hut, sitting on bamboo and woven sisal cots, and staring at the dim-witted peasant, who stared back at us as if we were two more dumb animals for him to watch over. His countenance was devoid of compassion. It was more of restrained tolerance. Buckets of water, apparently from the horse trough, were brought to us by his son to wash up. It wasn't enough for a proper job, and there was no soap, but complaining to the cretin in front of us was useless. I doubt they even knew what soap was.

Evidently, this was to be our hiding place for the next several days. Rork didn't say a word. I sat with my head in my hands. Despondency can rob a man of all judgment and stamina. It even takes away fear.

But alas, what was in our souls was far less depressing than what was in our stomachs. That afternoon, Rork and I discussed the subject and agreed that, given the rotting dung we'd had cover us, the mush we were given to eat, the rancid air we had to breathe, and filthy water to drink, that we'd definitely get it, eventually.

For the first day we ate and drank nothing, but there was no way around the inevitable and, sorely famished, on the second day we ate and drank just a little. The only question became "When?" On day three we had the answer, for that morning Rork and I came down with what we'd dreaded.

Dysentery.

I'd been sick with malaria and dysentery before and hated it. Both diseases are common to sailors who visit the tropics, though recruiting posters neglect to mention that facet of a naval career. Both can, and will, kill you, unless you receive decent medical attention immediately after the onslaught. Needless to say, medical attention where we were was a fantasy.

So we laid there on the cots provided us, sweating and shivering, vomiting and voiding. Most of the time we made it to the alley behind the hut to relieve ourselves, but sometimes it was too far. An old hag of a woman, whose breath smelled worse than even we did, came in to "clean up" once, but within hours we were beyond any feeble effort she could make. By noon that day, neither of us were mobile, the energy draining steadily out of our bodies, our minds slowing with weakness.

In a puny burst of willpower, Rork and I urged each other to remain steady, that the next two days were crucial. We knew that from sad experience, for as veterans of dysentery and malaria, we knew that when weakened by the dysentery, our recurring malaria would revisit us. That would be the difficult part, we agreed, choosing not to use the more accepted term—mortal.

At sunset on the fourth day of our odyssey in the custody of Gallo Sosa, grand cock of the walk in that area, he came to see us. Sosa showed no sympathy, instead clucking in Spanish at our condition in a chastising manner, as if our miserable state of affairs were our fault. In a dismissive tone, he then said in English, "No good, die here. No die here." Then he shook his finger at us.

Well, that got Rork's blood moving. From his sickbed he yelled at the thug with astonishing vigor, "You bloody arrogant damned bastard, don't you *dare* get uppity with me!"

He was feeling no pain or weakness now as rage took over and he sat up, cocking back his good right hand. "I've *killed* bigger sonsabitches than the likes o' ye, ya half-pinted, poxy-faced bag o' scum."

Rork, who hadn't the strength to say twenty words in the previous twenty-four hours, amazed me even more when he then stood unsteadily—eyes watery and reddened, but blazing with anger—and proceeded toward Sosa. I couldn't lie there like a lump at that point, so I managed to stand, a shabby reinforcement to my stalwart friend.

Sosa's reaction to all of this was not what I expected. He laughed, then stood there, arms akimbo, with that disgusting grin and said, "Good! Good man!"

We'd been foxed by a bandit.

I looked at Rork, and he at me, and both of us broke out laughing, which came out more like gasps, which hurt. Sosa joined in. He'd pulled an old bosun's trick: get the crew angry and united—even if it's against the bosun himself—and they can accomplish anything.

"Go . . . now. Go," said our gangster acquaintance, motioning that all of us should leave. He then pointed to the paper by my cot. "Read. Go now."

So, soiled, stinking, and emaciated, Rork and I, with Gallo Sosa trailing, trudged out of our shack and through the slum in the gathering night, not knowing where we'd end up, but pretty sure it would be in a better place. I say trudged, but that is too fast a portrayal of our speed. Dysentery, for those of you thankfully unfamiliar with the ailment, not only makes you weak, but it causes aches and pains in one's joints and muscles. Every step is agony.

I noticed Sosa didn't know where we were going. That much was manifest at the start, when he waited for me to lead. I got the idea he was coming along to collect money for his work of nabbing and keeping us. That gave me some hope. But to lead, I had to see the night sky, so we walked to a slight rise in the terrain above the hovels around us, where I could spy out my surroundings.

I soon evaluated where, in relation to the city, we'd been kept originally. It was near the slaughterhouse yards, southwest of the old city and east of the hill country that forms the backdrop to Havana. When I enlightened Rork as to the reason for the stench at that first way station on our exodus, he said he was swearing off beef and pork for the rest of his life. Said that the mere whiff of them would remind him of our ordeal, from both the slaughterhouse and the dung cart.

Now I understood that we'd been brought on the dung cart to farming slums covering the low hills inland of the Santa Clara fortress on the coast. Wherever we were bound, it would be up and down those hills. Sosa, who I was beginning to think knew more English than he let on, just grunted impatiently at me for taking too much time.

Ignoring him, I gazed around the horizon again to orient myself better. Miles away, in Havana's harbor, lights winked, while the downtown section blazed with electric illumination. It was a gay scene—off in the distance. All around us, however, was the hopelessness of the poor. I saw by my watch the time was seven-thirty in the evening. It was time to find our way out by the stars in the message.

The night sky was providentially clear and I found Saturn first. Orange, tinged with gold, it radiated in the eastern sky, about forty-five degrees up from the horizon. That told me we had a while to go until it reached its zenith at ninety degrees, which was good, because we weren't moving too fast.

Then I saw the three silver twinkles of Orion's belt, just to the right of reddish Betelguese, almost on the same elevation as Saturn. So far, we'd spotted the initial indicators and knew we had to walk east-southeast. I led the way.

We'd gone perhaps two miles as the crow flies, but twice that through the gullies, when I first spotted Mars coming up over the mountain east of the city at a quarter after ten P.M. We kept walking east-southeast and were now in some serious hills, slowing our progress even further. Orion's belt was higher than, and at an angle to, Saturn. I thought for a moment I'd misunderstood and, in my lessened state, emotions overcame me. I began to tremble with doubt and shame. The other two looked at me quizzically, and I realized I had not the luxury of showing weakness or ignorance in front of Gallo Sosa. He would cut his losses, literally, right then and there. I kept moving, silently praying I had guessed correctly, ordering my legs to go on.

And then, at twenty till eleven, Jupiter mercifully appeared in the east and completed the pathway pointing to our destination. It was an uncommon configuration, one I hadn't seen in the sky before. Golden Saturn, red Mars, and brightly silvered Jupiter formed a slightly curving line. It wasn't pointing east-southeast anymore, however. It was pointing us farther around, at south-southeast. I altered course. We continued dragging ourselves uphill, one step at a time. The hills became mountains. No one was speaking by this time.

A half moon rose, orange at first, growing white and gently overpowering the closest stars' light. By then, I'd already established a landmark toward which to steer, however. It was a distant rock outcropping, darkly silhouetted against the lighter sky. My navigation was no longer the problem, but internal strength was. My steps were getting smaller and smaller until I was shuffling along. My mind was losing focus, heart not caring. Everything was slowing down. Mutiny was taking over my body, begging my mind to lie down and sleep, to forget its duty to lead the body to safety. I heard Sosa grunt again, long and slow. It came out as an animal sound, more of a growl, like a final warning. I was past the point of caring.

Then we crossed a rise and saw it.

Sosa shook his head and swore in Spanish. Rork smiled, looked up at heaven, and crossed himself. I sat down on the ground and tried, unsuccessfully, not to cry.

10

The Hurricane Man

Tuesday, 23 February 1886
The mansion of Roberto Nutonio
Outside of Havana, Cuba

Before us, shimmering in the moonlight only a hundred yards away, over a substantial mansion, fluttered a white banner showing a black daggerlike cross with three large letters—IHS—superimposed. The symbol of the Society of Jesus. Safety for Rork and me.

But it was a hundred yards too far.

I couldn't get up. God knows I made an effort, but my legs wouldn't do it. Rork sank down beside me. Sosa was still shaking his head—obviously he'd done a contract to get us out of Marrón's clutches without knowing exactly who'd provided the deposit. Now that he did know, he wasn't pleased. Or was he just confused?

I could imagine Sosa's mind analyzing the situation—was this somehow a government trap to get him? Priests were paid by the imperial government. Even in my debilitated state, I fleetingly wondered the same thing. Maybe Sosa already had taken money to kill us, then decided to double his money and ransom us? Marrón wouldn't like that, and was capable of anything.

That was when I decided Sosa needed to understand I spoke Spanish. With my last ounce of dignity, I hauled out my quarterdeck voice and ordered him, *"Sosa—vaya a la casa para ayuda. ¡Ahora!"*

Rork showed him a wild glowering face to support my command. The outlaw comprehended our meaning completely. He started off for the front door and was halfway there when Rork and I dropped our heads on the muddy ground, panting for breath, hoping that for once in his disgusting life Gallo Sosa would really act like Robin Hood.

I faintly heard him pounding on the doors in the distance, then all went blank.

It is so strange what the mind can do, how it can conjure illusions, crystal-clear sounds, vivid sights, wonderful smells, within pleasant dreams. An Islamic scholar friend of mine in North Africa once told me that pleasant dreams were God's anesthetic for the mind, allowing it to heal from the harshness of life.

"Commander Wake? Can you hear me, sir?"

The dream kept repeating that same refrain: "Commander Wake? Can you hear me, sir?"

The vision seemed so real. A man in white robes in a white room. Or was it a cloud? A soft breeze washed over me, bringing the scent of flowers through flowing curtains of cottony gauze. Ah . . . heavenly. Lightheaded, a beautiful feeling. Yes, I was in heaven. Floating in heaven . . . I'd finally made it.

Then Rork destroyed my reverie with rudely ill-timed humor.

"Aye, Padre, he'll come 'round, not to worry. Just slide a wee bit o' rum under his sniffer an' he'll pop to like a jack-in-the-box!"

I slowly opened my right eye and saw Rork in a bed next to mine, propped up on one elbow and grinning at me like the proverbial cat. "Nice little nap, Peter?"

I moaned.

"You've been in bye-bye land for two days."

"Huh?"

"It's now the twenty-fifth, an' you're shirkin' your duties, Commander. But no more o' that sort o' gundeckin', lad, for there's work to be done."

I wasn't in the mood for his mirth. "Rork, you old—"

He almost fell out of bed laughing. "Nay! Belay that! Careful what ye say now, Peter. We're in the house o' the Lord, yes we are. An' ye shan't be strikin' me in here, neither, so gentle up your words, me friend, o' the padre here will have to chuck ye out with the rubbish!"

"The who?"

From my other side I heard a calm voice. "I am Father Benito Viñes, Commander Wake. Very pleased to meet you." I rolled over and saw a thin, older man in white robes. He wore spectacles atop a long nose, and had a quiet smile. He was the man in my dream. But I wasn't in heaven. For an instant, I felt disappointment.

"Commander Wake? Can you hear me, sir?"

My mind came alert and I looked at the priest again.

"Yes, Father, I can hear you. You saved us . . . thank you."

Viñes smiled again. "My son, it was not I, but a combination of events directed from heaven—Gallo Sosa took us to where you lay in the dirt that night. I am glad you received my message and understood it. I apologize for the secrecy, but discretion was called for and I thought you, as a sailor who knows the celestial sky, would understand the riddle. However, I am so very sorry that you were both extremely ill, my sons. But now you are better."

I couldn't get my brain to grasp it all. I looked to Rork, but he shrugged. "We'll explain later, Peter."

"Are you better?" I asked him. "You were sick too."

"Me? I'm doin' much better, courtesy o' the Jesuits here. The malaria didn't come to either o' us, thank God, an' we got medicines for the dysentery jus' in time."

Viñes touched my shoulder and said, "Your constitution will improve markedly during this day. Tonight we will all have a simple dinner in my quarters here. I know you have many questions. I can provide answers then. Until dinner, I bid you a gentle day of rest."

Rork, not stricken as badly by the dysentery, recovered faster and showed more vitality, but I was still a little shaky. A medical doctor came in and administered various medicines to us, some of which I didn't recognize. Beyond the usual lime and grapefruit and cinnamon treatments, he explained he was using native herbal remedies to calm our internal constitutions and fight the disease: holy basil, ginger, alum, dhatura, chirayata, and fenugreek. He assured me I would be better by the evening and strong again by the next morning. He was right. By late afternoon, I was able to walk and was hungry for food. It had been four days since I'd eaten.

Dinner was arranged at a colonnaded balcony overlooking the city in the distance. The bronze and pink sunset, reflected among the hills and the mansion itself, was nothing short of gorgeous, providing an added bit of medicine for me.

Waiting on the balcony, Viñes bid us a gracious hello and saw us to our seats. Servants poured a sweet red Spanish wine and laid out a tray of fruit, then were dismissed. With a brevity I wasn't used to in Latin America, Viñes got right to the point.

"We are at the home of my friend Roberto Nutonio, man

of means, who, for reasons you have no need to know, will not betray us. It is far safer for you here than my monastery in the city. I am so very pleased to see your recuperation proceeding so quickly. There is a nice dinner being prepared, but we have some time to converse beforehand, so I will do my best to answer your questions now, Commander. I am sure you have many."

I had hundreds, but decided to start with expressing our appreciation. The man had saved our lives. "First, please know that Rork and I thank you so much for all you've done to help us. We are in your debt, sir."

He waved away my thanks, so I went to my first question, one that had been building inside me since that afternoon. "Was it you who sent the message to Roosevelt in New York?"

He showed no alarm. "No, but I learned of it later, through a friend."

"Who sent it?"

"Why, Colonel Marrón, of course." He laughed at my reaction.

"Commander, Colonel Marrón is in charge of Spain's imperial intelligence apparatus in Havana. His tentacles extend everywhere, including, from what I hear, your country. They keep track of who is working against the Spanish occupation of Cuba."

He said it casually, as if it was common knowledge, but I'd never heard of Marrón before my encounter with him. I also noted Viñes's use of the word "occupation." Unusual for a Spaniard, or *peninsular,* as the Cubans called them. It was the sort of word used by anti-Spanish revolutionaries.

"Father Viñes, you are sure Marrón has agents in the U.S.?"

"Yes, my sources say he even has them within U.S. government."

I quickly asked, "Who? Where?"

"I only know that I've heard he has people in Key West and New York. But I do not know who his agents are, except that my source believes that one of them has a government function. It is an impression, my son, not a certain knowledge."

The Judas of Roosevelt's message. "A Spanish spy *inside* the American government?"

Viñes nodded while he peeled an orange.

"But how do you know all this, Father?"

"I have sources in unique places, Commander." He stopped at that, but seeing my frown he went on, his hands spread wide with paternal patience.

"My son, in the sixteen years since I was named director of the royal observatory and college, I have developed many acquaintances, some of whom give me information because they know they will not be associated with it. We Jesuits have an affinity for information, a thirst for knowledge, and not just the academic kind. We like to know what is going on around us in secular life. We also know how to keep a secret."

I already was well aware of their thirst for information. And I knew that they pass it along to their superiors. The Jesuits have the most extensive and effective intelligence network in history. "Does your source have a reason the colonel sent the message to Roosevelt?"

Viñes popped an orange section in his mouth and nodded thoughtfully.

"It was a clever ploy, a piece of bait to draw out his target—the American financial supporters to the Cuban revolutionaries. They would be arrested here, embarrassed in public, and possibly arrested for violation of laws in the United States about filibustering against a foreign country. The other money men in the U.S. would then become intimidated and the rebel cause would wither without its American backers. The theory was brilliant. In this case, however, it attracted the wrong target—you. Colonel Marrón is quite adroit at his intelligence work, but he did not anticipate that."

Earlier in the afternoon, I'd mulled over the possibility that this entire affair was a Spanish government set-up, but discounted it as too far-fetched and dangerous for the Spanish authorities. It still sounded that way—an incredible gamble.

"Why Roosevelt?"

"Well, I am not in the colonel's mind, but I presume because your Republican politicians in New York have been sympathetic to the Cuban revolutionaries. Roosevelt is rich and influential, also young and impetuous. I would imagine that Marrón thought Roosevelt would respond in person and the Spanish could catch him on Cuban soil, thereby embarrassing the Americans. As I said, my son, the *theory* was brilliant, but it was stupid to think that a man like that would get involved directly himself. Rich men do not do that. They have other men bleed for them."

I wasn't so sure of that. Viñes had obviously never met Roosevelt. The next question in my mind was: "You paid Gallo Sosa to rescue us?"

"Yes, to effect your escape and to hide you. He is very good at kidnapping and that sort of thing. But I sincerely regret the fact you grew ill, my new friend. I wanted you to stay . . . how do you say? . . . *incommunicado* . . . *bajo* . . . to stay *low* . . . for a while and hide after escaping from Marrón's hands. But I did not think they would give you bad food and water and you would become ill. Sosa was paid enough to give you decent refreshments, but unfortunately, he appropriated those for his own use."

The priest arched his eyebrows. "Naturally, I deducted that from his final fee."

"What would've happened if we'd stayed in government custody?"

He wagged his head. "I am not sure. But I was not hopeful at all that you would survive. The government is desperate, as demonstrated by Marrón's false message sent to the political man in New York. They wanted to catch a civilian, whom they might put on trial. But a military man of the United States? That would be too much, possibly inviting war. Still, who knows? They are doing more and more desperate things these days, many of which are not wise, and some of which are sins beyond redemption."

The priest's sad eyes regarded me closely as he sighed. "I am sometimes appalled by the barbarity I hear is going on. By people professing to be Christians, no less."

That sent a chill through my blood. "But how did you know Rork and I were taken into custody, or even in town? And why help *us?*"

"Mr. Rork went to the monastery several days ago and inquired about a brother in our order who had transferred. Word got to me that an American named Rork, on behalf of himself and a man named Wake, was asking questions around the monastery. That was a very unusual occurrence, so we checked your names via cable with our order's home, the Curia Generalizia in Florence. They sent a very concise reply: '*Wake and Rork are dear friends.*'"

He held up a bony finger and grinned.

"My sons, to a Jesuit that is all that is needed to be known. We then checked at the hotel, but found you were gone, disappeared. That was disturbing to me and I began to ask around. Sources informed me that you had been with Reverend Lefavre and a friend informed me that you later had run afoul of Marrón. Well, that is certainly not a good experience for a *dear friend* of the Society of Jesus. So, without further delay, I had a person go to your room at the hotel and retrieve your belongings before a more malevolent force searched your room and took them. We were lucky—Marrón's men arrived only minutes later. You have everything now that you left in the hotel room, I believe?"

"Yes, sir. We do. Thank you."

"And your cable from a Mr. Mondongo in New York? It was in plain sight on a table, so my man put it in your bags and brought it with him." He flashed a sly glance at me. "Mondongo, such an odd name."

"A friend in New York, sir. The cable must've been delivered after we left the room that night." I didn't elaborate, though I could tell Viñes wanted me to. When I'd unpacked my seabag that afternoon at the mansion, I'd read the cable message.

Mondongo's—alias Martí—reply to my telegrammed request for a social contact was ironic: *Avoid the Church. Someone will contact you.*

Avoid the Church meant the Catholics. No one other than Reverend Lefavre, the Methodist, had contacted us. Were he and Martí connected? Would that mean that Raul Leon, friend of Lafavre, was connected to Martí? My mind swirled with the implications of such a link. But I dared not ask Viñes any of that.

The priest let it go and offered, "It would appear that Mr. Rork's inquiries at the monastery set a beneficial succession of events in motion."

I nodded at Rork. "You must've made quite an impression, Sean."

He laughed and said, "Well, I gave it me best try."

The wine tasted better now that my mind and stomach were more at ease. There were many more questions, but one major concern in my mind. I was now a week late in sending that cable report to Porter in Washington.

Evidently clairvoyant, Viñes swallowed another piece of fruit and said, "Oh, and I thought your superiors might be concerned if they thought you had vanished. So don't worry. Please know that I sent a message to Florence explaining that you are well and—"

I blurted out, "In plain language? All the cables are being read!"

He put a hand on my arm and said, "Commander, please. I am a *Jesuit*. We always use a code, one that even others in the Church cannot readily understand. No one but my old friend Father General Beckx, the superior general of our order, knows of this. He sent a cable—without details—to a member of our order in Washington who then went by your naval headquarters and had a chat with an admiral to let him know that you and Mr. Rork are well and would communicate soon. A confirmation came in yesterday. Let us thank the Lord for transoceanic telegraph cables."

I sighed. "Was it Admiral Porter?"

Viñes' beamed. "Why yes, I believe that was the name. Do you know him?"

"Yes. I know him." I felt sick again. Porter knew about my dealings with the Jesuits over the years. He thought them quaint. He probably no longer thought it quaint. I couldn't envision what Secretary Whitney thought.

"I need to send a cable to them, myself. Can I write it out and ask you to have it sent, sir?"

"Of course, it will be our pleasure. Write it now and I will have it sent immediately."

He handed me a pen from within his robes and offered the back of a nearby piece of paper. I wrote to "Sales Manager Walker," at the private company street address in New York used for special communications, which would then be sent by courier to the Navy department in Washington. With no time to encode—a lengthy process I detested—I put it in plain words: *Am well. Will send further. Sale was a speculation and did not go thru. W.*

Viñes called for a servant and gave him instructions in rapid-fire Spanish. The man hurried away with the message. "He is a reliable man," said Viñes to my unasked question.

I proceeded to the next issue. "Thank you, again, Father. And I need to arrange transport for us, but I'm concerned about reappearing in Havana to try to board a steamer at the docks."

"I thought about that, Commander. We are in luck. There is no need for you to take a commercial steamer, or even to depart surreptitiously by small boat, for a U.S. warship is in Havana as we speak. It just arrived this morning. Pow . . . hate . . .tan?"

Rork perked up. "The old Pow Scow? *Powhatan*."

Viñes nodded. "Yes. I thought perhaps you could be quietly rowed to her tomorrow night. She is to sail away the next morning, from what I hear. If we get you to her, will they take you aboard?"

It was the best news I could hear. "They'd better, Father Viñes."

"Very good, my friend. And now I must request you use my first name, Benito. We have a unique bond that would allow that, I think. Do you agree?"

"Only if you use ours also, Benito. Peter and Sean. I must thank you again for everything. I am stunned at how this has evolved. We are very lucky."

"It is nothing. Ah, I see that dinner is ready. May I suggest we turn to other, more pleasant, subjects, Peter? Roberto's cook is very good and I think we could all benefit from some food right now."

But there was another question in my mind. One that couldn't wait.

"Benito, I must ask one last thing, though. In helping us escape and hiding us here, you have gone against the authority of the Spanish government, and therefore against the established policy of the Catholic Church in Cuba. You've also given me information that is confidential. What if this gets out and Bishop Piérola is told what you did? I fear you'll be in professional, or physical, peril for hiding us here. What will you do?"

I'll never forget his reaction. There was no apprehension, not a sign of worry, no anger. Instead, he sagged his narrow shoulders, a frail man with the serenity of a resting lion.

"Peter, my son, because of that telegram from Florence, I *trust* you with my confidential information. I think you understand better than I why my superiors have faith in you. Who am I not to do the same?"

He sipped his wine, savoring the flavor for a moment, then continued.

"And as for the potential views of the local Church and governmental leadership should they ever discover I helped you, well, worry not, my son, for I am not worried. The establishment sometimes expects the worst from us anyway. You see, Jesuits' opinions are not always in accord with local *administrative* authorities of the Church—but we like to think that someday those praiseworthy souls will gain enlightenment and catch up with us.

"And as for anyone in the colonial government wishing to do harm to me or my career, well, I happen to fulfill a function here that many characterize as quite needed and somewhat successful. A few have even gone so far as to call me *irreplaceable*, an embarrassing term for a mere priest."

"As director of the observatory?"

That distinctive smile, a combination of sly and innocent, showed again on his thin face. Behind the glasses his eyes glimmered as he answered, "Why, Peter, do you not know? I am the Hurricane Man . . ."

And thus started the topic of the dinner conversation. Benito Viñes told us how he and other Jesuits had been studying the world's weather patterns, specializing in hurricane storms of the tropics, with a view to coming up with better predictions of landfalls and giving advance warnings for affected populations. He hoped he could save lives. Father Viñes in Havana, and his friend Father Frederico Faura in Manila, were the world's experts in predicting the routes of hurricanes. Already they'd had successes over the last ten years and had, indeed, saved lives. Now they were working with the U.S. Army's signal service, which handled American weather forecasting.

It was an incredible evening—a huge contrast to the squalor and fear we'd known in the shanty slum. Before letting sleep take over that night, I marveled at the Divine Hand that, when Rork and I were in such peril, had put us in such care. The Hurricane Man saved two more lives that February in Havana.

11

That Impertinent Fool

0300, Saturday, 27 February 1886
U.S.S. Powhatan
At anchor in the harbor
Havana, Cuba

"Well now, this is quite unusual. Say, are you the same Wake that had the discipline problem with your captain off Panama? Back in sixty-eight, wasn't it?" asked Captain Gaston, commanding officer of the *Powhatan*. The executive officer, Lieutenant Commander Will Brown, stood stone-faced in the corner of Gaston's great cabin. Only the three of us were in the cabin—Rork was in the chief's quarters forward, explaining himself to a far more receptive crowd there.

Hiding my disgust, I replied as respectfully as I could to the captain. "Sir, it was eighteen sixty-nine and yes, I had to relieve my captain from duty because he'd become ill."

Gaston tilted his head in disbelief. "The way I heard it, you were court-martialed for mutiny afterward."

Rumors surrounding that incident had plagued me for seventeen years. There were still a few in the navy who believed them. It was frustrating, but I had to defend myself one more time.

"It was a court of inquiry, sir, and they found no violations. Captain, I wouldn't still be in the navy if there were anything improper about my actions back then. I've been promoted twice since then."

The captain nodded reluctantly. "So tell me, Commander, *why* again did you and a bosun, both of you out of uniform, suddenly show up at my ship in the middle of the night," he pulled out a pocket watch, "—make that at *three in the morning*—and demand to the quarterdeck officer of the watch that you be brought aboard? And while we're at it, Wake, have you been drinking? You don't look or sound too steady."

"No, sir, I have not been drinking. We had a bad bout with dysentery ashore and are recovering from it, so I don't look my best. Our uniforms are in our seabags, but we were rowed out to the ship clandestinely in civilian attire at this time in the night to preclude any suspicions by the local authorities."

"All right, then, I'll accept that you're not drunk. But why are you and that bosun in Havana doing *anything* clandestine? And why would the local authorities be suspicious of you for anything?"

"I'm in the Office of Naval Intelligence, sir, under Commodore Walker at Bureau of Navigation. Bosun Rork and I are on a confidential assignment."

"Naval Intelligence? Those are the people who keep pestering us for these ridiculous monthly information reports that no one could or will use."

Gaston huffed in annoyance and I knew, just knew, what his next question would be. He raised an eyebrow. "Confidential assignment, eh? By your appearance, your naval intelligence work doesn't seem to be going very well. What might that assignment be, Commander?"

He would be really annoyed now, but there was no other answer I could give.

"An assignment that is confidential, sir. By order of Commodore Walker and his superiors."

Brown coughed, or was it a snicker? Gaston drummed his fingers on his desk, hard, as his eyes blazed into mine.

"I *see* . . ." he said, which meant that he didn't see at all, and didn't very much care to at that point. But he had another question to fire at me.

"And what, pray tell, do you propose we do now, Commander Peter Wake, of the Office of Naval Intelligence?"

He was going to hate this part. "Delay sailing, sir, until a detailed cable to Washington can be sent, and the reply received. Probably a day, maybe two."

That did it.

Gaston slammed a fist down. "Confound it *all!* Wake, I will *not* be dictated to by a jumped-up staff *idler* from Washington who comes aboard like a bumboat *pimp* in the middle of the night from this gawdawful *cesspool* of a city! Get out of my cabin this instant. Brown, get him a berth and food and put him on the ship's muster bill for the noon watch as officer of the deck. And get that bosun to work, too."

I began to acknowledge, but the captain wasn't finished just yet. Cheeks livid, he leaped out of his chair, leveled his arm at me, and roared in the loudest voice I'd ever heard below decks on a ship.

"You are back in the *real* United States Navy, *Mister!* The one that goes to *sea,* like *men,* instead of playing with papers in Washington and skullduggering around with the scum of the earth in foreign fleshpots. Now get out!"

As his ranting got louder, I realized it was nothing compared to what Porter was going to do to me, so, with that sense of perspective, I calmly looked him in his bulging eyes and said, "Aye, aye, sir."

It set him off again, but I had already saluted, about-faced, and marched smartly out the door into the passageway, leaving poor Brown to deal with the overheated captain of the U.S.S. *Powhatan.*

For me the important thing was that Rork and I were physically safe at last. Everything else was minor and could be adjusted to—even Captain Gustavius G. Gaston, whom I was beginning to intensely dislike.

I went forward after fleeing the captain and talked to Rork, filling him in on my reception and our new work aboard. He'd already heard I was in trouble and that we were assigned to duties aboard, which neither of us, as seamen, minded. We stood near the starboard forechains and went over the possibilities for us.

"Me mates amongst the gunroom mess say we're bound east along the coast to Matanzas for a society port call at the request o' the consul, then we's off to Panama, to check on American merchant citizens down there who've made more complaints, Commander," reported Rork, reverting to naval discipline aboard ship by calling me by rank. "So I suppose it mixes in nicely with the mission's cover."

I shook my head. "That was the original mission. But now it's changed.

"Changed? We got new orders from Commodore Walker?"

"No. Changed by me. I've got questions I didn't have when we started."

"Oh, sir. Me old bones're actin' mighty pained on hearin' that. The commodore will not fancy that one little bit."

"As much as I appreciate the value of your old bones' premonition, the commodore isn't down here, Rork. There's a large conspiracy of some sort going on here, Rork—among Americans and Cubans, Catholics and Protestants. And much of it centers in

Key West. In the United States."

"An' you think dear Useppa is involved."

"Yes . . . I'm afraid she is, somehow."

"Well then, after Matanzas, me thinks we'd better get our old arses to Key West, Commander."

Powhatan got underway at ten that morning, after receiving fruits and vegetables from shore. I wasn't able to send a message to headquarters before our departure. Leaving the Plaza de Luz to port, we exchanged salutes with the signal station at Cabana Castle to starboard while steaming slowly through the cut at the entrance to the harbor. Gliding through the calm water past massive Morro Fortress and its lighthouse, Gaston ignored me as he paced the starboard deck. I did my best to stay out of his line of sight. As the Audencia prison slid by the port beam, I stood by the starboard main pinrail and peered around the mainmast, scanning the upper windows of the building for Colonel Marrón, but not seeing him. *Probably still interrogating his men who let us escape,* I thought.

Minutes later we were at sea, beyond the cliffs and fortresses, out of the reach of my enemies in Havana. Six miles out we caught the edge of the Gulf Stream and turned east. Gaston—following standard U.S. naval orders not to use his engine for anything other than harbor entry and exit—stopped the engine, set all sail, including the stun's'ls and moonraker, and we wallowed our way downwind. It was a light air day, and even with the current helping, we took over ten hours to make the fifty miles to our next Cuban port of Matanzas. Halfway there, the Spanish ram cruiser *Jorge Juan* steamed up from astern and passed us effortlessly, the crew waving gaily at our relic of a ship. Humiliating.

I did my deck time, as co-senior officer of the watch, with executive officer Brown. It was an easy watch. The navigation was simple, the ship's work routine. Gaston was below and I actually enjoyed it, gamming with Brown and an ensign about various ports and ships in our careers. Even at our snail's pace, it felt good to be at sea again, among my own. Up forward, Rork had been put on the same watch, and he spent most of it showing off his stump and its accoutrements to the other senior petty officers.

The sun was setting when we let go six hundred feet of chain in ten fathoms at Matanzas Bay. Within minutes, a boat carrying the consul for Matanzas, who was also vice consul for all of Cuba, came alongside. The diplomat climbed the side ropes and was on the deck before the captain or Brown could properly greet him, an uncommon state of events. Usually, naval officers reported in ashore. I happened to be standing there and he, recognizing the three gold sleeve rings indicating my rank, addressed me.

"Good evening, Commander. I am Vice Consul David Vickers, and I have an urgent telegraphic message for the captain. Would that be you, sir?"

"No, sir. I am Commander Peter Wake and aboard in transit. The ensign of the watch has run to fetch the captain and he'll be here very shortly, if you would like to deliver the communication to him personally. In the meantime, would you care for coffee from the wardroom?"

The man looked like he was seeing a ghost, or maybe a jackal. "*You* are Commander Wake?"

Sensing big trouble dead ahead, I admitted the same.

He said, "The message is about—" but was stopped by a great commotion erupting behind me. I recognized the voice.

"Stand aside there! The consul's here to see *me*, Wake!"

Captain Gaston deftly slid his bulk in front of me and snatched the envelope from Vickers' hand. I retreated three steps and went to parade rest while the captain spoke, a bit too loudly, in my opinion, to the consul.

"Thank you, sir. I am the commanding officer of this ship. Captain Gustavius G. Gaston. And you are the Mr. Vickers who is expecting us, I presume?"

The man recognized the captain's animosity toward me and became hesitant. "Yes, I am, Captain. Ah, well . . . I know it's highly unusual to come out to the ship, especially so early, but this message came in this afternoon. A telegraph cable from Washington. It was in plain text and marked urgent for you, so I thought I'd better deliver it now. I'll take my leave now, Captain, and oh, don't worry about the events that were planned."

"What? We had some amiable social affairs planned for tonight, the twenty-eighth. A dinner and dance with the local leading society, I thought."

"I believe this communication may trump that engagement, Captain. Another time, then." Seconds later he was sliding down the side ropes—clearly he'd had some sea time himself by the way he knew a ship—and the boat was away and pulling for shore.

Gaston, disconcerted by an unanticipated visitor for the second time that day, ripped open the envelope and read the paper inside, his face growing more contorted as he went along.

"Mr. Brown!"

"Here, sir," replied the executive officer, who'd raced from his cabin to the main deck and was still buttoning his coat.

The captain never looked at me, but I felt his rage like a blast furnace. "Weigh anchor instantly and set a course *directly* for Key West. I want to be there as fast as possible. Permission to use all coal needed for full speed is granted. We'll only be there *five minutes,* then we'll return to our duties here."

And with that said, Captain Gaston disappeared below. I never saw the message, but was later told the contents by Brown, who added that it came from Commodore Walker.

"Get Wake to Key West immediately."

Rork and I were mystified as to the reason for our sudden

luck. How did Walker know we were aboard *Powhatan?* And why were we ordered to Key West? Soon, however, we realized our good fortune was not appreciated by anyone else aboard the Pow Scow.

Out in the middle of the Straits of Florida, we found the wind had piped up to a gale. It and the Gulf Stream were now foul against us on the course to Key West and doing their nonlevel best to make all hands as miserable as possible, which was saying quite a lot regarding that old barge. Seas rose from nowhere to curl over and smash down on our bow, shuddering the entire ship from stem to stern. *Powhatan* was an infamous wreck of a ship anyway, her seams loose before the pounding. Now, smashing into the waves at full speed under engine and staysails, they were opening everywhere, making the men labor at the pumps incessantly to empty the hull of seawater. It was back-breaking work, bringing out the worst tempers in both officers and men.

Much of that ill will was directed at the cause for the ship's uncomfortable course and dangerous speed—namely, me. It took perhaps an hour for the ire of everyone aboard to be focused on the Jonah that had recently arrived in the trappings of a street beggar, which had already engendered opinions as to my identity and occupation. Before we'd made Matanzas, I was a curio. Now Rork and I were *personas non grata.*

On the afternoon of the next day, the first of March, we finally steamed past the reefs at Sand Key into calmer water and slowed to bare steerageway at Man of War Anchorage, a quarter-mile from the waterfront of Key West. Slowed was all we did—we never even stopped, much less anchored. The guard boat came out from the harbor station and came close alongside, expecting to show us to our mooring. Thirty seconds later, Rork and I were on the boat, facing an astonished coxswain. At a yell from *Powhatan's* main deck, the boat was sheered away from the ship, the old warship belched a cloud of black smoke, her propeller went into gear and bit the water, and she heeled over in a turn to get back to sea.

Not a man aboard waved, or even looked our way, but I did hear Gaston's roar that now he was "free of that impertinent fool."

The boat coxswain was flabbergasted by the whole performance, gaping at me but afraid to ask. Rork assumed the neutral gaze of the veteran petty officer, though I thought I detected the slightest smugness. The boat's crew glanced between me, Rork, and their coxswain, waiting for orders. In the background, the warship was charging out the channel, her bow wave nearly swamping a fishing smack. Finally, the coxswain could stand it no longer—this apparent marooning of an officer beyond his powers of comprehension—and he said, "Ah . . . orders, sir?"

I indulged his inquisitiveness by saying, as imperturbably as I could muster, "I needed a ride to the naval station from Cuba. Could you please get us to the dock to complete the journey, Coxs'n?"

Rork winked at me. It had been a very long forty-eight hours.

12

The Tangled Web

Tuesday, 2 March 1886
Russell House Hotel
Key West, Florida

When we'd arrived the night before, Rork and I had secured our previous room at the Russell House Hotel, but forgone dinner. I didn't even notify my daughter that we were in Key West. Instead, physically and mentally exhausted, we gave way to the temptation of soft beds and clean sheets. They are a luxury only a sailor or soldier can best appreciate.

But our morning duties on Tuesday could not be delayed, and with it the requirement to tell all to Porter and Walker, safely enciphered in a telegram. The cipher was necessary even though we were no longer in Cuba. You see, Key West wasn't exactly the United States, either. As Father Viñes had confirmed, many foreign eyes and ears roamed the island, and I assumed some of them had access to the cable messages at the International Telegraph

Company offices on Front Street.

After a good old-fashioned Southern breakfast, which we lingered over in decadent gluttony, Rork and I retired to the room to tackle the demanding job of encoding my summary of the situation. I'd say considerably demanding, for back in those days we were in the learning stages of encrypted telegraphy. The Europeans were well beyond us, as usual. You could read their telegrams and never have a clue as to the true content within, not even guess it was in code, but we had been slow to adopt such measures.

Reading another's private communications was thought to be sordid and ungentlemanly by many of the old horses in the navy—merely doing intelligence work at all was considered beneath a naval officer's dignity, hence Gaston's opinion of my ONI work. But the fact that foreigners had read *our* private Panama traffic the year earlier put to rest those quaintly innocent notions. Recently, the naval leadership had begun insisting that their private communications actually remain private. Being quaint and trusting others just wasn't practical anymore in our so-called modern world.

The U.S. Navy even went to the unprecedented extent of hiring a foreigner for assistance in the matter. One day at the office I met a gent named Hawke—an alias if I ever heard one, and probably derived from the silhouette of his nose—sent to us from our friends, the ever-perfidious British. He was supposed to be a cipher expert on special short-term assignment to teach us the intricacies of secret messaging, but I always wondered if perhaps we were teaching *him,* and thus his countrymen, a little too much about our weaknesses in that area. Or were we deliberately sowing incorrect impressions to decrease the Old World's apprehension of us? Maybe Porter and Walker really were three steps ahead of everyone else? Oh well, obsession with suspicion is an unavoidable trait of my business, though I still try not to be *too* scornful.

So Rork and I sat there in our room, conjuring up the code

words we'd committed to memory before our supposedly low-key Cuba journey. It wasn't complicated, just time-consuming. Back then, ONI used a simple one-time code. It was memorized in advance, good for one month, and tailored to fit the man's disguise assignment for communication purposes—ours was about the rum trade, which raised a chuckle between us that morning. It also addressed specific issues on our mission. The one-time code for February of 1886 consisted of having the fourth word in every sentence as a code word.

But the calendar was not on our side, for Monday was the first day of March, and brought in a new monthly code I'd never been given. I used the old code anyway and hoped for the best.

Each paragraph of the message also had a special purpose. The first paragraph was about the condition of the ONI agents— Rork and me. The second was about the condition of the targeted subject or country—the Spanish government in Cuba. The third paragraph described the situation regarding the main matter at hand, be it a new weapon, or a country's war mobilization, or, in my case—the activities of anti-Spanish revolutionaries. The last paragraph portrayed the agent's opinion of the mission's outcome and/or requests for additional funds, time, or assets.

To be sure, one had to be good at recounting things, for a mistake in remembering the code could alter the message. Therefore, Rork checked my memory and I confirmed his. We agreed, and set out to compose what Porter, et al, had been waiting on for over a week.

I must add, for the reader's confidence in our navy, that ONI's methods of telegraphic communication have completely changed since that year. They are now far more complex and impenetrable with the standardized Navy Secret Code system introduced in 1888 by Commodore Walker. Thus, with no danger of betraying current or future secrets, I will display the code we'd memorized, what it meant, and the message into which it was inserted.

1st paragraph code about the ONI agent:
Distilled = *safe*
Undistilled = *unsafe*

10 casks = *able to communicate*
20 casks = *unable to communicate*

2nd paragraph code about the target subject:
Good quality = *strong*
Best quality = *weak*

Sales are good = *target knows about mission*
Sales are bad = *target does not know about mission*

Volume discount = *target has spy in U.S. government*
No volume discount = *unknown if target has spy in U.S. government*

3rd paragraph code about mission itself:
10USD a cask = *revolutionary situation what we thought*
15USD a cask = *revolutionary situation not what we thought*

White rum = *good chance of success for revolutionaries*
Dark rum = *little chance of success for revolutionaries*

Cane drought = *revolution soon*
Cane pest = *revolution in distant future*
Cane monopoly = *no revolution wanted by Cuban people*

Rain = *Americans in New York involved heavily*
Tornado = *Americans in Key West involved heavily*

Hurricane = *Spanish agents active in Key West*
Doldrums = *Spanish agents active in New York*

4th paragraph code about mission outcome/requests
Transport by wagon = *continuing mission until directed
    otherwise*
Transport by rail = *discontinuing mission*

Harry = *need more money*
Bill = *need more time*
Tom = *need more people*
Lincoln = *need a warship nearby*
Pierre = *need extraction*
Gunther = *need to communicate in detail—code
    inadequate*

My message couldn't give details, but did provide broad information. I completed it with the false company address and one of my aliases. And so, our telegraph communiqué to Walker and Porter emerged as:

TO: CANNON/ANDERSON SPIRITS/NEW
YORK
FR: GOMEZ/KEY WEST
2MARCH86/1135/ROUTINE

1)X—ORIGINALLY RUM HERE
UNDISTILLED—X—NOW FOUND RUM
DISTILLED FOR SALE—X—SO FAR HAVE
10 CASKS—X

2) X—IT IS DEFINITELY GOOD
QUALITY—X—IT APPEARS THAT SALES
ARE GOOD—X—BUT I SEE NO VOLUME

DISCOUNT YET—X

3)X—PRICE GIVEN AS 15USD A CASK—
X—PRICE MOSTLY FOR WHITE RUM—
X—THIS DESPITE CANE DROUGHT—
X—BUT PREDICTION IS RAIN—X—ALSO
PREDICTION FOR TORNADO—X—AT
LEAST NO HURRICANE IN SIGHT—X—
RAIN GOOD BUT DOLDRUMS BETTER
RIGHT NOW—X

4) X—WILL TRANSPORT BY WAGON TO
PORT—X—PLEASE SEND TO HARRY THIS
MESSAGE—X—SHIPPING HANDLED
BY BILL—X—SEND INQUIRIES TO
GUNTHER IN BOSTON—X—END—X

I expected an answer that afternoon. Being Monday, my daughter was busy with school functions and afternoon children's events. So my intention was to talk to Useppa that evening about the man in her life. First, however, Rork and I needed to take time to think, to reason out the maze in which we found ourselves.

After sending the telegram at the cable office and taking a stroll down by the naval depot, we had lunch at Richard Curry's Saloon near the foot of Duval on the corner of Wall Street. Getting a table on the upstairs verandah overlooking the streets below, where we could be alone, Rork and I quietly went over what we knew for certain, and what we suspected.

I started. "First, we're pretty sure that Marrón started this mess with the message to Roosevelt, in an attempt to catch Americans conspiring on Cuban soil against the imperial government. Second, we know that the Protestant clergy in Havana and Key West are strongly connected. Third, we know Useppa has connections among the Episcopal and Methodist clergy in both cities. Fourth, we know Martí was going to have someone contact us in Havana, and that Lefavre did, though he said it was because of a message from Leon. Was that coincidence or connected? Last, we know, or suspect strongly, that some of the Protestant clergy is anti-government."

"Right so far, sir." Rork sipped his coffee. "But maybe Lefavre got messages from both Leon *and* Martí. An' one more thing— Viñes. The vicar planned an' executed our escape, an act against the government. Methinks he's involved far more than he lets on. An' we never asked him point-blank, now did we?"

"Yes, I know, I should have, but didn't want to turn him against us. Now, who are the connectors in this pattern? In Havana, Lefavre knows us, Raul, and maybe Martí. In Key West, it's got to be Useppa,"—I hated even mentioning her name in the context—"for she knows Raul, us, and Lefavre."

"Raul is the common link to everyone in Key West an' Havana. An' I reckon he lied about knowin' Martí too."

I contemplated the name. "Raul Leon . . . *lion*. He does seem to be the nexus of many parts of this thing—"

Suddenly Rork touched my arm to get attention, then tilted his head toward Stillman's Saloon, a block up Duval, on the corner of Front Street. A man was leaning against a lamppost on the corner, watching us. When he saw us looking at him, he walked across the street into Sariol's store. Middle-aged, thin, dark features, with a bowlegged gait, he appeared familiar somehow.

"Remember him?" asked Rork. Seeing I didn't, he said, "Well, I do, plain as day. Saw him that night in the dungeon of the Audencia—one of Marrón's officers. Aye, that's him, an' the bugger's name comes to me now. *Teniente*—Lieutenant—*Boreau*, somebody called him." Rork tone lowered. "Oh, yeah, that little bastard fancied gettin' rough with me, when I was shackled like a trussed pig. I could tell by the look in his eye, but Colonel Marrón walked in and took over. Mark me words, sir, that's the same man—an' Boreau's his name."

It came back to me then, and I recalled seeing him in a passageway in the Audencia as Rork and I were taken to the wagon. An evil leering sort. You could just tell.

Spotting him in the United States was unnerving. "Damn it, Marrón must've figured we'd come to Key West."

Rork rubbed his left arm and growled, "Aye, he sent that slimy bugger here after us. Ta' tie up a loose end for the Dago gov'mint. Boreau'll put an ounce o' lead between our ears to save his bossman the trouble o' explainin' our escape. Then they'll blame it on Key West outlaws o' some such."

I couldn't see that. "No, I don't think they'll try to go after us here, but I'd wager he'll follow us to see who our contacts are, and they might go after *them*."

But Rork was adamant. "Aye, *then* he'll try to kill us. I tell ye, he's up to no bloody good. I say we do unto him first. Interrogate *his* friggin' arse straight away, an' find what's what 'round here with *their* bloody spies. Just get 'im in an alley an' me spike'll do the rest o' that wee bit o' a job."

"Nah, Sean. This tangled web needs deciphering before it's destroyed. Brains first—then brawn, my friend. Let's follow *him* and learn what and who *he* knows."

Ducking out the back door of the café, we circled around the block, approaching our observer's last position from the rear. He'd moved, but we spotted him a block further north, at Duval and Greene Streets. Having lost sight of us on the verandah, Boreau became a dodgy character, indeed. Periodically stopping, backtracking, and starting up again, he worked his way east, then down Whitehead toward the harbor. Boreau veered into Sweeney's Billiard Parlor on Front Street. I decided we would wait. Five minutes later he emerged and started walking again.

After an additional half-hour of wandering through Key West, our quarry ended his meandering. Turning right from Duval onto Fleming Street, he then ducked left into a little alley that ran south between Fleming and Southard streets, just four buildings west of

Duval. Rork advised me he thought it was San Carlos Lane, so called by the Cubans who lived in the area. Seventy yards into the alley Boreau stopped suddenly, examining a shadowed area on the west side, where several old crates were piled. After glancing around for observers, Boreau edged himself back down behind the crates. Periodically, he peered around a corner of the crates, his attention centered on one door, the rear entrance to a relatively large two-storied building that fronted on Fleming Street.

Rork and I backtracked on Fleming toward Duval. We lounged against the wall of a mansard-roofed rooming house, where several other men, evidently the boarders, stood discussing Cuban politics. I nodded in vague agreement with my new companions' opinions of the Spanish while Rork wandered around and tried to keep Boreau under scrutiny. The building Boreau was watching had a small balcony overlooking Fleming Street, and an ornate sign over the front door. Unfortunately, the sign was in the shade of the balcony, so I could not make out the lettering.

Just as the men around me were growing suspicious at my unfamiliarity and lack of conversation, Rork reported back from his short walk. He said that it was difficult to see the Spaniard from Fleming Street, that we'd have to split up and seek more advantageous positions. That seemed logical to me.

He went around to the southern end of the lane near Southard Street. I slowly maneuvered my way toward a frangipani tree just inside the alley's northern end near Fleming, perhaps sixty feet from our man. I sat down in the shadows behind a latticework fence and waited.

At a quarter past three, the Spanish agent stiffened up, his concentration on the back door of the building in question, which was opening. Two young men emerged. I didn't recognize them. Boreau began writing on a notepad. A third man came out the door, looking up and down the alley.

I did recognize *him*. Father Raul Leon. He turned and conversed in Spanish—I couldn't get the words in detail—with someone unseen inside, then nodded his head in agreement. The first two men also nodded their heads. By their deferential gestures, I guessed that a senior colleague was about to emerge from the doorway. The door opened a bit more and I was able to read the placard on it—*Instituto San Carlos*. I knew of the group—Cuban merchants and cigar workers mostly; many were revolutionaries. It was their private social club, where they raised money and plotted offensives against their sworn enemy, the Spanish crown government. Boreau's government.

Then the mystery man emerged. It was none other than my acquaintance Reverend Lefavre, the Methodist from Havana. Boreau scribbled furiously.

Lefavre gave an apparent order to the other three and they set off down the alley, south toward Rork's position, but the Spanish detective didn't follow. I couldn't see Rork, but hoped he would follow Raul Leon. Meanwhile, Boreau stayed in his concealed position, glaring at the man in the doorway. After the others left, Lefavre smiled at someone inside the door and beckoned them out. Seconds later a form in red and white cotton plaid came out into the sunlight. I felt my stomach go cold.

Useppa.

Boreau recorded her too. I slid deeper into the shadows as Lefavre and Useppa walked north past my post, onto Fleming Street. They were followed fifty yards behind by the Spaniard, who in turn was trailed by me. Making their way east on Fleming, they separated at the corner of Duval, the minister heading south and Useppa heading east toward her church.

To my relief, Boreau followed the Cuban, while I stayed behind my daughter. When she entered the Methodist rectory, I decided not to confront her at that point. That would come later, after Rork and I had conferred. I wanted his opinion. I also needed to know what our instructions from Walker would be. I suspected Rork and I would be ordered to return to Washington.

Thirty minutes later, I went to the telegraph office and found my guess incorrect, for the decoded order from Washington was just the opposite.

TO: GOMEZ/KEY WEST
FR: CANNON/ANDERSON SPIRITS/NEW YORK
2MARCH86
1) X—YES BUY THE 10 CASES—X
2) X—KEEP WORKING ON VOLUME DISCOUNT—X
3) X—CONTINUE ADVISORIES ON WEATHER—X
4) X—COMPANY MANAGEMENT APPROVES TRANSPORT BY WAGON—X— SALES APPROVED BY HARRY AND BILL— X—SALES COMING BY GUNTHER—X— END—X

Section one said they wanted me to stay in communication. The second section ordered me to continue working on the spy in the U.S. government. The third told me to continue working on the general spy network. And the fourth said that the mission was to continue until otherwise directed, that money and time were approved. That more detailed communications were needed, and that a messenger would be en route.

We were a fair distance from Washington. It would take probably four days at least for a courier to get to the island from naval headquarters, via train to a southern port, then by steamer. Until he got here, I was on my own, a state of affairs I always appreciated, for it increased my flexibility to get things done.

By the time the courier arrived, I intended to know exactly what Useppa's part in any of this was and to end it swiftly. On the other side of the espionage equation, I would determine the extent of the Spanish spy problem in Key West. And with any luck, I might even ascertain the identity of the Spanish spy within my government.

But therein lies a lesson—flexibility does not always result in success. Sometimes, it just gets you deeper into the trap.

A Disquieting Discovery

Tuesday, 2 March 1886
The African Cemetery
Southern beach, Key West

Dinner at a restaurant, as a setting for this conversation, was dismissed from my mind once I saw Useppa at the Instituto San Carlos. I wanted to talk with her at a place guaranteed to invoke emotion, and therefore candidness. So I left a note at the church for her to meet me at a time and location I knew would serve my purpose—sunset at the old African cemetery on the south side of the island. Useppa loved the place for its sentimental value. I wasn't thinking like a father at that point, however, for a perilous part of the world had intruded upon my family. There wasn't time anymore to be delicate. Or sentimental.

The cemetery was actually an unkempt collection of mainly unmarked graves, mostly for the Africans that died after the U.S. Navy rescued them from slave-runners off the Cuban coast just before the Civil War. The slave-runners had been arrested and the Africans who'd been liberated, some fourteen hundred of them, were taken to Key West. They'd been deathly ill on the crossing, and upon landing on the island were put in crudely constructed huts—dumped in a locale utterly foreign in every way. The U.S. Marshal built the shelters out of his own pocket, and missionaries fed and cared for them, but three hundred of the Africans didn't make it and were buried by the sea, on the opposite side of the island from the town. Ironically, it is the side that faces their homeland.

That had been almost thirty years earlier, and now, in addition to the old African burial sites, there was the occasional Negro American or Bahamian grave, signified with a simple cross. It was a sad place, said to be haunted by the wailing of those poor souls from the slave-ships. Whites seldom visited it—their dead were laid to rest in the center of the island, nearer to town and their loved ones.

Sometimes when I visited Key West, Useppa liked to walk with me along the African beach at sunset, and hear again the story of her parents exchanging their vows there during a similar sunset. And she had another connection to the site. My daughter cared for some of the older Africans that had stayed on at Key West, parishioners of Reverend Artell. A few of their grandchildren were her students at the Douglass School. So she, better than most, understood the poignant spirits of the graveyard, whose soul was purest Africa.

I got there first and waited. Rork was back at the hotel. Down the beach, beyond the West Martello Tower fortification, the sun was copper tinged, just above an inked horizon. Useppa walked up to me through sea oats waving in a warm easterly trade wind. My little girl's lovely auburn hair was highlighted by the sun's last rays.

She smiled, a look of genuine warmth, while passing the same sabal palm where Linda had stood on that evening long before.

Useppa embraced me. "Daddy, I didn't know you were on the island. Back from Panama so soon?"

I didn't say anything at first, and saw her smile wilt during the pause. My heart was breaking, but I dared not show it.

"I never made it to Panama. I came here from Cuba. We need to talk, Useppa. I know what you're involved in."

Her intended look of surprise failed. Then my Useppa, devoted Christian missionary, almost lied to me. "Daddy . . . I don't know what—"

I stopped her right there. "Don't say another word before you think about it, Useppa. And think about this first. I love you. I'm here for you. Your brother Sean, you, Uncle Sean, and I—we have only each other in this world. We'll always be there for each other. Understood?"

Her eyes cast downward and she was twelve again. "Yes, Daddy. I understand."

I pulled her to me, felt her trembling, and desperately wanted it to all go away, to not even have to think about it anymore. But things had gone too far for that.

"Useppa, we're going to sit down here together, and you're going to tell me everything. No yelling on my part, no leaving anything out on your part. You are involved in a deadly situation that now involves me too. I'm used to that. You aren't. I need the truth, right now."

She nodded and we sat down on a little ledge of sand, the sun's final glint flashing off the sea like a signal from God to proceed. High above us, faint clouds brushed across the sky, edged with lime and lavender. I heard a conch shell sounding from somewhere. So many memories here. Even that tangy smell of the sand. As I sit here writing this I can smell that beach.

She reached for my hand. "Daddy, I didn't mean to get so involved."

"I know that, dear. Let's start from the beginning, when you first learned about the Cuban rebels."

After a sigh, she started. "Actually, everyone on the island knows about them, Daddy. But the first real interaction I had was through the church. The Methodists and Episcopalians—we're all friends here—have close ties to their sister churches in Havana. The Protestant churches have been harassed and closely watched by the authorities there. Some of the Cuban people who attend our churches in Havana are working for independence. They visit here sometimes, and over dinner the conversation turns to that topic."

She was still hesitating. I needed specifics. "When and how did it go from dinner conversation to you actively participating, dear?"

Useppa took a breath. "I suppose it was when Reverend Lefavre, of the Havana Methodists, was visiting Reverend Sparks of our Methodist church. He told us over dinner that he needed to get some friends out of Cuba to safety, so we helped him by arranging a home for them to stay in. Reverend Sparks had done it before, but that was my first time—about a year ago. That was when I met Raul. He would bring people on fishing boats to and from Cuba." A second went by, then she added, "We were saving lives, Daddy."

"I understand that, dear. What happened next?"

"Raul and I, well, we talked and talked, and found we liked the same things and, well, spent some time together, and we . . . well . . ."

I searched for a word that wouldn't embarrass either of us. "Became enamored?"

"Yes, enamored. He's a good man. A very good man. And he told me of his work with Mr. Maceo and Mr. Gómez and others in Cuba. I got to meet Mr. Maceo last October, at dinner here in Key West. Raul wants me to meet Mr. Gómez too."

My God. I'd no idea she was *that* far into it. "Antonio Maceo?

Máximo Gómez?"

"Why yes, Daddy. Do you know them?"

"Maceo is a general in the rebel army. Gómez is the head of the rebel army."

I didn't add that indeed, Rork and I did know Maceo. I had heard that he'd been in Key West the October before, brought out of Cuba to escape another Spanish attempt on his life.

Useppa followed up with, "Raul has a wonderful vision for Cuba, Daddy—someday it will be a free democracy, with equality for all."

My daughter, the philosopher. The dreamer. It would be a long time before the Spanish left, and they wouldn't leave quietly. "It's a war, Useppa. A dirty, deadly, civil war. You're now involved in that, courtesy of Raul."

"Yes, in a way, I suppose I am, but Raul hasn't killed anybody, Daddy. He's a minister of the Lord."

I could hear the pleading in her voice, trying to convince herself Raul wasn't involved in any bloodshed. I had to admit, it *was* hard to imagine him in combat. Just didn't seem the type. More of an intellectual, the kind that spurs others to action. Gets *them* killed.

"And Raul asked you to help out by doing what?"

"Simple little things, really. Take a message to someone, arrange a boat or a house, store some supplies."

It sounded innocuous, but I needed to know more. "Boats to or from where?"

"Tampa or Key West or Havana."

"Who went on the boats?"

"I didn't ask, Daddy. That would be rude."

Rude? Useppa'd never met Colonel Marrón and his thugs. "What kind of supplies did you store for them?"

"I don't know. They were boxes."

"What kind of boxes?"

"Oh Daddy, they were *boxes,*" she said with exasperation.

"Different kinds of boxes—some were small, some were big, some were long."

"Any writing on them?"

"No, not on most of them. I don't remember what anything said on the boxes."

"What did they tell you was in the boxes?" She gave me that look again.

"Oh, they didn't tell you and that would've been rude to ask, right?"

She said, "Don't be *mordant,* Daddy." My daughter sometimes uses her extensive vocabulary to intimidate me. She knew I had no idea what *mordant* meant. My education was limited, far inferior to hers. "And yes, Daddy, that would've been rude."

Ignoring that taunt, I thought about what she'd said about the boxes. Long boxes—rifles? And that probably wasn't the least of it. "And now you're with the Cuban revolutionary committee at the Instituto San Carlos."

Her eyes instantly widened, while I continued, "And I know you heard what happened to me in Havana, know that Reverend Lefavre had seen me, and know that I was working on an assignment there. Stop playing games with me, Useppa. I need to know *exactly* what is going on."

Her voice was tiny. "Yes, Daddy, I just found out. I was so scared for you."

"And you know that I was at a place in Havana—a place like this, in fact—used by the rebels as a rendezvous point."

I searched her eyes and knew instantly. "It was a set-up, wasn't it, Useppa?"

Tears streamed down her checks. "Oh Daddy, you weren't supposed to be involved in any of this. I didn't even know you were going to be in Havana. I thought you were going to Panama."

"Well, I *am* involved, Useppa. And I'm waiting."

She spoke between sobs. "We sent a message to a man in New York a month ago—a politician Raul thought could sway opinions in Washington . . ."

What? Raul Leon sent the message and not Colonel Marrón? I completed her sentence. "—by the name of Roosevelt."

She cringed. "Yes, Daddy. That's the name. Raul and the others thought that if we could get the Republican leaders to recognize the independence movement in Cuba, then the U.S. government would follow suit. That would speed the day when the Spanish leave forever."

"Why Roosevelt, a Republican? They're not in power. You follow politics in the papers. You know that."

She shrugged. "That was my idea. The Republicans were pro-independence when they were in power, though, and I thought the younger ones could influence Congress. Roosevelt has a reputation for being . . . enthusiastic . . . about causes he believes in. We were desperate, Daddy. There's going to be a lot of people hurt if Cuba doesn't gain independence *peacefully,* so I suggested trying Roosevelt. Besides, we knew the Democrats would reject it right away. They don't want to get involved. So it had to be the Republicans."

I sighed inwardly. This was beyond my fears. Far from being an unwilling dupe blinded by love, my twenty-one-year-old daughter was the political consultant for the Cuban revolutionary committee—motivated by altruistic notions and love, no doubt. Of course, she certainly had that last part about the Democrats correct. President Cleveland's administration was distancing itself from Cuba fast.

"But why send the message to Roosevelt in a riddle?"

"Raul wanted to for security, but it turns out that didn't work out anyway. The Spanish government has spies everywhere here, and up in New York, too. Somehow, they intercepted the message, but let it go through after they deciphered it."

Useppa choked as her eyes filled. "We didn't know that at the time, though. Nobody knew that until the night you were caught in Havana, Daddy. That's when we knew everything had gone terribly wrong."

"How did the Spanish see the message?"

She shook her head. "Raul thinks they pay a man at the telegraph office here. The Spanish knew where the meeting would be in Havana and got you there—right after they arrested the man, Raul's friend, who was the real contact. His partner ran away and told us what happened. We think Raul's friend is . . . dead. His name was Marco."

She was crying hard now, but I couldn't let up.

"Who is the Judas from the message—the one in the U.S. government?"

"I'm not sure. But Raul thinks maybe it's one of the federal officials here in Key West."

"And what's this about how something will happen soon—the slaves will rise up and go after the masters with bloodshed?"

She had been through so much, but I knew I couldn't put my arm around her just yet. Useppa took a moment to compose herself. "It's something they won't tell me, Daddy. All I know is that it's got to do with an Indian leader named Hatuey, from when the Spanish first arrived in Cuba. His name is some kind of rallying point for a big uprising. That's when the bloodshed will start. Raul is worried that a lot of people who have been loyal to the Spanish government will be killed. He thinks the revenge will get out of control. That's why he wanted the Republicans to start pushing for Cuban independence in Congress, and maybe lessen the violence."

"When is this uprising supposed to happen?"

"I don't know. They didn't say and I didn't ask. They just use me . . ." she stopped, realizing what she'd just said, then set her jaw and went on, " . . . for minor things, and for political opinions on policies in Washington. I don't know much detail of what goes on."

"Useppa, before I arrived here and had dinner with everyone, did they know what I do for the navy?"

While my children didn't know specifics, they had known for

the past few years that I worked in "gathering information from around the world" for the navy's intelligence division.

"Yes, of course, Daddy. I'm proud of what you do. I told my close friends here that you work in naval intelligence for Commodore Walker. Did I do something wrong?"

Oh, just wonderful. So much for the Cuban insurgents, and probably many others, being ignorant of my real work. Now I understood how Colonel Marrón knew enough about me to have sent his lieutenant to Key West—from their spies in the independence movement. Probably everyone on both sides of the conflict in the whole damned island of Cuba knew about me by now. But worse, dreadfully far worse, was that without a doubt the Spanish knew about Useppa's role too.

I kept the façade up. "No, dear. But in the future, why don't you leave out the intelligence work part; just tell folks I'm a naval officer and let it go at that. It'll be easier for you, and for me. So what's Raul doing next?"

"He sailed on a fishing smack today to go to his church in Havana with Reverend Lefavre. He'll be back in a couple of weeks."

"Anything planned to happen soon?" I asked as casually as I could under the strained circumstances.

She wasn't fooled in the least. "Not that I know, Daddy."

I changed the subject back to the supposed bloody uprising. "So Hatuey will be the rallying point, you say?"

"Yes. That's what they said. Do you know anything about him? A martyr, I think?"

She was near the breaking point again. It was time for that hug. "Yes, he was a martyr, dear—back against the original Spanish *conquistadores.* When the Spanish conquered the island of Hispaniola, Hatuey was a Taino *cacique,* an Indian chief, who escaped with four hundred of his people across to Cuba and warned the natives there about the Spanish. But the natives in Cuba ignored him. Hatuey fought the Spanish in Cuba, but was captured, then executed by burning to death at the stake. The Indians of Cuba were soon killed or enslaved too. Yes, Hatuey's a good choice for a rallying symbol against the Spanish. Did they tell you what his last words were?"

"No."

"A priest offered to convert him to Catholicism prior to the execution, so that his new Christian soul would go to heaven as his body burned. Hatuey asked if there were Spanish Christians in heaven. When the priest said yes, Hatuey said that in that case, he never wanted to go to heaven or be a Christian. The Hatuey rally cry for the revolutionaries might have an anti-Catholic church sentiment too."

I held her trembling body close. "Useppa, I think it's time you took some leave from your work and stayed at Patricio Island for a while. Unwind a bit, away from all this."

"Daddy, I can't. I have work here. The children, the church . . ."

"You haven't taken much time off at all. You've earned it. I'll talk with your pastor."

She pulled away. "Daddy, no, please don't do that. I know you mean the best, but I'm a grown woman and have to make my own decisions. I'm not leaving the school children."

"Useppa, listen to me—you're involved in something very dangerous. This isn't an intellectual exercise. People have been and will get killed. And Raul Leon can't protect you from them."

That was the wrong thing for me to say. Linda and I had raised her to be strong willed, and there was anger in her words now. "I'm not some child that needs protecting! Or a girl that's been foolish. Obviously, I know the revolution is dangerous, Daddy. I also know that it's the right thing, the only thing left to do, for the Cuban people. I'm staying right here and yes, I'll continue to help Raul and the Cuban people. They need my help."

"Now, dear . . ."

Useppa held up a hand. "No. It's *my* decision and I've made it, Daddy."

It was apparent to me that Father Raul Leon was not some young, naïve romantic, a minor figure in the rebel cause who had fallen in love with my spirited daughter, inspiring her to follow his notions of liberty and equality. No, I was beginning to understand that this was far more complex, more *calculated,* than youthful enthusiasm. And that Raul was a very smart, very busy, young man.

But at that point, looking at my defiant Useppa, I still had no idea just how busy he was. Or what the consequences would be for me, my daughter, and my country.

Two days later, when the messenger arrived, I began to understand.

14

Orders

Thursday, 4 March 1886
Schuerer's Bakery
Southard & Whitehead streets
Key West, Florida

Rork and I asked around for days, but no one could, or would, give us information about Cuban revolutionary activities, or Spanish government activities. I had to be careful whom and how I was asking, naturally, so the inquiries were couched in connection with nondescript trade terms—for rum and tobacco and such. In the end, the only new fact I learned was the name of the Spanish consul in Key West, Joaquin Torroja, who was rumored to be the point man for Spanish counter-revolutionary operations in Key West. I determined to go and meet him, to gauge the man, if nothing else.

But early Thursday morning my situation changed. A front desk clerk's note, slid under the door of my room, said simply,

"Mr. J. G. White will meet you at Schuerer's for lunch today at noon." I didn't know a Mr. White in Key West. It had to be the messenger from Washington.

I arrived early to get a table. Schuerer's was a small grocery-bakery on the northeast corner of Southard and Whitehead streets. It served simple meals to people from the offices nearby. The county courthouse was just a block down Whitehead Street and the shop was full of people—the movers and shakers of Key West. Not a good place for an important meeting to pass along confidential information. Taking the last table available, semi-secluded in the back corner, I settled in near a window on the Southard Street side.

Five minutes later, while I was perusing the menu, a shadow loomed over me and I looked up to see a twin-spiked salt-and-pepper beard of at least ten inches leaning over me. I inadvertently groaned. It was one of the most famous, and feared, beards in the navy.

"You look surprised to see me, Wake."

I was more than surprised. This particular courier—taciturn Commodore John Grimes Walker, in the flesh—could only mean grim news. I almost jumped to attention out of habit, but both of us were in civilian attire and I came to my senses just in time.

"I am, sir. Please sit down."

As he did so, I suggested, "Another place, without so many people, would be better, sir. This is the courthouse crowd."

Walker, as usual, was not in a jovial mood. "No, this will do. And belay the 'sir.' I don't want to call attention to us." He looked around. "Politicians, self-centered windbags. Same everywhere. All right, we'll just be two more in the crowd. I leave on a Morgan steamer for Pensacola in two hours, so let's get on with this."

We ordered sandwiches from Mrs. Schuerer, and afterward Walker's thin eyes narrowed even further as his voice dropped in volume. "All right, Peter, I need concise answers fast. First, who sent that message?"

Omitting my daughter's role, I told him it was sent by a Protestant clergyman who was sympathetic to the rebels and had ties with Methodist and Episcopalian churches in Havana and Key West. I explained that they thought American recognition of the revolutionary groups would influence the Spanish government to understand its days were limited. That they hoped it would influence the Spanish to turn over power peacefully to the Cubans. I included the clergymen's fear about a bloody uprising coming soon.

Walker listened but seemed preoccupied. "Very well. Now, what happened to you and Rork in Havana?"

I decided to be careful about what I would say. "Spanish government agents intercepted the message to New York, probably at the telegraph office here. They decoded it and sent it onward, figuring they'd catch Roosevelt in Havana meeting with the rebels in the cemetery. That would embarrass the United States, dry up the financial and political support for the revolution in New York and Florida. Good plan, but they ended up with me and Rork in custody instead. That wasn't part of either the Spanish or the rebels' plans."

"And then what happened?"

"We were interrogated by a Colonel Marrón, head of the counterintelligence department there, at the Audencia in Havana. He seemed very surprised at finding naval men and at odds as to what to do with us. However, he didn't let us go. They were moving us to another location when the prison wagon was stopped and we were transferred to another wagon, which took us out of the city. That was when I realized we were abducted by a notorious bandit named Gallo Sosa, who kept us hidden for several days in the slums. We were delivered to a Jesuit priest—you know my ongoing relationship with them—who got us to *Powhatan*. The Jesuits also sent word to you and the admiral that Rork and I were alive."

Walker nodded pensively. "Yes, I remember when the priest

visited headquarters. That's why Admiral Porter decided to have Gaston get you up here, where I could meet you in person. We thought you'd try to get to his ship, so we sent the cable to the consuls in Havana and Matanzas."

"Rork and I got aboard in Havana. The captain received the cable as we pulled into Matanzas. I'm afraid Captain Gaston doesn't like how all that came about, sir."

"That's his problem. So there's been no press on your arrest in Havana?" asked Walker.

"None that I've heard about. Of course, we were arrested quietly and weren't in their custody long. And, in point of fact, we weren't caught meeting with anyone, much less the rebels. We were merely strolling through a cemetery at midnight."

Walked nodded, without smiling at my satirical addendum. "Yes. What about the Judas in our government?"

"Maybe a federal official in Key West, but that is mere supposition. I'd hoped to have an answer for you, but don't have a name or anything solid yet."

"And the extent of financial and supply support for the rebels here in Florida?"

"Extensive, sir. Mostly through the tobacco workers here and in Tampa. Transport is mainly through the Cuban fishing boats that work the Florida coast. As for the money, I heard when I was here last year that the revolutionaries were getting tens of thousands of dollars donated through the cigar makers in Florida. It may be even more now."

The commodore growled his next question. "Spanish agents in Florida?"

"I know of one named Boreau. He works for Marrón in Havana, and I've spotted him here in Key West in the past few days. He was watching me and Rork. He knows who we are. There are probably others."

Walker was clearly upset with the turn of events. "I see. Obviously, this thing is worse than we thought and something needs to be done. You're not going to Panama. You've got other things to do right here."

He paused and glanced around again. "This is going to be *delicate,* Wake. The new administration doesn't want to antagonize the Spanish any more than we already have, but we can't ignore this Cuban revolutionary situation within the United States any longer. Plus, evidently we have foreign spies running around here, on American soil, and possibly one of our people in cahoots with them. We certainly can't have that sort of thing going on.

"The senior national leadership wants something done, Wake, and done now. So Admiral Porter and I went to Secretary Whitney with a plan. He approved it and went to *his* superior . . ." Walker glanced around again before continuing, "who has also—reluctantly, I might add—approved it. That set the wheels in motion."

He waited while I digested the significant reference to the president.

Then Commodore Walker continued, "So now I've come down here to personally explain it to you, because Peter, you're right in the middle of this whole mess. And we, from the highest levels on down, expect *you* to figure it out and clean it up. *Quietly.*"

Uh, oh. That didn't sound good at all.

It got worse. Walker then proceeded to tell me what my orders were. He pulled a document from an inside pocket and put it on the table in front of me, but didn't wait for me to read it. Instead, he explained it himself, *en sotto voce* so others couldn't hear.

"That is a warrant from President Cleveland, naming you as a special investigative agent of the Treasury Department. It will give you the legal authority to carry out your mission."

"Agent? You mean like a lawman?"

Walker conveniently ignored my disdain and replied, "Yes, you will be a federal lawman."

Mrs. Schuerer delivered the sandwiches to our table. I waited until she departed, then asked, "But there's that law they passed in the late seventies, the Posse something-or-other law against federal military taking action against civilians. That prohibits me from doing this, from enforcing civil law within our country."

"It's the Posse Comitatus Act, Peter—and you're wrong on its legal restrictions. It was enacted back in seventy-eight, when Reconstruction ended in the South, to prohibit a return to military occupation of the South again. It refers only to personnel of the army, Wake. Not to us in the U.S. Navy. Therefore, you are entitled to be designated as a federal lawman and to take action against citizens of the United States who are acting in violation of laws, but your orders will be to do that *only* as a last resort. As a treasury agent, you can also take action against foreigners within our country who are violating our customs laws—also *only* as a last resort. Rork is not getting a commission. It will only be you. He can assist you, but will have no independent authority."

"But why me?"

"Because of that damned Judas factor. We don't know who else to trust, so we'll trust no one totally until your investigation is completed."

I was attempting to understand this bombshell when he added, "By the way, the only person in the Treasury Department who knows of your appointment is Treasury Secretary Manning. Admiral Porter, the president, and I are the only other ones that know. That's it, just four of us, at this point. Rodgers in ONI doesn't know anything about any of this—it's way above his pay grade and he's not to learn of it. Understood?"

"Uh, yes . . . I guess so . . ." I almost added *sir* out of habit.

"Do you understand the *political* consequences of this; should certain people in Congress or the press find out?"

I was beginning to comprehend, and get a headache. "Yes, I think so. But what am I supposed to *do?*"

"The orders to you and Rork are verbal, and as follows: you have two objectives. First, you are to ascertain the extent of Cuban anti-Spanish revolutionary activities in Florida, then follow up on them with a view to eventual arrest and prosecution of any Cubans, Americans, or anyone else here, who are violating federal laws. Do not arrest them yourselves. And do not, unless in an emergency situation, reveal your federal agent status to anyone, including federal authorities. I repeat, work alone, not with federal authorities. The reason for that brings me to your second objective."

One can readily imagine what immediately dominated my mind—Useppa's role in all this. Could I protect her and still do my duty? If the others were eventually caught, they would certainly tell of her involvement. I was absorbed in the intricacies of my dilemma when Walker continued with his orders, startling me.

"Wake? Your second objective is to ascertain the extent of clandestine Spanish *governmental* activities in Florida, and any Americans who are acting in concert with them. I want to know how large and active their intelligence network really is, and if there really is a spy in the American government working for the Spanish. But, and remember this, you will take *no* action against anyone in that network. This is to gather intelligence only. We do not want them alerted to the fact we know about them.

"You will then hand-deliver two *separate* confidential reports to me at headquarters, and only to me—one on your first objective, and the other on your second objective."

Even aside from worry about my daughter's connection, and my career's future, it was a huge assignment. I tried to grasp the logistics of it. Money, time, travel.

"Ah, what's the time frame to get those reports to you?"

"You're not known for lollygagging around, Wake. Get the reports to me as soon as you can. I would think that April first would be a realistic date. That gives you four weeks. I know you'll have travel and other needs, so operational funds have been increased at your current alias account at the Bank of Key West. Use discretion with that account. You never know who is watching it."

I instinctively said, "Aye, aye, sir."

He gave me a perturbed look and went on, "You hopefully have figured this out already, and Secretary Whitney said it before, but I'll make the point again anyway—this is a strictly *confidential* mission. You got very lucky in Havana. There is *no* more room for error. Understand?"

I bristled—the Havana debacle wasn't due to anything I did—but said, "Understood."

"Good luck on your assignment, then."

Walker pushed his half-eaten food across his plate. "This sandwich is terrible, Wake. Must be the damned heat down here. I hope the other food on this rock is better. But, that would be *your* problem, because right now I'm leaving for up north, to a civilized part of the country."

Assimilating everything just said to me, I belatedly realized that his last comments were an attempt at humor, but by then Commodore John G. Walker had straightened his twin-tailed beard, stood up, and begun walking out.

"Good-bye . . ." I said to his back. Then I looked down.

The document, dated four days earlier, was of the fancy variety, full of flourish and elegant language, like a university diploma. My name was in the middle, right over the part proclaiming me to be "a Special Agent of and for the Treasury of the United States of America." It was more elaborate than my naval commission. At the bottom was a signature I couldn't read at first, so I concentrated on what was printed below it: President of the Unites States.

That did nothing for my nerves. I folded the damned thing up quickly before anyone else could see it. Mrs. Schuerer came over and put the bill on the table. I had to take care of that too.

A Far-Fetched Notion

Friday, 5 March 1886
Russell Hotel
Duval Street
Key West, Florida

It was six o'clock in the morning. Rork and I had been awake for an hour, discussing the amended assignment. He wasn't impressed with my new credentials, opining that it just muddied the waters and got more people involved, or angry, with us. More importantly, our chat yielded no solid idea as to how to accomplish our task without implicating Useppa. Which was paradoxical, considering what occurred next.

The knock on the door was soft, the voice following it softer still.

"Daddy, are you there?"

Rork offered to leave, but I waved him no, then told my daughter to enter. Her face was puffy and red, and she wasn't her usual confident self.

"What's happened, Useppa?"

She shook her head. "No, it's not what *has* happened, but what will happen. Last night I heard something." A thin hand rose to stop my impending question. "I can't tell you how I know, who told me, or where I learned it, Daddy."

"All right, dear. But there is something important, right?"

"Yes. I think I have to let you know, now that you're involved in all of this."

That sounded like judgmental disappointment, which I ignored and said, "And?"

"At Sugarloaf Key tomorrow night, I think around nine or so, there'll be Cuban fishing boats coming in to get supplies and people. They're taking them to a place near Havana."

I knew Sugarloaf from my days patrolling the Keys for blockade-runners during the war. About fifteen miles east of Key West, it's a low marshy mangrove island, maybe three miles by four, with a large, shallow saltwater bay in the middle.

I hadn't been there since 1865, so my information was dated, but from what I knew, the only inhabitants were some charcoal-burners, mostly black Bahamian squatters. They lived near the swash channel on the east side, farming some fruit and burning buttonwood and red and white mangrove to make charcoal. The charcoal was sold to buyers in Key West. From time to time, they've also sold some sponges from the flats near the island.

"Any idea who is doing this?"

"A man named Doyle is involved, but I don't know him or how he's involved. I just heard his name in conjunction with the supplies. No, wait—I do remember hearing his name before. I think he sometimes goes to your coast, and sometimes further up near Tampa, and delivers people from there."

I looked at Rork, who shook his head. He didn't recognize the name either.

"And the people to be picked up?"

"I don't know names or numbers, but my impression is only one or two."

"Useppa, are you supposed to be there tomorrow?"

"No, Daddy. I only help out around here."

"And what are the supplies?"

"I don't know what they are. Perhaps they're medicine or food."

Not likely, I thought. *Most probably something in a long box.*

"Yes, perhaps they are. Is there anything else, dear?"

"Not that I can think of."

Rork walked over, sat on the bed next to Useppa, and put his left arm, the one with the rubber hand, around her shoulders. Clearing his throat, he asked, "I've a wee question, darlin'. Was there to be anyone from Key West there?"

She thought about that. "Well, I forgot that part, but yes, there is. But I don't know his name. They just said there'd be someone heading over there to make sure it went well, so I presumed they meant he'd leave from here to go to Sugarloaf."

Rork asked, "Anglo o' Cubano?"

"I don't know, but I got the impression it's somebody important to the cause."

An idea came to mind and I asked, "Do you know anyone who lives on Sugarloaf these days besides those old charcoal men?"

"No—except I heard a while ago that there's some farm land there. Would the charcoal burners farm the land too?"

"They might."

I suppose I looked disappointed, for Useppa gave me that sad look that melted my heart. "Daddy, I'm telling you this because I don't want anything bad to happen to you, but I don't want anybody else hurt either."

"I understand that, dear, and I appreciate how difficult this was for you. Thank you. One last question. You heard this from people who would know, right? Not some rumor, but a definite person who said these definite things?"

"Yes." She stood up, flustered. "I've got to go to the school now, the children will be arriving soon."

After she left, Rork sat back down on the bed. "Where do you want to get a boat?"

"How about Pinder's, over at the foot of Caroline Street? We can get some provisions there too."

"An' go by way o' the naval depot? For a pair o' horses?" he said with raised eyebrow.

Sailors are notoriously bad horsemen, and Rork wasn't referring to the equine mode of travel. "Navy Horses" is slang for standard naval-issue sidearms—.36-caliber Colt revolvers. We'd lost ours to Colonel Marrón.

"Yes, Rork. I think that'd be a good idea."

"Peter, you didn't ask her about old man Malinovsky. Remember him?"

The man to whom Rork was referring was a Russian immigrant to the South in the late '40s. During the war he ran guns from the Bahamas into the Confederacy along the Florida coast, a contemporary of my old Confederate nemesis, Jonathan Saunders. Never caught, at the end of the war I'd heard Malinovsky was up at Jacksonville, and a man who'd made a considerable amount of money off smuggling.

"The rebel blockade-runner? I didn't think of him. He was at Jacksonville last I knew. What's he got to do with this?"

"Aye, Alex Malinovsky, one an' the same. Methinks he's farmin' over on No Name Key, jus' a couple o' miles east o' Sugarloaf. I knew him after the war, in sixty-eight, when I was in Key West an' you were stationed up at Pensacola. Alex went to settle about then on No Name Key with that Bahamian girl he married. Alba's her name, if me memory serves rightly. Pretty little lass, a bit too saucy, though. The kind that'll get a good man in bad trouble. I think he's still there."

"From what I heard during the war, he was pretty rough himself."

"Aye, an' after the war he wasn't a wallflower either. Anyway, we've time to pay him a bit o' a visit an' see if he knows about any smugglin' goin' on these days. We'll do it right, come in from the north along the back way, Spanish Channel, then no one at Sugarloaf'll see us sailin' to No Name. Then, after we see old Alex, we—"

"Wait a minute, Sean. This sounds pretty far-fetched to me. Why would a former enemy smuggler talk to us about any current smuggling that's going on near him now? Especially a mean old cuss like Alex Malinovsky? Hell, he's probably part of the Cuban gun-running."

Rork flashed that grin of his. "Because, Peter, me boyo—the dear lad owes me a favor, a considerable favor. Oh, he'll not be overjoyed to see me, but by God he'll tell the truth when I ask. O' that you can be as sure as a misty day in Cork."

I had to ask. "Why?"

He scratched his chin and looked thoughtful for a second. "Hmm . . . well, let's just say that some things are better not to be told, Peter Wake, but it started with a wee bit o' rum an' went downhill from there . . ."

Mr. Pinder, scrutinizing me over the rim of his spectacles, seemed dubious of my ability to come up with the funds to use his boat. She was tied up at the fishing boat docks behind his store on Caroline Street, where William Street ends. Like the preacher who had married me in Key West, he was of Bahamian descent, but this Pinder was white—well, mostly white. His accent still had a bit of the northern Bahamas in it. Abaconian.

"Ah, that'll be thirty dollars, *cash* money, for the boat's week-long charter, and also another five dollars for your provisions, Mr. Wake."

Pinder didn't usually charter his boat—he was a grocery

man—but Rork knew that he had in the past and would now for cash. I handed him the money in silver dollars and watched his attitude improve markedly. The man actually got friendly, asking about our destination, which I said was the Marquesas Keys, to the west. Rork, who had been an acquaintance of Pinder for years and had arranged the charter, was already on the boat, ready to cast off for our "fishing expedition," which I thought an apt description. Pinder waved us goodbye from the dock, no doubt eager to tell his family about the fools from up north who'd just paid twice the going price for a week charter of his thirty-three-foot sloop, the *Royal Victoria*.

The sloop was very similar to my *Nancy Ann* and typical of the Keys and west coast of Florida—broad-beamed, with a straight stem, low freeboard, long-boomed gaff rig, and most importantly, a centerboard that allowed the boat to only draw a few feet when the board was up. The cabin was tinier than mine, but the hold was bigger. Rork had stowed our gear and provisions there under a tarpaulin.

Ten minutes later, at two o'clock in the afternoon, we had the forestays'l and mainsail set and were slogging into a west-sou'westerly wind, steering nor'west past Frankfort's Bank. Rork tended the sheets while I steered her across the Middle Ground of Key West's harbor on a close reach, bearing off to the north toward the Calda Bank. Once there, we could slack sheets and head around the bank to the nor'east, with the wind at our backs. That was the back way to No Name Key, around the northern edge of the Florida Keys. The westerly breeze was pushing dark blue-gray rolling clouds along our course, which in early March means the wind is about to veer nor'west, then north, and that a nor'easter would soon follow.

The occasional dull thud of distant thunder reached us from the southwest, but no flashes were seen. With any luck, I told Rork, we'd be at No Name Key in time to beat the foulest of the weather. Timing was important. There were thirty-five more miles to go, but at the six knots the sloop was making, I figured we'd be there around nine that night—not good. You don't go sailing among those reefs, especially in the shallow back channels, at night. So I informed my one-man crew that we would stay in the deep water of the Gulf of Mexico until sunrise, then find and follow the winding Spanish Channel for the last eight miles to No Name Key.

Sitting on the weather deck, he nodded absentmindedly at me. My friend was lost in thought, apparently planning how he was going to approach Alex Malinovsky—a man known to be hospitable or ruthless, depending if he liked you or not. It wasn't until later that Rork told me about the perimeter of gun traps Malinovsky had laid out to kill interlopers on his island. If I'd known that at the beginning, we would've passed by No Name Key.

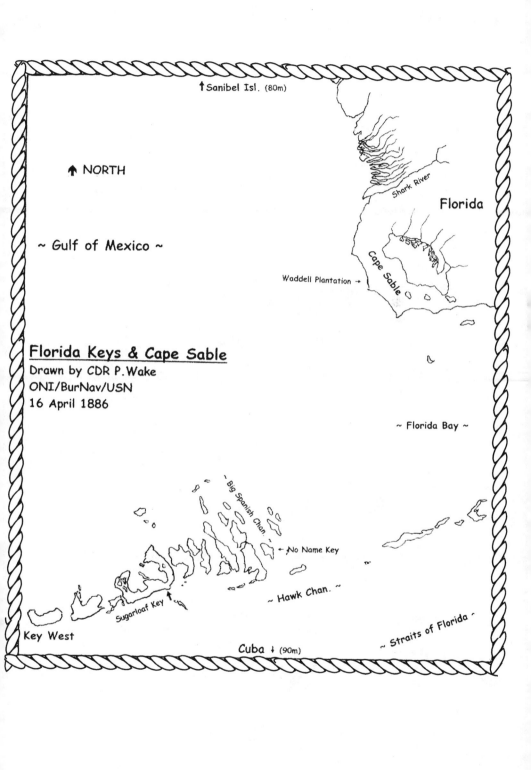

↑Sanibel Isl. (80m)

↑ NORTH

~ Gulf of Mexico ~

Shark River

Florida

Waddell Plantation →

Cape Sable

Florida Keys & Cape Sable
Drawn by CDR P. Wake
ONI/BurNav/USN
16 April 1886

~ Florida Bay ~

Big Spanish Chan.

← No Name Key

~ Hawk Chan. ~

Sugarloaf Key

~ Straits of Florida ~

Key West

Cuba ↓ (90m)

16

No Name Key

Saturday, 6 March 1886
Malinovsky Plantation
No Name Key

The sun rose but didn't come out to shine. It couldn't. Thick clouds stretched in a huge formation across the horizon, scudding along at thirty or more knots from the nor'west. Everywhere else was overcast. Even the water had turned light gray. The seascape was funereal. Not a good sign.

The run south from the Gulf of Mexico through Spanish Channel, with coral-strewn shoals to the left and right of us, was nerve wracking for me. There are no channel markers, but in good weather that's not a problem. Usually, the area's colors help you navigate, but that morning there were no greens and blues for deep water, or tans and browns for shallow. It was frustrating, not the least because Rork was still pensively quiet, which made me even more agitated. Usually he can be counted on for some tension-relieving humor—that famed Irish wit. Not this time.

Our chart, a yellowed thing of dubious value, showed reefs all around us, so we steered by eye and took bearings off the islets, difficult in those low-light conditions. Rork and I hadn't done this sort of thing in these islands since the war, but finally what we took to be No Name Key hove into view. We rounded up into the wind, close to the eastern mangrove shoreline of the island, and at ten minutes to nine in the morning, exhausted mentally and physically, the hook went over the side to the sandy bottom.

The waves were two feet and rising with the wind where we'd anchored, the sloop bucking like a bronco on her anchor rode. Rowing ashore in the dinghy seemed foolish to me. The *Royal Victoria* had a small dinghy, a plain affair, little longer than Rork is tall. Not appropriate for those conditions at all. I suggested we go around to the shoals at the southern, or lee, side of the Key and anchor there, but Rork said no, he had to go ashore here. He said that we were already under surveillance, tensely adding that any attempt to shift anchorage would seem hostile to Malinovsky.

Rork headed off toward the rickety dock, fifty yards away in the mangroves. What I presumed was Malinovsky's large rowing punt was tied up at the dock. I stayed aboard at the stern, Colt hidden in my coat but ready to provide covering fire if needed. Though, on my unsteady perch, I had small confidence in my marksmanship at that range.

"Shtoop right zere, or you vill die . . ." came out from the tangle of mangrove trees, the words sounding disjointed in the wind. The baritone voice had a sinister accent, not angry or frightened, but matter-of-fact, which was more disconcerting.

Rork kept on rowing, yelling back, "Alex! You know me. It's Sean Rork, o' Key West. Permission to come ashore?"

A wave sloshed into the boat, but Rork didn't have time to bail. To stop in those waves would mean he'd swamp the boat completely.

"Come to zee dock und stand up shtraight. Show me who you are."

Rork finally made it to the dock, climbed up, and hauled himself erect, hands outstretched, facing the invisible man in the trees. "Remember me now, Alex? You should."

"She sent you?"

"No, she didn't send me, Alex. Alba doesn't even know I came here. I haven't seen her in almost twenty years."

Rork knew the man's wife? This was a turn I hadn't expected. Rork walked to the foot of the dock, right among the trees. I could see him talking to someone, his hands gesticulating, no longer needing to yell against the wind. He returned to the end of the dock and yelled across to me, "I'm comin' to get ye, Peter!"

Then, using the punt at the dock, he rowed out and I dropped down inside for the ride back. Rork said nothing beyond, "Stay calm, an' do as I say, Peter. Alex's a wee bit more touched in the head than I recall from our last time together. Suspicious o' people."

Then he shook his head slightly, signaling me to stay quiet as well as calm. It was a struggle to do either, so I started bailing. Once we got to the dock, Rork took off his rubber hand, exposing the marlinespike beneath. As he tossed the hand into our dinghy, he muttered, "A wee bit o' dissuasion for the Russian."

"Bring him int heere, Rork," called out the man filling the doorway of the stilt shack. His tone could best be described as resentful.

We'd walked a short distance from the dock, but it was enough for me to understand the lay of the land. Malinovsky had cleared fifty or sixty acres of land from the mangrove and planted various types of fruit trees, green with pastels of color hanging on them. There were no orderly groves—the trees were in haphazard clumps, everywhere overgrown with weeds. An open-sided, thatch-roofed shed, what the Seminole call a *chickkee,* tattered and worn, housed some plows and tools. A fence of bamboo and buttonwood held a few sickly goats and a cow. But in the main, the establishment was a run-down endeavor. Malinovsky Plantation was nothing like the ones in the romance books. It was as dismal as the weather.

The fifteen-by-ten-foot sun-bleached shack, a board-and-batten affair set four feet off the sandy ground, had a crude ladder, which we then climbed. Next to the doorway were two five-foot-long rattlesnake skins spread out on the exterior wall, apparently to dry out, in spite of the wet weather. Once inside, we faced Malinovsky himself, seated at a table at one end, on the wall behind him was an imposing display of shotguns.

The man himself was huge, a solid block of beef, with the biggest hands I've ever seen, almost freakishly large. I immediately wondered how he'd ever get those fingers inside the trigger guard of the shotguns. Then I noticed there were no trigger guards—they'd been sawn off.

Malinovsky growled, "So, vaht ya vant?"

He was speaking to me, but it took me a while to understand his Russian accent. Rork nudged my foot, a sign to not dally.

"I want to know about the Cubans running guns at Sugarloaf."

Malinovsky showed no surprise at my question—which was pure bluff, for I had no proof the supplies were guns. Obviously Rork had prepared him for it. The Russian allowed a slight shrug of his shoulders. "Vat about dem?"

"Where are the guns? Who is running them?"

He snorted in disdain at my dumb questions. "Dey are at Harris's place. De Cubans undt de blahks store dem dere. Und de Cubans run dem in de fishink schmahks."

"Harris? Is he from around here?"

"Key Vest."

"Doctor Jeptha Vining Harris? The collector of customs for the port of Key West?"

"Yah, yah, de same mahn. At his lahnd, dere on de Sugarluff Aylundt—at Cudjoe Bay."

"Does he participate?"

"Vaht?"

"Does Harris run the guns himself?"

Obviously Malinovsky thought that a dumb question too. He waved a dismissive hand. "Nah, nah . . . de Cubans undt de blahks do zat."

"Any Anglos involved?"

"Vaht?"

"Any *white* people involved?"

"Nyet."

"What about you? Do you run guns?"

Malinovsky swung his gaze to Rork and grumbled something. Rork shook his head and turned to me. "Alex an' I already talked about that, before you came ashore. He sometimes makes trips to Cuba, but not recently o' in the near future. He told me he only runs rum, not guns."

The Russian's forearms were tensing. He looked as if about to launch himself toward me. I got the hint and changed targets for my next question, "Do you know the next time those other people are running the stuff?"

The answer was a mixture of no and nyet and nah. Then the giant pounded the table and stood. Rork said, "Thank ye, Alex. We'll be goin' now," and started down the ladder, me right behind him.

Behind us, as we headed back to the dock, I heard a loud grunt and saw Rork wave a hand back to Malinovsky, but not stop walking. As we approached the dock he whispered to me, "Don't turn to look or stop, but out o' the corner o' your eye, take a gander to the right an' left along the ground."

I did, and saw in the bushes on both sides of the path a disturbing sight. The double barrels of four shotguns were trained on the foot of the dock. They were arranged in such a way as to not be seen when someone first came up the path from the dock.

That was when Rork remembered to inform me about

Malinovsky's penchant for security, backed up with a ring of trip-wired shotguns around his farm. I nodded acknowledgment and kept walking, wondering why anyone would have that kind of security to protect *fruit* on a run-down farm in the middle of nowhere?

But there was another question in my mind. After we'd weighed anchor and were scooting along under forstays'l toward Hawk Channel, I asked my friend, "You ever going to tell me what happened with you and your friend Malinovsky years ago, Sean?"

His eyes were sad when he turned to look at me. "He's not me *friend*, Peter, an' no, I'd rather not speak on it. 'Tis done an' gone, long ago, so let's just let it go."

"All right, I'll let it go. Thank you for arranging that interview—at least we have some idea of who is involved and where. Black Bahamians and Cubans, using Harris's land on Sugarloaf. It's not proof of the customs man's involvement, but it is an indicator."

"Aye," agreed Rork, but his mind was still far away.

"Alex's got all those shotguns around to protect something more than fruit, doesn't he?"

Rork slowly wagged his head. "Not certain o' anything with the likes o' him. Could be the guns're for protectin' his ownself from an imaginary enemy. His mind's had far too much time to dwell on sad memories, an' conjure up scapegoats."

That reply wasn't the answer I expected. "Are you one of the scapegoats?"

"Aye, maybe that I am. . . . But all o' that's long in the past."

Clearly, Alex Malinovsky and Sean Rork shared a dark moment in their pasts. Everyone has some mistake of commission, or omission, in their history, created from lust or greed, or fear or sloth or gluttony. I'll never know what happened, for I never asked again. Rork's never explained.

There is no such requirement between friends.

Revelations in the Dark

Saturday, 6 March 1886
Cudjoe Bay
East of Sugarloaf Key

Though our future was uncertain, I was glad to be quit of No Name Key with its bizarre Russian. Now we were heading for the leeward side of the Keys. The sky was a solid, steady series of rain-laden curtains of wind now, hurrying down from the north, veering farther around to the nor'east and getting stronger—force eight at least on Beaufort's scale. With only that forestays'l showing, we flew around Spanish Harbor Keys, swerved to starboard, and ran westerly down Hawk Channel, close under the lee of Big Pine Key.

At the Newfound Harbor Keys, we ducked in to the shallows off the beach, thinking we'd await dusk before our final approach to the east side of Cudjoe Key. Once at Cudjoe, next to Sugarloaf, we'd anchor and dinghy over in the dark.

Just after four o'clock, we weighed anchor again and set a reefed-down forestays'l, so as to reduce our silhouette to anyone watching from Sugarloaf. Slowly working our way west, we crossed the opening for Newfound Harbor, sailing along the edge of the shoals south of Pye's Harbor Key and those nor'east of Loggerhead. It was a narrow, snaking channel, demanding intense concentration and quick work with the forestays'l sheets in repeated tacks. Finally, in the eerie amber half-light of a drizzly early evening, we rounded up and slid to a stop among the mud flats east of Gopher Key, off the southern point of the big island of Cudjoe. Rork loosed the halyard and set the anchor in a few feet of water between two tiny islets.

We both sat there, wondering if anyone had heard the staccato tattoo of the sail luffing as we'd come into the wind. We waited for the challenge to our presence, but none came. The shores of Cudjoe and Summerland keys were dark green, with no houses, boats, or lights. In fact, there'd been no vessels or sign of man since departing No Name Key. We'd arrived unnoticed.

The storm had concealed us, and kept others from sea, but it was now our nemesis, for we had to use that dinghy to go the last mile across Cudjoe Bay to Sugarloaf Key and spy upon the gun-runners. Rork got in the bow thwart and I in the stern, with him rowing and me using a third oar to steer. We set out two hours after darkness.

One unfamiliar with Rork may ask how in the world he can row with a false hand. The rubber hand is formed into a gripping posture, for gripping a bottle. My friend can hold almost anything of that size, and the loom of an oar—the handle—usually fits well. This one was a little too small, however, allowing some leeway in his grip, and I observed that Rork had to apply extra energy to make sure it didn't slip out. Even then, he was twice the oarsman I was, and wouldn't think of letting me do the work. Rork was a bosun, will always be a bosun, and that is that.

At first we were under the lee of Cudjoe, but soon we were

a quarter-mile, then half a mile, then more, from the shelter of the land, propelled rapidly by rowing and by the ebb tide and breeze. With Rork rowing downwind amongst the two- and three-foot waves, and cold water slopping in at every heave of the oars, I strained in the cramped quarters to steer the damned thing without broaching.

The overcast eliminated a sunset, and darkness fell quickly upon us. No stars shone through the murk and no lights at Sugarloaf peeked through, so I guided us by the feel of the wind on my right cheek and the lines of waves rolling under us. That is a poor way to steer a course, but the best I could do at the time. Aggravated by a considerable ebb tide and wind, we ended up farther to the left, or south, than was correct. Or safe.

Once I saw the ocean end of Sugarloaf come into view, well off our starboard bow, and getting farther away by the second, I knew the next land we'd see would be the unfriendly island of Cuba, ninety miles to the south. Bad navigation on my part, to say the least. Poor Rork had to row additional ground to windward to set us right again. That, in turn, brought waves over the bow into the boat.

Now that my plan to hit shore on Sugarloaf north, and to windward, of the gun-runners was dashed, I resolved to put the rapidly filling dinghy into the nearest mangrove beach that looked semisafe. I saw one in the gloom and we headed for it. After what seemed to be hours, but was actually twenty minutes, we tied to the root of a red mangrove on Sugarloaf. Sloshing ashore at the mouth of a small creek, both of us crumpled down on a three-foot-wide shell beach—two cold, wet, and thoroughly miserable lumps in the dark.

Rork, who had remained silent during the row, and was noticeably affected by his exertions, spoke in a whisper. "We're already friggin' wet through an' through, so why'n't we jus' wade 'round the island along the fringe o' the mangroves, an' sneak up on the buggers that way."

It was pitch black, so I had to come within inches of his face to see and hear him. He peered inland at the mass of twisting mangrove roots and continued, "Oh, laddie . . . methinks we're both a wee bit too old to be messin' with likes o' that in there."

"No problem, we'll wade around. It'll be faster, and we've lost too much time already. It's getting close to nine o'clock now."

Rork had another concern, holding up his right hand to make the point. "An' by the by, gov'nor, how the hell will we be gettin' back to our boat?"

He only says *gov'nor* when he's tired, worried, and sarcastic. I think he was angry about my navigational failure. It was time for some levity.

"Rork, I'm surprised at such a silly question. Why, we steal one of *their* boats, of course. I thought you were Irish."

I could see him grin in the dark, his teeth bared as if to bite, and heard him grunt, "Cor blimey, how damned silly o' me, indeed. Sorry for me lapse o' judgment, sir."

I was growing worried about my friend. Rork had been the physical stalwart for so many years that I tended to overestimate his limits. He wasn't sounding—I couldn't *see* him in any detail to be sure—very good at all.

"Quite all right, Rork. Now, if I've answered all your apprehensions and you're ready, we'll get to the really fun part of all this."

"Aye, aye, sir. Lead on, MacBeth, an' let's get the soddin' party started . . ."

He sounded better then, and I switched my mental focus to the enemy, for that was how I thought of the gun-runners. I led the way in the waist-deep water.

"Only a half a mile to go, Rork. I think . . ."

I thought I heard a groan, but then again, it could've been the wind.

We crouched amongst pickleweed, behind a crape myrtle and a buttonwood, our lair overlooking a path that opened onto a clearing in the mangrove jungle. A dozen men sat around a campfire, its flames sputtering in the breeze. The men were passing a bottle and warming themselves in the chill, wet air. Along the shore fifty feet away was a small beach, open to the wind with waves crashing on it. Beyond the beach, four small Cuban fishing smacks were anchored, shadowy dark forms against the darker bay. They were rolling and pitching in the waves. The wind was getting worse. You could tell the smacks were Cuban, their long, low, live-well fish holds differentiating them from American boats, which had a higher freeboard and rig.

The men were mostly dark skinned and conversed in the Afro-Creole Spanish of the lower-class Cubans, or the lilting Celtic-tinged English patois of the northern Bahamas. Short, hard words among leather-skinned fisherman and charcoalers. No one seemed to be in charge. We waited for sixty long minutes, until my pocket watch showed ten o'clock by the flickering light of the fire.

So far, the gathering of men hadn't done anything but act and sound like an impromptu meeting of typical islanders. Tedious. My right leg cramped and I stifled a groan while straightening it. Rork, the appliance carefully laid in the shadows, massaged that left stump of his, confirming my worry about the toll of that rowing on him. The trip back to our boat against that wind would be terrible. I would have to row, and wondered if I could make it that far.

Just as I was beginning to rethink my decisions for the evening, one of the men asked loudly in Spanish when the *commandante* was supposed to arrive. Another one answered him with an angry, "When de mon get here from Key West, fool."

A few minutes later, I heard a rustle up the path. The sound of running feet got louder, attracting the attention of the entire congregation. A young boy ran past us and into the firelight, explaining in Spanish that the *commandante* was not here but a *teniente*—a lieutenant—was just approaching.

Two men strolled down the path and emerged into the clearing, twenty feet from Rork and me. One looked Cuban, mid-twenties, the handsome, refined kind; the other was an Anglo, same age but a disheveled sort. Neither looked like they were known by the others around the fire.

The Cuban surveyed the wary men, then solemnly began in good English, "Commandante Caldron is still at Key West, prohibited from attending by the storm. I am Lieutenant Reyes. This is Thomas Doyle, a sailor and supporter of our cause. He will show you the position of the munitions cache, then you will load it into the boats and leave for Mantanzas tonight."

I registered the names: Commandante Caldron and Lieutenant Reyes, of the revolutionary army; Doyle, the name Useppa had heard. Validation of what we had learned, and new information for the file. Right alongside Dr. Harris. We were making some headway, finally. And who was Commandante Caldron? I'd heard of a merchant in Key West named Caldron.

The oldest of the black men stood up and shook his head, gesturing to the blustering sky above us. His accent was from the Abaco Islands of the Bahamas, a busy blockade-running area during the war. "Dis storm is too damn big, mon. 'Tis folly to go out now in our liddle boats. De Stream will be in a rage. Give it another two o' three day."

The circle of men grumbled their support. It was a rough crowd, but the lieutenant showed no fear.

Reyes turned on the older man and simply said, "No."

He backed up that by saying, with an edge of controlled anger, "You were contracted for *this* date. Plans have been made in Cuba that cannot be changed. You will do as you promised. Only then—at Mantanzas—will you get the rest of your money."

The men, Cuban and Bahamian, joined their leader in standing and facing Reyes. They weren't buying any of *that*. Several grumbled and fidgeted, glancing up at the wind-bent treetops. The man called Doyle added in a twangy south Florida drawl, "Hey, it ain't much. We can get it loaded in a hour, maybe two, an' then all y'all can be on your way. The wind is piped up, sure, but fair fer Cuba right now an' it'll be a fast overnight sail. Hell, this here little-bitty storm'll even keep the Spanish navy in port for ya'."

But the old Bahamian wasn't playing along. "We go now, but get storm money. Two times de fair weather money—up front . . ."

The group, which had formed a semicircle around Reyes and Doyle, grumbled their agreement with that proposition. Some of them started to show the handles of concealed pistols and knives. Reyes, in a smooth move showing some previous practice, slid his own pistol out and aimed it at the face of the group's spokesman. The lieutenant's hand was rock steady, holding that muzzle a foot away from the old man's eyes.

Reyes didn't wait for a reaction but informed them, "This is *not* a civil contract. This is a *military* contract. It is not negotiable. You will follow the orders of Mr. Doyle, load the boats, and sail now."

That was followed by Reyes clicking back the hammer. Even in the wind, I could hear it.

"Hmm, the dago fella's got a Schofield Model Three. Forty-five caliber. Single-action. Nasty weapon," whispered Rork, Navy Colt in his right hand. "Those other lads've only got pocket guns. Aye, they can wound Reyes, but he'll *kill* six o' them afore he goes down."

His point was corroborated when the assembled men quietly returned their weapons to their hiding places. Their leader got the message too, saying to his men, "We do what de mon say now, jes' to get de money dis time. But no more in de future."

The Bahamian then gave Reyes a defiant pose, but the Cuban kept the pistol aimed as before, and said, "Just get the cargo to the contacts in Matanzas. Whatever you do after that is no business of mine."

Reyes lowered his pistol, but kept it out and at the ready, his gaze constantly on the Bahamian. Doyle told three men to follow him into the woods, tramping close to our position. We lay still as the young American pointed out an area to dig up, not fifteen feet away from us. Then he showed them three other places to dig. A hurricane lantern was brought forth and hung from a tree, its light casting weird shadows in the trees, and a few minutes later we watched as they hauled a long crate out of the first hole. The wood was in relatively good shape. It hadn't been buried long.

Illuminated by the lantern light, on the side was a stenciled notice:

Ten Rifles—U.S. Army
Model 1873, Caliber .45—with bayonet
Springfield Federal Armory
Springfield, Massachusetts

Under his breath, Rork whispered into my ear, "Springfields, stolen from the friggin' U.S. Army?"

"Stolen, then sold on the black market," I replied.

Ten crates came out of the first hole, which wasn't deep due to the low nature of the island, perhaps three feet down. But it was wide; the containers were buried beside each other. Doyle came back to the digging operation as they were being hauled away. "There's even more in them other holes, boys, so let's get 'em up an' loaded, so y'all can go. I can't be waitin' ferever on y'all. I got to go too."

Reyes, still glancing at his adversary, joined Doyle in the circle of weak light. In the woods the wind wasn't as loud, so I could hear much better when the revolutionary lieutenant quietly asked Doyle, "You are still heading up the coast for the other load, right?"

Doyle was perturbed with the haughty lieutenant. "I'm doin' what I *said* I'd do, but I can't go upwind aginst a storm, like these fellas can use it to go downwind. Gotta wait till the wind goes east—about two, three days. Then I'll go up the coast an' we'll get that load down here, don't you worry none on it, Lootenant . . . *sir.*" He raised his hand in mocking salute.

Reyes wasn't much thrilled with Doyle either. "I don't have time to go up the coast with you, Mr. Doyle. I am needed back in Key West. But you know Monterojo. He will meet you up there. It is already hidden at the designated place, correct?"

"If your boys up on the coast did what they's supposed to, it is."

Reyes nodded decisively. "They did."

"Good, then you'll have yourself another thousand guns in a week er so. Then you can start shootin' every Spanish grandee in sight, for all I care. Just so's I get the rest of *my* money."

The two of them walked away as the men around them began hauling up crates from the second hole. We stayed and watched. I counted thirteen. Fifteen came out of the last hole. Three hundred and eighty new rifles. Plus there'd soon be another *thousand.* Enough to arm two Cuban infantry regiments with modern weapons.

The holes were empty, the lantern gone. Most of the crates were still piled on the beach, being ferried out to the smacks by small boats. Rork nudged me in the dark.

"About time for a bit o' larceny, ain't it? We can swim out an' nab a boat afore they get too many lads aboard, but we'd better do it quicklike."

I'd been thinking about that. We knew where those fishing

boats were going, we knew where Reyes was going, but we didn't know where Doyle was going, except that it was somewhere up the coast, presumably the Gulf coast. Our orders were to concentrate on the Florida end of the revolutionary operations. From what I could deduce, Doyle was our best bet for that.

"We're not stealing one of the boats just yet, Rork. Plan's changed. We need to know more about this Doyle fellow and his boat."

"An' how're we goin' to do that, pray tell, sir?" he asked while adjusting the rubber hand over his marlinespike. "We don't know where the little bugger has his boat. An' we're gonna have one hellova time tryin' to get back to *our* boat against that wind in that bloody awful excuse for a dinghy."

"Reyes and Doyle's boats must be on the southern, leeward side of the island. Doyle said he's waiting for the wind to veer easterly, so there's no hurry. We follow him and Reyes back to their boats after these fishing smacks leave. Reyes will go downwind back to Key West, but Doyle will have to stay around here. Once we know where Doyle's boat is, we head back to the *Royal Victoria* and get around the island where we can watch his boat and wait. When he heads north, we'll head north after him."

"All well an' good, sir. But you still haven't let me in on how we're gettin' back to our boat in that tiny cockleshell."

"Same as before, only delayed a bit. We just borrow a charcoalers' dinghy after they're all passed out from rum. That dory-bowed one should do nicely. Hopefully, when they sober up tomorrow morning they'll think the tide took it. And I'm rowing this time. You steer. That's an order, bosun."

"Well that sounds simple, sir," Rork said rather doubtfully, as he slapped a bug on his face.

I knew it was time for me to exude some command confidence—which is damned difficult when you're soaking wet, cold to the bone, hungry, thirsty, and somewhat lost on a dark, stormy night on a mangrove-jungled remote island, all the while surrounded by people who would kill you in a heartbeat if they found you sniffing around their hideout.

"Yes, it is simple, Rork," I said with a smile that he couldn't see. "The best plans always are."

18

A Long-Lost Friend

March 1886
Along the west coast of Florida

It turned out that Doyle wasn't nearly as scrupulous as he'd promised to Lieutenant Reyes. On the third day the wind laid down and came easterly, fair for a fast broad reach to the north, but the lad still couldn't let go of the girls—apparently professional ladies of joy, from the conversations I could hear from shore—he had aboard his fifty-foot cutter, off Sugarloaf's south beach. It wasn't until the following Thursday, the eleventh, that he departed Sugarloaf, having spent the intervening five days partying with his two-man crew of ne'er-do-wells while at anchor.

Just as I was about to admit defeat and return our chartered boat to her rightful owner at Key West, Doyle set sail along Hawk Channel, the route that parallels the Keys on their southern shore. Once he passed our hidden anchorage, Rork and I maintained a position several miles behind, where we could barely see Doyle's sails ahead of us. But once again Doyle didn't do as I expected. Instead of sailing for the middle Gulf coast of Florida, just north of the Keys he altered course and slogged close-hauled to the northeast.

The next dawn, staying on the western horizon and using the rusted telescope we found aboard our boat, Rork spotted the cutter stopped at Waddell's huge coconut plantation at Cape Sable, taking on a cargo of coconut meat and copra. Side business or a cover for gun-running? That night we sailed inshore, beached the dinghy a half a mile away, and crept close to where Doyle's crew and the plantation's workers enjoyed some raucous merrymaking ashore. The talk was of the copra, not guns. The work conversations ended when the girls came ashore. It appeared that Doyle's girls were the first white females seen there in quite a while, and were fully appreciated by the local overseers and laborers. At the end of an hour of giggling and moaning, Rork dryly observed that, so far in the surveillance, our man Doyle was having far more enjoyment than we were and suggested that perhaps we were on the wrong side.

When the sun rose over the palm tops on Saturday, the thirteenth, Doyle's cutter was sailing northbound on a fast broad reach past the mouth of the Shark River, with us tailing along far in the rear. Late on the following morning, Doyle's cutter neared the lighthouse on the point at Sanibel Island. My hope for something definitive to happen began to seem more possible. It was about time. Over a week had passed since I'd decided to follow the Cubans' American connection to the north, and *Royal Victoria* should've been returned back to Pinder several days earlier.

But it was a false hope. Doyle got within a mile of the outer buoy at San Carlos Bay and sheered off to the nor'west, to go around Sanibel Island. The wind had gone light, drifting up from the sou'east. The cutter, with all sail set and winged out abeam, was making slow headway with the wind coming from dead aft. I immediately altered course myself to the nor'west—farther out to sea—and deliberated destinations with Rork as the *Royal Victoria* rolled from one side to the other.

"Peace River, through Boca Grande Passage?" he suggested.

"Tampa?" said I. "Remember, Doyle mentioned *up* the coast, as in a long way. Farther than Boca Grande. Reyes's men had done something there to make the next load ready."

Rork disagreed. "Nay, not Tampa. Too big. Too many witnesses. Nay, it'll be Cedar Key. There aren't many people there, an' they've got a good rail connection. But, o' course, that means another two hundred miles o' this bloody rollin'."

"Maybe, but there's a rail line at Tampa now too."

"Aye, that new one o' Plant's. But what about this boat? What'll Pinder do? We're a couple o' days late now, an' he don't strike me as the kind o' lad that'd wait afore he called the sheriff on us for theft."

"Yeah, I've been worried about that too. We'll just have to pay for the overage on the charter."

"We could tell 'im the fish kept bitin' an' we followed the slimy buggers up the coast."

"Good line. I'll use that on him and see if it works. Think he's gullible enough?"

Rork laughed. "Nay, it won't wash with that evil-eyed shark—but it did sound good, even if I do say so meself."

Ten days after Doyle told Reyes he would be up on the coast in a couple of days, I at last determined his destination. It was none too soon. Completely out of our original provisions, Rork and I had been eating the few fish we'd caught—ironic, considering my suggested excuse to Pinder—and were down to using the none-too-clean water in the sloop's emergency cask. If Doyle had sailed past the mouth of Tampa Bay, I was ready to cancel the plan and return *Royal Victoria* to her owner. But he didn't. He sailed around

Anna Maria Island with a sou'westly sea breeze building up and made a nor'easterly course for Gadsden Point.

That meant Tampa.

At last, one of my guesses had been right. Rork congratulated me as the sloop moved slowly across the bay under all sail. By sunset on Tuesday, the sixteenth, we'd arrived and tied up to a transit dock a quarter mile up the east bank of the Hillsborough River, past the remnants of old Fort Brooke. I thought our story cleverly couched with just enough truth: we were northern fishermen who were taking a break from sampling some of the Gulf coast's famous game-fishing. That we were terribly unsuccessful fisherman and starving as a result, I did not add. In any event, we were met with smug, knowing smiles, but also with a modicum of courtesy, the locals clearly hopeful for some added income off us.

Doyle's cutter was docked a hundred yards farther upstream, his crew already supervising Negro laborers manhandling burlap bags of copra into carts and taking them away. Foul-smelling stuff, that copra. It reminded me of durian fruit in French Indo-China. Somebody at Waddell Plantation must've already had buyers waiting in Tampa, for Doyle lost no time is getting rid of it. I found that interesting, because Waddell Plantation usually transported its product through the brokers at Key West, where Waddell was a successful merchant. It appeared that this load was a little side business for the overseer—something to file away in my brain for future retrieval. It also meant that Doyle was agreeable to opportunistic deals. Perhaps I could offer him one.

Now that we were ashore, my expense account money could come into play. Rork and I immediately concurred that the first order of business was to eat, and eat well. After that we would gather information about Doyle's Tampa connections.

I just happened to have an old friend in Tampa from the war, Michael Bain, who could help us with both. That is an alias, the necessity for which will become obvious.

Michael grew up in the area of Tampa. When the war came

NORTH

~100 yds~

Town of Tampa, Florida
Drawn by CDR P. Wake
ONI/BurNav/USN
11 December 1886

Ybor's City →

~ pine woods ~

~ Railroad ~

vacant

fields

Harrison

Tyler

Spring

Cass

Water

Polk

Hillsborough River →

Zack

vacant

Twiggs

fields

Monroe

Ashley

Tampa

Franklin

Madison

Marion

Morgan

Pierce

Jefferson

East

~ swamp ~

Dix →

Lafayette

Café →

Jackson

Doyle →

pine
woods

Washington

Victoria →

The Scrub →

Whiting

Old Fort Brooke
Reservation

~ swamp ~

along in '61, he was pro-Union—a very unpopular position, to put it mildly. He left the Confederate stronghold and went to Useppa Island with other political refugees. For the first two years of the war he helped the U.S. Navy—mainly me—with his knowledge of the coast. In December of '63 he helped to form the pro-Union militia regiment formed at Useppa, fighting at many of their battles along the west coast of Florida.

Now Michael was a middle-aged merchant, relatively prosperous and slightly portly. Though I hadn't seen him in five years, I knew he'd help. The little boy I sent to find him returned on the run to our dock. He had a scrawled note from Michael: *Delighted you and Rork are here. Will meet you at the café at the corner of Jackson and Ashley at eight. Dinner on me. Michael B.*

We sat ourselves down at the nondescript café overlooking the docks, where we could observe our quarry. Rork and I had last seen Michael in '81, a brief stop when bringing my children to Useppa Island from Washington to scatter their mother's ashes. We'd written to each other once right after that, but not since. Michael hadn't known of Rork's horrendous wound from three years earlier, and listened in stunned silence to the sanitized version of how it happened. Once that was done, the good stories came out, about times of chaos and laughter, of personalities and victories. The rum flowed and the food was good. It was a great evening among men remembering the few good times during a horrific war.

Our quarry, however, proved dull. Doyle never left his boat that evening, instead occupying himself by lounging about the deck with those same girls, showing them off to the dockside idlers. Laborers, steamboat men, fishermen, boys from the town, they all ogled the show.

Fortunately, in response to my gentle inquiries, Michael provided a bit more excitement with his information. He knew everyone and everything in town, including the growing Cuban connection. He explained that the previous fall, two cigar manufacturers, Vicente Ybor from Key West and Ignacio Haya from New York, had decided to get away from the union conflicts in their respective cities and build new factories in a new place—one they would create from scratch. Haya, he said in answer to one of my questions, had connections with the Spanish government and Ybor had connections in the revolutionary movements, so they were comfortably in the middle of the Cuban civil war.

The two friends chose an area of savannah pineland east of Tampa and north of a swampy area by the bay. In the space of six months, Ybor and Haya had done what they told everyone they would—laid out and built a town named Ybor City. Factories and offices, homes, a church and a school, a light rail line to Tampa. It was, said Michael with genuine awe, amazing.

I asked how the locals felt about the immigrant influx.

"Those that will make money are for it. And more Spanish money's coming. Hell, the Spanish government just set up a new consul for Tampa. American fella by the name of Ethelbert Hubbs. Former customs inspector at Key West. As Spanish consul here, he works for the main consul down there."

What? Rork and I looked at each other.

I asked, "A former customs man at Key West is now a representative of the Spanish government? When did he come here?"

"Few weeks ago. He was in Key West until then. Why?"

I ignored the question and asked one of my own. "You know him?"

"Met him, but don't really know him. He's a little older than us. Union man during the war. Knows his way around Florida. Friendly with Haya and Ybor."

"And the Cuban rebels? Any of those up here?"

"Yep, a few. And they say more of 'em are coming when the workers from Havana and Key West get here. Ybor's bringing 'em."

"Ever heard of a fellow named José Martí?" I asked him on a hunch.

"Martí . . . that writer fella up in New York? Yeah, I've heard some of them around here speak of his name. They like him. Writes anti-Spanish revolutionary stuff, that sort of thing. Hubbs mentioned him once too. Why?"

"I ran into him up in New York. Interesting man. Say, I'd like to see that Ybor village place, Michael. Can you show it to me?"

Michael chuckled. "It's Ybor *City,* Peter. And just wait until you see it." He paused a moment. "Hey, hold up a minute. You and Rork aren't really here on any fishing vacation, are you? Or maybe you're fishing for something on *land?*"

"Just curious about the Cuban influence in my adopted state, Michael—that's all. If you don't have time . . ."

"Yes, yes, I've got time. I'll show you the place tomorrow morning."

"All right, how about we meet at the boat at eight? By the way, ever heard of a young fellow named Doyle? Thomas Doyle. Or somebody named Monterojo?"

"No, neither of them." Michael was wary now, but curiosity overwhelmed any reluctance. "Enemies of the state?"

Rork changed the subject. "By the way, Michael, whatever happened to the Fort Brooke military reservation? Ever used anymore by the army? Last time I was here, they still had a battery stationed there in the summertime. Looks from the river like it's now in ruins."

"It is. The buildings were never completely rebuilt after the bombardment in the war. They sold off part of the federal reservation a couple of years ago. The army had an artillery battery from Key West up here in tents every summer until eighty-three, then they stopped even that. No, the old large reservation's mostly gone now. But not all—part of it's still around. It's pretty much deserted, but it stretches northeast from the river's mouth all the way out toward . . ." His voice faded away as he turned from Rork and looked at me oddly.

"Toward where, Michael?"

"Just south of Ybor City."

The morning sun was just clearing the rooftops of the town, illuminating the oak trees lining the opposite riverbank, when Michael arrived at our boat. He was eager to show us around—and discover why we were really there, no doubt. Rork and I were ready, but there was a new development with Doyle.

"The Stud," as Rork was now calling him, was at last providing some incentive for the ever-lengthening surveillance. Just as Michael stepped aboard *Royal Victoria*, Doyle stepped off his boat onto the jetty, climbed the riverbank, and walked east, up Jackson Street. That move caught me unprepared. I was sure Doyle would sleep in until noon after the previous night's performance.

Rork moaned under his breath, "What now?" and Michael, seeing us eyeing the distant figure, asked, "Who's he?"

I quickly filled him in while jumping onto the dock and heading for the street. "Oh, he's a strange-acting bird we're kind of curious about. Nothing definite, Michael, he just acts a bit too shifty for me. Maybe we're just getting bored around here. Do you mind if we trail along behind him for a while?"

Michael's expression told me he didn't buy my explanation at all, but he also didn't protest. "Only if I can come too. I presume that is the man Doyle you asked me about?"

"Hey, the more the merrier, and yes, that's Doyle," I said, trying to sound nonchalant as the three of us trotted along Ashley Street to Jackson to catch up with Doyle.

Based on his prior behavior, I naturally assumed our boy was heading to some den of iniquity for a change in feminine scenery, although it did seem a bit early in the day for that. Rork mentioned the same as we walked. Michael agreed, explaining that if we continued in that direction we would arrive at the infamous "Scrub" area east of the town. He further described it as a "shanty-ville of good-for-nothings," where prostitutes made their living, near the northeast end of the military reservation of old Fort Brooke.

"I'm ready to forget this idiot," I grumbled to Rork as we carefully leaped across a foul-smelling gully running through the street at the intersection where Franklin Street crossed Jackson. My enthusiasm was waning fast. I was convinced by then that Doyle was probably more of a hindrance to the revolutionaries than a help, and that this whole endeavor was wasted time.

"Rork, if this fool doesn't do something significant in the next fifteen minutes, we'll stop and head over to Michael's Ybor City."

"The Stud is headin' to the Scrub," muttered Rork with a sigh. "Aye, this thing's gotten too bloody peculiar. An' I've no fancy for dealin' with a bunch o' poxied trollops at this time o' morn, even if 'tis Saint Patrick's Day."

Michael stayed cheerful—this was probably the most interesting thing he'd done in years. "I'm with y'all, Peter, whatever you want to do, but it sure does look like your friend is heading for some female entertainment."

I shook my head. "He's not *my* friend. Fifteen more minutes—that's it."

My watch indicated eight thirteen A.M. At eight twenty-eight, we'd abandon Doyle for a tour of Ybor City, then return to the *Royal Victoria* and get under way.

Four minutes later, just before Jackson Street devolved into a sandy lane into the pinelands, Doyle turned left onto East Street and headed north, away from the prostitutes. Intrigued, we followed. Nine minutes after that we found out how wrong we were about Thomas Doyle's intentions that morning.

Dead wrong.

19

Little Havana

Wednesday, 17 March 1886
Ybor City, Florida

At Polk Street, Doyle suddenly stopped and looked west, awaiting for someone or something. It turned out to be a trolley car, one of two pulled by a small steam engine named Hattie, on a narrow-gauge track running from the docks along the river. I hadn't even known Tampa had trolleys.

Michael laughed when he saw it. "Well, I'll be damned. Boys, looks like your fella's heading to Ybor City himself. This here is Mr. Ybor's new trolley line. The engine's named for his daughter."

Following Michael's lead, we jumped on the back of the crowded second car. Doyle was in the front of the first car. Both cars were full of workmen carrying construction tools. A flatbed piled with lumber brought up the rear. At little faster than a brisk walk, we lurched and swayed on a narrow-width railroad parallel to the heavy-gauge rail line on one side and a rutted wagon road on the other. The trolley dipped and rose, like a ship at sea, through thick sand in the pine woods northeast of town, slowly ascending a slight rise in the land. A mile and a half later it jerked to a stop at a dirt street in a cleared-off area.

We'd arrived at Ybor City. At first glance, it wasn't much. Then I surveyed it more carefully and changed my opinion.

The passengers disembarked, bound for a two-story frame structure a block away that seemed to be the headquarters of the operation. Just up the street was a huge three-story building under construction, which Michael confirmed was Ybor's future factory.

Several dozen long, narrow cottage homes lined the surrounding streets, each set up on brick or concrete pillars, and surrounded by a white picket fence. I saw other houses, two-story affairs, presumably for many men or several families. Dust was everywhere and the March sun reflecting off the sand made it uncomfortably hot. There were no trees, no shade. I wondered what August would be like there.

Other houses and buildings were under construction— stretching as far as one could see. Michael was right, the place was amazing. There were hundreds of workers toiling, many speaking the rapid-fire Spanish of Cuba. Some were erecting the structures, others were stockpiling material, a few were clerical types checking on progress. Unlike what I'd seen elsewhere in Latin America, this whole operation radiated energy. It reminded me more than anything else of Washington, D.C., during the war, when army encampments for tens of thousands of men were built in weeks. The scale and vigor were extraordinary.

Just as the trolley's passengers arrived at the office building, which a rather grandiose corner signpost let me know was at Virginia and Fourteenth streets, Rork squeezed my arm. "Uh-oh—take a look at the bloke on your starboard bow."

Three paces behind Doyle was a lanky, tall man in drab black coat and broad-brimmed dark hat. He was olive skinned, with long black hair that hung past his collar. Intently staring at Doyle, his face was lined and grimly set, his right hand poised inside the coat, as if about to pull something out of a pocket. I asked Michael if he knew him. He didn't.

Our mutual prey was oblivious to it all. Doyle entered the picket fence around the office, then stopped and said hello to another young man. The new man was in his late twenties, scraggly like Doyle, and spoke with a flat Midwestern accent. Doyle called him Smith and they both laughed. An alias?

Rork, Michael, and I—and the stalker—were still in the crowd of workmen standing around and gabbing, waiting for orders. In the commotion, Doyle and his new companion stepped out to Virginia Street, then walked south, down Fourteenth. The mystery man followed. This street, a thoroughfare with deep, loose sand churned up by wagon wheels, had buildings on it for two blocks. Past that point it lost any urban pretense as the houses thinned out. About two hundred yards farther south there was nothing but sand and stunted weedy bushes as it sloped downward toward a tree line in the distance.

It was as if we'd entered a desert, so thoroughly had the land been denuded. Rork and I picked up several pieces of siding lumber from a pile by the last of the houses, put them on our shoulders, the better to hide our faces, and headed south. Michael got into the spirit with his own load and walked behind us. The mystery man, who was following Doyle and his companion a hundred yards ahead of us, didn't bother with any subterfuge and kept marching on.

A lone cottage, well out of town, stood ahead on the left. Doyle and Smith, chattering away, continued to lead the drawn-out procession through the sand. At the cottage, they turned off the road and entered the front door. Without knocking, I noticed. The stalker turned at that point to look our way. Presumably dismissing us as local workers, he went across a field of plowed-up palmetto debris and made for the back of the cottage. Once there, he crept close to the outside wall and peeked in a window.

Rork made a "hmm" sound, then said, "Methinks that lad's up to no good, sir."

Hearing that, Michael couldn't contain himself any longer. "Peter, who the hell *are* these fellas? I agree with Rork—that one sneaking around over there is up to no good."

I was about to reply when the man in black dashed through the cottage's back door. A split second later there was a shout and the crack of gunfire was heard. I counted two pairs of quick shots, then the front door burst open and Doyle ran out at full speed, arms pumping as he crashed through the gate, rounded the cottage's picket fence, and ran northbound past us. I saw blood splattered on his shirt, his eyes wild with fear. He never slowed or spoke to us. Just kept running.

Rork whipped his revolver out, scanning for targets. Michael yelled, "Sweet Jesus!" and crouched down. I checked behind us. Seven blocks to the north, the company office crowd was taking notice of Doyle now. People were pointing, several were coming toward him. It wouldn't be long before they went to the cottage. We didn't have much time.

"Come on, men. We'd better see what happened up there."

Michael, to his credit and my thanks, reverted to the old discipline and kept right behind us. As Rork and I entered the front door with pistols drawn, the rear door slammed. Through a side window I saw the stalker running across the fields to the south, leaping like a deer over the bushes in a display of surprising agility. I looked beyond him toward his destination—a collection of hovels clumped together half a mile away in the tree line.

Michael said, "Peter, that ol' boy's heading over to the Scrub. If he don't get snake-bit trying to get over there, he can get back to town that way."

Hearing a loud click next to me, I turned to see Rork squinting along his Colt's barrel sights at the fleeing figure, right hand balancing the pistol on the left arm's appliance. The hammer was back, his finger poised on the trigger. "How 'bout I wing the bastard afore he gets too far away?"

"No. Not the right time. Let's put our guns away before the company people get here. Remember—we're visiting businessmen on a fishing trip accompanying Michael here, looking at investing."

Michael was shaken, staring at Rork's trigger finger backing off the pressure. He nodded agreement. "Whatever you say, Peter."

"Aye, aye, sir," Rork said as he lowered the pistol, clearly frustrated.

I was frustrated myself. Or was it fear? No, it was anger. This wasn't some far-off two-bit jungle country of savages; this was America and the state where I had my *home*. Somebody was *assassinating* Americans in Florida.

The body was in the back room, slumped against the splattered wall where he'd slid down after being shot. From two holes in his forehead, blood leaked down his patterned blue shirt. The eyes were wide in fright—death had been instantaneous.

"Hmm . . . good grouping, an inch apart," concluded Rork, as he examined the wounds. "Double-action revolver for rapid fire. An' remember the sounds? They were booms, not a bang or a pop. Significant . . ."

Michael asked before I could. "Why?"

"By that sound an' these holes, I'd say the shooter was using a forty-five caliber. But the sound indicated the cartridge load was light, not a standard American load, which is heavier. Nay, 'twarn't a U.S. weapon that made this. Make you a wee wager it's one o' them Orbea model sevens." He paused and dramatically arched an eye at me. "The *Spanish* army's version of the Smith an' Wesson. Seen an' heard 'em afore. It's issued to commissioned officers. But the fellow who did this ain't no average commissioned officer, no sir."

Spanish army? This time it was I who asked. "Why?"

"This killin' is the work of a man who's had practice. It was done quick at real close range—almost touchin' the head. See the star-shaped wounds an' powder burns? The killer walked right up to him an' shot the poor bastard afore he even knew what was happenin'—boom, boom—no reaction or defensive move on the part o' the target means no hesitation on the part o' the attacker. Most officers couldn't do that outside o' battle. Aye, me lads, this killer's done it afore. Many times."

Rork stood and looked around the wall, toward the front room.

"Aye, an' lookee there. Them's the second pair o' shots, right there in the doorframe. Just' missed ol' Doyle's head as he ran out."

Michael was staring at the dead man and looked unwell.

"Excellent points, Rork. Very scientific," I offered.

He shrugged. "Jus' me own experience, an' a little observation, sir."

We conducted a little more observation. Smith's boots were off, his trouser buttons undone and underwear opened, trouser pockets and socks turned inside out—a quick but thorough search job. I wondered what the killer was searching for, and if he'd found it. And what did the killer make of us? He'd seen us enter the house. Were we in his sights now? Would he search Tampa for us? Useless to speculate. I heard voices outside. Time was running out.

"All right, there's nothing more here," I said to Rork and Michael. "We'll tell the officials what we saw, then get the hell out of here. Remember, just give descriptions of what you saw on the street and in the house, but nothing else, especially that we know of Doyle."

Michael said, "Yes, sir. I'll only give a description. But I have a question, Peter."

I said, "What?" rather abruptly. People were clomping up the front steps.

"Will you ever tell me what I was part of here today?"

I looked my old friend in the eye and shook my head. "No. Probably not, Michael. And you know enough not to talk about it. Now, let's get this done. We've got to get back to Tampa so I can send some telegrams."

We never did get Michael's detailed tour of Vicente Ybor's new city that day, for we were instantly busy with company officials who were aghast that potential investors had to see such violence in the new town. Then Sheriff J. P. Martin's lawmen showed up at the scene and began questioning everyone. It was a mob scene inside the company headquarters office, what with company officials, policemen, two newspaper men, and the coroner's official all talking at once. Outside, a crowd of lookers-on gathered along the fence. Doyle was sequestered right away, interrogated at length by the sheriff's men in a supervisor's office.

When it was our turn, Rork and I did not lie, we just omitted our profession. We told the investigator our real names, our addresses in Washington, and that we were on a fishing trip and in Tampa to visit our old friend, who persuaded us to see the new city with a view toward investing in it. Then we told, in a horrified manner, what we saw of the killing. The detective, tired and harassed, seemed satisfied with that. After finishing our interviews, the three of us were about to write out statements of what we saw during the incident, when Rork quietly groaned and nudged me, then brought my attention to the crowd outside the window. I saw the man straightaway—his expression of malevolence so distinct from those around him.

It was none other than Boreau.

The Spanish agent didn't come inside, but stood by the picket fence, periodically pacing like a predator waiting for dinner. At length, Michael, Rork, and I finished our statements and were released. We departed out the rear door, with Rork keeping a weather eye out for anyone following us. No apparent surveillance was spotted by the time we reached the trolley, and half an hour later we were back by the Hillsborough River, saying good-bye at the dock.

After shaking hands all around, Michael went home to his family. His last words to me were, "Exciting, like the old times, eh, Peter? But you know what—I think I'm too old for this anymore . . ."

You're not the only one, my friend, I thought, but didn't say it.

Late that afternoon, I sent three communiqués from the telegraph office. The first one was to Commodore Walker in the February monthly code about rum sales—he'd forgotten to bring me the new March code. It was uncomplicated: *Getting information; will continue operation.* I put an addendum in plain language: *Rum is of high quality and volume, and ready to go. Competitor lost a salesman in Tampa. Details later.*

The next telegram went to Pinder in Key West, explaining we still had the boat, would be back soon, and would pay the overage on the charter. I did not give any details of what had happened, when we'd return, or where we were, though he'd know it was sent from Tampa. That should confuse him entirely, I imagined.

The last was a long shot. To "Mr. Mondongo" I sent: *Do you have any friends in Tampa I can speak with? Please reply immediately by 10 A.M. on Thursday, March 18.* I sent it priority. That was expensive, but it meant a delivery boy in Brooklyn would track him down as soon as possible.

That evening Doyle stayed on his boat, down below. I got a glimpse of him only once, shooing his disappointed girls away and checking his crew posted on watch, openly armed with a shotgun. The girls, unceremoniously thrown off the vessel, acted surprised, then angry, as they stormed off down the street toward the nearest tavern. Their language, as blue as any sailor's, echoed off the wooden buildings. The dockside idlers laughed, but none followed. It took money for that entertainment.

Aboard the cutter, it looked like Doyle and the gang were staying put, but I wondered why he'd remain in Tampa when someone, presumably a Spanish agent, was out to get him. Then again, maybe the murder had disrupted his rendezvous with the rifles and he was afraid of returning to the Keys to face the iron-willed Lieutenant Reyes empty-handed.

The only reason *we* were still around was the long-shot telegram to Martí. By noon the next day, I intended to be heading south, hopefully to discover more rewarding avenues for our investigative efforts.

A steam whistle jolted us just as the last purplish shade of light was leaving the sky. Moments later, the revenue cutter *Dix* chugged by us, an old side-wheeled former navy gunboat from the war. For the last twenty years she'd been a treasury department ship; for the last six she'd patrolled the Keys and Gulf coast of Florida. I'd met her commanding officer years before at Key West. Captain Fengar was known for being a very determined man.

Dix tied up at the Madison Street wharf, where larger steamers docked. Within thirty minutes her steam died away and we saw some of her crew on liberty ashore, walking down Ashley Street, searching for something to do on Saint Patrick's night. "Those lads'll either find a pint o' pleasure o' a ton o' trouble," Rork commented with a grin. "O' maybe both!"

After supper ashore, Rork and I sat on deck in the evening, debating what to do next. The Hubbs revelation in Tampa was important and disturbing. I thought it worth some inquiry in the morning. But Rork brought up a good point that dampened my enthusiasm—Hubbs was too obvious to be a current spy for the Spanish, or even a past one. Everyone knew his Spanish connection now. Was he a spy before he quit federal service? Maybe, but why would the Spanish then overtly employ him now and invite suspicion? And the federal authorities in Washington, especially at the treasury department, would've thought of him immediately once they read the message to Roosevelt. No, Hubbs was probably always inclined toward the Spanish, but the real Judas had to be someone else.

And what of the Tampa revolutionary connection? There had been Cubans in Tampa for years, but no real overt activism to the point of violence. Now it looked like thousands were coming to Ybor's community. How many would be revolutionaries? What would the Spanish government do? Had they already started? Were they behind the murder or was it an internecine killing by other revolutionaries? Or was it a local crime of opportunity?

Boreau's presence was ominous. Havana, Key West, now Tampa. Had he been looking for us? Had Hubbs reported us in Tampa? Was Boreau connected to the murder? The last point seemed certain.

It grew cold out on deck; the wind was veering around to the north again. So we continued our deliberations in our boat's minuscule cabin. We broke out some recently acquired decent rum to properly observe Saint Patrick's Day, while pondering each factor of the noxious web of personalities and politics in which we'd become enmeshed. In the end, after several glasses, we deduced no brilliant hypothesis to solve the riddle of what was happening in the Cuban-Spanish conflict in Florida. But we knew this: a Spanish agent and an anti-Spanish gun-runner had both showed up in Tampa at the same time that an acquaintance of the gun-runner had been killed.

The discussion led to more questions than answers. My mind was overwhelmed with possibilities of investigation, so I resolved to ignore all that took our concentration away from those thousand rifles. Where the hell were they? Time was running out, according to the agenda we overheard at Sugarloaf. And skinny little Doyle, as idiotic as he was, plainly was the key to those rifles. Rork agreed and we began to go over the possible locations of the cache. By the dim glow of a cabin lantern we perused the coastal charts.

By nine o'clock, we'd narrowed it down to four or five sites, and were looking at the chart when we felt the boat list with the weight of a man quietly boarding our boat from the dock. Both of us took up our Colts and swung their muzzles toward the closed companionway hatch above us. I doused the lantern.

A slow double knock sounded on the cabin top, followed by a deep voice with a Spanish accent, "Message for Peter Wake."

Boreau, or one of his men? I slid open the hatch slowly, Rork covering me, and saw a large man attired in a black cape leaning over the companionway. He didn't flinch when he saw the revolvers aimed at him. In his hand was a piece of paper, which he handed down to me.

It contained a message that would influence the rest of my life.

20

The Prince of Wales

Wednesday, 17 March 1886
Ybor City, Florida

The message was simple:

> *Dear Mr. Wake,*
> *A distant acquaintance of my friend has asked him to meet with you. My friend does not speak English, so he has asked me to interpret for him. Please meet us this evening, so that you and my friend may discuss matters of shared interest. The driver who delivers this message will take you immediately to us and provide return transportation.*
>
> *Thank you in advance,*
> *Eduardo Manrara*

The carriage ride took me through the dark streets of Tampa

alone, for I asked Rork to stay aboard the *Royal Victoria* and watch Doyle's cutter. No activity was apparent on his boat, but I had an odd inkling something might happen with Doyle—perhaps he'd have a visitor or would go somewhere ashore. I told Rork I'd probably be gone for no more than an hour. Just long enough to see what the writer's friend, apparently a man of means by the style of his carriage, had to say. The driver, a large, scowl-faced man, wouldn't tell me who sent the note or the name of his employer, even when I inquired in Spanish. In fact, he wouldn't say anything during the journey.

The carriage passed through the quiet streets of frame houses under live oak canopies and was soon on a dirt road along the river, north of town. We turned into an old-growth copse of orange trees. The grove was fragrant in the crisp evening air.

A house, two storied with verandahs all around both, loomed up before us. It smelled sweetly of flowers and newly cut yellow pine lumber. Lamps and lanterns lit the verandahs outside, and from inside came the hesitant notes of a violin student.

The driver pulled up in front and spoke for the first time since handing me the note. "He waits inside."

The driver escorted me to the front door, then disappeared around a corner. A maid curtsied and ushered me in without a word. It was quite a house. Not ornate, but comfortable, with many side rooms off the main hall. Left alone in the study, I inspected the surroundings for a definitive clue as to my host's identity, though I had pretty much deduced it by that point. Bookshelves lined the walls below portraits of stern-faced men. A globe sat atop a massive desk devoid of paperwork. In the fireplace, pine logs sputtered low flames. Sawdust, tangy lamp oil, musty books, sweet cigar smoke. A cozy refuge. I was examining some of the books when the floor creaked behind me.

"Welcome, Mr. Wake—or I should say, Commander Wake."

I turned around and faced an older man with a balding

head over a bushy moustache. The man did a slight bow and continued.

"I am Eduardo Manrara, Commander, and I thank you for making this spontaneous journey. As you can tell, English is a second language for me, and I am sorry to say that I have not mastered it well. But my friend asked me to be a confidential interpreter, to facilitate a meeting with you that he has been asked to do by a distant acquaintance in New York."

"Thank you for the invitation, Mr. Manrara. Your English is just fine. Who might be the gentleman in question, sir?"

The floor creaked again, and behind Manrara a man filled the doorway. He was in his sixties, strongly built, impeccably dressed, with a perfectly contoured handlebar mustache. The eyes were evaluating but not demonstrative. Shaking hands with me, he began speaking in Spanish, his manner indicating a man clearly used to authority.

After he spoke, Manrara translated word for word.

"Commander Wake, I am Don Vicente Martínez Ybor, and I most humbly beg that you please forgive the unconventional method of invitation, sir. And also that we must use my friend and business associate *Señor* Manrara as an interpreter, for regrettably, I do not sufficiently possess the English language. As for the timing, I must explain that I received word of your presence only in the last two hours, from our mutual acquaintance in the North. It took Manrara that long to ascertain your whereabouts. Understanding that your time is limited, I judged it necessary to impose upon your evening in order that we might meet in these private surroundings. This is not my home, but rather the winter residence of a dear American friend that I use while in Tampa on business. He owns a vast collection of orange groves in the area. However, now he has returned to the North and kindly allowed me full use of it."

I decided to keep my Spanish dormant for the evening, and remained in English. "Your note—"

Interrupting Manrara's translation, Ybor raised a hand. "Please, I am sorry. My rather enigmatic message was to preserve the privacy of our meeting, should it fall into the wrong hands."

"Enigmatic or not, thank you for the invitation, Don Vicente. I am delighted to meet a man of your reputation and success. But I am afraid you have me at a considerable disadvantage, sir. Who is our mutual friend up north?"

His mouth allowed the slightest smile as he opened a cigar box on a side table, extracting two. I didn't much like that smile. There was a hint of controlled anger in it. "Why, he is the man you telegrammed in New York today, Commander—the writer, José Martí. Due to the political sensitivity of the times, we have not met and seldom correspond. A distant compatriot. I understand that, unlike me, you have the honor to know him personally."

Just what I'd thought. That Martí fellow had his hand in everywhere. A thought flashed through my mind—*was it really a coincidence that we'd met that day in Brooklyn? But it must've been, right?*

Accepting a proffered cigar, I asked, "And what did José tell you, if I might inquire?"

Manrara even mimicked Ybor's inflections and gestures, complete with shrugs.

"Oh, not much. The telegram said that you are in the United States Navy and interested in the situation in Cuba. He asked me to assist you in understanding that situation. Please, sit down, Commander. Would you care for a glass of sipping rum to go with that cigar?"

"Yes, thank you." I sank into a silk-upholstered wingback facing the fire. Ybor produced a bottle from a paneled compartment in the wall and filled two snifters. It was Matusalem—a high-priced rum from Cuba. Handing me one of the glasses, he lowered himself in the other chair with a sigh. Ybor waved the cigar in one hand, the other raised the snifter in a salute.

Standing in the corner, Manrara said, "To a free Cuba. I hope you like the rum, Commander."

I raised mine to Ybor. "I'm sure I will. Thank you, Don Vicente."

I could understand much of Ybor's meaning, but waited for Manrara's English version that followed. "It was awarded top honors at the international competition five years ago. The company is relatively new for Cuba—only thirteen years old, started by the Camp brothers over in Oriente, the eastern end of the island. Like me, they came from Spain. It is a very smooth, sweet rum; created by way of the old Solera process of southern Spain. As I am sure that you know, the Solera is a process which creates some of the finest Spanish wines and brandies."

I nodded agreement, even though I had no idea what he was talking about.

Ybor continued, through his friend. "*Matusalem,* by the way, is our word in Spanish for Methuselah, from the Bible. It is a play on words, as is so much in Cuba. It refers to the rum-making process by way of an old Spanish proverb: *Esto es mas viejo que Matusalem.* 'It is older than Methuselah.'"

He went on about various rums for some time. As he spoke and was translated, I sipped the Matusalem. It slid down my throat, mellowing my outlook as its warmth spread through me. I sipped again, then let the cigar fill my lungs with smooth sweet smoke, complementing the rum. It was a brilliant combination, though I don't usually like cigars.

"This is excellent, sir."

My cultured host continued on in his velvety fashion. "Commander Wake, I presume, since you've presented a story to the people of Tampa that you are a visiting northern fisherman— and did not include your true occupation—that you are engaged in somewhat clandestine naval duties here in Tampa. Probably regarding the aforementioned 'Cuban situation.' I am correct, am I not?"

That last comment was slipped in without apparent rancor.

Just part of the friendly conversation. Ybor was as smooth as his rum.

"You are most certainly *not* correct, Don Vicente. I am on leave, on vacation, with my friend. We live on an island near Fort Myers and are sailing the coast, fishing and relaxing. Your new project intrigued me. So does the situation in Cuba."

Ybor's face crinkled into mock surprise as he exhaled several smoke rings from his cigar. "Really? Hmm. . . . Well, to return to my New York friend's request that I help you—what *exactly* do you want to know about the Cuban situation, Commander?"

I decided to try candor and see his reaction. "The revolutionary connection between Tampa, Key West, and Havana interests me. I know there are connections, and would like to understand them better."

Manrara hesitated for a moment. Ybor's wicked smile showed again. "Oh, I think you know the connections by now, Commander."

I smiled back. "Why don't you humor me, Don Vicente, and start with your own connection?"

He stood—the man was an imposing presence—and slowly paced along the bookshelves behind the chairs, forcing me to turn around to look up at him. An old trick. Some of the more obnoxious admirals I've known do the same thing. I stood and leaned indifferently against the mantelpiece, then raised my rum in salute to him.

He acknowledged my move with a nod of his head. As Manrara put it English, Ybor watched me closely. "Very well, Commander. I was born in Valencia, a beautiful part of Spain. But my heart . . . my *heart* is in Cuba. My family went there when I was fourteen, and I worked my way up in the cigar business. First as a clerk, then as a broker, and finally as an owner, when I opened my first factory. The cigar you are enjoying is one of mine—the finest grade of *Principe de Gales.*"

Both Ybor and Manrara pronounced it *principay day gallays.*

I'd vaguely heard of the name, but didn't know what it meant. Seeing me confused, Manrara explained, "It is named for the Prince of Wales. The royal house of Great Britain holds a certain fascination for Don Vicente."

It was my turn to study Ybor. "I see. So you are a cigar seller . . ."

He didn't like that word. His indignation showed through Manrara's English.

"I am a cigar *manufacturer,* sir. Ten *millions* of my cigars are manufactured each year, Commander, for the discriminating gentlemen of Europe and North America. However, the land that I love, and the people that have helped me make those millions of cigars—"

His voice weakened, and he paused for a moment. At first I thought it more theatrics, but he wasn't faking. It was genuine emotion. "My people are not free. They are trodden down by a system and attitude from the past. Even slavery, an abomination eliminated over twenty years ago here in the United States, is still legal in Cuba. The Spanish colonial government is sick, Commander. It is living inside its past glories, a type of grand cultural dementia. It refuses to see that the modern light of liberty has illuminated its government's arrogant abuses of the people of Cuba."

Ybor's voice lost its refined tone. He almost snarled with rage, "The *idiots* even imposed a tax on *tobacco* in Cuba. On tobacco, of all things! They are not content with stifling even the most basic tenets of liberty for my people. Oh, no, now they are stifling the trade—the economic lifeblood—of the island. Those pompous bureaucrats are bleeding us dry with taxes to prop up their own corrupt way of life."

That was a widespread belief among the islanders. But what about *him?* "Besides the tobacco tax, what did they do to *you,* to make you so angry at them?"

He shrugged. "Well, they tried to kill me, for one thing. Back in sixty-nine. I was warned just before they arrived at my home. And why would they want to kill me, you will ask? It was all for the crime of having friends who were believers in liberty. Yes, for the fact I had friends who favored independence. My friend Vicente Galarze hid me—at great personal peril—and got me to Key West on a schooner, saving my life. I worked hard at Key West. Within five years I was producing millions of cigars. Within nine years, I had factories in New York also. This country gave me a new opportunity."

"But you never forgot the Spanish tried to kill you."

"One does not easily forget such a thing. I want my Cuba to be free of thugs that would kill a man for his *ideas* of liberty. It is barbaric, an indication of their desperation."

"So you, and Martí, and many others, support the revolution with money and supplies. And you provide a place for Cubans who escape from Havana."

He was less strident now, calmed down. He refilled my glass, then his. Manrara was eerily good at this translation business. Obviously Ybor had used him many times.

"I do not really know Mr. Martí, and cannot speak for him or anyone else. But yes, of course I do want Cuba to be free of the imperial yoke. So would you, Commander. Your reputation is that of a man of honor. I think you understand my position well, for in your career you have made decisions, and taken actions, based on the concept of honor. Even when in distant lands around the world, among people who do not understand honor. And though some of those decisions threatened your life and your career, you still chose to do the right thing."

What the hell was *that* about? Martí didn't know about my career, so how did Ybor? "I appreciate the kind words, Don Vicente, but am mystified as to how you know about me. That must've been quite a long telegram about me from José."

"Oh, I already knew of your reputation, Commander. It wasn't all from José."

I could tell from the superior look on his face he wanted me to ask the question burning in my mind. "Then who has been talking about me, Don Vicente?"

He took out a beautifully engraved pocket watch, checked the time, spoke, then waited impatiently as Manrara said to me, "Quite a few people in Key West and Havana, Commander. They have already helped you significantly. As long as you do not interfere with liberty for Cuba, they are your friends."

Useppa and her chums. But there was more in what Ybor said.

The reference to receiving help indicated he knew about what Father Viñes had recently done for me in Havana. That meant Ybor, and Martí, were somehow tied in with Raul Leon, Lefavre, and the rest of them in Key West and Havana, even if loosely. It confirmed what I'd suspected—the pro-revolutionary people knew all about me, and maybe my mission. The logical extension of that meant that, through their spies, the Spanish authorities probably did too. Damn it all . . .

And that last part—*as long as you do not interfere with liberty for Cuba.* Intimidation? I don't react well to that sort of thing. "Did Martí suggest that thinly veiled threat, Don Vicente?"

Once he got it in Spanish, Ybor held up both hands in innocence. "Oh, no, not at all, sir. He is but a romantic writer and philosopher. I am not threatening you, Commander, only passing along the views of others in Key West, meant as a request or a hope, not as a threat. I am a man of means in Key West, and hear many things. I am merely passing along what I hear.

"And as for José Martí, he is but a young writer—a dreamer who has become disillusioned with the hard policies of the military leaders of the cause, Maceo and Gómez and the others, so he is now separating himself from their efforts. His writing advocates civil reform, a change in cultural attitudes, in addition to the victory of the battlefield. He wants true freedom for the people when Cuba gains her independence, not merely a different form of dictatorship. As do I, of course, but without the flowery liberalism, for I am a businessman, not a poet. No, Commander, there was no threat from him at all. No one in the revolutionary movement wishes you harm."

I wondered if he really meant that. It was time to bring up some things from earlier in the assignment, to shake the tree a bit. "But, Don Vicente, there are some in the cause, radicals, I suppose, that wish the Spanish extreme harm, to the point of invoking violent Biblical verses. Or perhaps ancient Indian warriors. I suppose anyone, including me, who got in their way would be considered an enemy."

Ybor didn't react to my provocation. He would've been hell to play poker against. Instead, he shook his head sadly. "Quite the contrary, Commander. Your *enemies* are the Spanish government agents in Florida. You saw evidence of their work today."

"You know that the murderer today was a Spanish agent?"

"We *believe* so. The victim was a pro-revolutionary American, an Anglo. So is the man who got away. But then you knew that already—you've been following him."

That took me aback. When I regained my wits, I asked, "I was walking down the same street, that's all." I quickly changed the subject. "What about this man, Hubbs? Was he supplying information for the Spanish before he was appointed consul for Spain in Tampa?"

That got another shrug. "You mean, was he a spy when working in the customs house in Key West? I think not, though there was conjecture about that. I've seen no proof, though, and I have lived in Key West for many years. No, he is simply, like my dear friend Ignacio Haya, an aficionado of the Spanish ideal and traditions, not a Spanish spy. There *are* rumors the Spanish have a spy among the American federal authorities in Key West, but I do not know the identity. It is only a rumor. And, as you may know, Cubans do love gossip."

Ybor downed his rum, and I followed suit. He took out his

watch again. "I see it is late now, after midnight. I have imposed upon your valuable time far too long, but I find you an intriguing man, Commander. It is my hope that we shall be friends."

I agreed, feeling quite congenial in spite of the fact I'd learned nothing solid but merely confirmed my suspicions. "Most certainly, Don Vicente."

Ybor wasn't so bad, I decided. Maybe we could be friends. He would be a good source for information, if I could breach that guardedness, which would be difficult while using an intermediary. Watching him stand there in front of his bookcases, it gradually dawned on me that I'd had several glasses of rum, lost track of exactly how many, and that they weren't being sipped anymore. Damned if I wasn't drunk. And what time did he say it was, anyway? After midnight! How the hell did that happen?

My host moved to the liquor cabinet and poured a final round of rum, filling my snifter before I could protest. He spoke lightheartedly and Manrara echoed it, "Now, I know you must be tired after your stressful day, so I will have you driven back to your boat. But before you leave I must pass along something important, which I have kept to the last."

Ybor's face tightened again, the tone somber. Concern was apparent as he waited for Manrara's interpretation. "I said earlier that the Spanish are your true enemies. That was not an idle comment, Commander. I have been asked to pass along some important information to you and also to assist you. Remember, my position here in Tampa is quite delicate, as you can well imagine. I am not a public member of the revolution. I am merely a cigar manufacturer, who has invested much money in this town on the faith that it will succeed. This information, and that fact I am telling it, must be kept very confidential. Will you agree to that? I am informed that you are used to dealing with such conditions."

I nodded. "I agree—no one will know where it came from."

"Thank you. A Spanish agent named Boreau, a lieutenant, is

here to kill you. He has been asking about you in Key West lately, and now is in Tampa. He must have seen you at my company offices today, for I am told he was inquiring there of your local address. I have taken the liberty of providing him, through a third person, answers to his questions about you."

Oh, no. Ybor told him where my boat was? "Please, do go on, Don Vicente."

He glanced again at his watch. "Two hours ago, right after Martí's telegram about you reached me, I made sure Boreau was informed that you were staying at the Orange Hotel in Tampa and that you had left on the afternoon train, bound for Jacksonville via Bartow and Palatka. He is a quite cynical man, however, and insisted upon personally observing your name on the hotel's guest register and the train depot's passenger list . . ."

Ybor puffed his cigar haughtily, enjoying the moment far more than I was.

"Fortunately, we thought of that ahead of him, so he saw what he needed to see at both places. But Lieutenant Boreau was too impatient to wait for the next train. You must have made Colonel Marrón in Havana quite angry, Commander—congratulations. So Boreau decided to go by specially hired express coach to Palatka in an attempt to intercept the train. It is a very uncomfortable journey, which I am afraid will add to his considerable distress. And, naturally, he will fail. But, my new friend . . ."

Ybor stopped, looked at the ceiling, and nodded ruefully. "That irritation Boreau feels now will be nothing compared to his state when the stage arrives at the railroad station at Palatka and he does not see your name on the passenger list *there*. I would actually pay money to enjoy the look on his face at that moment."

This was unbelievable. A respected businessman was sticking his neck out, way out, to save my life? The rebel network wanted me to live. Because I was Useppa's father, or because they thought I could be useful to them? Probably the latter.

"Thank you for that, Don Vicente. Why did you take that chance for me?"

"Because you are admired by people that I respect, Commander."

Ybor waited for a second, then added some more in an almost jovial tone, which Manrara included in his translation, "Well, I wish you good luck, Commander. And now, though I do not want to be rude, I have other duties to attend to and must reluctantly bid you goodnight. My driver will take you back to your boat."

Still bewildered, I shook his offered hand. Manrara said, "It was an honor and a pleasure to act as interpreter, Commander. I present my own best wishes for you."

Ten seconds later, Don Vicente Martínez Ybor and Eduardo Manrara walked out of the room, replaced immediately by the driver waiting in the doorway.

I wouldn't see Ybor for another three years, but yes, we would remain friends. Seven years later, I would be in Don Vicente's city with Martí, on the day he was poisoned. That, however, is another story.

As I departed the grand house into the chilly night, my mind churned with what had just transpired. Belatedly, I recognized it was a tacit assumption by the revolutionary movement that I had chosen sides—their side—in the Cuban conflict, against my orders and government's policy. I thought it arrogant of them.

But then, as we made our way back to the riverfront in Tampa, I gradually realized they were right. I *was* in favor of Cuban independence. I was antislavery in Cuba. I was pro-revolutionary. And it wasn't because of Useppa's recent involvement, or Colonel Marrón's efforts against me. No, I'd fought against slavery in this country. I'd been anti-Spanish colonial government for a long time. I'd seen what they'd done in Cuba for the last twenty-three years. That experience had made me pro-Cuban. Now, in 1895, nine years after meeting Don Vicente, I am even more so.

The driver rounded the corner of Madison and Ashley streets and we clomped along the waterfront, deserted and dark. The wind was rushing down the curve of the river, getting colder near the water, the biting air penetrating the carriage blanket the driver had thrown over me. *It's a cold night out at sea,* I thought as *Dix* came into view at the wharf. The duty watch was huddled on the lee side by a lantern.

I looked for Doyle's cutter, but didn't see her. Searching the other docks, I still didn't see her.

What did that mean? Wait. I remembered Don Vicente suddenly looking at his watch, announcing our meeting was over. Was I set up? Had I been duped into leaving the docks so Doyle could depart and get the weaponry unobserved? Did that mean Ybor's story of deflecting Boreau away from me was a lie? Maybe. Maybe he was more involved in the revolutionary movement than he portrayed.

In any event, Rork and I would have to get under way quickly and try to find Doyle. But where? Earlier that evening, Rork and I had determined several potential places where the arms cache might be hidden. The salient factors we considered were depth of water, nearby land transport, and remoteness. As the carriage continued along the riverbank, I went over them in my mind. They would take days to check.

The driver pulled up at Ashley and Jackson streets in a squeal of brakes. The rude halt interrupted my concentration on Doyle, bringing me back to my surroundings. I followed the driver's gaze. Far icier than the air around me, a chilling dread overwhelmed me. Good God, what a fool I'd been—allowing myself to get drunk, losing track of time, letting my friend down.

The *Royal Victoria* was gone.

21

The Bluff

Thursday, 18 March 1886
Aboard the USRC Dix
Tampa Bay, Florida

The carriage driver snapped his reins and rolled the vehicle away. Standing there, I forced myself to be calm, to think like Rork. My watch said it was almost one in the morning. How long had Rork and the boat been gone? *Dix*—maybe her watch had seen something. Did Rork give them a message for me? I ran along up the riverbank shouting for the officer of the watch.

A lieutenant appeared at the revenue steamer's gangway along with a seaman, both clearly displeased by the drunk or lunatic bothering them so late at night. They left their relatively warm spot out of the wind and stood there, arms folded, glaring at me. Well, I must admit that bounding up the gangway, I *did* look like a lunatic, but there was no time for niceties.

I pulled my well-creased naval identity document from my wallet. Another folded paper was in there, the treasury warrant, but that was a last resort, for the captain's eyes only. I addressed the young officer as I thrust the paper into his hand.

"Lieutenant, I'm Commander Peter Wake, U.S. Navy. Sorry for the intrusion, but I urgently need to speak with Captain Fengar, right away."

"Lieutenant Grogan, third lieutenant of *Dix*, sir." He held my paper to the dim lantern, trying to read it and evaluate me at the same time. His face was pursed in thought. It is not a minor decision to rouse one's captain in the middle of the night while at dock. He sent the seaman below to notify both the executive officer and the captain.

"Lieutenant Grogan," I asked. "Did a man from the small sloop docked down the riverbank leave a message for me tonight? He was Sean Rork, a navy bosun. It would've been probably right after that fifty-foot cutter got under way this evening."

"No, sir, not on this watch." He opened the deck log. "Nothing in the log from the previous watch either, sir."

The seaman came back and reported that the captain was coming. I thought about Rork. No messages. That meant he got under way too quickly to leave me any indication of where they were headed.

"I'm Captain Fengar."

The captain was as I remembered him from several years earlier—taciturn, middle-aged, weathered from many years at sea. He scrutinized me while waiting for a reply. This would be difficult.

"Commander Peter Wake, U.S. Navy, Captain. I need to talk to you on a confidential matter immediately. Privately."

Fengar's brow furrowed. It was apparent he considered my presence an ill-omened event, but he muttered, "Follow me," and led the way aft to his cabin.

Once there, he sat behind his desk. I stood. "Captain Fengar, I am with the Office of Naval Intelligence, investigating the Cuban revolutionaries and the Spanish government agents that are operating along our coast."

Fengar made some sort of grumbling acknowledgment.

"I was here on a chartered sloop, the *Royal Victoria,* with a navy bosun, Sean Rork. This evening Don Vicente Martínez Ybor had me visit him ashore. I left Rork on the sloop, watching a man named Thomas Doyle, who had docked his fifty-foot cutter, no apparent name on the stern, just upriver from us. Doyle is suspected of dealing in stolen army weapons and transporting them to Cuban revolutionaries in the Keys. When I just returned from Ybor's house, both vessels were gone. Rork is probably following Doyle."

He wasn't impressed at all. "And?"

"I need your help."

"How?"

"I need you to take me in search for Doyle. I have some ideas of where he might have gone to pick up the weapons, which I have reason to believe are due to be handed over to the revolutionaries within days. When we find him, we'll also probably find the guns and my bosun."

Fengar leaned back. "Let me get this straight in my mind, Commander. You want me to turn this revenue cutter over to the navy to search for a smuggler of weapons on the coast of Florida? The enforcement of which applicable laws would, of course, come under United States Code fifty-eight, section six. From March of eighteen-seventeen, if I remember correctly."

As one would guess, I had no earthly idea of what law he was talking about, but I nodded and said, "Yes, sir." I was treading on thin ice as far as legal knowledge, but by the look in his eyes, I was sure of what was coming next. Fengar didn't disappoint me.

"Commander, don't you think you're a little confused? The United States Revenue Service patrols the coast for smugglers—not the United States Navy. You only come in when *we* ask you for assistance. And we haven't. Therefore, you have *no,* I repeat, *no,* jurisdiction here, *no* authority over me, and *no* damn sense at all in hopping aboard my ship in the middle of the night demanding I do anything for you or anybody else. Frankly, I find it surprising for a man of your rank and experience."

I sighed in exasperation. Fengar sounded like an ill-mannered echo of Captain Gaston of the *Powhatan*. But I had that other paper in my wallet now. It was time to use the last resort. I pulled out and unfolded the commissioning paper from the secretary of the treasury, the Revenue Service's cabinet-level boss, and handed it to him.

"No, Captain Fengar, I am afraid you are mistaken. You see, in addition to being a naval officer, I am also a commissioned treasury special agent, so I *do* have jurisdiction for these laws"— this next part was a pure, undiluted, ruse—"and authority over you."

When he'd completed his third examination of the paper, Fengar looked up at me. "This looks real. Why the hell didn't you tell me right away about it?"

I'd been hoping to keep it quiet for use as a last-ditch defense against whoever the Judas was. But Fengar deserved an answer. "Well, this is supposed to be a clandestine investigation. My commission is for last-resort use only. Yes, I know it's unusual."

"Unusual? It's pathetic. A navy commander, stumbling around the coast under sail, looking for gun-runners to Cuba? Why the hell did they send *you*?"

I could not tell him about the Judas, but I had to tell him something. "I've asked myself that question a lot lately. It's complicated, but maybe it's because I served on this coast during the war and now I live near Pine Island, on the coast by Fort Myers, so I know the area a bit." Fengar untensed a bit, nodding an acceptance of my reply. I was making headway. Maybe this could work out and he wouldn't have me thrown off his ship.

"Look, I'm not here to cause problems for you, Captain, but I have a navy man who is in danger, and a gun-runner who is picking up a cache of stolen army rifles. I need help and I need it right now."

Fengar nodded, then growled toward his cabin door. "Have the executive officer come in!" Seconds later, *Dix*'s executive officer, a Lieutenant Dobson, strolled in and stood at the revenue service's version of attention. "You called, sir?"

Fengar, as I was beginning to get used to, was brief. "Mr. Dobson, this is Commander Peter Wake, U.S.N. We are going to assist him for a while in tracking down some gun-runners. Call the liberty party ashore and make preparations to get under way as fast as possible."

Dobson, a tired middle-aged veteran of the U.S. Revenue Service who looked like he'd seen it all in his years, swiveled his head toward me then back to his captain, saying, "Aye, aye, sir." As Dobson left to rouse the engineering crew and get steam up, Fengar took a rolled chart from its bin overhead and spread it on his desk. "By the way, Commander, where is it that we're heading?"

I ran a finger along the coast from Tampa Bay to San Carlos Bay. "Several places, Captain. Just guesses, deduced by the actions of Doyle so far, and what we've heard. The first location is the head of Hillsborough Bay, where it comes closest to Ybor's new town. We also need to check a couple places in the Charlotte Harbor area. Then the Punta Rassa area."

"Yes, there's Cuban fishing smacks at all those places. But what about Sarasota Bay, Commander?"

"I didn't think Cuban fisherman were in there."

Fengar shook his head. "Occasionally they are, not often though. No, I was thinking about the remnants of the Sarasota Assassination Society, also known as the Sarasota Vigilance Committee. They might hook up with these fellas, just to bring in some cash. They're a little worn down since a bunch of them went to jail last year for those murders. You know about that?"

"Yes, sir. I know a little."

I did indeed know a little about the subject, but not much. One February morning back in 1885, while opening mail at my office at the Navy Department, one of my colleagues interrupted me and gleefully inquired if my home on Patricio Island was near Sarasota Bay. He then showed me an article in *The New York Times* from the day before, exposing the nefarious activities of a brazen gang of murderers running riot in the area of Sarasota village, in Manatee County. I remembered explaining that yes, I vaguely knew of them—everyone in southwest Florida had heard of the Assassination Society.

That, of course, was a fancy name given to a bunch of vigilante bushwhackers from the Sarasota area who'd threatened many, and killed several, men they didn't like during the past few years. Some of the crimes revolved around the victims being Republicans, the assassins being avowed Democrats who considered all Republicans as "land-grabbing nigger-lovers." Revenge, after twenty years of Republican rule, was the order of the day. The Republican postmaster of Sarasota had been killed, as was a man who had tried to warn him.

But not all the twenty-two hooligans who took the secret oath of the "Society" were your common thugs. Oh no, some of these boys were supposedly upstanding members of the frontier—farmers, store owners, ranchers—headed up by a physician, no less. The community, tired of years of bullying capped by two murders, with more promised, reacted strongly. In 1885, the leaders and half the followers, nine in all, had been rounded up by Manatee County Sheriff Watson, tried, and convicted of murder. Since then, the rest had laid low.

Hmm. I supposed it was a distant possibility. Very distant.

"I never thought of them, Captain. Where would the guns be hidden there? They'd need a road nearby if they brought them overland. Some place remote, but with deep water."

Fengar smiled for the first time. "The same place the Rebs used to get their Confederate secretary of state out of the area, back in the summer of sixty-five—Whitaker Bayou."

He did have a point. Yes, there was a trail leading down from

Tampa to that area. We could check on our way south. "We'll put it on the list, Captain. And thank you."

He grunted. "Hey, you've got that magic piece of paper, Wake. Never heard of such a thing, myself. But damned if they didn't go and make you a real, live treasury agent. So now you outrank me, you're in charge, and everything that happens from here on out is *your* responsibility. We'll be under way as soon as the boilers steam up. About fifteen minutes. Ol' *Dix* still's got some gumption—she can do about twelve or thirteen knots in calm water, with the current."

I tried not to show my relief at Fengar accepting my authority over him. The bluff worked. Now all we had to do was find Doyle, the guns, and my friend Rork.

22

The Search

Thursday, 18 March 1886
Aboard U.S. Revenue Service Cutter Dix
Along the middle west coast of Florida

The beach along the upper rim of Hillsborough Bay appeared empty of people and boats. We couldn't be sure about the people—it was three in the morning when we got there. But a landing party, led by me, searched the marshy area in the moonlight and found nothing. Not even footprints.

We departed for Sarasota Bay soon after, steaming through the starry night with the rising wind coming from aft. The patent log indicated thirteen knots as *Dix* began rolling downwind. I decided against checking the Manatee River, which opened off the southwestern part of the bay. Too many people lived there now. It wasn't remote enough. I hoped I was right.

The captain and I paced the bridge deck, which literally bridged the ship between the two side-wheel boxes and reverberated with the incessant smacking of their paddles. Fengar weighed the possibility of setting some sail for more speed, then thought better of it. Still, he cut every corner of the bay's channel as we charged out past Passage Key in the blustery pre-dawn, the wind now blowing a small gale and whipping our coats around us.

The shorelines of Anna Maria Island and Passage Key were pencil-thin black silhouettes as we steamed by. I started to think about Manatee River again. No, Rork and I thought the guns would be loaded farther south. I didn't tell Fengar of my doubts.

Captain Fengar surprised me by getting into the spirit of the chase. He seemed jovial as he yelled into my ear, "We'll catch 'em with this kind of help from the wind and tide. Sarasota Passage in a few hours. Whitaker Bayou thirty minutes after that."

He proved accurate. *Dix* rounded the curved sandbars at Sarasota Pass and pushed inside to the relatively calm water of the large bay of the same name. We arrived off Whitaker Bayou, three miles from the pass, at eight that morning. The sun was already warming the air as the wind died down and veered to the east.

The settlement of Sarasota, a loose assemblage of crude huts and framed homes along an attractive elevated shoreline of orange trees, was to our south. About two dozen people lived there. Several fishing vessels were anchored or under way near the settlement, but none were Rork's or Doyle's. The vast orderly lines of citrus groves and pineapple fields I surveyed in the binoculars belonged to the slain postmaster, Charles Abbe, the Society's last victim.

It was difficult to imagine the tranquil scene before me being the site of a foul murder just two years before, but rougher ways of life were common then on that coast. The place is different nowadays, but back then the most common description of Sarasota I remember was a head-shaking, "The Devil's in that soil." Mostly, a different kind of people live there these days. I say mostly, because there are still some remnants of that dark-hearted clan around to this day.

But back to the moment at hand. As *Dix* drifted a hundred

yards off the low bluffs at its mouth, I peered up the bayou. It was a narrowing creek that twisted its way into the pinelands and groves beyond. There was a dock of sorts on the south bank. No vessels, though. Fengar ordered a boat lowered and sent up the bayou. Upon returning, the coxswain reported they'd seen nothing substantial, but plenty of locals were watching. Another dead-end for the investigation. Minutes later, we were bound south across the large bay, bound for the pass and the Gulf of Mexico.

Standing there, looking forward over the bow, Fengar suddenly spun around to the portside, stepping back so he could see around me and the paddle box. Shielding his eyes against the morning sun, he squinted toward a small ketch that had all plain sail up, a quarter-mile away. She was close-hauled, headed up the bay, fighting the tide and the wind. I swung the glasses around, saw the name on the bow, calling it out, "*Phantom.*"

"Aha! I *thought* that was Hamlin! Bring her around to starboard and lay me alongside that ketch, Mr. Dobson."

Fengar had his own glasses out now and was waving to a brown-burned white man with a huge, floppy straw hat, sitting aft on the ketch. The man waved back lackadaisically. Fengar explained to me that the man sometimes favored him with information, a rarity in those parts.

"Ahoy there, Will Hamlin!" the revenue officer called out.

The man waved back again and luffed his sails, slowing the ketch. When we were alongside him, Fengar called down. "Good morning, Will. Hope all is well. Say, have you seen a boat called the *Royal Victoria* here last night or this morning? Or a strange cutter, about a thirty-tonner, no name on her?"

Hamlin didn't hesitate. "No, Cap'n. No strangers 'round here this morn but y'all. Watcha lookin' for 'em for?"

"Nothing much, Will. Just overdue at Key West. Have a good day, sir."

The captain leaned toward Dobson and gave him an order. We steamed onward, increasing our speed, but weren't headed for the pass anymore. Fengar whispered to me, "Hamlin's seen something, I can tell. But he's hiding it. Will's a good man, even testified against those assassin thugs in court, but even he won't be seen talking to a federal lawman in the open. It was too much to expect, I guess."

Fengar cocked an eyebrow and nodded to a smaller sloop also heading north in the bay. "But *this* fella coming up will. That's A. J. Adams's boat. He's the current judge for Manatee County and a former Union army major. He's also the commissioner for the federal courts in middle Florida and was the first to investigate the Assassins a couple of years ago."

We came alongside the sloop. Fengar was friendlier with this man than with Hamlin. Adams explained he was sailing his boat up the bay to the town of Manatee, by the river of the same name. Fengar introduced me—without my rank—and described the boats we were looking for. Notably, Adams didn't ask why, but he did regard me carefully. I presume he thought I was connected to Fengar in an official capacity.

He reported seeing no unusual vessels himself, however, his friend Peter Crocker had. Crocker'd told him, not an hour before *Dix*'s arrival, that he'd seen two strange vessels leaving the pass that morning at sunrise. Evidently, Crocker had been fishing near the pass the previous evening and had not seen them then, so he'd suggested to Adams they must have slipped in during the later hours of the night. He also told Adams that he heard Spanish coming from the larger boat and therefore had the impression they were *aguardiente* smugglers—rotgut rum from Cuba.

"Crocker's a good man. Spoke out and testified against those villains," Adams told us.

That meant the Assassination Society. So we now had third-hand information that vessels, probably Doyle and Rork, were two hours ahead of us. I hadn't made a mistake about the Manatee River. Relief flooded over me. But we needed more information.

When asked where Crocker was now, Adams said,

"Somewhere south of here, down near Osprey, I should think. He's gone home."

Osprey—ten miles away in the southern part of the bay. There was no time to track down the witness. We had to go, I told Fengar, but he had one more question.

"Judge Adams, you think the leftovers from the Assassination Society are mixed up in Cuban smuggling? Just to be ornery or make money, or something?"

"Well, hmm. Could be, Captain. They never did before, but some of 'em are just dumb enough to try it. *Aguardiente* and such? Yeah, they might try it."

That got me to thinking. I called out to Adams as the vessels drifted apart. "Do me favor, if you would, Judge. If you do hear of anything like that, then please send a telegram to me at the Russell House in Key West."

He glanced at Fengar, who said, "It'd help me if you did, A. J."

"Then if I hear of anything to do with Cubans, I'll do just that, gentlemen."

After thanking the judge, Fengar ordered *Dix* to head for the pass again. As she gathered speed, we discussed Crocker's information and did the applicable navigation: If the sailing vessels had departed Sarasota Pass at sunrise, two hours prior, with that fair wind and the ebb tide helping, they would be probably ten to fifteen miles away. We would have seen them if they had headed north toward Tampa, so they must be headed south. *Dix* could catch them in two hours.

My worry was growing for Rork. Obviously he was dogging Doyle, no longer trying to be covert. That had dangerous consequences. Two vessels making the passage from Tampa for Sarasota could be seen as coincidence. Both leaving Sarasota at the same time for the south would alarm Doyle.

And the Spanish speaker aboard the larger boat? We never noticed one with Doyle at Tampa. Was it the man Reyes referred to on Sugarloaf as Monterojo? Did they pick up the weapons at Sarasota? No, they couldn't have, I concluded. There wasn't enough time to load a thousand rifles. But they did have time to stop and pick up a man, a Spanish-speaker, someone important to their plan.

My heart was pounding as we dashed out Sarasota Pass at full speed and ran south, a quarter-mile off the line of white sandy beach stretching as far as the eye could see. Perhaps some of Rork's intuition was rubbing off on me. We were closing in, I was certain of it. Everything earlier that had seemed disjointed, unrelated, or just plain stupid was starting to come together.

There was one last area to search. The guns weren't at Tampa or Sarasota, and probably not at Punta Rassa—it was too crowded there, too. No, they were somewhere at Charlotte Harbor. But where?

Fengar knew the shoreline very well. We stayed close in to the beaches of the long, thin coastal islands; mile after mile of jade water, dazzling white sand, yellowish-green buttonwood trees, gray-trunked sabal palms, and dark green myrtle. For two long years during the war I'd patrolled for blockade-runners from Sarasota to Shark River and beyond. Just down from frigid New England then, the view of those beaches never tired me. A tropical paradise—a scene from one of my friend Pierre Loti's popular novels about the South Pacific. Usually the unending beach was tranquilizing for me. Now it just made me impatient.

Dix drew six feet, too much to actually enter the treacherously shallow passes south of Sarasota, but we got much farther inshore than I would've dared. We decided to err on the side of caution and examined each of the little passages along the thirty-eight miles between Sarasota Bay and Charlotte Harbor. Passing the gaps in the barrier islands slowly, we scanned the back-bays behind for any sign of Rork or Doyle. No vessels, no distant masts. Nothing.

I hadn't counted on those delays, so it was afternoon when we reached Boca Grande Passage, rounded the outer buoy, and chugged up the entrance to Charlotte Harbor, my home waters. Named after Queen Charlotte by surveyor Bernard Romans in 1774, it was almost an inland sea. Along the perimeter of that huge bay, twenty miles long and five wide, there were hundreds of islands, dozens of creeks, and two major rivers, the Peace and the Myakka, for Doyle to hide. From the war, and from living on Patricio, I knew the waters and shorelines of Charlotte Harbor very well. It was made for smugglers.

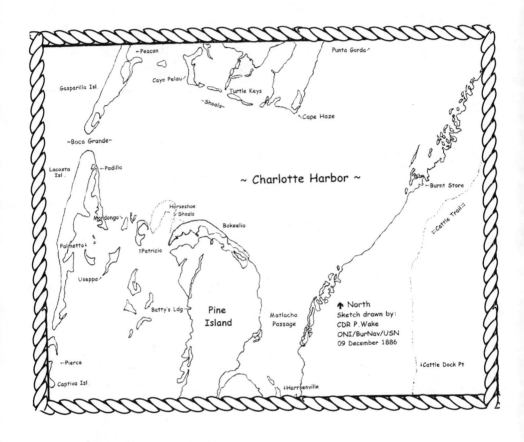

~ Charlotte Harbor ~

Gasparilla Isl.

←Peacon

Cayo Pelau

~Shoals~

Turtle Keys

Punta Gorda↗

~Cape Haze

~Boca Grande~

Lacosta Isl.

←Padilla

Mondongo↘

Horseshoe
↘Shoals

Bokeelia

Burnt Store

Palmetto↓

↑Patricio

~Cattle Trail~

Useppa↘

Batty's Ldg

Pine
Island

Matlacha
Passage

↑ North
Sketch drawn by:
CDR P. Wake
ONI/BurNav/USN
09 December 1886

←Pierce

Captiva Isl.

↑Harrsenville

↓Cattle Dock Pt

23

The Ambush

Thursday, 18 March 1886
Charlotte Harbor
Southwest Florida

We found Rork immediately, just east and south of Cayo Pelau. The *Royal Victoria* was aground on a small spit of sandbar coming down out of Turtle Bay. She had deep water all around, but had stuck hard. Rork, sitting on the cabin top, was smoldering when Fengar and I got to him in *Dix's* launch. He explained that Doyle left Tampa an hour after I'd headed off for my nighttime social call. I filled him in on what I'd learned from Ybor. Rork said that at the time, he too figured Doyle's departure was connected to my absence.

Rork sighed and gestured around *Royal Victoria*. "Aye, the bloody bastard got me by the bullocks, I'm ashamed to report, sir. He skirted the shoals here, close-hauled to the east an' up the bay. Doyle knows the water here like the Devil knows hell, that's for certain sure. I followed him two miles astern, shaved it a wee bit too close, an' ran her right up an' on this hunk o' sand—at low tide, thank you, Jesus. So I'll have her floatin' in an hour on the flood. Meanwhile, Doyle's up ahead there somewhere. Damn all."

"All right, what's done is done. It happens, Rork. Now, where did he stop on the way here?" I inquired. Rork's reply confirmed my suspicion about Doyle picking up the Spanish-speaker at Sarasota. It had been a brief stop, just long enough for a boat to row out to Doyle, who then sailed out of the bay, southbound, with Rork behind. From there on, Doyle knew he was being chased.

Fengar asked, "Where did you last see him here in Charlotte Harbor, Rork?"

"Headin' east from here, sir. Last sight o' him was at Cape Haze there. He rounded it to the north, so he must be farther up Charlotte Harbor. Aye, them guns're 'round here someplace. I can feel it in me right foot."

Fengar continued. "No other vessels near him? Not Peacon from Gasparilla Island, or Padilla from Lacosta?"

He was referring to fish camps. Captain Peacon's was a Key Wester—Conchies—camp. Pappy Padilla's camp, on the back side of Lacosta, was mostly Cuban. Both had been known to smuggle *aguardiente,* especially Pappy. Rork shook his head; no other vessels were seen.

I thought it over aloud. "Well, it looks like Doyle could be at Punta Gorda, or up the Myakka River, or up the Peace River."

Fengar nodded. "Most likely the Peace. It's deeper. Close to the road and railway at Fort Ogden."

Rork suggested the old landing at Burnt Store. "He could hide back o' those little islands an' take on some cargo through the shallows. That's what the Rebs did in the war."

There were only a few hours of light left in the day. I was concerned Doyle could slip out past us in the darkness. "Either way, there's not much time, so a decision has to be made. Captain

Fengar, please take *Dix* up to the top of Charlotte Harbor. Look into the mouth of the Myakka River, then look around Punta Gorda up the Peace River a bit. I'll stay here with Rork on the sloop, get her under way with the tide, and examine the islands and creeks down this way. He could be hiding behind them. Tomorrow morning at ten o'clock, let's rendezvous off Bokeelia, at the northern end of Pine Island. Agreed?"

"Very good, Commander. See you tomorrow, hopefully with this Doyle character and his stolen rifles in custody aboard *Dix*."

Dix had disappeared behind the point at Punta Gorda, fifteen miles to the north, by the time *Royal Victoria* got off the bar and sailed the three miles east to Cape Haze. Once at the cape, I decided to follow Rork's instinct, and we crossed Charlotte Harbor to the fringe of mangrove islands on the east side. Starting at the mouth of Matlacha Passage, east of Pine Island, we sailed north along the shore, scanning everywhere for a sign of Doyle. By early evening, we were approaching Burnt Store.

Burnt Store had a ramshackle jetty, a renovated version of the dock used at the beginning of the war to load cotton and turpentine on Robert Johnson's blockade-running schooners. There hadn't been a "store" there since Seminole chief Billy Bowlegs burned down the trading hut in 1849, in retaliation for drunken soldiers trampling his banana groves. In the thirty-seven years since, it had been just a dock with a path to the cattle trail a mile inland. That cattle trail, always a minor one, came down from Fort Ogden on the Peace River and was very seldom used lately. Most of the drovers used the main trail much farther inland, to the east. So Burnt Store sounded perfect for Doyle's purposes.

By the time we spotted her, I estimated the cutter had been there several hours.

Doyle may have been a fool ashore, but he was a wily

character afloat—young, yes, but evidently using tricks learned from the rebels who'd been in the war. His cutter was anchored in the shallows by the shoreline and behind two tiny islets that screened him from the main bay. Tree branches sprouted from his masthead, decorated the rigging, and hung down along the sides—breaking up the straight lines of spar and deck, blending it with the green jumble of mangroves around the vessel. Using the telescope, I swept over the area several times before the movement of a man on the deck attracted my eye.

The cutter was no doubt sitting on the bottom, especially with the heavy load being brought aboard. There were still several hours of flood tide to come, but even then it didn't add up. If there were ten rifles in each crate, that added up to more than a hundred fifty pounds per crate. For a thousand rifles that would be a hundred crates, with a weight of somewhere around seven *tons* or more. Could the cutter carry seven tons of cargo? Rork and I found that incredulous. Doyle must be doing the smuggling run in turns, perhaps three trips, I thought.

Upon confirming her, we immediately slacked sheets and bore off, sailing so our small forestays'l, the sole canvas set, would present only an edge-on aspect to a lookout ashore. That diminished our profile. We steered nor'westerly toward the opposite shore of the bay above Cape Haze, to have it behind us so we wouldn't be silhouetted against a sunset on the watery horizon below Cape Haze. My whole intent was to appear like we'd given up and were going away. After dark, we'd come back.

I remembered a few tricks from the war too.

We anchored a mile north of Cape Haze and waited. Five hundred feet behind us was the mangrove-jungled western shore of Charlotte Harbor. From the direction of Burnt Store, four miles away, we were practically invisible, but any vessel sailing out of there would be easy to see with the full moon rising in the east behind them. That bright silver light—*midnight, with the light of day* repeated itself in my mind—seemed to make the easterly wind even colder.

An hour after full tide, around eight o'clock, Rork said, "Damned if that ol' boyo ain't good." He handed me the telescope.

Doyle had surprised me so many times. Now he had again. Doyle had all seven tons of rifles, but not in the cutter's hull alone. She was towing three boats, flat-bottomed bateaus. All four vessels looked low in the water. Doyle was gambling—trading speed and safety for the slow exposure of a single run. He had the full mains'l, tops'l, forestays'l, and jib set. His sheets were eased and Doyle was going as fast as he could downwind. It was still slow—three, perhaps four knots. I predicted he'd sail out of the bay, through Boca Grande Passage into the Gulf, and south to the Keys. It was Friday night. By Sunday afternoon or evening, at the latest, he'd be at Sugarloaf Key.

I looked north, but there was no sign of *Dix*. She was up in the Peace River. We debated signaling her with gunfire, but figured our pistols wouldn't sound that far. Besides, she'd take several hours to return, during which Doyle could get under way.

Next, I reckoned the probable angle of intercepting Doyle near Cape Haze. About forty to fifty minutes for him to get there, at the most. We'd swoop down on him at six, seven knots, from our position a mile away from the cape. No need for us to get under way for another twenty. Plenty of time.

Royal Victoria had her forestays'l and mains'l set, jogging along fast on a broad reach toward the line of boats a mile ahead. At any second now they'd see our sail, but by then it would be too late. We'd surprise them. The odds were the two of us against the three or four of them. Acceptable.

Rork cocked an ear to leeward, then turned to me. "You hear that, sir? A steamer?"

Yes, I did hear something. A muted but rapid *thud-whoosh, thud-whoosh, thud-whoosh*. Barely perceptible in the wind. Waves on the shore, or an engine? Far too fast for surf. And it was getting louder. Yes, closer. Moving fast.

"Yes, that does sound like an engine. Could it somehow be *Dix*? Where away exactly do you hear it, Rork"

"Methinks from downwind, sir. From the west, well beyond Cape Haze, near Boca Grande. Nay, 'tis not *Dix*. She's well north o' us, by Punta Gorda."

"A coastal steamer, headed up Charlotte Harbor for Punta Gorda then?"

"Nay, methinks not. 'Taint a regular steamer, by that sound, sir. No local steamer is that fast. Gotta be somethin' else."

Doyle must've heard, or seen, it too. He altered course further south, no longer heading west for the pass and the Gulf. He was heading for Lacosta Island, south of the pass. The change in course gave him more speed. I deliberated setting the big flying jib to catch him close in and avoid a chase.

Rork grabbed my arm. "Doyle's comin' round! Well, how 'bout that? He's trying for the back channel."

That he was. The cutter was now sailing due south, toward Horseshoe Shoal, just west of Bokeelia on Pine Island. There was a shallow back channel at Horseshoe Shoal that led south into a broad swash channel between Pine Island and the smaller islands in the bay. I knew that channel well. It led to my home.

I couldn't believe it. Chased by something around Cape Haze we couldn't yet see, Doyle was heading straight for Patricio Island.

"Send up the jibs'l, Rork. I want to catch him before the shoals."

Fortunately, I made that decision too late. Before Rork made it forward to the halyards on the mast, we arrived at Cape Haze and were able to see what it was out to the west that had spooked Doyle.

The steamer was about fifty or sixty feet long, low profiled, and fast—very fast. Like nothing I'd seen on that coast or the Keys. No, she was definitely from out of the area. Her bow wave made a brilliant flash of white in the moonlight as she crested the small waves in the bay, the spray exploding into mist in the air. I estimated she was doing fifteen knots at least, probably more. Smoke poured out of a single-raked funnel. By the moon's illumination, I could see it was thick black smoke, blotting out the stars. That meant bituminous coal. Therefore, not from the South. The sound of the engine was now continuous—an ominous loud thudding, like an Indian war drum. She was headed straight for Doyle, a mile ahead of us.

Rork and I both saw the flashes on the steamer at the same time, spontaneously uttered together, "Oh, hell!" and ducked down. The bangs, there must have been about a dozen, came a second later across the wind and engine noise, sounding like children's pop guns. Flashes and bangs erupted from Doyle. Rifles.

Rork looked at me. "Revenue steamer?"

"No, the only one on this coast is *Dix*. That's somebody else."

"The Spanish? Boreau? I thought he was heading the wrong direction on a train?"

"Hell if I know, Rork. Anyway, they haven't seen us yet from the steamer. We'll tack away from them and watch what happens. Slack off the stays'l sheet and drop the main."

The steamer was almost on Doyle. But he was game, returning fire and continuing on for Horseshoe Shoal. By the flashes, I estimated six or more men aboard—his original three, the Spanish-speaker, and maybe some others picked up at Burnt Store. I was glad I hadn't blundered into trying to board them.

The steamer *was* boarding them, though, crashing into the side and blowing off steam in a screaming wail. It was followed by a rash of gunshots, pierced by two shrieks of pain. Deeper booms, shotguns, echoed from the steamer. The night air transmitted somebody swearing in Spanish. Then the shooting stopped. I heard a man with a south Florida twang proclaim, "They's all dead, Cap'n." Seconds later, we heard the sound of an axe chopping wood. Several axes. An angry shout in Spanish, "*¡Que próximo!*"–What next! "*¡Dése prisa!*"—Hurry up! More chopping. Splashing. It went on for several minutes, then nothing.

We stayed a mile away, back by Cape Haze, our sails down, drifting away to leeward, the northwest, staying bow onto the steamer. We dared not show ourselves, hoping instead to blend into the shoreline behind us.

The steamer's engine started up again with a belch of smoke and cinders, and then she edged off the cutter. In the telescope I could see the cutter's mast above the silhouette of Pine Island. It was listing heavily. None of the barges in tow were visible in the darkness. The mystery steamer picked up speed, westbound for Boca Grande Passage. Ten minutes later, it was gone from sight and sound. We raised sail and cautiously approached the cutter.

The blood covering his shirt was black in the moonlight. A large hole, blossomed by radiating tears, centered his forehead. Doyle's eyes were hooded in death, his mouth twisted into a leer, as if to show he didn't care. Beside Doyle, two bodies were draped across the cutter's deck, all of their torsos turned into bloody messes. The shotgun sounds we heard. Point-blank. Quick, effective. As if the rifle fire weren't enough.

The two other bodies were the original crew. But, based on the gunfire I'd seen coming from the boat, and the report of a Spanish-speaker aboard, there should've been more bodies than that. At least one or two, maybe more. Where were they? Did they fall overboard? Did the attackers kidnap them? Did they swim away?

Doyle's boat was awash and would be down in seconds. I sloshed into the flooded cabin with a lantern, looking for anything that would give me some sort of information. Water was rushing in from several holes in the hull. I could feel it flowing around my legs. There wasn't much room at all. Crates were stacked up to the deckhead, the same kind that I saw at Sugarloaf.

I found a crumpled copy of *Voz de Hatuey,* a Key West Cuban revolutionary propaganda piece, floating among the debris. I glanced at it quickly. Below the newspaper's masthead, dated a week earlier, most of the ink had run, and the text was illegible to me. Did it contain information important to Doyle? I didn't have time to ponder the question. Rork called down to get out, that she was going down now. Feeling her starting to sway to port, I climbed up to the deck and stepped off as she rolled over, then sank.

The men on the steamer had done an effective job of scuttling the barges and the cutter with the axes. I remembered from the war that it's harder than it looks to have the vessel go down rapidly, even one heavily laden. And they'd also destroyed the scene of their crime. No evidence of the attackers' identity was apparent. Except for one thing. A spent rifle shell, left on the deck near Doyle's body. It was in my pocket when I stepped away.

"Let's get out of here, Rork. Right now. We'll head for Patricio, where we can think this out before our rendezvous with *Dix* at Bokeelia."

I could tell he was stunned too. "Aye, aye, sir."

He got the main and forestays'l up, and in the moonlight we slid downwind across Horseshoe Shoal for our island, a few miles away. When I looked aft, there wasn't anything left to show that a battle had taken place. Just black water reflecting the moon.

I fished out the shell from my pocket and examined it while Rork held the lantern. My suspicions were verified as to the attackers. It was a reloaded brass .43-caliber cartridge—you could see two previous firing-pin strike marks on the base plate—and had the mark for Fabrica de Armas de Ovieda, the royal Spanish armory that manufactured rifles and ammunition in Spain. Standard issue. The Spanish army was known for reloading previously used cartridges. My hand holding the shell began trembling.

That steamer, the rifle shell. Evidence I couldn't ignore. The closest place I'd seen a fast steamer like that was Havana—the *Guardia Costa* of the Spanish colonial government. Everything was becoming obvious, pieces connecting together in a web. A web being pulled tighter and tighter by a man determined to hunt us down.

Boreau.

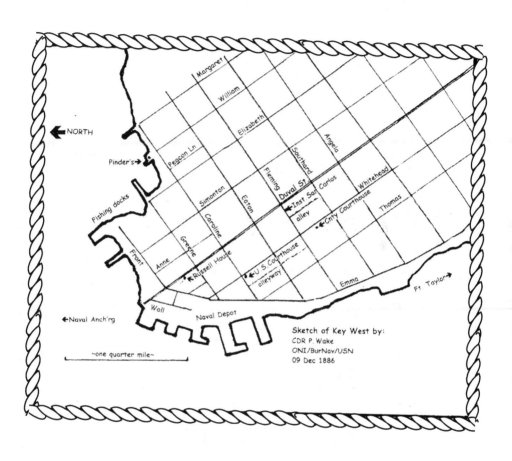

NORTH

Pinder's

Fishing docks

Margaret

William

Elizabeth

Pecon Ln

Simonton

Fleming

Southard

Angela

Duval St.

Inst San Carlos

alley

City Courthouse

Whitehead

Thomas

Caroline

Eaton

Anne

Greene

Russell House

Front

U.S. Courthouse
alleyway

Emma

Ft. Taylor

Naval Anch'rg

Wall

Naval Depot

~one quarter mile~

Sketch of Key West by:
CDR P. Wake
ONI/BurNav/USN
09 Dec 1886

24

Tree-Shaking Time

Saturday, 20 March 1886
Key West, Florida

As *Dix* approached the Customs House dock, I saw that part of the fleet was in. The two tired big boys of the Atlantic Squadron, *Tennessee* and Gaston's *Powhatan,* lay on their hooks just off the town of Key West, their worn teak decks covered over by sun-faded canvas awnings from bow to stern. Both needed new paint, their hulls showing various shades of blanched wood and brown rust.

The weather was abnormal—usually March and April were the windiest months, but that day Key West was in the doldrums. From the warships' stern staffs, the red, white, and blue of the national ensigns drooped as if exhausted by the heat and despondency. Rear Admiral Jouett's command pennant hung like laundry from *Tennessee's* main mast. It was as if the air itself had been suffocated at Key West, replaced by a threatening vaporous presence. Had it been August, I would've predicted a hurricane was coming. My general sense of unease intensified.

Around each warship, launches and cutters swung on their moorings from the boat booms. By the waterfront, the officers' barge headed away from the navy depot wharf for *Tennessee*. It was hot already at eight in the morning. Few figures in navy white were moving about the decks, and those that were went slowly. No smoke issued from the stacks. The ships were motionless that Monday morning, baking in the sun.

By contrast, in the near distance, a three-masted, schooner-rigged steam yacht, glistening and energetic-looking even at anchor, was a beehive of activity and color. The paid crew, splendid in red jerseys and blue trousers, were setting out deck chairs and readying a launch, which, by its livery, was apparently the tender to the ship. And what a ship. The yacht's canvas was snow white, the masts raked at a jaunty angle, the varnished wood of the long deckhouse gleamed in the sunlight. I could hear the lilt of women chattering gaily as they descended into the launch, evidently for an excursion ashore.

Fengar saw me mesmerized. "There's that famous yacht of Mr. Gould's. She's called *Atalanta*. Two hundred and thirty-two feet on deck. Crew of fifty-two."

He chuckled at my apparent ignorance.

"That would be Jay Gould, Commander, the famous New York City financier. You've read about him, I'm sure. He's the one that young crusading politician went after for corrupting New York judges a few months back. Did the judge in pretty good, and damn near got Gould, too. Gould even got blackballed by the New York Yacht Club for his shady dealings, but he just went off and founded his own new club. Money talks, my friend."

Oh, of course, *that* Gould. Yes, I did know the story and one of the men involved. It was the same crusader who'd gotten me roped into all of this—none other than Theodore Roosevelt.

Gould and Roosevelt's hatred for each other was well known and great fodder for the press.

"I wonder why he's down here?" I asked.

"Pleasure voyage to escape the cold up north. Took her to the Med for the winter back in eighty-three, but Florida's a lot closer. Yep, he's down here to relax, and probably also to check on what Flagler and Plant are doing with their railroads and such. *Atalanta* was here when I left for Tampa. Gould fishes during the day, parties at night. I think he may be due to depart soon. Getting too danged hot for him around here. He'll be heading back up north now."

"That lifestyle's way beyond me," I said.

"Richest of the rich. It's beyond all of us. That ship's more modern than anything we've got in the revenue service."

As we nosed *Dix* into the naval depot pier, I thought about the mission's strange turns. What a change—from the abject terror of the gun battle to this languid place, all in the space of the last forty-eight hours.

The morning following the attack, Rork and I sailed *Royal Victoria* from Patricio Island to the rendezvous with *Dix* off Bokeelia. Briefing an astounded Fengar on what had happened, I announced that Key West was our next step. He asked whether we should drag the bottom and try to recover the guns, but I determined that there was no time for that now. It could be done in a few days, but for now *Dix* would take Rork and I, towing *Royal Victoria*, back to the center of this entire mess—Key West. Fengar acknowledged my decision, and I could see his mind at work, wondering what would happen next—gun battles with smugglers were rare. So far, I'd managed to liven up *Dix*'s existence.

Once we were secured at the navy dock, Rork cast off *Royal Victoria* and sailed her around to Pinder's store. He had with him a sizable amount of coin to procure Pinder's good will. I didn't envy him that duty. Rork's second mission was to take passage to Punta Rassa on the packet schooner and bring the *Nancy Ann* to Key West. Future efforts were likely to revolve around the Keys, and we wanted our own vessel handy. I figured he'd be back in four days, maybe five.

Meanwhile, I thanked Fengar, released him from assisting me any further, and went ashore. The first stop was the Russell House to obtain a room and check on messages. As I walked the two blocks to the hotel, I heard rhythmic shouting coming from the harbor. Altering course to the foot of Duval Street, I searched for the source of the sounds and groaned when I saw it. Around me townspeople were shaking their heads in disbelief.

Incredibly, in that mind-numbing heat, it was a boat race. The admiral, or somebody high up, was making boat crews from *Tennessee* and *Powhatan* row a race for the pleasure of the officers seated on the decks, and probably for Mr. Gould and his ladies in the launch. Stupid. Perhaps mortal, in that heat. I was glad to be out of uniform at that moment.

At the hotel, the third-floor corner room was available. There were three separate messages, dated from within the week, from a man named Dort, asking for a meeting with me, with no reason given. I'd never heard of him, didn't understand the lack of explanation, and found it more than slightly disturbing to have some new factor to deal with.

His last message read:

255

Mr. Wake,
I hope this note finds you well. I've been trying to get
together with you on a matter of mutual interest, but
you've been out of town. If you get this in time, could
you please go to the Russell House bar, at 7 o'clock on
this Saturday evening, the 20th? There you will find
an invitation in your name to a social event that I
am attending. We can meet once you enter the party.
Regretfully, my schedule precludes me from meeting
you earlier. I am affiliated with your new position,
and have greetings from up north.
                                        W. Dort

My new position? Did he mean treasury agent or man on
the run? And who the hell was Dort? He just might be a Spanish
provocateur, trying to lure me out. I put Dort's notes aside and
read the one from Useppa, which had been at the front desk for
a week.

Daddy and Uncle Sean,
Please see me when you get in. Time to pray again,
for a miracle is what's needed. Things aren't what
they used to be.
                        Love from Useppa

More riddles. And from my own daughter. God help me, but
I was sorely tired of silly riddles. I wrote a note to her for the hotel
messenger boy to deliver. It was simple—*Meet me for breakfast at*
six A.M. tomorrow at the hotel. Father

The last message was a telegram form. Expecting something
from Washington, I didn't recognize the name at first—then it
struck me.

TO: P. WAKE/ RUSSELL HOUSE HOTEL/ KEY
WEST FLA
FROM: AJA/MANATEE FLA
XX—RUMOR SAYS EXSOCTY UNK WHO
MET W FST STMR ON 19 APR—X—LEFT
EARLY EVE AND BACK LATE SAME NITE—
X—NO MORE INFO—XX

The day after we'd met with Judge A. J. Adams, a fast steamer
had been at Sarasota to pick up a former assassination society
man, then returned him late that night? The same fast steamer as
the one in Charlotte Harbor? The timing was correct.

I suddenly realized that I'd gotten it completely wrong at
Sarasota Bay. Former members of the Sarasota Assassination Society
weren't helping the revolutionaries get guns out of Florida—they
were helping Boreau kill people inside Florida! It was the perfect
solution for the Spanish agent. He stayed at a distance and let
American criminals, with known violent pasts, do his dirty work
for him. Damn, why didn't I think of that earlier?

But how did they know where Doyle would be? Another
revelation suddenly came to me. Somehow, those local boys had
a spy in the revolutionaries' Sarasota connection, someone who'd
found out what the Spanish-speaking man knew—where Doyle
was to find the rifles hidden. Maybe one of them was part of the
delivery crew that'd brought the crates down to southwest Florida.
Or had heard somebody talking.

So now I could piece it together better: the Guardia Costa got
word by telegraph message to send the fast steamer to Sarasota and
pick up the final information of where to go, along with a coastal
guide—I remembered hearing that Florida accent after the shots
ended. The Spanish steamer then arrived at Charlotte Harbor in
time to eliminate both the shipment and the rebel gun-runners
themselves. Afterward, the Spanish returned the local man to
Sarasota, probably with the promise of more well-paid work in

the future, and finally made their way back to Havana at fifteen knots or more.

I did the arithmetic—at that speed, it would've taken about nineteen hours or so from Sarasota to Cuba. They would've been back at the Arsenal docks in Havana by five in the afternoon the day after the attack. Total length of steaming time would be approximately fifty hours, the high speed necessitating a lot of coal per hour, probably two to three hundred pounds at least, for a total of five to six tons. The steamer must've been filled to the main deck with coal.

It was an audacious gamble on the part of Colonel Marrón, but wickedly brilliant. It made me wonder how many other times they had dashed in, eliminated revolutionary enterprises, and disappeared back to Cuba in a flurry of foam and spray. And how was the spy in the federal government helping them?

For decades, the Russell House was not only the best eatery and hotel in Key West, it was also the most popular locale for family gatherings, business meetings, and society balls. Thus, when I entered the bar at seven that evening to obtain my reserved invitation, courtesy of the enigmatic Mr. Dort, I wasn't surprised to see a poster announcing that the main room was closed for a private function—Mr. Gould, of New York City, was having a soirée at seven, by invitation only. I further learned that a chosen few would be invited to *Atalanta* for late-night moonlit cognac. It was, the poster advertised, *Atalanta's* last night at Key West, before they departed for Charleston and points north.

A final sip of rum and I departed the bar, armed with my invitation, making my way toward an uncommon sound in Key West—a string quartet playing Beethoven in the main room of the Russell House Hotel. I walked into the artificial perfumed gaiety of people pretending to be what they weren't—important on a grand scale—so they could meet a man who was, Mr. Gould.

There were ladies with coiffed hair and bosoms draped in pastel satin. Dandified gents in black and white, along with a sprinkling of naval officers' blue and gold, provided a sea of color—each privately wilting under the heat but trying their best not to show it. Those productions always disgust me, but I wasn't there for them. I was there to meet Mr. Dort, and see what his part in this unfolding tragedy was to be. It didn't take long.

"Mr. Wake, I presume? I am William Dort. Very nice to meet you, sir." He spoke loudly, above the music and the noise of a hundred people talking but not listening. Then his tone dropped considerably and he winked. "Mr. Daniel Manning gave me a piece of paper like yours, so we're colleagues. Mine's signed by Grover, too. We get them renewed with each incoming boss. In my shop, only Mr. M. and I know of your efforts. I've already talked to your Mr. Walker up north and I stopped by today to say hello to Fengar down here. He mentioned you being aboard. Both gentlemen spoke well of you."

Daniel Manning was the secretary of the treasury. Grover would be President Grover Cleveland. Which made Dort, unlike my temporary status, a *real* special agent for the treasury department.

He allowed me a second to assimilate the information, then said quietly, "I understand you've had a rough time lately. We're working on similar things. We need to find a place to talk."

In an alcove near the back corner, he showed me his commission papers. Then he spoke and I listened. Ten days earlier he'd received a cable to contact me and had been trying since. His purpose was to brief me with recent intelligence, and also take back to Washington what I'd found out.

He was in the Keys for another purpose also—an investigation into the activities of one Jeptha Vining Harris. The Spanish government, in the person of the local consul, Joaquin Torroja, was accusing Harris of violating U.S. neutrality laws by assisting

Cuban revolutionaries in sending guns to Cuba. Dort had been in Key West for a month, at first covertly, but for the last two weeks openly in society, trying to gain intelligence.

My mind flashed instantly to Useppa and her involvement—did Dort know?

Two waiters stopped and stood nearby, so we walked into the main room, standing by the quartet. Dort added with a bemused smile that both of the main actors of his investigation were present at Gould's party, not twenty feet away. He indicated with a nod Harris and Torroja to me. It wasn't hard to find them. They were conversing pleasantly by a window, with none other than the man of the hour, Jay Gould. I recognized him from the newspapers.

All three were of the same age—mid-fifties; each had the same attire—expensive white satin and black silk; and each spoke in the same tone—confidence. Their conversation looked animated but not heated. I resolved to get closer to engage Torroja in talk, but Dort turned my attention back to him, asking me what I'd learned so far.

I passed along the basics of what I knew about the revolutionaries' endeavors in Havana, Key West, and Tampa—minus a certain young lady. I also told him about Boreau, whom he'd already heard about.

Dort took it all in, nodded, and said, "Thanks. Here's what I've got for you. Spanish government activity in the U.S. has gotten more brazen lately. There was a murder of a Cuban revolutionary in New York last month—most likely by Spanish agents. Spanish gunboats—the *Sanchez* and *Magallanes*—are now patrolling just off the Keys and have been spotted up the Florida Gulf coast, intercepting Cuban fishing smacks heading to and from Cuba. They've also hired Allan Pinkerton's company to spy on the rebels and provide security for Spanish diplomats. He's mostly operating in New York."

That last surprised me. "Pinkerton, Grant's secret service fellow during the war? I thought he died."

"The very same. And, yes, he did die two years ago. Poor fellow slipped on the sidewalk in Chicago and bit his tongue. It got infected and killed him. Talk about a bad way to go. But his company is alive and well, and their services don't come cheap."

"So what about Harris? Is he involved with the rebels?"

Dort wagged his head in a so-so gesture. "Yes. No. He has close friendships with the exiled Cubans, but social interaction isn't a criminal offense. I don't think he's dumb enough to be running guns himself, and certainly don't have enough to charge him with specifically violating any law. Your information about his place at Sugarloaf supports what I've heard, but it's not conclusive. I need to show he *intentionally participates.*"

Dort added, "By the way, for what it's worth, I found out he has several dozen acres of land near Fort Myers. Not sure where, but I think it's north of a Caloosahatchee River and south of some place called Punta Gorda. Also heard mention that there's a man named Monterojo in that area who's involved with the Cuban rebels, but I don't have any more on him. And I think Harris also has some land over near the old Fort Dallas, at the mouth of the Miami River.

"Harris has decided to step down anyway, so my investigation is a moot point. Fellow named Livingston Bethel is going to replace him on April first."

More pieces of the puzzle. Dort's description of Harris's land up on the Gulf coast placed it in the general vicinity of Burnt Store. A useful, hidden way-station for supplies to be covertly taken south to the Keys and Cuba. And the mystery man Monterojo was known to be in the Fort Myers area. The Spanish-speaker? The man who led Doyle to the stash of rifles at Burnt Store? Things were coming together. What about the Judas, though? Some questions formed in my mind.

"Say, do you know if Torroja is friendly with any federal officials here? Anyone who might be helping him with inside information?"

"Not that I know of. Most folks are polite, but not overly friendly to Torroja."

I noticed Dort didn't use the word Judas, so I assumed he hadn't been let in on the riddle, or maybe even that part of the mission. I asked if Torroja ever associated openly with Boreau in public and was told no. Boreau came and went quietly.

"What about Hubbs, the Spanish consul in Tampa? Any word that he used to pass information along to the Spanish when he worked in customs down here? Really friendly with the Spanish?"

Dort's surprise showed. "Hubbs? No, he's not the disloyal type at all. He was professional with the Spanish consul, but I've heard nothing else."

"Mr. Dort, I've got this feeling that something's going to happen soon," I said. "Not sure when or where, but this is escalating on both sides."

"Yes, I think you're right. Unfortunately, I'm due back in Washington. I only stayed to get your opinion so I can pass it along. Tomorrow I'm gone, so you'll be alone here until your friend Rork gets back."

He paused, taking in a breath, thinking about something. "Tell you what—I have a local man who's helped me out, and will contact you if he hears anything. He'll leave a message at the hotel for you—from Mr. Ferro. That is not his real name. No sense in him trying to reach me twelve hundred miles away, not when you're right here."

"Thank you," I said, noting that Dort didn't tell me how to find Ferro, only the other way around.

"Good luck. Please watch yourself. So what're you going to do next?"

"Shake some trees, Mr. Dort. Right now, over there."

As I've described earlier, occasionally I lose all patience, self-discipline, and subtlety. Frustration gets the best of me. I've discovered that when that time comes for me, I either make a bad situation horrific, or I gain insight as to how to solve the situation. Well, I'd reached that point. I walked toward the trio of men by the window.

Ignoring the two Americans, I stepped close to the consul of the empire of Spain, where I could gauge the resulting effect on him, and said, "Good evening, *Señor* Torroja. Why exactly are you trying to kill me?"

25

Información Importante

More than a week later, while watching an alleyway at the dreary hour of three o'clock in the morning, I still found it entertaining to reflect back on the various reactions to my inquiry of the Spanish consul. Gould's upper-class lower jaw dropped as he cleared his throat repeatedly. Harris turned to the window, trying unsuccessfully to hide a grin. And my target? Torroja appeared baffled by my inquiry, his eyes showing confusion, but no indignation about the blatant allegation. I thought that significant. Oh yes, Torroja knew about Marrón, Boreau, et al. He just wasn't sure who I was.

He made some hemming and hawing sounds until I finally said, "Oh, I'm sorry. Did you think I meant *literally?* No, no. I meant my business. You Spanish are killing my business of cattle shipping to Cuba from Florida. The import taxes are exorbitant.

Well, I just wanted to let you know that, and now I bid you a good night, sir."

Then I walked away from them. The reader will notice that I omitted my name, for understandable reasons. What I didn't notice, however, was that Captain Gustavius G. Gaston was standing in all his glory a mere fifteen feet away. Seconds later, in his gruff and unfortunately loud manner, my former reluctant sea-going chauffer blurted out what I had just concealed.

"Is that you, Commander *Wake?* What in tarnation are you doing still *here?* And don't you *ever* wear your uniform?" He shook his head in aversion to my presence. "Are you *spying* here these days, or just lollygagging away from your desk politics in Washington?"

Torroja, Gould, and Harris each gave me another once over, this time in far more detail. Well, so much for my identity. Concerning Gaston, one cannot walk, and never run, away from a superior officer—not in front of others, at least—so I had to turn and use the single excuse available by naval custom to leave his presence without permission.

"I'm on leave, sir. And now, I must beg your leave, for I really *must* find the head around here."

The subsequent week was spent in frustration. Fengar took *Dix* out to sea on patrol of the east coast of Florida. Rork had gone to fetch the *Nancy Ann* and was late returning. Dort, my only reinforcement left, embarked aboard a steamer the next day for the north, to present a brief outline of his investigation and my progress, or lack thereof. My own detailed report would be forthcoming.

In the meantime, I'd received no message from Dort's informant, Ferro. My attempts at watching the Spanish consul and discovering whom he might be linked to locally had been frustrating and fruitless. No word had reached me regarding Boreau and whether he had been aboard that attacking steamer, or whether he was still chasing aimlessly after me in northern Florida. It was nine days alone, contemplating my failures, and my superiors' response.

But the most devastating part of that time was the fateful meeting with my daughter. Useppa adamantly refused to leave Key West and Raul, using some hateful language I'd not heard from her before.

"Stop it right now, Daddy. Just stop trying to run my life, like you always run everyone else's. I'm not in the navy and you are *not* my commanding officer. I love Raul and I love what we are trying to do together—bring freedom for all the people of Cuba. So stop harassing me about it. Please go back up north and leave us alone."

Her eyes held real contempt for me. She was seething with anger. When did I lose her? I walked away, not trusting myself to say anything, not really even knowing *what* to say. Three times I walked back toward the church to try to patch it up, but each time the memory of those eyes stopped me and I turned around. I hoped she'd cool off given time. I hadn't seen her since.

The only tangible result of that period were two long, handwritten reports documenting my failure—one on each aspect of the mission—which I kept in a safe-deposit box at the hotel. In three more days, on April first, I would be sending an encrypted telegram with the overview to Commodore Walker, then I'd catch a steamer and begin the journey northward to hand over the written reports in person. I still hadn't included anything about Useppa's role.

Three more days to figure it out, and there I was, reduced to watching Torroja's house in the dark hours of morning. He lived on the south side of the town, out by the Catholic convent on Division Street. I rubbed my eyes awake for the tenth time and lifted my head over the trash barrel I was behind to check the rear of the home. No sounds, not even a stirring of tree branches. The only smells were the garbage in the barrel and horse droppings in the alley. The moon was nearly gone, just a sliver now, so there was little light. I scanned the scene, but I saw nothing, again.

It was the fifth morning when I'd gotten up early to satisfy an intuition that Boreau would contact Torroja. I *knew* he would, that he had to. Events were churning, and his consul must be kept apprised, if for no other reason than to use the diplomatic communication route to his superior in Havana. Boreau wouldn't chance an office visit, the telegraph, or the mail within Florida. No, it would have to be in person somehow. That left either a secret location to drop off and pick up messages, or a personal meeting away from public sight. Since I was known to both of them, I couldn't trail them around town in an effort to spot a drop site—that left covertly watching the house. Distant odds, yes, but that was exactly what I was down to. A dispiriting state of affairs.

I stretched my aching muscles—I was getting far too old for this sort of thing—and lay back down, massaging my right knee. Mulling over what to do next, I heard a dog bark from inside the house. It was hesitant at first, an inquisitive yipping. Then the dog grew resolute, growling continually. Looking over the top of the barrel, I saw movement outside, a dark form by the house's back stoop. I strained to see.

The form was short and bowlegged.

It was Boreau.

Near him was another man, not so visible. They waited until the back door opened slightly and Torroja's voice queried softly, "*¿Quién es? ¿Señor Boreau? ¿Blanco?*"

I slithered closer inch by inch, moving behind a bougainvillea bush, the thorns cutting the skin of my left hand as it parted them. Who was that second man?

Boreau answered the Spanish consul. "*Sí, señor, es Boreau y Blanco. Tenemos información nueva. Es muy importante, acerca los rebeldes y sus planes.*"

So the second man's name was Blanco. And they had new information, important information, about the rebels and their plans.

Torroja beckoned them inside. "*Entonces vengan, señores.*"

As Blanco entered the doorway, I caught a fleeting glimpse of him. It was enough. Tall and thin, with long black hair. He was the man I'd seen at Ybor City stalking Doyle and his companion, "Smith." He was the killer.

I didn't dare creep closer to the house to eavesdrop with that watchdog of Torroja's. Instead, I stayed put and waited. Five agonizing hours later, after the sun had risen, Torroja left his house for work, but Boreau and Blanco remained. People began walking around the town and I was forced to vacate my observation post, lest I be seen. Ever so carefully, I stretched my cramped legs and began the long walk back to my room, staggering like a bum. No matter, for I now had more names, connections, and locations. I was getting somewhere. The new information was entered in the report.

Rork docked the *Nancy Ann* at the fishermen's docks at five that afternoon and met me at the hotel shortly thereafter, explaining his tardiness in a disgusted tone. His passage up—he decided to take the monthly coastal steamer to get there faster—had been lengthened by a boiler failure, which caused them to drift for days until another steamer happened along and took them in tow. His troubles weren't through. The voyage back on *Nancy Ann* had been in light to no wind, taking five hot days. To put it mildly,

Rork was not in a good mood.

We sat at the corner table in the Russell House bar and drank the hotel's dwindling stock of Matusalem. I filled him in on the latest and asked if he'd heard any talk up the coast about the gun battle in Charlotte Harbor. He said that yes, people heard the sounds, but that no one was a witness. The rumor among the islanders? A personal fight between drunken Cuban rum smugglers.

I asked his opinion on what to do next. It was simple. Keep doing what I'd been doing. But now Rork could expand our efforts. He said he'd watch the rebels while I watched the Spanish. Rork was right, of course, but it meant more twenty-hour days. My right knee and lower back ached at the thought.

He asked about Useppa. I told him what had happened and that I hadn't seen her since our argument. I told him my worry was growing. Obviously, the rebels were planning something soon. The evidence was clear: Reyes's and Doyle's efforts to get the guns to Cuba; Useppa's overhearing about Hatuey as a rallying point soon; and Boreau's comment at Torroja's back door. She was in danger from the Spanish and we had to sail her out of Key West, but I couldn't get her to believe it.

Rork volunteered to give it a try, adding, "If that lass don't listen to logic an' the best wishes o' her father an' uncle—why then, the only thing left to do is kidnap her an' sail her to Patricio Island, trussed up like Thanksgivin's turkey."

26

Hatuey Lives . . .

Wednesday, 31 March 1886
Key West, Florida

Useppa rejected Rork too. At breakfast he told me about their meeting an hour before, at sunrise, when he'd caught her on the street by the Methodist church.

"Oh, she was listenin' just as nice as you please, Peter. But the moment, the very *moment,* I said, 'Well darlin', there's nary more to say—you've got to go,' the lass went into a tirade about me not understandin' that she was a grown woman an' all o' that. Aye, me friend, Useppa's got more than just a wee bit o' her mother's distant Irish temper. Told me to mind me own *damn business.* Yes, sir, an' that's exactly *how* she said it too."

Rork shook his head. "I'm not pleased, not one little bit. Dear ol' Reverend Raul's got her committed to the rebel cause o' Cuba, lock, stock, an' great big barrel. Why, she's more devoted than the bishop o' Kerry."

"So we'll have to use force to get her away," I moaned.

"Bound an' trussed, no doubt," he sighed.

I took a breath for strength. "Tomorrow then, on her way to school," I said, dreading it more than anything in my life.

My plan, which sounds sadly inadequate now, was to send the ciphered telegram message to Walker early the next morning, then take—I still couldn't use the word *kidnap*—Useppa to the *Nancy Ann* and depart for Patricio Island.

But as I had become tiredly used to, my plan fell apart. It started to come undone when I found a note slipped under the hotel door that morning, after Rork and I'd returned from breakfast.

Southard and Whitehead, in two hours.

I didn't know when it was put there, but guessed no more than thirty minutes earlier. It was nine o'clock in the morning by that point, and would take a few minutes to walk to that location. Rork agreed we should go, with him in the lead by five minutes, to scout out the area, just on the off-chance it was an ambush for me by Boreau or his henchmen.

I stood on the southwest corner, near the café Walker and I had lunch at. Rork sat in line of sight on a bench by the courthouse, a block away to the north. I loitered, trying not to look like I was waiting for somebody.

A little Negro boy came up to me several minutes later, announced shyly that he was Cedric, and handed me a note. He said a man had given it to him, showed me the penny paid him, and added that no reply was needed. I immediately asked the boy where the man was who gave him the note. Cedric spun around and proudly pointed west, across Jackson Square, where the county courthouse and jail were located. But there was no one there. He looked surprised, afraid he'd get in trouble for fibbing, but I patted his head and said, "No problem, and by the way—what did that man look like?"

Cedric said that he was a white man, old like me, with gray hair and wearing a tie and coat. That was all he could remember, so I gave him a penny too, and told him to run along. Then I read the note.

Innocent lives are about to be lost—I think tonight. I find out more later today on when and where. I will let you know at your room. Act fast when I tell you. F

"F" . . . Ferro.

I walked over to Rork and sat down, showing him the note. He thought it could be a ruse to keep us in the hotel room. I asked him, by which side? Either side, was his answer. He thought that F must be a veteran in the art of intrigue—for he'd been extremely careful to conceal his true identity, and probably now knew both of our faces.

The "innocent lives" part bothered me. It was an eerie echo of Roosevelt's message, but I remembered Marrón knew of that message, so he could've inserted that in this note to get our attention. But why would they, any of them, want us to stay in our hotel room? Rork suggested it was to keep us from following people, or to tether us to a locale so they could kill us more easily. Then there was the option that didn't occur to us straightaway—that it was a legitimate note of warning. We discounted that instantly, naturally. Jaded attitudes are an occupational hazard.

Rork and I ended up returning to the hotel room to wait. Each of us sat with a shotgun in our hands—he covered the door, I took the window. For hours we sat there, deliberating our situation in whispers, prepared as well as we could be for either another note or an attack upon our lives.

Thankfully, I can report it turned out to be the former. At five that afternoon, a paper slid under the door. Immediately, we heard someone of small stature run down the hallway stairs. Rork dashed out in full but fruitless pursuit, raising a racket far in excess of his result. By the time he got back empty-handed, I'd read the missive, noting the common characteristics with its predecessors. All three notes were in the same hand—a clear male cursive—and fluent in English, concise to the point of urgency and lack of time to write it. Given what we'd learned over the last month, this one was ominous.

Hatuey will be reborn at 2 A.M. It all starts then. But they will make sure it will die then and there. They know about all of you. This is all I can give you—they will kill me too if they find out I know. F

Rork sat on his bed, reading the note. I spoke first, thinking aloud while pacing, as I'm prone to do when trying to deduce a thorny issue. My friend is well used to that and he let me ramble on.

"Well, to begin with, Rork, this appears to be a warning that the catalyst for the new uprising in Cuba will be tonight, or more precisely, tomorrow morning—at two A.M. on Thursday, April first. Secondly, that Hatuey will be used as the rallying cry for a new declaration of independence, as we heard from Useppa. Thirdly, the opposition to the uprising knows about it and will stop it right there. A preemptive attack, as it were. Fourthly, that the opposition knows about us. Fifthly, if 'F'—who we presume is Ferro, an alias assigned to him by Dort—is found by the opposition to have this information, they will kill him. Am I correct so far?"

"Right as the Pope, sir. So may we assume the buggers in opposition to the Hatuey uprising, the ones doin' the killin', would be Boreau and company?"

"Yes, I think that is logical."

"An' the location of this big event?"

A couple places came to mind, but only one was the most likely. "Rebel headquarters. That means Instituto San Carlos. I would imagine there would probably be some sort of a revolutionary committee meeting to finalize the declaration prior to releasing it to the press tomorrow. The senior leadership, gathered to give their final approval."

Rork agreed. "Aye, them Spanish could catch 'em all in one spot. Do you think Máximo Gómez and Antonio Maceo will be there?"

"Could very well be; however, we've no indication they're here on the island. But those Spanish agents would certainly like it if they were, wouldn't they? A chance to kill the leaders. Yes, Rork—tonight is definitely the night. A preemptive raid to stop a proclamation that would rally all of Cuba. Incredibly dangerous if the Spanish are caught doing this on American soil. Huge consequences. But they must feel it's worth it."

It *was* amazing. "Think of it, Rork. A *Grito de Hatuey* would be even more powerful than the *Grito de Yara* back in sixty-eight. It would inflame the passions of all the people of the island in a way that nothing has before. It took the Spanish ten years to defeat them after the *Grito de Yara*, and even then they damn near failed. This time the revolutionaries would have modern weaponry and supplies, the symbolic specter of Hatuey as a rallying cry, and perhaps simultaneous attacks on Spanish targets . . ."

"Aye, 'twould be overwhelmin' an' bloody. Followed with a bit o' Old Testament revenge afterward."

"Quite so. This all adds up with everything we've heard to date."

Rork frowned in thought. "Then a good question is—who is this lad 'F' who's givin' us this stuff? An' more important, *why* is he tellin' us this?" He shook his head. "Hmm. You know what's in me mind on this?"

"Sean, your mind is a wondrous place, but I seldom can penetrate its workings. Please save me the effort."

He cocked his eyebrow and did a half-bow. "I'll take that as a compliment o' me Irish gifts. Methinks our Mr. F ain't no Cubano at all. Remember, your impression from Dort was that he'd not met his Ferro in person. They'd just passed notes. The notes we got were written by an Anglo, an American Anglo—'tis too natural in the appearance o' the words for a foreigner, certainly for a dago."

"All right, I'll accede to that. The name Ferro is an alias of ethnicity. Then who is he?"

"The only American who might know the dagos' plans, sir. Ferro is the Judas, o' course. Who else would know this information?"

He took advantage of my reaction to press his point. "Think on it, Peter. He arranged us to get the note near the county's courthouse at Jackson Square, courtesy o' little Cedric. The boy described him as a white man in a suit—old like *you*. So he's a courthouse man. Nobody else wears suits here."

Rork held up two fingers, before continuing. "But there are two courthouses in Key West, an' the Spanish wouldn't need a spy at the county courthouse, would they? No, they need one in the federal system, the one that deals with foreigners an' customs cases an' the laws that go after smugglers an' foreign revolutionaries. Probably a clerk o' somethin' like that.

"Aye, we've been thinkin' the spy's a senior man, but methinks we're wrong. 'Tis probably a low-level man. The sort that senior government people don't pay attention to, but that handle the messages and reports an' such—jus' the kind o' spy the dagos would need an' use for their own ends."

That was logical, but one part of Rork's explanation was losing me. "But we got the note at the county courthouse, not the federal one down near the waterfront."

"*Exactly*, sir. He did it to conceal his identity. The federal court is in that big buildin' at Whitehead and Caroline, three blocks to the north o' where we were. Ah, but we forgot the alley, now didn't we? The alley behind the federal courthouse heads south the three blocks to Jackson Square. The informant could head out o' his office, nip down the alley, give the boy the note, an' be back up the alley in his office, in three shakes o' a trollop's bottom. An' the beautiful part is that it makes it look like the little devil's from the Jackson Square area. But he ain't. Oh, quite a fancy brilliant one, our man 'F' is. Aye, methinks he's got some

Irish in him, for sure."

Damn. Why hadn't I come up with that? "I think you're onto something, Rork. But why give Dort any information, and send *us* these notes, if he's really working for the Spanish?"

"Simple. The lad's had a change o' heart. Back in Ireland, sometimes the local stool pigeons for the English army would regret their actions an' beg forgiveness o' the rebels. They couldn't stand the blood o' their neighbors on their hands, an' then'd come cryin' to the lads to warn o' a comin' raid or arrest. Maybe our boy Ferro realizes what's about to happen an' doesn't want Key West blood on his hands. He's reached his limit o' sellin' his soul an' his honor."

"That makes sense. So now what?"

"Aye, indeed. We need to ponder that a bit. A wrong move now . . ."

"First, we get Useppa out," I said.

"Right. That we must," he agreed.

"Second, do we warn the rebels? I say yes."

"Well, 'twould be a violation o' orders, o' course, by taking sides. 'Tis not our fight, sir. That's what some'd say up in Washington." Rork loved to play devil's advocate and take the official position in a quandary, usually in a mocking tone.

He saw my look. "But, o' course, I say bollocks to that notion! 'Tis the right thing to do to warn the rebels, an' I've no doubts on that. Let's save some lives."

"Agreed. And there's a third thing for us to do. Surveil the place tonight, and see who is in the Spanish gang when they show up. I want to know who our personal enemies are and what they look like."

"Brilliant idea, sir. An' I've just thought o' a fourth. We find little Cedric early in the morn, walk him 'round the courthouses, an' get him to point out the man who gave him the note. That way we find out who Ferro is, an' where he works. If he works at the federal courthouse, then me wager's on him as the Judas."

"Right, very good idea, Sean. You're in rare form today."

"Oh, well, jus' doin' me job, sir."

"All right, it's almost six o'clock. Let's invite Useppa to dinner and go from there. I'll tell her I'm sorry and want to put the past in the past. At dinner we'll figure out a way to get her to stay away from her boyfriend and his pals tonight, but meet us in the morning, after we send the telegram and find Judas."

My melancholy had dissipated, as it does when action presents itself. Time was advancing rapidly and we had a lot to do. What we faced would require not only our wits, but stamina too.

27

Terror

Useppa was gone. We checked the Methodist church and rectory, St. Peter's African Episcopal Church, the Douglass School, the regular white Episcopal church. Nothing. We asked the local ministers, the church caretakers, and the other schoolteacher who worked with my daughter. No one had seen Useppa in two days. They also hadn't seen Raul Leon or Martín Lefavre, didn't even know if they were on the island. Rork, who we hoped was less well known by the various local factions, went to the Instituto San Carlos to see if she was there. He banged on the door, calling for her. No one answered. No light shone through the window. The door was locked.

We retraced our route, asking everyone again. Still nothing. By this time I had all the Key West ministers frantic as well. They began walking around, asking for Useppa. Reverend Sparks of the Methodist church, who'd been out of town during that first evening with Raul Leon, confided in me that he thought Useppa was becoming obsessed with the young preacher. Everyone knew Leon's cause and most supported it, but Sparks shared my concern regarding the young man and Useppa. I couldn't get him to go further in his description of their relationship, delicacy intervening on both our parts, but he did say he doubted that they eloped. That didn't make me feel better—for it was the last benign reason I could think of for her disappearance.

By eleven that night, all logical explanations for her disappearance had been examined and disproved. We went to the county sheriff's office at the jail on Whitehead and reported Useppa missing, rousing Sheriff Demeritt himself out of bed. Yes, he knew Useppa, he said. Practically everyone on the island did, and she was well liked and appreciated for her work with black children. No, he had not a clue as to what might have happened, except to say that crime against ladies was rare. He knew there were Cuban rebels on the island, but didn't think they would hurt Useppa. She was known to be their friend. Neither did he think the Spanish would do anything to her.

He suggested that perhaps she had gone sailing with friends downwind to the Marquesas Islands for a picnic and couldn't get back as fast, now that the breeze had piped up. The sheriff's attempt to calm me didn't work. Panic set in.

Rork and I sat on the steps of the jail. The pitch-black night had a kinetic feel to it. Nervous, portentous. Fear can heighten the senses, and mine were fully alert. I mentally registered the weather, which was changing. The static doldrums were over; a storm was coming. It was still far away, but the velocity of the southerly wind told me the storm would be bad when it arrived in two, maybe three days. Clouds were starting to come in from the south, riding a rising wind that brushed against the laurel and fig trees, making their limbs sway above us.

We sat there silently until Rork said, "I say we stop at Russell

House an' check for messages from everyone who's out lookin' for the lass, then we need to put our minds at work, Peter. We need to start watchin' the Cuban club. Sooner or later, somethin' will happen tonight. It might provide us answers."

He was right, but it seemed so . . . so *wrong* to stop searching for my daughter. There was one more place I knew to look. I didn't think she'd be there, but wanted to intimidate the man into understanding that my daughter had better be safe or he would have an assassin going after *him*—and it would be me.

I didn't know the whereabouts of Boreau or Blanco or the rest of them. But I did know where their boss would be. Rork shook his head when I told him what we were going to do. He said he thought it would probably be counterproductive at that point and surely come back to bite us later.

Then he said he'd be right next to me.

The dog began growling even before I got to the front porch. Rork was out back, in my previous lair, next to the barrel of trash, in case anyone tried to abscond. No one did.

I pounded on the door, even giving my name, demanding it be opened. Neighbors' lamps went on in response to my incessant clamor, but there was no light from within, no sounds of movement except for the enraged dog, who clawed at the front door to get at me. Torroja wasn't at his home. What did *that* mean?

We walked back downtown and looked in the windows of the darkened Spanish consulate on Duval Street. No sign of anyone, just a forlorn gesture, really. Around us, Key West was sleeping on a Wednesday night. We made one last check at the hotel desk. No messages. Rork checked the room for any notes, then came downstairs shaking his head. We left the Russell House, each carrying a sack with a shotgun within. They were our navy-issued Winchester .10-gauge double-barrels. Rork brought them back from Patricio with him on board *Nancy Ann.*

Heading south on Duval, I noticed how deserted and shabby it appeared at that time of night. Tired, really—the whole place looked tired. Or maybe it was my own weariness. The increasing wind accentuated the sad impression. At Fleming Street, we turned right, bound for the club of the Cuban revolutionaries, Instituto San Carlos.

It was well after midnight when I settled into a position behind the Cuban social club. After making sure that Boreau's previous surveillance spot was unoccupied, I moved halfway down the alley and found a secluded corner several doors down on the east side. I sat behind a barrel of food slops, of all things, where I could see the club's rear door. Rork took the west side of the building, behind the latticework fence I had originally used, where he could watch the front door and still vaguely see my position in back.

In the gloom, my mind was frenzied as I went over and over my last words with Useppa. I sat there beside the rotting garbage, the worst images invading my mind, sinking me deeper into despair over what I'd done, and not done, to cause this.

I'd failed at it all. I hadn't warned the rebels they would be killed. I hadn't identified the Judas. I hadn't stayed covert. I hadn't discovered Doyle's depth of involvement with the revolutionaries. Or the full extent of the revolutionaries' Florida network. Or Boreau's organization in the U.S., for that matter. Nothing was working correctly, and it looked like it might get worse. Manifestly the most important of all, I hadn't gotten Useppa out of Key West to safety. My daughter was in mortal danger, and I didn't even know where she was.

I sat there in the dark, beneath palms rattling in the building breeze, drowning in terror.

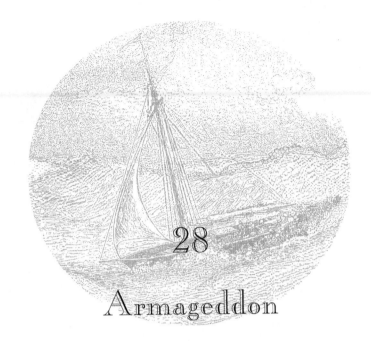

28

Armageddon

Thursday, 1 April 1886
Instituto San Carlos
Fleming Street, east of Duval
Key West, Florida

I held the pocket watch close to my face. The hands showed two A.M., the time indicated in the note. But around me nothing was happening. I heard an owl coo, the sounds blending with that hot southerly wind, then heard it again. Rork had chosen an ironic signal, for in Cuba the coo of an owl is a bad omen, a sign to be wary.

I could barely see him as he gestured to a rear window on the second floor overlooking the alleyway. A lamp was being turned up. I gestured back to him—*anyone at the front?* He shook his head. Then I saw it, out of the corner of my right eye. A light came on in the little café in the alley, next to the Instituto San Carlos. It was opposite Rork's post. More light glowing in the café now, showing through several windows. The sound of Cuban-accented Spanish voices—men greeting each other, accompanied by laughter—came from the lit windows. I waved to Rork and pointed toward the café. He saw it too. The Instituto San Carlos, except for the light in the upstairs window, was still dormant, but men were up and about at the café.

Rork darted quickly behind a gumbo-limbo tree, crossed the lane so that he was under the shadow of the Instituto San Carlos, then crept along a bougainvillea hedge. Duck-walking, he made his way past my spot and got closer to the café. Moments later he sprinted over to me and whispered, "Nary a soul's gone in the Cuban club from front o' back, but there's men in the café on the other side of the club. A party, by the sounds o' the buggers. They must've come in the café's door on the east side. Can't see it from me position."

"Maybe the rebel meeting's in the café?" I said, keeping my voice low too.

"Want me to scout it out further, sir?"

I nodded yes and Rork darted behind various boxes and bushes up the alley to where he could see the far side of the café. He disappeared behind a wall, and seconds later I saw him back in the alley, motioning hurriedly for me to join him. Just as I arrived, he turned around and pointed down the alley, beyond my last location. His eyes were blazing with intensity.

"Look, they're coming," he whispered hoarsely.

Moving slowly from the Southward Street end, through the shadowy murk of the alley, were figures carrying long objects. I counted out six of them, staying to each side and away from the open ground in the middle. Their movements were furtive, heads swiveling in vigilance from flank to flank. Professionals. Men that had done this before, a combat patrol in enemy territory. They were led by a man in front who pointed at the light in the window of the Cubans' club. The leader was only a blacker form in the inky dark, but even then I instinctively knew him from his lopsided gait. Boreau.

Rork nudged me and swung his head toward the café, then held up five fingers. Five men were inside. He put his mouth to my ear and whispered, "I . . . saw . . . Raul . . . and . . . Lieutenant Reyes . . . in . . . there. Talking . . . about . . . Hatuey."

Rork isn't fluent in Spanish. I'm not either, but mine is better than his.

"Stay here, Rork. I'll get close and listen in. You watch *them*." I pointed down the alley toward the approaching Spanish. He nodded and withdrew his shotgun from the sack. Boreau and his men were still a hundred feet or more away, slowing their advance. It looked like I might have two or three minutes.

"Just before Boreau gets here," I whispered, "I'll warn the revolutionaries, and we'll get out of here. But I want to hear as much of what they're saying as I can."

The window shades were pulled down, but the door to the café was slightly ajar. Creeping closer, I got down and crawled forward on the planked porch, so I could peer around the doorway into the café at floor level, the less likely to be seen. I was able to observe about half the interior.

Inside, four men sat around a table listening to Lieutenant Reyes, who was attired in formal civilian clothes, speaking somberly. Two large lamps, one on the table and another in the corner, gave off a yellowish light. A small bottle of cheap-looking rum with a red rooster on the label was on the table. An amber-filled glass sat before each man. Raul was there in clerical black, the white collar stark against the background. He gesticulated to Reyes, agreeing with him on a point of discussion. The other three, all dressed well, I didn't recognize. Generals Gómez and Maceo weren't there. With profound relief, I saw that Useppa wasn't at the meeting, either.

The oldest man in the room, distinguished looking, with a trimmed white beard, said something about the Spanish viceroy of Cuba. It was a joke, eliciting a round of laughter. Another man, his face grim, said something about a declaration, pointing to a pile of papers. Then he held up a document from the pile. It was elongated mustard-colored parchment, with calligraphied writing covering it. The man added something about the quality of the paper, that it would last a long time. Then he paused a moment and murmured word *posteridad.* Posterity. Everyone nodded solemnly.

Reyes glanced at his watch and motioned for silence. Standing up, he began speaking. I concentrated on translating what he was saying. Fortunately, he spoke slowly, giving a military-style briefing, which I could understand more easily than the usual rapid Cuban lingo. I murmured his words in English to myself, to better memorize them for inclusion in my report later.

"Gentlemen, it is now ten minutes beyond two o'clock, on this first day of April, a day that will be remembered forever by our countrymen. And so, we must begin. All of our military and civil forces are ready and waiting. As soon as our telegrams proclaiming the Grito de Hatuey declaration of independence go out later tonight at eleven o'clock, General Antonio Maceo, General José Maceo, and General Flor Crombet will strike their respective targets across the island.

"Four hundred copies of the declaration were printed here at Key West, and secured in this café during the last twenty-four hours for safekeeping, since we know that the Spanish tried to break into the club last week. These copies will be taken by steamer to Havana later this morning and disseminated across Cuba tonight—after the attacks at eleven—for public posting tomorrow in all the major cities and towns."

The older man asked, *"Are you sure the Spanish don't know?"*

"To the best of my knowledge they do not, sir. We have kept this as secret as we can, but to be sure, we cannot let down our vigilance in these final hours. These copies of the Grito de Hatuey must be protected, for if the Spanish hear of our plans, they will disrupt them. The patriot generals are waiting for the telegraph announcement at

eight o'clock tonight to attack the Spanish occupation troops. If we find our plans are compromised, the telegrams will not go out and there will be no uprising." Reyes pulled out a watch. *"We have only a little more than twenty hours to go until eleven o'clock and the uprising that will end the subjugation of our people."*

The old man swallowed some rum and shook his head. When he spoke, it came out in a doubtful tone, almost accusatory. *"But Boreau has been spotted back here in Key West, Lieutenant. The Spanish bastard has been very successful lately—killing our associates, attacking our arms shipment. We lost a thousand rifles in that attack, Lieutenant. I have a feeling he is getting far too close for us to proceed."*

Reyes nodded his acknowledgment. *"Well, sir, our friends in Tampa did their best to divert Boreau—he was after a yanqui friend of Martí's up there—but unfortunately that diversion did not last long. Yes, you are correct, he has returned to Key West. And, yes, we have had setbacks."* Reyes spread his arms and glanced around the room. *"For you other gentlemen who do not know, let me explain. Boreau had one of his people, Ramon Blanco, kill our American contact up in Ybor, then used local Florida outlaws to kill Doyle and his crew and sink the weapons at Charlotte Harbor. We know that because one of our people got away from the attack by swimming ashore and sent us a telegram from Fort Myers.*

"And now we have word both Boreau and Blanco are here in Key West. But we do not think they know about the Grito de Hatuey, certainly not about the timing. If they did, they wouldn't have waited this long to prevent it. So yes, let us never forget that Boreau is a very dangerous man. However, only twenty hours of continued vigilance, my friends—twenty hours—and we will be victorious. Our people will overwhelm the Spanish completely and Cuba will be free. By that time, Boreau will be far too late to stop anything. Less than a day, and revenge will be ours."

I let out a breath and willed myself to stay calm, not believing my luck. So Vicente Ybor really *did* send Boreau on a false trail to save my life. And the Spanish *did* use the remnants of the Sarasota assassins to attack Doyle. This was an incredible intelligence coup—and I was hearing it all from insiders.

Remembering my resolution, I was about to intrude and warn them of Boreau's attack force coming up the alley, but I decided to wait just a few seconds longer when I saw Reverend Raul Leon lean forward on the table and ask, *"What about the Yateras Indians in Oriente? Does General Gómez have confidence that they will renounce their work as scouts for the Spanish army and finally join us when they hear of the declaration in Hatuey's name? They are, after all, the descendents of Hatuey. The guajiro peasants will follow their lead."*

Fascinated, I wanted to hear Reyes' answer, but felt Rork jabbing me in the arm, pulling me back from the doorway. We crouched by an unhitched wagon, where he said under his breath. "Boreau's almost to us! Let's warn the rebels an' get the hell out o' here!"

He was right, of course, damn it all. We'd run out of time.

"Agreed, Rork. I'll approach the meeting, you stay here and watch Boreau."

No need for stealth now, so I stood up on the porch. I was about to enter when I heard Rork howl in anguish, "No! Useppa— don't come out!"

Baaooooom!

Shotguns barraged at once in the alley—their thunderous blasts blotting out all other sound, stunning me. Everything happened instantaneously as I spun around to face the danger. To my left, by the corner of the café, Rork was already moving. He fired one barrel of his shotgun down the alley in reflex, then fired the other toward targets I couldn't see from my position. Inside the café, the men scrambled out the door. Raul was in the lead. I saw the table and a chair go over, heard glass break, and caught a glimpse of lamp oil gushing across the floor, erupting into a wave of flame.

I ran to Rork and yelled, "Where's Useppa?" but he couldn't hear me in the din.

Gunfire, shouting, cries of pain—the alley filled with sound. Rounding the rear corner of the café, I fumbled with the damned lever on the shotgun, and got ready to fire. I couldn't see Useppa in the alley, but a woman's scream oriented me toward the Instituto. She was at the back door of the club, slamming it shut. A man holding a shotgun was trying to open it. I fired from the hip and he jackknifed, crumpling into a squirming heap.

More shots—pistol fire from Boreau's men. The gun flashes made fleeting tableaus around me: Rork leaning over a crate, shooting deliberately as he balanced his pistol on the fake hand, marking the targets. Reyes firing his revolver rapidly. Raul running in front of me, hysterically shouting for Useppa.

The tall form of Blanco appeared before me, near the social club's door. I swung the barrel and tracked him, firing at the same moment he did. My blast hit him from fifteen feet, plowing the buckshot into his gut, knocking him back and down. A brief wave of ecstasy went through me when I realized he'd missed me, incredible at that range. I threw down the emptied shotgun, no time to reload now, and drew my Colt.

Pulling at the back door, I found it locked. Calling to Rork, I headed for the club's front door on Fleming Street. I had to get my daughter away from this.

Suddenly, the shooting stopped. The night went from pandemonium to deathly quiet in an instant, except for the wind and a crackling noise. Boreau was retreating, limping away for his life toward Southard Street, three others with him, one of them swearing in Spanish. Rork stood in the alley, covering us from a counter-attack with his reloaded shotgun.

I called out for Useppa, shrieking for her.

"Daddy, I'm up here."

She was in the second floor window, the one I'd seen with the dim light earlier.

"Honey, are you okay? I'm coming in to get you. Go to the front door."

Rork staggered over to me, his eyes wide. "Get her out quick—look! It's spreadin' too bloody fast to fight."

I followed his gaze behind us at the café and saw what he meant. The crackling noise I'd heard seconds earlier was fire consuming wood. Rapidly spreading fire. Every window in the café was glowing like a giant, evil living thing, flames reaching out, the wind curling them far into the alley. A whoosh came from the roof as it collapsed, sending a huge cloud of red hot embers flying across the neighboring roofs. Firelight instantaneously flooded the alley, crazy shadows dancing everywhere, and I saw the carnage clearly for the first time. Two of Boreau's men lay on the ground, lifeless piles, oozing gore from their massive shotgun wounds. No one survives a full hit from that weapon at close range.

Beside them lay two other bodies. Lieutenant Reyes still held his revolver, the top break opened to reload fresh cartridges. His face was set in grisly determination, a young patriot who'd gained the poignant distinction of being the first man to die in the latest Cuban war for independence.

Stepping over Reyes and seeing the body next to him, I suddenly realized Blanco's shotgun hadn't been aimed at me. Raul Leon's hand was outstretched toward the back door of the club, his eyes plaintively staring up in death, searching for my daughter. The blood-spattered white clerical collar was undone. I had the illogical urge to straighten it, but Rork's second shout brought me to reality.

He was already running around to the front of the building, screaming now. I couldn't make out his words. Above me, the San Carlos was on fire, the roof engulfed and upper walls jetting smoke out of their seams. It was all going up in flames.

I started running for the front, but I was stopped abruptly by pain—for I couldn't breathe. A solid sheet of flame, spirited by the breeze, literally bridged the alley over my head to the houses on the other side. I felt it suck the very air out of the alley. It seemed that in mere seconds, everywhere around me was on fire. The sound of wood being *eaten* by the blaze was overwhelming. I'd never heard fire so deafening.

There were other sounds now. Church bells clanging, people shouting, horses screaming. Inhabitants were dashing out of their homes to join others in the street, pointing at the fire and sobbing. I slowed down, doubling over with a searing agony in my lungs. My skin felt like it had an instantaneous sunburn. Then it started cooking. "Oh God!" came out of my mouth as I watched my skin *cooking* before my very eyes. Smoke eddied up from my sleeves, to be borne away on the wind. No, it wasn't my skin burning, it was my clothing.

I kept walking, each step more sluggish from the pain, along the side of the club toward Fleming Street. Toward my daughter and my friend. I saw them standing in the middle of Fleming Street. Useppa was weeping but safe, held up by Rork.

Rork shouted angrily at me. I was taking too long.

The fire crossed the street over me to the boarding house. Embers filled the night sky—red glowing dots everywhere. Time slowed, my mind ridiculously reporting to me that the whole thing, from Rork's warning to Useppa, until now, must've only taken maybe five minutes, but in that brief period *everything* was changed. When I reached them, I understood for the first time what Rork'd been screaming at me.

The air is on fire!—we were in a firestorm.

Key West had become Armageddon.

29

Tears through the Ash

Thursday, 1 April 1886
Caroline Street fishing docks
Key West, Florida

Black mucous dripped from our nostrils and lips, and we coughed and gagged our way to Duval Street, then followed the crowd instinctually heading north toward the waterfront, five blocks away. Someone threw a bucket of water on me, dousing the wisps of smoke from my coat.

At Front Street, we turned and ran east to the fishing docks. I say ran, but the chaos was such that no one could run. Flaming debris—shingles, intricate trim pieces, fabric from walls and furniture—flew above us, propelled by that evil wind. People poured out onto the streets, watching with stunned horror the parade of flames soaring along the rooftops faster than a man could run.

Increased by the heat of the fire, the wind became a force in and of itself, sucking the flames up into it, expanding the blaze to new areas, devouring the city. Like a great caldron, smoke and flames shot up, roiling in luminescent copper-colored clouds across the island. Giant banks of chokingly thick black smoke blotted out the stars and rolled along the streets.

A few town constables and some sailors from the fleet were shouting orders on Duval Street, where Greene intersects, but no one paid them any attention. Desperate cries of *How? Why?* were everywhere. The church bells rang incessantly, long past alerting everyone, now calling out in pain, as if Key West were begging God for help.

Houses, cigar factories, stores, warehouses, churches—*everything*—was going up in flames. First they smoldered, then openly smoked, then abruptly burst into fire as we ran by. Entire blocks of the tinder-dry town, which hadn't seen rain for weeks, were alight within twenty minutes. I found out later that the hulls of ships in the harbor blistered from the heat radiating from the town. Sails and rigging smoldered until doused by sailors hauling buckets of water up the masts.

When we arrived where *Nancy Ann* was docked among the fishing smacks, we found her covered in ash. Some of the shops on Front Street were already smoking. Useppa was almost catatonic and even I, for some reason I still cannot fully fathom, was strangely slow witted, nearly insensible, even as I knew what should be done. I allowed Rork to take the lead, stumbling along meekly in his path. It must have been the seared lungs that did it, robbing me of my strength. The scene was beyond comprehension then, and description now. As I sit at my desk, nine years later, I can still feel those flames, hear the screams, smell the overpowering odor of burning wood.

Nancy Ann was tied up outboard of three fishing smacks.

Their crews were trying to get under way amid a desperate chorus alternating between cursing the fire and begging for God's mercy. We clambered across them to get to our sloop, my energy draining with every leap, and I damned near didn't make it.

Once aboard, I cast off the boom lashings, my fingers fumbling with the knots, taking twice as long as usual. Then I moved to the tiller while Rork hauled on the halyard. Useppa got the forestays'l and jib ready. Around us, dozens of fishermen were doing the same, colliding as they got under way, turning their terror into anger at each other. They worked with one eye on the blazing wall of doom advancing toward the docks. It was only three streets away now, consuming buildings like a Jules Verne monster, spitting them out in huge flares of glowing debris as it roared toward the water.

From the harbor nearby I heard, "Wake, by God in thunder! What are you doing?"

I turned to see who'd beckoned me. I shouldn't have—it was Gaston, in the sternsheets of *Powhatan's* launch. The ship's other boats were astern of him, all of them crammed full of bluejackets rowing madly for shore.

"Answer me, man! What are you doing, Commander Wake?"

There was no time for the full explanation, so I croaked out, "Saving my family's life, Captain!"

Gaston shook his head in disgust, then pointedly ignored me as his launch slid past us in the other direction—toward the fire. At the seawall he leaped ashore, calling out to his sailors, "Follow me, men! Get those pumps over there. Form the bucket line from the water's edge."

My heart sank even lower. Rork got the mains'l up and drawing, set Useppa to work dowsing it with water lest the embers light the canvas, then came aft to me at the tiller.

"Forget him, sir. He doesn't know we're protectin' Useppa from Boreau as much as from the bloody fire. No tellin' what

Boreau'd do if he caught any o' us ashore now."

"Yes," was all I managed to say in return. I was so tired, arms and legs alive with pain as I steered through the mass of fishing and navy boats. We hit several, fended off others. The firelight was so intense that even the harbor was lit up. A quarter-mile from shore glowing strips of wood still wafted on the wind, like a summer fireworks celebration. Up forward, Useppa, her dress in tatters, threw more water on the sail. She looked unlike I'd ever seen her, old and weak, moving by rote. I'd seen men look that way after a battle. The body still worked, but the mind was blanked out, numb.

"How is she?" I asked Rork. He said he'd quickly told her about Raul when she'd gotten out of the building, so she knew of her loss. I'd not had time to talk to her during our escape.

"She's busy now. It'll hit her later."

"We'll sail directly for Patricio." My voice was distant, small.

Nancy Ann picked up speed, sailing downwind around the edge of Frankfort Bank for Northwest Channel. Useppa sat on the cabin top by the mast, staring with lifeless eyes to the town behind us, the fire reflecting in her eyes. I turned to see the whole of Key West alight, from near Fort Taylor all the way to the fishing docks we'd just escaped. Plumes of fire whooshed up here and there as a taller structure succumbed. From the distance it didn't look real, or even possible. A painting of a famous battle, set to life.

"My God, Rork, did we really do that?"

"*No,* not us—Boreau an' his friggin' bunch o' cutthroats are responsible. They did the attack. That oil lamp . . ."

I tried to think. "We've got to get Useppa away from this. Must ride this wind while it's fair for sailing north. This is the front side of a nor'wester and it'll veer onto our nose pretty soon."

I felt Rork's right hand on my shoulder. "Aye, aye, sir. I'll send up the mains'l with a reef. An' after that, I'll spell ye a while on that tiller. Useppa needs to put some jelly on those burns o' yours afore it gets worse."

My arms and face felt odd, a tingling sensation mixing with the heat of the burns. Movement of my head caused the skin of my face to spasm. "Yes. You're right, Rork."

Though I felt weak, the pain wouldn't let me doze off, jerking me wide awake as I strained to steer down the waves. Useppa came aft with a jar of sea grape jelly from the cabin and held my hand as it gripped the tiller. Tears streamed down her face, making rivulets through the coating of ash, her eyes pleading as she pried my fingers off the wood.

"Daddy, let me help you."

Rork sat down heavily on the deck next to me and took over steering.

"I'll give ye an hour, Peter, an' then I'll kip some sack time me own self." He glanced astern. "'Tis time to go home."

30

A Last Resort

Thursday, 1 April 1886
At sea in the Gulf of Mexico
Off the lower coast of Florida

Later in the black night, the wind veered from southwest to west and increased even further, to a force-seven gale—a typical spring storm pattern, which can be frightening in a small vessel. The roasting air of Key West was behind us, displaced by cool temperatures and heavily laden clouds, which unloaded cataracts of icy cold rain from high above us.

Rork let me sleep under the tarpaulin on the deck beside him for two hours, not one, until the eastern sky began to lighten. Then I in turn allowed him four hours. He desperately needed it. Rork's always been stronger than me, but even he was dangerously worn out. Useppa had collapsed in a bunk below, emotionally and physically drained by the ordeal, thankfully insensible to the world around her.

The rain, which continued all that next day, rejuvenated me somewhat, washing the piled ash off the decks and some, not all, of the stink from our clothes. I let both my companions sleep as the sun rose like an illuminated orange, filtering through the walls of dark clouds. My arms and face—the areas exposed when that sheet of flame swept over me—were still quite painful, but the jelly Useppa spread on them had a calming effect, mitigating the worst of the throbbing. I thanked God above that Rork had thought to bring it along for provisions. Pappy Padilla's wife over at the fish camp on Lacosta Island had given us several jars for Christmas. I thanked God for her too.

Rork had dropped the mains'l during his trick at the helm. The storm's wind and seas wouldn't allow it to be carried any further. No longer under the lee of the Florida Keys, the seas had grown to dangerous proportions, but were fortunately on our port quarter—the best aspect for a small boat in those conditions. Most importantly, they weren't cresting yet. The sloop rolled deeply, requiring constant attention to the helm to keep us from broaching. So we charged along at five or six knots under forestays'l, each rippling hill rising astern of us thrusting *Nancy Ann* forward with a rush of bow wave and a humming vibration of the rudder.

Around noontime on April first, Useppa made an appearance briefly on deck, glanced at the scudding clouds above us, and returned to her bunk without a word. Not knowing what to say or do, I let her stay there. On deck, Rork and I took turns at the tiller, and throughout the day we plowed northbound through the Gulf of Mexico, eating the provisions he'd stowed aboard and getting closer to our refuge at Patricio.

At sunset, thirteen hours after fleeing Key West, I spotted the long white beach at Marco Island. We followed it north, up the desolate coast toward San Carlos Bay. Twenty minutes afterward, it was lost to sight, covered in rain and cloud. There was no beauty in that sunset, only a dim glow descending behind the dense overcast. Once that token of light was gone, we were immediately plunged into another night of impenetrable blackness. We had a lee coast to our starboard, so I guessed our leeward drift and set a conservative course to remain at least four miles offshore, steering nor'westerly.

We saw no one at sea this whole time. Vessels from the fish camps on Marco or Estero must've been snugged down at anchor behind their islands. That was a wise decision, for, now rested and more fully alert, I registered that the storm was progressing beyond the usual parameters of the usual spring storm. Far from elation at escaping death to our south, I began to have doubts about our ability to survive the maelstrom we'd entered.

Rork felt it first. Hail, a bad sign of particular malevolence in a storm, pelted the deck, stinging our arms and faces, making Rork and I huddle even deeper in our slickers. The wind increased to a complete gale, fully forty knots of wind, and we worried about our landfall at Sanibel Island. That island does not follow the coast— it sticks out at right angles to it, a barrier to coastwise navigation. There was a new lighthouse at the east end of the island. In benign weather, once we saw it at the entrance to San Carlos Bay, we would sail up Pine Island Sound to Patricio Island.

But beyond the fact that this wasn't benign weather, and that our navigation was reduced to guessing, there was another difficulty. *Nancy Ann*'s seams were working open from the stress on the hull and water was rising in the bilge. Rork worked the handle on the tiny pump and soon gave up. It was a toy of a thing, not equal to the task at hand. Useppa was regretfully woken up and pressed into bucket brigade service below deck. She and Rork began lifting the two small buckets kept aboard and pouring the water on deck to run overboard through the scuppers. She did the work without outward expression, as she had doused the sail in

Key West harbor. Rork's legendary humor emerged as they bailed. "Well, damn all an' pass the rum—'twarn't a couple o' hours ago when we was pourin' water onto her an' now we're pouring the bloody stuff out. Aye, what a fickle lass our *Nancy Ann* is!"

We tried to laugh, even Useppa, but it came out in dripping coughs, our lungs still full of black sooty phlegm. The attempt at raising spirits was short-lived, though, for after twenty minutes of their hard work, it was obvious that the water was still coming in just as fast.

We were sinking.

It was grossly unfair. We were so close, and yet I knew *Nancy Ann* wasn't going to make it to Patricio Island. After we'd run the proper distance and time, and still didn't see the lighthouse, or anything else in the murk, I made the decision I'd been mulling over. It was the last resort all seamen shrink from. When I informed the others of my verdict, they just nodded their heads. They'd already known what it would be.

We'd steer due northeast, riding the waves downwind until we hit Sanibel Island, literally, and ride *Nancy Ann* right up onto the beach. It would be the death of her, but maybe, just maybe, we would live through it. It was our only chance.

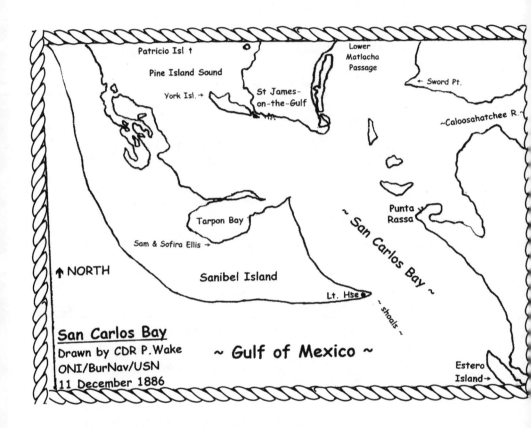

Patricio Isl t

Pine Island Sound

York Isl. →

St James-
on-the-Gulf

Lower
Matlacha
Passage

← Sword Pt.

~Caloosahatchee R.~

Tarpon Bay

Sam & Sofira Ellis →

Punta
Rassa

~ San Carlos Bay ~

↑ NORTH

Sanibel Island

Lt. Hse

~ shoals ~

San Carlos Bay
Drawn by CDR P. Wake
ONI/BurNav/USN
11 December 1886

~ Gulf of Mexico ~

Estero
Island→

31

The Electric Man

Friday, 2 April 1886
The lower Gulf coast of Florida

Normally, under the idyllic conditions so prevalent in the tropics, you can hear the surf as you approach a reef or a beach at night under sail. Accompanied by earthy feminine scents from the nearby land, Nature's perfume, as it were, the sound of gentle surf stimulates a sailor's best memories. It brings a smile of appreciation, and of anticipation, for the sound means liberty ashore. The voyage is ending. Even low surf has a loud, rhythmic rumble of symbolic import, the weight of the vast sea falling upon the very edge of the land—two worlds mingling, like a man and a woman meeting for the first time, evaluating the other, touching, hoping something good will come of it.

It's a majestic sound, really, far more than merely a sign of land. To me, the gentle surf along a tropical beach is a metronome of life—calming, inspiring, a constant measure of time. This primordial stimulus, subtly sensual to the inner core of a man, ignites a response deep inside, like when that demure girl looks you in the eye while she hums a romantic song.

When you get close enough at night, the surf provides a visual feast too. The phosphorescent glow of tropical surf is a silvery green, bursting against rocks in radiant showers and stretching out in lines running along the beach. The water is alive around your hull with shapes, some sauntering and some darting, all of them illuminated by shimmering skins, sometimes so bright they light up the bottom below. Sights and smells and sounds—those were my soothing reminiscences of approaching an island in the darkness, but they were mere memories now.

The beast in a storm makes a joke of beautiful senses.

You see, in a storm, the sailor never hears the surf, for the beast around you doesn't want you to hear it. The storm overwhelms your ears with mindless noise, numbing your brain to the outside world. Its wind is a living, breathing entity, physically tearing at you, screaming and moaning at you, beating your eyes and ears until you can turn neither toward it. The color of a storm at sea is uniformly gray—the top of the sea and the bottom of the clouds are plastered together in a seething stew of grayish movement. All other colors are stolen from you, not to be seen until the damn thing ends. And what of the smells of a storm? There are only two: the thick, acidic tang of wind-blasted saltwater above decks, and the sweetly rotting stench of sloshing bilge water and disintegrating wood down below.

Aye, mark my words. A storm at sea is the sailor's personal adversary, a monster of gigantic size that makes you live every single second, of every single interminable minute, in terror of the ultimate dread of sailors—being washed overboard, watching your ship rush away downwind, and floating there, waiting to die, all alone. A storm on land can defeat your efforts to live comfortably. But real storms at sea are not the stuff of romantic novels or intellectual lectures. They hate you. They try their best to *kill* you. They defeat your efforts to live at all.

Sailors are rough men who wear their salt-cracked skin and bruised arthritic knuckles and scornful attitudes like badges of achievement. Used to enduring the punishment of an angry sea, they know from their first storm as a boy that you cannot expect to win against the sea, you can only work your guts out to not *lose*. Losing means you die.

But even the toughest, saltiest tar can wither under an incessant assault. Age and ailments and other worries can tip the scales even before the fight begins. The most sun-leathered seaman can be weakened—outwardly and inwardly—to the point where the beast and the man both know what comes next, and they both know there's not a damn thing the man can do about it.

That was where I was, both physically and in my mental state, in the midst of that cold, wet hell as I steered us toward the upcoming collision with the island that was out there somewhere, waiting for us. Neither the storm, nor I, nor the island, could alter history. The only question remaining was how long it would take to unfold.

Not long, as it turned out. It was anticlimactic when it happened. I had everyone on deck, ready to jump for it the moment we hit. Well, jump was a fanciful word. They, and I, didn't look like we could jump very far, much less during the grounding and wreck of a vessel driving ashore.

The new day, Friday, the second of April, began with the storm reducing the morning sunlight to a gauzy gloom. In the few clearer patches, one could see perhaps half a mile. Useppa was beside me, her head lolling against my shoulder with the boat, gazing blankly past the bow of the boat while I fought that damned tiller. My arms were about done in, and I found myself wishing it was all over—dear God, just let us hit the friggin' beach and get it done. Rork was sitting against the back end of cabin top, drooping eyes staring at the seas coming from abaft our beam. I watched the waves closely for any sign they were rebounding off a shallowing bottom, a tiny forewarning of our coming impact.

Rork turned his head and muttered something, the words torn away by the storm. Annoyed, I told him to speak the hell up.

"Uh? . . . Oh," he replied, barely audible this time. "Well, methinks *that's* it, right over there."

Rork was looking off our port quarter, behind us. That annoyed me even more. He knew the island would be in front of us. I assumed he'd gone mad and was imagining things.

Then I looked to port myself.

There, a quarter-mile away, through the wind-blown mists, a lone column of black iron, supported by a spiderwork lattice of rods and beams, rose ghostlike above buttonwood and crepe-myrtle trees. Sanibel Island lighthouse. My God—it was *behind* us.

We were already in San Carlos Bay.

Somehow, beyond all logic, we'd crossed the shoal that hooked out from Point Ybel and had not wrecked, as so many others had done over the years. I had managed, quite against my will, to fail to hit an island fifteen miles wide. It was unfathomable. I sat there astounded.

The seas quickly laid down under the lee of the shoals and the island. Now all I had to do was bring *Nancy Ann* to port and we could sail close-hauled into the bayside beach under the lee of the point. Then ground her in calm water. No shipwreck, no death.

With Rork tightening the sheet, I put the helm down a bit and dear old *Nancy Ann* did the rest, coming up into the wind with a Gatling-gun clatter of the sail's leech. Heeling over hard with the wind on her port bow, she was even more sluggish—the water was sloshing back and forth well above the cabin sole boards now. But the extra weight helped her smash through the waves, and we bludgeoned our way over to where the flat water spread out off the beach, sliding to a gentle stop in the sandy shallows a short way down the shore from the lighthouse. The wind roared through the trees from the other side of the island, but *Nancy Ann* just quietly sat there, as in a millpond. I could hear snatches of a bell sounding at the lighthouse. It was the signal of a wreck ashore.

Rork loosed the halyard and let the forestays'l fall into its lazy jacks, then collapsed to the deck himself. Useppa and I clutched each other, not believing our surroundings or our fate. I don't know how long the three of us remained there in a semiconscious stupor, but our lethargy ended when Dudley Richardson, the lighthouse keeper, and his assistant, John Johnson, waded out in the water and yelled ask if we were all right. With them was Captain Ellis, who'd walked along the beach more than a mile from his place at Tarpon Bay.

I suppose the audience spurred my sense of pride, for I answered Mr. Richardson with ridiculous bravado that yes, we were quite all right, just stopping for rest and minor repairs. That repartee managed to get me Rork's disgusted look, and I quickly amended my statement to admit that we'd need *major* repairs, for we seemed to be sinking. I added that we were bound up through the islands for our home at Patricio Island.

That got a laugh from Ellis, who pronounced me with slurred words as, "Daft as a lunatic, but a bloody good egg." Keeper Richardson asked what I had in mind for the repairs, explaining that it was high tide and our vessel probably would fall over as the tide ebbed during the next few hours. He suggested we push her into a little deeper water. I agreed.

What I had in mind was an old sailor trick. We couldn't do it at sea, not with only two exhausted men aboard, but there in calm water with five men I thought it might work. I told everyone we were going to *fother* the hull—spread an extra sail under and around the hull, then tighten it. We could then bail the water out and the resulting inward pressure of the seawater upon the sail would somewhat plug the leaking seams. It worked better with an actual hole in the hull, but it was the best I could devise.

Fortunately, the three islanders were old sailors and understood. So, with their greatly appreciated assistance we passed the spare jib around *Nancy Ann's* bottom. With three more buckets from the lighthouse, the six of us then started to get most of the water out of her. The bailing work took hours, while around us the sun began to burn away the clouds.

To their astonishment, we told the islanders about the fire in Key West and our escape, leaving out the cause. Ellis reported that the storm had also forced Thomas Edison, Fort Myers' new celebrity resident, to wait overnight at Schultz's place at Punta Rassa. He'd seen him there the day before, before sailing across the bay for home, ahead of the worst of the storm.

By midmorning, *Nancy Ann* was floating again, lighter by over a ton of water, as well as two bottles of rum we usually carried aboard, which were presented to Ellis and the lightkeepers. All the men took a taste, declaring in a toast that it was the best we'd ever had. Even my temperance-touting daughter didn't begrudge Rork and me *that* tot.

After breakfast at Mr. Richardson's cottage, we got under way, with Useppa steering. Still tired, but fortified by food and the knowledge that our home island was just up the coast, we set sail with renewed vigor. *Nancy Ann* short-tacked west through the bay toward the lower end of Pine Island. While passing the hotel dock at St. James, I went below and saw that our hull was still leaking, but not nearly as bad as before.

Until York Point, that is. The wind had gone nor'westerly, and once we poked our nose past that point at the west end of York Island, we were laid over right down to our gunwale. I tried again, and again, but couldn't get anywhere to windward under that forestays'l. The triple-reefed mains'l was too much and the forestays'l too little. We were only ten miles from home, but we couldn't get there.

We were attempting it for the sixth or seventh time when Useppa came on deck and made two announcements. First, the hull was visibly opening up again from the stress on it, and second, the water level below deck was rising.

To that dismal news she added a third revelation after glancing aft, then focusing on something. "There's a steamboat coming up behind us. It's going fast."

You can imagine what Rork and I instantly thought, and why we cringed. Rork blurted out, "How the hell did the dagos find us here?"

We found out we were fortunately wrong, however, when we focused the glass on a very nicely decked out little steam launch—a yacht and not the notorious Spanish steamer, cutting through the water from San Carlos Bay, heading right for York Point.

As it slid by us in the little area of calm water behind the lee of York Island, a well-dressed man sitting under a canvas canopy amidships raised a small speaking trumpet and called over, his voice sounding tinny from the instrument. "Hello there. Are you in trouble? Do you need help?" Then he held it to his ear for our reply.

Well, there are times to maintain a semblance of dignity and soldier onward alone against the odds, and then there are times to ask for assistance.

"Yes!" I answered. Rork gave me an approving nod. Useppa's relief showed clearly on her face.

The man at the tiller in the stern took the trumpet and bellowed over. "What is your problem?"

"Taking on water. Can't get to windward. Need a tow to Useppa Island or Patricio Island."

There ensued a conference between the man in the stern,

obviously the captain, and his passengers, evidently the yacht's owners. The man who first spoke to us seemed in charge, gesturing toward us, then speaking stridently to the captain. I suggested to Useppa that she become prominently seen—the better to play the damsel in distress. To her credit, she swallowed her pride and did just that. Parading along our deck, she pleaded, "Please help us." Her performance would've melted an ogre's heart.

The captain bellowed, "Stand by for a tow!"

The pretty little steam launch—her name was *Lillian*— wasn't slicing so effortlessly through the water at twelve or more knots once she rounded that point with us under tow. Oh, no, she earned her money that day, slogging forward at perhaps four knots, taking water over her bow and using fuel at a prodigious rate. *Lillian's* side canvas was lowered to protect her well-heeled passengers, but they still reached out periodically and waved back to us. The captain was not amused, I could tell by his scowls, but the passengers were quite pleased with their adventure in rescuing locals in need.

Once they got us to Patricio Island in midafternoon and *Nancy Ann* was grounded safely at the dock, I invited them all up to the house for refreshments and a moment of rest. I also offered some of our cordwood as fuel. They looked like they could use some hot tea as a respite from the cold and wet. Eager to hear from Useppa the tale of our maritime woe, the ladies agreed at once, forcing the gentlemen aboard to acquiesce.

The entire entourage, under the meager cover of three umbrellas, trooped up the hill through our fruit trees to my bungalow. And what an unusual group they turned out to be. The owner of the yacht and his wife, Mina, were a wealthy couple on their honeymoon, visiting their new winter home on the Caloosahatchee River near Fort Myers. He called it "my little jungle," but she said quietly that its formal name was Seminole Lodge. The man was a bit younger than me, and fully twenty years older than the bride. His friend, a silent older man named

Gilliland, was with them.

They also had with them the groom's precocious twelve-year-old daughter, Dot, from his first wife, who had died. The boating trip was to pick up the bride's parents at the railhead at Fort Ogden on the Peace River and bring them back to Fort Myers.

Young Dot prevailed upon me to tell the tale of how we came to be waterlogged, so I told them briefly of the fire, our escape, and their own providential arrival. Dog-tired doesn't describe accurately our condition, and I suppose we showed it. Mina and Dot were captivated by the story and our island home, and insisted on helping Useppa with the stove and the tea. A proposal to fortify their tea with something made from corn or cane was politely declined by the group, taking their cue off Useppa's rather brusque refusal.

After my sea story, Dot roamed the bungalow, examining my trinkets from around the world and asking questions, as did her father. An accomplished man, he expressed an interest and knowledge in things naval and scientific. He was particularly intrigued by Rork's arm appliances and their uses, and enjoyed hearing some of my friend's lighter tales, the ones he can tell in fair company.

In the confusion, we were still wearing our clothes from the fire, filthy and reeking. Poor Useppa had none stowed at my bungalow. Well, once that was learned, nothing else would do but that Mina would give Useppa some of her own extra clothing, packed for the trip. That was carried out with great fanfare among all the females down on the yacht, while the men remained on the verandah, talking about the weather. Now the rain was ending, but there was still a cold wind from the north.

After a few minutes, the captain reminded his employer, a bit too gruffly for my taste, that they still had a long way to go, against that frigid wind, to reach Fort Ogden, and the head of the group reluctantly said good-bye. As our new friends departed the island, everyone agreed to meet again in the future, under more pleasant conditions.

Thus it was, in such extraordinary circumstances, that I got to know our rescuers, who were led by none other than Thomas Alva Edison, the most famous electric man in the world. Sadly, Tom and Mina haven't been to their Fort Myers home, Seminole Lodge, for a number of years now, evidently the result of acrimony with their former friend and neighbor, Gilliland.

Edison and I still correspond, however. Our communications nowadays center mainly around potential naval applications of his amazing inventions. And each letter always contains a humorous reminder of that treacherous day on the water, when the inventor rescued the sailor at sea.

32

Recuperation

Saturday, 3 April 1886
Patricio Island
Lower Gulf coast of Florida

The next morning, after a hot-water wash-up for all hands, Rork came to my home for breakfast. Useppa organized the meal from what little was in the larder. The rain had stopped completely and the sky was mostly clear, but the thirty-knot cold breeze made us stay inside. However, between Rork's stack of orange wood burning in the fireplace and Useppa's breakfast of hot potato hash with vegetables from the garden, by midmorning we were clean, warm, dry, and feeling somewhat human again.

As we sat there at my table, I fidgeted, trying to figure out a way to broach what'd happened in Key West. Useppa did it for me.

"We didn't do anything improper, Daddy. I want you to know that. Raul and I are Christians. But you should know that he asked me to marry him, and I said yes. We are going to . . ." Eyes filling, she steeled herself and continued, "We *were* going to . . . have the wedding in Key West in June. You can guess where."

"Honey, I'm so sorry he was killed. I know you loved him."

"*Love,* Daddy. I still love Raul. I always will. I realize that you thought of him as a revolutionary, but please understand that I loved him as a caring Christian man who was trying to liberate his people."

"I do understand that, dear. But I was worried to . . ." I almost said *to death,* " . . . to the point of *madness* when I couldn't find you. Where did you disappear to? Why?"

"There was an emergency at the committee. On Wednesday morning they asked me to help with getting some paperwork completed because they were running out of time—"

I interrupted, "The *Grito de Hatuey* declaration of independence? It needed to be printed by the thirty-first, so they could get it to Cuba and disseminate it there the night of the first of April."

She couldn't conceal her reaction. "How do *you* know that?"

"I was outside the committee meeting that night and heard them talking, just before the Spanish opened fire. So you were in the Instituto San Carlos that whole time?"

She sat there looking at me, clearly overwhelmed by my revelations. I could see her mentally processing the ramifications of what I'd said, but she asked no question as to *why* I was outside the club that night. I was grateful, for I couldn't tell her about Ferro and his warning. Instead, she answered my question.

"Yes, I got there after school on Wednesday. Worked upstairs, in the office. But I didn't work on the declaration itself. That was already done. I worked on the English translation of the communiqué that would be sent out to American newspapers. I'm so sorry you got worried, Daddy, but I didn't know you were looking for me."

That all made sense. She'd headed for the Cuban club just before

I'd started looking for her. We'd been minutes apart. If only . . .

"Useppa, I had a feeling the Spanish were going to do something and I wanted to get you away—yes, before you say anything, I know you would've refused, but I had to try."

Rork touched her hand. "Useppa, why did they meet in the café next door an' not in the club?"

"Because it was just a short meeting—a celebration—only long enough to get the declaration copies to Lieutenant Reyes, who would then take them over to Havana on the morning steamer."

"Did the lads in the committee have any notion that the Spanish would do what they did? Did you hear o' anything else the dagos—excuse me, dear, I mean the Spanish—have done lately?"

"No, Uncle Sean. I didn't hear anything about the Spanish doing anything lately, but everyone at the club has been getting very quiet around me on a lot of things. I know Raul and the others were worried about Spanish break-ins at the club, or maybe an isolated assault on one of them away from Key West, but not about anything like the attack that night. Not that I heard, anyway."

I asked, "They had the declaration printed in Key West for security reasons?

"Yes, we already had four hundred copies ready to go, with more to be printed in a few days. The editor of the Cuban newspaper arranged that. The night of Thursday, April first, was when it all would be made public. Oh, Daddy, we were so close, so close to everything working out."

She sighed, then detailed her fiancé's plan. "Raul was sure it would happen, that a *Grito de Hatuey* would rally all the Cuban people, not just the educated and rich. He was convinced that the United States would recognize the revolution as a legitimate entity, even if our plan with Roosevelt had failed. That Congress would support the Cubans and pressure the president to do the right thing. Recognition of the Cuban patriots as 'belligerents under international law' was the term he used. Raul said that was the same thing the British had done with the Confederates. Once that happened, and the patriots had secured some surprise victories around Cuba, he said that the Spanish would realize their time was over. He was certain there could be a minimum of bloodshed, and perhaps no killing at all, if it was all done properly."

"And the revenge bloodlust killings against the Spanish?"

"That wasn't Raul's vision. There were hotheads who demanded that. Raul told them to stop using the Bible for justifying murder. Our plan with Roosevelt was an effort to preclude that."

Useppa had been clear-eyed while explaining the revolutionaries' plans, but now they filled again as her chin began to quiver. I reached for her hand as her voice broke.

"Now my Raul's dead. They killed him, Daddy. They killed him in *our* country, for believing in freedom for his country."

Yes, they had. The Spanish felt they were at war, and Useppa's man was a target. Key West was no longer a sanctuary. There were no guarantees of safety for anyone involved. I assumed that Rork and I were targets. Useppa as well.

Raul Leon had known his international law. Recognition of belligerency was one step below recognition of sovereignty. I thought it a brilliant plan by the rebels—one that came within hours of fruition. What more could I say, or do, than to hug my brokenhearted daughter?

"And after all the work, all the sacrifice, it didn't happen, did it, Daddy? They didn't send the telegrams to the patriot generals, the declaration burned up so it wasn't disseminated, and nothing was started, was it?" she asked me, knowing the answer.

"No, I don't think so, dear. I have Edison's copy of the *Fort Myers News* from yesterday morning. He got it at Punta Rassa before they got under way. It mentions the fire, but nothing about an uprising in Cuba. They would've gotten word over the telegraph—Punta Rassa's the first stop in Florida of the Havana telegraph line."

"So everything Raul and the others did was for nothing, and

no one will ever know."

"No, dear, that's not true. A few like us know, and possibly someday many will know about what Raul and the others tried to accomplish. They are Cuban heroes, dear. But for right now, I think they need to be silent heroes. There are dangers out there for those who have survived. We are among them."

I'm not sure she heard my gentle warning, for she said, "Raul's body . . . needs a funeral."

"A memorial, not a funeral. His body is gone, Useppa. That fire consumed it completely along with the town. You are a Christian, so you know that a physical body is a temporary home. Raul is alive and well, in a life beyond ours."

The newspaper had a telegraphed report of the fire. Well over half of Key West was burned to the ground, engulfed and destroyed by that firestorm. Incredibly, no one was reported killed by the fire, though scores were hurt. I had found that last part significant. No bodies were found—the firestorm had cremated them.

We talked for hours—about Raul Leon and his Episcopalian ministry, about Cuba, about the fire that night in Key West. I discovered that my daughter, my little girl, had been a grown woman for some time, carving out her own path in life, a path that was far more detailed than I had known. The blind innocence of fathers, I suppose. That afternoon, while my Useppa gave in to sleep, Rork and I had a talk about what to do next. There was a lot to discuss.

First, we needed to get the boat fixed. My burns were healing, so I could help with that. He figured two, perhaps three days at the most, to caulk the seams aft of the main chain plates that he'd identified as the culprits causing most of the leakage. The rig and hull flexing had loosened them. We could get them done while she sat in the shallows at low tide.

After that was accomplished, I needed to get in touch with headquarters, which meant sailing to Fort Myers and using the telegraph there. I would see what I could find about J. V. Harris' land in the area. I was three days late on the report and feared Washington would assume we'd been hurt in the now world-famous fire. I'd also send a telegraph to Reverend Sparks and Sheriff Demeritt in Key West, thanking them for their concern and explaining that Useppa was no longer missing, that she was recuperating and safe with me.

Rork and I talked about the report. All along I'd been worried Useppa's name would be exposed by an informant, or mentioned in someone else's account. Now it appeared that her connection to the revolution might be sufficiently obscured by the enormity of the events. That connection was through Raul and now he was dead. I surmised that the Cuban rebels had scattered and were laying low. Plus, Useppa would, hopefully, not be participating with any of them for a while, if ever again. So I could still omit her name and no one would know enough to ask.

The report itself would have to be redone. In the storm aboard the *Nancy Ann,* it had been soaked through and made illegible. I'd have to sit down and rewrite it. There was a lot of additional information to add, as well. That reminded me that we'd never finished our effort to identify Ferro, who we were convinced was the Judas, by taking little Cedric to the courthouse and having him point out the man who gave him the note. With Key West in chaos—we didn't even know if there *was* a courthouse anymore— that would have to wait. It was enough that Ferro's information was correct on all points, a solid indication of his clandestine endeavors, and perhaps new disaffection with the Spanish.

All this was bound, of course, to take a while. Once it was done, then all of us would head to Washington. Rork and I needed to check in and present the report to Walker, and Useppa would stay at Boltz's for a while and convalesce. While up there, my son, Sean, could join us from Annapolis, and everyone could relax for a weekend. We'd be a family again, if only for a few days—a soothing vision to this overwrought father.

33

Reporting In

Friday, 9 April 1886
Frierson House Hotel
First Street, near Jackson
Fort Myers, Monroe County, Florida

Nancy Ann handled well, our job of filling and caulking having evidently done the job. I worked on the seams from inside the hull while Rork paid and pounded them from the outside. Then all three of us bailed her out for the third time in a week. This time she stayed dry. I suppose that dry isn't the right word, for the dampness remained below decks, impregnated into everything in the cabin. *Nancy Ann* would take her own time to truly dry out.

Desiring some different scenery, I arrived at the Caloosahatchee River by the back route. A brisk sea breeze from the west facilitated the decision, and I decided to forgo the usual way to the river, down Pine Island Sound, and headed for the river via Matlacha Passage, which separates the mainland from eighteen-mile-long Pine Island.

Rork stayed with Useppa back at Patricio Island, his stump an alarming color of crimson and quite swollen. No infection, but definitely an inflammation. That painful condition required muscular rest. I flatly insisted upon it, making it a naval order. My judgment was confirmed when he didn't even begin to argue.

Departing Patricio Island after a generous breakfast on a sunny morning, I broad-reached under main and forestays'l on a westerly wind across Horseshoe Shoal, then bore off around the houses at Bokeelia on the north end of Pine Island. Continuing my course to the east, I wore the sloop over to the starboard tack when Matlacha Passage opened to view. Now heading south down the east side of Pine Island, *Nancy Ann* raced through the snaking swash channel of Matlacha Passage.

Halfway down the Passage, several mangrove islands narrow the waterway, from two miles wide down to a few hundred yards. On one of them lies an old Indian mound, maybe eight feet in elevation at the most, atop which cluster a few shacks ostentatiously known as Harrsenville, named for J. O. Harrsen, the head of the fishing family who lives there. I waved at his young son Hans, who was poling a bateau out of a creek. Hans' father is the local postman for all of the scattered fishermen families of that area, and his home serves as the post office and meeting place.

Without a doubt, word would spread that Patricio Island's odd Yankee navy man was back on his island and sailing to Fort Myers or Punta Rassa, I thought with a chuckle. My reputation in the area was one of recluse naval officer. Continuing south, I hauled the centerboard up, for the water gets quite shallow between Harrsenville and the entrance to the Caloosahatchee River, down at San Carlos Bay.

This is a safe course, provided the winds are westerly. When they are out of the north or east, the tides aren't high enough to negotiate the shoals in the lower Passage. I proceeded slowly under forestays'l, arriving at the bay in the late afternoon. Deciding not to push on in the dark, I spent the night under the lee of a mangrove island in the middle of San Carlos Bay. It had a pretty little beach, upon which I built a fire and had my dinner.

After an easy morning's sail up the Caloosahatchee River, the glaring sun was high in the sky and heating up the day when I tied *Nancy Ann* up next to half a dozen other small vessels at the narrow jetty jutting out from the low marshy riverbank at First and Jackson streets in Fort Myers. The name was in flux back then. Some were calling it Myers, but many of the old-timers still used the military prefix, a moniker I favored, which has won out.

First Street stretched along the Caloosahatchee and was the center of activity then, and that Saturday afternoon you could see it all from the docks. Stores, hotels, lawyers, land agents, and other commercial enterprises were springing up all along the riverfront street. Little Fort Myers had four hotels for me to choose from. Straightaway I got a room and a meal at Frierson's hotel, a boarding house catering to the newest denizens of the region—northern sport fishermen after tarpon.

At that time, nine years ago, Fort Myers was a sleepy village with a hungry eye to the future. Only twenty years old then and built up with scrap lumber from the old Seminole War fort, they'd already snagged Edison as a new resident and were relentlessly flogging the place in newspapers as a palliative for northern ills and uncommitted money. Land was one thing they had plenty of. And sure enough, the bait worked. New settlers were arriving. There were less than a hundred inhabitants in 1875; by 1886 there were over seven hundred people in the town. Land agents were legion, and next to fruit farming, the biggest business was building houses. The growth was phenomenal; land prices doubled and tripled.

Those newcomers were not docile, either. They demanded service, be it from a shopkeeper or the county government, which was headquartered in far away Key West. The town was about half northern and half southern in population by then. Some of my former wartime adversaries—Powell, Hendry, and many others—were in charge, but apart from nostalgic stories of how they *almost* won the war, there was no animosity from the ex-rebels toward the newcomers. I've discovered across the world that money speaks a lot louder than politics, and that principle was alive and well in Fort Myers. Yes, it was a quaint and cheerful place back in '86. Progress was in the air. I liked it.

Though it's not part of my personal tale, I must report that the next year, in '87, those progressives in Fort Myers took things into their own hands. After an argument about the Monroe County commissioners refusing to rebuild the new schoolhouse on Jackson Street that had just burned down, the former Rebel and the Yankee residents banded together and besieged the state capital with petitions. It worked, and that year they *seceded* from Monroe County and Key West. The secessionists then set up operations as Lee—as in General Robert Edward Lee—County, a huge tract covering the entire lower Gulf coast, with Fort Myers as the seat. It was quite a coup.

They even spoke of having Henry Plant's railroad come down the coast to the town. Big talk then, but nine years later I see it hasn't happened yet. You still have to reach Fort Myers by inland cattle trail or coastal steamboat. Maybe that's why it's retained a certain charm.

Well, back to the story at hand. Minutes before the closing time, I arrived at the telegraph office on Lee Street just as the operator was leaving early after a slow day. He agreed to open up and displayed no curiosity about my cable to New York City—after all, those tarpon fish were bringing in more and more northern city businessmen. After he took down the message nonchalantly, he asked if I wanted it priority, to which I said yes.

The communication to the ONI cover address was simply veiled and short, letting the commodore know we had not perished in the fire and that I was still heading north to report in:

TO: ANDERSON/NEW YORK
FR: GOMEZ/FORT MYERS
10 APRIL 1886

XX—JUST RETURND FRM FISH
EXPEDITION—X—CAUGHT MANY
LITTLE ONES OF BOTH TYPES IN FLA
KEYS AND ALONG THIS COAST—X—
BIG ONE WE HEARD ABOUT GOT
AWAY—X—I KNOW HIS LOCATION—X—
SPANISH MACKEREL VERY ACTIVE ON
FLA COAST—X—PHOTOS DESTROYED
BY BAD WEATHER—X—WILL RETURN
TO TELL IN PERSON—X—MORE
LATER—X—GOMEZ—X

I also sent telegrams to Key West, identical ones to Reverend Sparks at Useppa's Methodist Church and Sheriff Demeritt.

TO: SHERIFF DEMERITT/KEY WEST
TO: REV SPARKS/KEY WEST
FR: P.WAKE/FORT MYERS
10 APRIL 1886

X—USEPPA WAKE SAFE RECUPERATING
FRM FIRE WITH ME—X—ALL WELL—
X—THANK YOU FOR CONCERN—X—P.
WAKE—X

Those duties done, I proceeded to the offices of Huelsenkamp and Cranford on First Street by Hendry, the most well known of the property brokers in the area. If anyone would know the answer to my inquiry, it would be Mr. C. L. Huelsenkamp. He had handled Tom Edison's acquisition along the riverbank, west of the town, and while he was visiting Patricio Island, Edison himself suggested that I use his broker if I was in the market to buy some land. I wasn't, but I did have a question. It turned out that Huelsenkamp was out that morning, but Mr. Cranford was in and answered my inquiry about Jeptha Vining Harris' land holdings with a friendly ease.

"Yes, sir, I do believe that Mr. Harris has various parcels near the coast up this way, but I've not been told he is releasing them for sale. Have *you* heard that he's selling, Mr. Wake?"

I decided a slight deception was in order. "Yes, word is that he's looking to divest himself of some property, but I only heard it in a vague way. I was wondering what you knew of the land."

"Well, I have no particulars about his land, Mr. Wake. Mr. Harris seldom comes here, but he's a very important man in Key West, so his holdings aren't being utilized at the moment. He's the collector of customs for the port and district, you know."

Evidently, Cranford spotted me for a military man and thought I'd be impressed with some added information about Harris. "And, of course, he is a *proud* veteran of the Confederate States Army."

Once a rebel . . . I said to myself. "Really? Interesting. Say, do you know *exactly* where Harris' holdings are, Mr. Cranford? I'd like to see them."

I could see him deflate. "No, not exactly. I regret to say that is all recorded in the courthouse at Key West. They had a horrible fire down there two weeks ago. Burned down almost the whole town."

"Yes, I heard about that. Could you tell me, did the courthouses burn down—the county and the federal?"

He shrugged. "They were damaged, but I'm not sure how badly."

"Well, thank you for your time, Mr. Cranford."

It wasn't definitive new information, but it did substantiate what I'd heard in Key West from Dort, the treasury agent. So Harris did indeed have land up near Fort Myers. Was some of it near the old Indian trading post at Burnt Store, very close to where Doyle loaded his boat with the stolen army rifles?

***

Before I left Patricio, Rork had given me a detailed list of mercantile provisions to obtain while I was upriver at "civilization," and Useppa had added a page of much-needed female under and outer clothing, along with various necessaries of the feminine world. So, after a stop late in the day at E. L. Evans' general store, where—to my utter amazement—Mr. Evans produced every item from both lists, I retired to Frierson's for drinks on the verandah. Conversing with some of the last fishing tourists of the season, I discovered that the Key West fire was big news up north, and found to my relief that Cuban revolutionaries were not mentioned in conjunction with it. That was just as well.

***

Sunday morning I shoved *Nancy Ann* off from the dock and headed home. It was another cool day, and with the wind fair from the east and an ebb to ride, I made good time downstream. The main and stays'l were wing and wing for most of the fifteen miles to the mouth of the river at Sword Point. There I wore the ship around and bore off on a starboard tack to the north, entering Matlacha Passage, reading that Saturday's *Fort Myers Press,* a surprisingly detailed sheet for such a small town.

The trip to Fort Myers for provisions, and to send a message to my superiors, was minor in every way. However, unbeknownst to me, in addition to the information I had gained there, I'd inadvertently *provided* some. You see, lulled by time and distance from my adversaries, I had made a fundamental mistake and let my guard down.

My enemies were not so complacent.

34

Kindred Souls

Monday, 26 April 1886
Patricio Island
Lower Gulf coast of Florida

It was a fine spring day, the sun bringing out the lush shades of the neighboring islands carpeted in green, the luminous aqua-jade waters, the brown pelicans and blue herons flying overhead. The morning land breeze was from the southeast, organizing the water into lines of small waves marching in formation across the bay. Disrupting that precision was a fin rippling along the surface by our dock. It was joined by another, smaller one, and together they cleaved an undulating path across to the islet nearby. They were porpoises, man's friend, on the hunt for breakfast. A reassuring sight.

I didn't want to go back to the world of the navy, especially in Washington.

But my wishes didn't matter. The next day that same breeze

would take Rork and me north on Whidden's boat to the railhead up on the Peace River, the first leg of our long journey to report in at naval headquarters in person. Useppa had decided to stay on at Patricio for another couple weeks. She wasn't ready to face people or the city crowd just yet, she said. She promised that when she was ready, she would head to Washington also. We'd heard stories that her school was badly damaged, so Useppa agreed there was no reason to return to Key West—she'd just be another person to feed and house in the midst of chaos. Perhaps in September they'd be ready to start classes again.

Two weeks earlier, Walker had replied to my cable from Fort Myers. I got the message two days later by island mail boat: *Expect you and full report no later than two weeks from receipt of this msg.* That would've put my arrival at headquarters no later than on April twenty-sixth—that very day.

Well, it didn't exactly work out like the commodore wanted. Whidden reported that the railroad had experienced some problems with the line near Fort Meade in middle Florida, and simultaneously, the locomotive working the last segment of the line had gone down for repairs. After sending Walker that update, which required another two-day sail to Fort Myers and back, he answered: *Delay acknowledged—proceed as immediately as you can via any transport.*

Obviously, he was not amused. I refused to be distressed, however. Were there other ways to get to Washington? Yes. But I didn't take them. My daughter and friend—and I, for that matter—needed rest. There was no urgency anymore, since, according to the newspaper accounts I read, there was no news out of Cuba—the revolutionaries had obviously cancelled their uprising and the Spanish were staying mum.

I spent the time waiting for the rail line to reopen by carefully rewriting my reports. On Friday, the twenty-third, the amended reports were finished. Whidden stopped by that morning to inform us the railroad would be running again on Tuesday.

Accordingly, I planned to leave Tuesday morning, allowing Rork and me one last weekend of maintenance on the house and the *Nancy Ann*. By leaving the island then, I expected us to probably be in Washington late on Thursday evening, enabling me to be in Walker's office bright and early Friday morning, the thirtieth, to explain everything that had happened since I'd left two months prior. I wasn't looking forward to it, but strangely, I wasn't unduly fearful. I suppose experience does that for a man— removes vague distant fears in favor of more visceral immediate ones. I didn't even have any close worries. The dangerous part was over for me.

Whidden returned to Patricio Island on Monday afternoon, delivering a letter from the post office, since he was sailing by the island. The next morning he was due to pick up Rork and me and take us up the Peace River to the railroad, so we asked him to stay the night, but he said he had plans over at Peacon's place at Gasparilla Island for the evening. I suspected it had something to do with romance. I'd heard there were some new women over there.

The letter was a pleasant surprise, from my son Sean in Annapolis. It was dated from just before the Key West fire. He was doing well in his first year at the naval academy, but admitted, without elaboration, how surprised he was at the amount of discipline and punishment. Sean asked about his sister Useppa and his namesake Uncle Sean. At the end, he alluded to a relationship with a girl, but I found that odd. First-year midshipmen had very little liberty time, and I suspected he might have gone "over the wall" a few times to meet this girl, hence the reference to punishment.

Rork read the letter and chuckled. "Aye, the lad's got it in his blood, he does. His daddy did the same with a pretty little lass named Linda in Key West. Remember, Peter?"

Useppa smiled as I admitted, "Hmm. Yes, I do. And I got in trouble for it too."

My daughter shook her head and added, "Oh, my little brother's a conniver all right. And now he's got a girlfriend when he's not supposed to? Probably told her he's an admiral." Her voice was light-hearted but I could tell Rork's comment had unintentionally taken her mind back to Key West. She saw my look of concern and snapped out of the melancholy. "My little brother's just not as smart as you were, Daddy. He'll probably get in *lots* of trouble!"

The three of us sat on my verandah after dinner that night, speaking of our lives and our dreams. Sean and I had plenty of twists and turns in our lives, which had evolved into completely different paths from youthful expectations. Now the same could be said for Useppa. Most of her girlfriends who had grown up with her in Washington were either married or still living with their parents.

None of them had experienced life as she had, she declared. Then, in an ethereal voice that sounded ten years older, she sighed, "I suppose I'm resigned to being alone, but at least I can say that I've loved a decent man." She took a breath and looked me in the eye. "Don't worry, Daddy. I'll use the strength he gave me to move on in life. And I still have Christian work to do."

It suddenly struck me that my daughter and I shared a common, and tragic, bond now. Both of us had our mates, our other halves, taken away from us. Words failed me at the enormity of that grossly unfair loss at her age. I beckoned for her to come to my chair, and she fell into my lap like she was twelve again. We held on to each other as she sobbed.

Rork returned to his bungalow. Time slipped away under the stars on a cool, still night in the tropics. It was so quiet I could hear the tiny anoles and geckos scampering along the walls and ceiling. The scent of jasmine and orange drifted from the trees. The half moon hadn't risen yet, but the starshine was so bright no lamp was needed.

Commodore Walker, Admiral Porter, the secretary of the navy, the president—all of them up in Washington—were the furthest things from my mind, right then.

Thirty minutes later, drained by an outpouring of grief she'd restrained for so long, my daughter trudged off to bed. I crawled into a hammock on the verandah. Within seconds, both of us were oblivious to our surroundings.

Normally, I can sleep soundly, yet be instantly aware of changes in my environment. An old sailor trait. A different sound of the wind, motion of a hull, smell of a bilge, slight nuances will alert me to an alteration of the situation around me. Not that night.

It was Rork who heard it first.

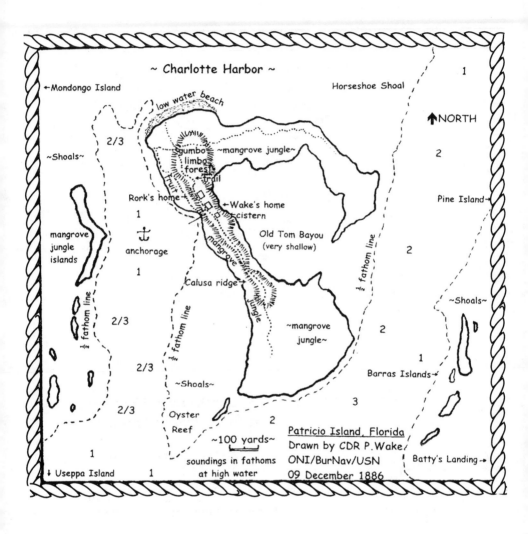

~ Charlotte Harbor ~

←Mondongo Island

Horseshoe Shoal

1

low water beach

↑NORTH

~Shoals~

2/3

gumbo limbo forest

~mangrove jungle~

2

Pine Island→

Fruit trail

Rork's home

1

←Wake's home cistern

mangrove jungle islands

⚓ anchorage

1

Old Tom Bayou (very shallow)

2

½ fathom line

Calusa ridge→

mangrove jungle

2/3

~mangrove jungle~

2

½ fathom line

2/3

~Shoals~

½ fathom line

2/3

~Shoals~

Barras Islands→

1

Oyster Reef

2

~100 yards~

3

Patricio Island, Florida
Drawn by CDR P. Wake
ONI/BurNav/USN
09 December 1886

1

↓Useppa Island

1

soundings in fathoms
at high water

Batty's Landing→

35

Venganza

Tuesday, 27 April 1886
Patricio Island
Florida

A sweaty hand covered my mouth. I lurched out of instinctive
terror, but felt iron pinning my right arm down, preventing
me from rising. Hot breath filled my ears.

"Peter . . . shssh . . . it's Sean. Listen to me. There's men on
the island. I can hear 'em."

I focused on Rork's tense face, willing my mind to stay calm,
and nodded acknowledgment. He released his grip.

"Where?" I whispered.

"North o' my place, up by the end o' the trail. Heard 'em
comin' through the mangroves, slow-like. I think there's maybe
three."

The half moon was a couple hours high, spreading a thin
silver glow around the hilltop, interrupted by long shadows from

the buildings and the trees. There was little light on the verandah, but still enough to see details. My eyes adjusted quickly and I instinctively checked my pocket watch, noting time and weather. Three thirty-four A.M. Wind was calm. A few clouds dotted the sky. Only the buzz of insects and croaking of a frog broke the stillness.

Rork had only trousers on, with two pistols and a cutlass jammed in his belt. His old Navy-issued shotgun leaned against a nearby table. As quietly as I could, I slipped out of the hammock, found my shoes, and made my way inside the bungalow.

I keep several weapons hidden in my home. In the parlor is a Navy Colt revolver, behind the books on the highest shelf, by the fireplace. Under the bed is a unique shotgun, one of Christopher Spencer's newly patented twelve-gauge, six-round, pump gun models. Mine was loaded with buckshot and had a small bandolier, with six extra shells, wound around the stock.

In my desk drawer is a Merwin Hulbert pocket pistol—a small but heavy, very effective six-shot .44-caliber revolver, with the notorious "skullcrusher" butt, made to resemble an eagle's beak. The kitchen had a cane knife and a cutlass hanging by the back door.

With Rork watching out the front doorway, I rushed through my home, arming myself as I went. Last stop was the bedroom, where Useppa lay sprawled asleep. I knelt down and removed the Spencer from under the bed, leaving it within easy reach on the floor. Shaking Useppa's shoulder, I quietly told her there were intruders on the island, and pulled her up from the bed. In the gloom, her eyes opened stark white, I saw her nod her understanding. By then we were already moving.

I led her by the hand to a corner of the kitchen, which had a diffused shaft of moonshine coming through the open door. I told her to sit still on the floor, and armed her with the Merwin and the cane knife. I took the cutlass. Still clad in her nightclothes, Useppa never said a word the whole time, responding only by gesture. The revolver trembled in her hands, her elbows balanced on her drawn-up knees.

I heard someone approaching outside. Two men behind the house, back by the roasting pit. Their deliberate footsteps crackled the dry sea grape and buttonwood leaves covering the ground. Cautious whispers in questioning tones came from the murkiness outside. Peeking around the corner of the open back door, the Colt following my line of sight, I couldn't see any movement. But they were there all right, probably farther back in the gumbo-limbo trees now, under the shadows. Watching. Taking their time.

Who were they? And how did they know where I lived? Their intent was undoubtedly hostile, but what was their motive? Why were they here? This was an organized, premeditated assault. The gun-runners from the Keys? The Chileans—enemies from my past? Boreau and his Spanish agents? The Sarasota gang? What the hell did they hope to gain?

I backed away from the door and ducked around the corner into the parlor. The moonlight hadn't penetrated the west side of the bungalow yet, and it was even darker than the kitchen. From the front door, Rork slowly motioned to me with his fingers—one man in front, two in the back. He shrugged and motioned to the north, the side toward his own home, as if there might be a fourth man over there.

I nodded understanding, pointed to myself and the rear porch and held up two fingers—I would deal with the men in the back. I pointed to the front and the north side, then to him—he would take care of them. He raised his shotgun in acknowledgment. I returned to the kitchen.

Useppa was still crouched in the shadowed corner, the Merwin held steadier now and aimed at the door at waist height. I got down on my knees, then my stomach, and crawled forward, assuming a prone firing position just to the left of the doorway, out of the dim path of moonlight on the floor. I slowly moved the Spencer up beside me, one hand on the pump mechanism, ready to jack the first shell into the receiver, then pointed it toward the verandah. Outside, it was quiet again. No footsteps, no whispers.

Glancing back at Useppa, I nodded confidently, wanting to boost her morale. She gave me a determined look that broke my heart. I've been in combat before, but this was completely different. The stakes were beyond measure. My daughter, my baby, was a target. In my own home. Emotions surged inside me, alternating between fear and fury. The very fact that my mind was diverted to sentiments made me angry. I needed to be in cold control, in command of myself and the others. To lead, now more than ever in my life.

My brain was churning, trying to *think*, to deduce who was out there, finally settling on Boreau and his crew as the most likely. Apparently, they thought we were asleep. That they would catch us defenseless, like hogs in a trap. But they were wrong. We were in a good defensive stance. And due to Rork's light sleep, we would have the element of surprise—*they* would run into the trap. We'd wait for however long it took for them to come in, whoever they were.

Ten seconds later, they did.

They had advanced much closer than I had thought. The two men in back had actually made it onto the rear porch, out of my line of sight. I had expected a stealthy entrance. I was wrong. They started shouting simultaneously and rushed the door.

"Venganza!"

I instantly knew their identity. "Revenge"—in a Spanish accent, not Cuban.

A form filled the moonlit entryway. I closed my eyes to keep my night vision, pumped the shotgun, fired a blast, and pumped another round into the chamber. I opened my eyes again as the man jackknifed and fell on top of me. Gore from his gashed-open abdomen splashed out, the intestines plopping onto my head. There was no time for revulsion, however, for Useppa was shooting from behind me. Her rounds went over my head into another figure in the doorway. It fell backward. My memory is eerily clear—she shot twice with no scream, no emotion.

Rising up, I walked onto the verandah, shotgun at the point-shoulder position, scanning the ghostly scene back and forth for a target. Smoke eddied around the door and out onto the porch, catching the moonlight and concentrating it into white wisps, making the scene even more unreal, like theatrical smoke at a play.

My eye saw a form dashing from the tree line in front of me to the corner of the cistern off to my right, on the south side of the bungalow. I swung around and tracked it with the barrel. Two shotgun blasts in rapid succession eliminated his cover just as he arrived at the cistern. Tabby cement and oyster shells disintegrated into a cloud of shrapnel. But damn it all to hell, I'd only closed my left eye when firing, and my sight was ruined in my right eye from the flare of the blast. A stupid mistake. Before I could aim again, the form fired a pistol and fled to the rear of the cistern, a better position for him. A grunt roared from the man. It wasn't from pain or weakness. It was rage, like a wounded and still very dangerous animal.

Behind me, the twin booms of a shotgun sounded from the front of the house, followed closely by three bangs from Rork's Colt. I suddenly realized that I was standing in the open on the verandah, and ran to my left, toward the gumbo-limbo trees, to get some cover. I wanted my opponent to lose track of me. For *him* to feel the terror.

Gumbo-limbo trees have no low limbs and lose their leaves in the winter and spring. This lack of obstruction allowed me to make some rapid distance in my flanking maneuver. But the lack of ground cover also allowed him to glimpse my shadow as I moved.

The first blast hit just behind me. Hearing the gale of lead tear through the tree trunks, I dove headfirst into a swale and rolled in the sandy shell-filled soil as the second blast shredded the trees directly above my head. So he had a shotgun.

I had fired three rounds from the Spencer, and still had another three in the gun, plus the six extras and my Navy Colt. My enemy had fired one round from a pistol, with five left. He probably had a double barrel and was reloading. It was time to attack.

Rolling even farther along the slope of the small hill, I jumped up ten feet from my last position and fired a blast where I thought he was, then charged. A pistol flash popped to my right, between me and the bungalow. I was at the cistern now, as another flash popped from further over to my right. Shell debris from the cistern wall showered me. A near miss. The man was smart—saving his shotgun for an open shot. And now I understood his plan.

He was heading toward the bungalow, and Useppa.

My eyes had lost their peripheral vision and I had little hearing left. It happens in battle. Everything beyond your immediate person and area is lost to your senses. I've felt it before during close quarters fighting with firearms, especially in the dark. But this time was different—I wasn't in some far-off land, with military men around, and an escape route behind me.

In a panic, I charged toward Useppa's position, not daring to fire without a definite target, and not able to see clearly enough to identify a target. Halfway there, I heard a gasp and a groan, then a thud. Metal into wood. Straining to see, I made something out in the deep shadow of the rear verandah, near the doorway. A big man, snarling unintelligibly, looming over another person.

Once there, I was finally able to see exactly what was happening. I lowered the Spencer, took in a great draught of air, and tried to control my shaking hands. My eyes adjusted to the dim moonlight again.

36

Right and Wrong

Tuesday, 26 April 1886
Patricio Island
Florida

The tall man was Rork. His right hand held a cutlass to the throat of Boreau, stretching the man's neck and head upward. I got close enough to see a dark line snaking down Boreau's neck from the cutlass's point, the blood looking shiny black in the shadowy light.

The marlinespike on Rork's left arm was stabbed through the Spaniard's shoulder and jammed into the wall of the bungalow. Boreau's eyes were filled with fright, seeing death coming, losing all dignity, trying to beg but unable to speak. I smelled the strong odor of his excrement. His mouth kept opening and closing, without words. Rork was savoring Boreau's reflexes, his eyes inches from the man's face, as he twisted the spike from side to side.

I called out to Useppa and she appeared silently in the

doorway like a phantom, grimacing, but still holding the Merwin revolver in both hands.

"Are you all right?" I bawled at her in fear.

"Yes, Daddy. I'm not hurt," was the reply, strangely composed.

Rork jammed the spike in further, making Boreau gasp, then swiveled his head toward me, apparently just taking notice of my presence. "I got the one in front an' checked for any others at my place, but 'twarn't any. We got every one o' 'em, sir. Four in all. An' all o' the bloody swine're dead, 'cept for this bag o' dago shite." He flashed an evil grin and put his mouth close to Boreau's ear. "An' methinks he'll wish he was already dead too, in a minute."

"Hold him there, Rork. I'll look around myself, just to make sure. Useppa, get some lanterns lit, dear. Stay inside. I'll be back."

After examining the boots of Boreau and the dead men, I searched the ground around the bungalows and along the pathways for footprints with a lantern. I'm no woodsman, but saw nothing that I couldn't account for. We'd gotten them all.

Rork was right on how they got ashore. There was a dinghy tied up in the mangroves near the end of the pathway at the northern end of the island's western shore. Anchored a hundred feet away was a Cuban fishing smack, apparently empty. I'd never seen one there before.

When did they get the smack into that spot? Boreau would've had to go right past our dock, in full view of anyone sitting on the verandahs of our bungalows on the hill. They must've watched from afar, waited until our lamps went out, then approached the island. A tricky proposition.

I returned to my bungalow. Useppa was inside making coffee, busying her hands and mind on a normal chore, meticulously ignoring Rork and the prisoner on the porch. Her countenance showed anger and sadness. She barely acknowledged me as I walked through.

Outside, I told Rork to lash Boreau to a leaning gumbo-limbo tree forty feet away, then to come sit on the porch—we had to talk. This he did, dragging the man over to the tree, roughly tightening the half-hitches around him, including one around the man's throat, so that Boreau's body was bent backwards along the tree trunk. The Spaniard was faced away from us, into the black woods.

We sat down in the chairs on my back porch. The moon was very high now, providing enough light to show the bodies crumpled together only feet away from us. Useppa stepped around them as she brought mugs of coffee out. There was a large dark stain on the wall where Rork had pinned Boreau. The blood trail led across the deck of the verandah toward the tree. The wound, along with the buckshot I'd put in him, was enough to cause great pain, but Boreau never screamed, as so many would've.

Rork was still shaking with anger, emitting a low continuous growl, the wrath at a level the likes of which I'd never seen in him. His eyes were locked on Boreau, and I knew what he was planning, could see it unfolding vividly in my mind.

Useppa displayed the opposite state of mind, appearing nearly catatonic in her calm. She turned a chair to face my direction, away from the dead men, and sat down, watching me. Her look made me nervous. She understood what Rork and I were about to discuss. What I would ultimately decide.

Rork leaned over to me and quietly said, "I've still some last questions afore we do 'im in."

"What did you find out so far?"

"The bastards came here to kill us. No news there, but first they were to interrogate you about what the American government knows. Then they'd do Useppa, to find out who all is in the rebel movement."

I took in a deep breath. It was as I'd thought. "And the Judas?"

"As we thought. A clerk at the federal court named Thadeus

Irons. Worked for them for three years. They took him out o' Key West in the chaos after the fire, when the Spanish gov'mint sent that cruiser, the *Jorge Juan,* there to evacuate the Spanish crown's subjects who wanted out. He's in Havana now. Bloody friggin' dago sons o' bitches pulled it off."

"Irons? Thadeus Irons? Incredible . . ."

"Why's that, sir?

"Remember Dort's name for his informant? Ferro. It means *steel* in Spanish. Pretty close to *iron.*"

"I thought *acero* meant that in Spanish?"

"It does. So does *ferro.* Dort didn't disguise the man's identity that much, did he? But I didn't even figure that out. I should have. And you were right on target back in Key West, Sean—Ferro, the informant, was also the Judas. Actually, a double Judas. He informed *us* about what the Spanish agents were about to do. And now he's escaped."

"Aye, courtesy o' that man o'er at the tree. An' that little poxied bugger wouldn't hesitate a heartbeat in hell to kill Irons if it came out he'd turned white mouse against the dagos."

Rork used the old sailors' term for stool pigeons—white mice. Irons must be terrified the Spanish would find out he warned us about the intended assault at the Cuban club. "So what else do you want to ask him?"

"The names o' their other agents in the States. But he's startin' to clam up. I think he's losin' his fear o' us. I can see it in his eyes. Thinks we won't kill his arse, anymore. We waited too long."

I nodded. We needed to know their names. Crucial. I also needed to make the other decision. The final one—what to do with Boreau. Or his body.

As if reading my thoughts, Useppa broke in, her voice deeper than usual, adamant. "No, Daddy. This needs to end. Now. Right here. No more killing."

I didn't appreciate her lecturing me, but I restrained my reply. "That animal came here to kill us—after he extracted information from me and from you. He would've taken his time with *you.*"

She shook her head, her eyes never leaving mine. "But he didn't get to, did he? We stopped him. I was part of that. I shot too. But now that's over. And now we need to let him live."

"Look, men like that don't stop killing, Useppa. Unlike us, they *enjoy* it. Boreau is a sadistic monster. He wanted to kill Sean and me in that dungeon in Havana. He tried to kill us in Key West. He tried again to kill all of us here, in my *home,* tonight. Boreau'll try again, if I don't kill him now."

"*No.* We're past that point, Daddy. It won't be in defense anymore, it'll just be cold-blooded murder. We'll be like him. I can't live that way."

I seethed with indignation—how dare she sermonize to me on behalf of bestial scum like Boreau? This wasn't some Bible lesson among children in Sunday school.

"I can," I said, with more edge than I should have. She didn't understand Boreau's culture of violence and hate.

She sighed sadly and put a hand on my arm. "Honor was always important to you, Daddy. Where is that, here?"

Good God, how naïve she was. "Honor? That's no longer a factor in this equation. It ended for me tonight, Useppa—when they tried to kill *you.*"

Rork had been quiet this whole time. Now he began to speak.

"Useppa, darlin', this ain't a game. This is the bastard who killed your intended, Raul. Your father's right. He'll kill again, sure as hell. You want that on your conscience? I don't."

"So we *murder* him? Why not follow the law and have the sheriff arrest him? That's the *honorable* thing to do, isn't it?"

Rork and I exchanged glances. There was no way we could allow this whole story to come out in a public courtroom.

"That can't happen, Useppa," I said.

"And why not?"

"Because there are parts of this whole story that would

embarrass our country. And embarrass Spain. That would lead to a bunch of hotheads on both sides calling for war in Cuba. That war would mean thousands of men dying on both sides. Men unlike Boreau and his thugs. Decent men. I'm not going to allow that to happen."

She stood and spoke firmly, regret clear in her words. "And I can't let you murder him in cold blood, Daddy. All three of us are Christians. This is the test of what we believe in, what separates us from the monsters like him over there. And I will *not* let you fail that test of faith, and of honor. So you'd better think of another way to end this."

Rork looked at me and raised an eyebrow. If Useppa hadn't been there, Boreau would've been dead already. But she was. And God help me—in my heart I knew she was right. I felt the hatred dissipating inside me. Yes . . . damn it, she was right. But what to do with him?

I reluctantly explained my decision to Rork. "He lives. Please go get his fishing smack and bring it around to our dock. We'll load the bodies aboard, have a heart-to-heart with Boreau, then put him and a message to Marrón aboard, and tell him to shove off for Havana."

He sat there, not moving. I added, "And pray to God that Boreau takes this chance and lets it go."

Rork still didn't move. Useppa looked at him and said, "You're not a monster, Uncle Sean, and you know it."

"God blast it all, sir. This dago sonovabitch ain't worth a drop from a fat-back candle. I don't agree a bit, but I'll do it. I warnin' ye, though, if he's tries anything—any damned little thing a-tall— I'll run through his eye with me spike, quick as crap through a goose, an' be smilin' the whole time he bleeds out."

"Understood, Rork. Just go and get it done for me. I'll go and write that note now."

By the time the eastern sky began to lighten, the three bodies had been shoved into the smack's fish hold. The rum found aboard was taken off, and just enough food and water for three days was left on the boat. We included some strips of cloth for bandages.

As Rork predicted, Boreau declined to tell us the identities of the other Spanish operatives in the United States. In fact, the only information he'd given us was already known or surmised by us. I knew that torture—well, that was the word for it—might gain us an answer, but with a man like Boreau, its veracity would be suspect. Thankfully, Rork didn't push me on the subject. He went about his business evenly, still tensed, and marched the prisoner down to the dock.

I went over my decision one more time. It had terrible potential for future harm, but I didn't regret it. Rork and I had killed men before, but we had never murdered in cold blood. And now that the hot flash of terror and rage was past, I knew we wouldn't start there.

My written note to Marrón was simple:

> Colonel Marrón,
> This senseless killing must stop. To further that sentiment and show my honorable intent, Boreau is being returned to you alive, even though he came here to kill me and my daughter. Let this stop now. Is honor among gentlemen dead? I hope not, but the opportunity is now yours. Send no more agents into the United States. If I see Boreau in the U.S. again, I'll do what I didn't do here and now.
> P.W.

Useppa stayed up on the hill, in the bungalow. The final

moment with Boreau was for Rork and me. I shoved the note into the Spanish lieutenant's pocket as he stood on the deck while Rork untied his hands, then hoisted the luffing mains'l up.

"If I ever see you anywhere in the United States again, I will assume you are here to hurt my daughter. I will immediately kill you without hesitation. Do you understand?"

I said it as matter-of-factly as I could—for I wanted him to see that it wasn't irrational rage talking. It was a cold, hard decision. His dark eyes betrayed no emotion as he said, "Yes. I understand you."

We shoved his boat away from the dock. Boreau lost little time in hauling in the mainsheet and getting the boat under way.

Rork walked up the hill, but I stayed on the dock for a long time, watching Boreau sail away in the pre-dawn. When the sail disappeared around Mondongo Island, heading for Boca Grande Passage and the Gulf of Mexico, I said a silent prayer to God, telling Him I hoped I hadn't made a huge, fatal mistake.

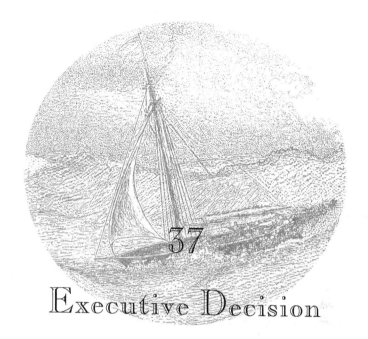

Executive Decision

Friday, 30 April 1886
United States Naval Headquarters
State, War, and Navy Building
Seventeenth Street NW & Pennsylvania Avenue
Washington, D.C.

I made it to my superior's office at the time I'd projected, but Rork wasn't with me. He was at the senior petty officers' quarters at the Washington Navy Yard. This meeting was for the officer in charge of the mission—me. I'd made the decisions that would now be scrutinized.

While I sat there in the anteroom of the office of the commanding admiral of the navy, I had plenty of time to reflect on what had happened since that night at Roosevelt's townhouse in New York City. Not much had gone well. Then I went over the events of the day we left, just hours after the gunfight.

In spite of the horror of that night, we continued my original plan. An hour after Boreau sailed away, Whidden arrived at Patricio. Rork, Useppa, and I jumped aboard his sloop without inviting him up to the bungalow for coffee. That was unusual, and in those islands considered impolite, but explaining the fresh stains on the verandah would have been difficult. Whidden knows full well what blood on wood looks like.

Useppa didn't argue with me about anything after Boreau's departure. When I told her she was coming to Washington with us, for an extended time, she nodded her head and packed her few belongings in one of my extra seabags. She didn't want to stay.

We'd had a talk on the train as it swayed through the pine-wooded hills of central Florida later that day. Seeing her gazing desolately out the window, I asked Useppa how she was feeling.

"Not very well. I feel dirty." She turned at looked at me. "Daddy, I shot a man."

In actuality, she'd killed him, but Rork and I had let her think that our shots were the mortal wounds of the second man on the porch. "You helped save my life, and Uncle Sean's."

"I know that, and I'm glad you and Uncle Sean are unhurt, but I never thought I'd be involved in something like that—violence against someone. I can't help feeling hypocritical. Like I failed to be a Christian."

"Useppa, dear, you were drawn into violence from the moment you helped the Cuban revolutionaries. They are at war with the Spanish, and they dragged you into it."

That was the wrong thing to say. Her eyes filled.

"And I got you involved in it . . ."

"No, you did not. I would've been there as part of my work, whether you were involved or not. And as for you feeling you've gone against your beliefs, I don't agree. If it was a bear or wolf or gator, or some other man-killing animal, you would've defended yourself and us without regret. Well, it *was* a man-killing animal. So you did what anyone would do. You did exactly what Raul would've done."

I held her hand. "Useppa, you are a victim, you are *not* a perpetrator. For the last six months you've been a participant in a dangerous situation, but that's over, and now you are a survivor. Simple as that. There are no morals to be won or lost here, so don't live your life in regret. Your mother and I didn't raise you that way."

There was something else I needed to say. "And Useppa . . ."
Her voice was stronger now. "Yes?"

"You were right about us not killing Boreau. That would've been murder. Sean and I realized that, once we calmed down. I'm glad you did what you did, and convinced us to spare him. Your mother would be proud of you. So would Raul. So am I."

She nestled close to me, my little girl once again, as the shadows lengthened in the dark train car. The next day, as we rumbled along through the Carolinas, I saw that she was more like her old self. Rork got her to smile, and to laugh once at some silly joke. My fears about her emotional state began to subside. She had a lot of Linda in her. She'd survive and put it all behind her.

Upon arrival in Washington Thursday evening, Useppa got a room near mine at Boltz's Inn. She planned on looking for a teaching position in the immediate area around Fairfax. She didn't mention Key West.

Still waiting in the admiral's anteroom, my focus progressed to the next priority. Patricio Island was as safe as I could make it from afar. I'd made arrangements for Whidden to stay at Patricio Island during my absence, explaining that some rough characters had been seen lately, possibly reconnoitering the place with mischief in mind. He'd make five dollars a month, payable upon my return. I hoped the stains would've faded a bit by the time he got back to the island.

If Whidden couldn't be there, he was to ask Captain Peacon to either stay himself or have one of his sons do it. I could have asked Pappy Padilla on nearby Lacosta Island to look in on my place, and he'd probably do it for me, but there were just too many rumors that the Padilla fish camp was involved in smuggling. Besides, Peacon was an old friend from Key West.

Rork concurred, opining bluntly, "Peacon ain't a dago, an' that's sayin' a lot after what all we've been through. I'm a-gettin' jus' a wee bit tired o' their kind o' treachery lately."

So, when I was finally called into the admiral's office some forty minutes after I'd arrived, I felt reasonably sure that my most important personal issues were solved. In retrospect, and after a lifetime of surprises, I think that it's a good thing we are not able to see into the future. I'd have run the other way, several times. What happened next is a fine example of why.

The instant I saw the admiral's face I knew this time was different. There would be no explaining, no maneuvering, no mitigating an apparently woeful result, no adroitly sidestepping various negative backlashes from my actions. I'd been very lucky in the past. Clearly, there'd be none of that this time.

As I walked in, I noted Admiral Porter shaking his head slowly as he read something on his desk, his finger racing along the lines, periodically stopping. Then a blend of moan and grumble came from his closed mouth, and he'd begin reading again. I saw that it was a report, but not nearly thick enough to be one of my two reports—the first, on the revolutionary activities, was twenty-eight pages. The second, on the Spanish agents' activities, was twenty-five. I could also see that it was typewritten. Mine had been written longhand back on the island, with an addendum written on the train ride north, covering Boreau's attack on the island. I had turned both reports into Commodore Walker's aide that very morning, to be transcribed by a typing clerk.

Upon this deduction, my spirits elevated cautiously. Perhaps the report Porter was reading wasn't about me? Maybe I wasn't in as much trouble as I'd feared.

Commodore Walker stood stone-faced at attention in front of Porter's desk. That wasn't a good sign. Commodores generally don't stand at attention. Upon my entrance, he motioned for me to stand beside him. I marched over, stood at attention also, and made the prescribed regulation announcement of my presence, which the admiral proceeded to ignore. The commodore and I remained like that for a minute, maybe more. Porter went through four more pauses and groans before he lifted his eyes and looked at me.

"Well, by all accounts, I see that you have gone far beyond your previous exploits, Commander Wake. Indeed, you have managed to get into a position so far beyond anything you've done before, that you are unsupportable by me, or by the United States Navy."

"Sir? I don't understand."

That was not the best thing for me to say.

"You don't understand? I think you understand only too well, Commander Wake. Your orders were to be, above all, *covert!* To specifically *not* excite the attention of the Spanish, to *not* take sides, and to merely observe and report on what was happening in Havana and Florida. You were to attempt to ascertain the identity of any U.S. government official who might be furnishing assistance to a foreign country, and the extent of foreign activities in our country. You were not to *kill* anyone, get involved in *revolutionary* activities, or *embarrass* this government in front of Spain. And you were to have your reports to us here on time."

The admiral stopped to breathe. "Well, none of that was done. You did embarrass this country, you did get involved in the Cuban civil war, you did kill people—within the borders of the United States, no less. You have not accomplished your mission at all in the professional manner that it was to be accomplished, Commander. Not . . . at . . . all."

"But, sir, I did get the infor—"

Porter's hand clenched into a fist as Walker stepped on my shoe, stopping me. The admiral's eyes narrowed into slits as his voice dropped an octave. "And now *I* am the one who has to explain this convoluted mess to the secretary of the navy and the *president* of the United States."

"Sorry, sir. It ended up more complicated and dangerous than I, or any of us up here, anticipated. But we did find out who the Judas was, the extent of the Cuban rebel operations in Florida, and quite a bit about the Spanish agents operating there."

"But you didn't do it *quietly,* as you were commanded to—by the secretary of the navy himself, and later by me, in this very office."

Walker spoke for the first time. "The official position of this administration is neutrality, Commander Wake. We are not to be part of the civil war in Cuba on either side. In addition to not maintaining a clandestine status and thereby protecting the United States' image, you took sides by attempting to warn the rebels about the Spanish agents, an endeavor that led to your killing men. I presume that decision on your part was because your daughter had already joined the rebels."

So they knew about Useppa . . . oh, God.

They didn't get that through my report, but probably from Dort, who'd heard the rumor through his informant. My hopes to keep the extent of her involvement quiet ended.

Walker's demeanor was the opposite of the admiral's. He was cold, monotone.

"Among the other salient things you failed to do on this assignment, you failed to mention your daughter's connection to the revolutionaries in your report, Commander."

I was trying to formulate an answer when Porter took over. "And on top of every other damned thing, I have a new report here, just in from Captain Gaston of the *Powhatan*," Porter held up the thin report I'd seen him reading, "that states he saw you 'running away from the fire in Key West in a state of panic.' He further reports that he considers your actions that night a 'gross example of conduct unbecoming a naval officer of the United States, and it borders on cowardice.' He suggests that charges be brought."

That was preposterous. "Sir, that is totally not true! Captain Gaston did see me, but I was evacuating my—"

"Yes, your daughter. We know, Wake." Porter's face turned crimson, in stark contrast with his famous white mane. He growled out the rest in rapid-fire. "This has gotten out of hand. Your position here in ONI has become untenable. Therefore, you—and Boatswain's Mate Rork—are hereby placed on official leave awaiting further orders."

I was beached, on half-pay. So was Rork.

"You both will still be under naval discipline, Commander Wake, and are hereby ordered to not discuss this entire affair with anyone. You are not to attend any professional functions in Washington, and will immediately be en route to your home in Florida, where you will await further orders from the department. You will not request nor inquire as to possible billets—the department will be in contact with you regarding any possible future assignment via official correspondence."

We were being sent away, out of sight, but still on the leash. Still under naval control. My reputation and career would be ruined. Then forgotten. It was over. Everything I'd worked for during the last twenty-three years was gone. Finished.

Walker said, "And please hand over your treasury department commission right now, Commander. You no longer have any law-enforcing authority."

I did so, fumbling to unfold it. "Admiral, I don't think things justify any disciplinary—"

Admiral Porter exploded. "Don't you *dare* even think about

playing sea-lawyer with me, Wake! There *is* no disciplinary action—not that I couldn't make that happen in a monkey's
heartbeat. Besides Captain Gaston's complaint about you at the
fire, there is more than probable cause to believe that during your
mission you violated articles fourteen and twenty of the Articles
of War of the Navy, regarding failure to obey orders and neglect of
duty. And your daughter has most certainly violated the neutrality
law—section 5288, of the United States criminal code—in aiding
and abetting a foreign military operation within the United
States."

Shaking with barely controlled anger, he went on. "I have
chosen not to follow the prosecution route, though it remains
an option, at *my* discretion. Do you understand completely the
ramifications of what I've just told you?"

I was overwhelmed by the ferocity in his voice, stunned by
the enormity of what he had just said. All I could muster was a
weak, "Ah . . . yes, sir."

The next words hissed out of Porter's mouth. "Then you are
dismissed, Commander Wake."

Walker and I executed a right-face and marched out of
the office. In the anteroom, he turned and informed me, "The
personal belongings from your desk at ONI are boxed and with
the senior clerk at my office. You will not return to ONI, but
will pick up that box at my office and depart naval headquarters
immediately, to await our communication at your home. Do not
doubt the admiral's anger, Commander. This could've been far
worse. I'm the one who talked him out of the court-martial."

And that was that. I was off active duty, exiled away, and all
hopes of continuing my naval career ended. My knees were so
wobbly I could barely stand.

When I exited headquarters minutes later and descended the
Navy Steps on the White House side of the building, I needed
to use the handrail like an invalid. With trembling hands and
pounding heart, I made my way across the presidential park

toward the Navy Yard. I needed to get with Rork and try to figure out the answer to the only question left.

What did we do now?

When I got there, Rork had just found out his fate and was sitting in the senior petty officers' mess. Bewildered is an understatement for our mutual state of mind. To get away from the onlookers, we took our belongings and went for a walk past the gun works, down to the river. Sitting on a bench near the launching ways, we went over what each of us was told, trying to decipher the meaning and our future.

Our stories were identical. We were both on leave awaiting orders. Both of us were told to immediately vacate our billets and go home to Florida where we would *eventually* receive orders. The reason given was failure to follow orders to maintain a covert status during the mission. That Rork shared my fate was unusual. Normally the officer would suffer the consequences of a failure and the enlisted man would simply be reassigned.

Rork thought that significant—in a bad way.

"Methinks we're to be on ice, sir. Out've sight an' mind. They don't want an official inquiry—'twould bring out too much they don't want known. Think on it—how would it look in the papers if all hands could see that dago agents are runnin' around this country, killin' an' such? An' with the notorious Pinkertons helpin' 'em? An' then there's the Cubans stealin' our army's guns and smugglin' 'em out easy as a stroll through the park at Limerick? Not to mention a federal man spyin' for the Spaniards? Nay, 'tis too much to be let out. Why, there'd be calls for war."

He was right. If the public got wind of it, the situation would spiral out of the administration's control. "And President Cleveland doesn't want any part of that, does he? Why the hell did they send us in the first place?"

Rork chuckled bitterly. "'Cause when they sent us on this mission they didn't think we'd find much! Thought Roosevelt's message was a hoax, an' they sent us to shut him up. But 'twarn't a hoax, an' we found out too damned much. So now we're to be stuffed, stowed in the back o' the closet."

Rork sighed and surveyed a gunboat steaming upriver. His seabag and hammock—rolled and lashed in the regulation manner with thirteen hitches—were beside him. I looked down at my box of office effects on the bench beside me. I never kept many personal items at my seldom-used desk. A photograph of my family, a *gahnjar* fighting knife from Africa, some quill pens from Italy, and a few other things. I hadn't examined the box when the old senior yeoman handed it to me. Humiliation made me take it quickly and escape the building. Now I saw that there were two envelopes atop my things inside. Telegraph envelopes. Both had been unsealed.

Rork was still watching the river when I opened the envelope and read the message within.

> 14 APRIL 1886
> FROM: T. ROOSEVELT/DICKINSON/ DAKOTA TERRITORY
> TO: P. WAKE/NAVAL HQS/WASHINGTON DC
> XX—REGRET DELAY IN COMMS—X— HAVE BEEN BUSY ATTDNG TO BOAT PIRATES AT MY CATTLE RANCH OUT WEST—X—RECVD WORD U DID JOB TOO WELL—X—CONGRATULATIONS—X— DON'T GIVE UP THE SHIP—X—SENDING LTR TO UR FLA HOME—XX

I showed it to Rork as I opened the other envelope.

10 APRIL 1886
FROM: MONDONGO/NEW YORK CITY
TO: P.WAKE/NAVAL HQS/WASHINGTON
DC
XX—GLAD YOU SURVIVED TROUBLES
IN YBOR & KW—X—MOVEMENT
STILL STRONG—X—WILL KEEP IN
CORRESPONDENCE—XX

Rork and I exchanged puzzled looks. That Roosevelt knew the situation didn't surprise me one bit. He'd probably pestered Admiral Porter mercilessly to find out what was happening on the mission. His comment about doing the job too well was odd, though. What did that mean? I suppose Martí's message didn't surprise me either—he'd been peripherally, and deniably, involved the whole time. But the timing of both messages added to our disorientation on the entire affair. I thought everything was over.

Rork disagreed. "Nay, sir. There's more ta this. I know not what, but there's more."

The next day we were aboard a train, heading for Florida.

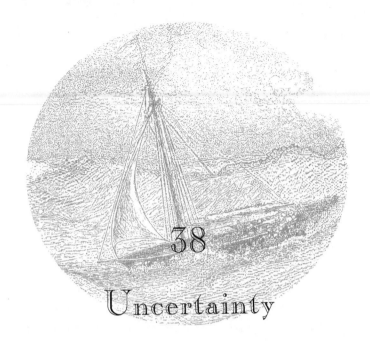

38
Uncertainty

Summer, 1886
Patricio Island
Florida

Useppa stayed in northern Virginia. She taught at a school near Fairfax and professed to be happy. I thought that false and mainly for my morale. Key West, and now Patricio Island, had too many grotesque memories for her, and I was relieved she had work to occupy her mind. I knew from personal experience that the nights would be the worst.

My son, Sean, having successfully endured the hardships of being a lowly plebe, was in his second year of struggle at Annapolis. He learned of events—a condensed version without details of our involvement—by letter. I counseled Useppa to not divulge her knowledge of what had happened to anyone. Sean's reply was full of questions, most of which I deflected or ignored. I worried about the repercussions of my situation upon his career. The navy was in essence a small town. Unfortunately, we never did get to see young Sean, since my stay up north was cut short.

Rork and I lived in our bungalows atop the hill at Patricio after our abrupt return from Washington. When we arrived, Whidden reported that no strangers had been near the island, but that a strange vessel had been seen in the area.

It seemed that a small steamer had anchored in the middle of Charlotte Harbor for two days. Whidden saw crew hauling up boxes out of the water. When he went alongside and asked what was going on, he was told the steamer was part of an army engineer survey of the coast. They were determining where channel marks and lights should be placed. The next day the steamer departed.

We settled in to wait for the call to return to duty. It was our longest habitation on the island since I'd bought the place three years earlier. Staying at the island through the summer was certainly not our norm. Late fall, winter, and spring are paradise there, but the summer and early fall—July to October—is a beastly hot and humid period. And worst of all, clouds of voracious insects penetrate all functions and facets of civilized living. But there was no choice. When on half-pay, one does not spend frivolously to go to cooler climes merely for comfort.

Even if we'd gone to Massachusetts, where I still had some family, it would have been more expensive to live. So instead, we stayed on the island and lived like our neighbors. It was a simple, hard existence, centered around daily scrubbing away the constant mildew, fishing for food, fighting the damned bugs, dodging the afternoon monsoon, and trying to keep a positive attitude.

Correspondence, and its weekly arrival via Whidden's boat, became the high point of our existence. Letters and telegram deliveries were pored over by Rork and me, with discussions in endless detail about meanings and ramifications. For some reason

I've never understood since, people we'd known for years from our jaunts around the world chose that period to write us. Even Rork, who never got letters, received notes from distant cousins in Ireland. Did the anguish of our banishment transmit some sort of a cosmic alert, like a central telegraph key sending out a call for help on all wires? It appeared eerily so, and we were grateful for it.

Two weeks into our exile, on May fifteenth, Whidden dropped off a telegram from Commodore Walker. It simply said our status would remain "on half-pay awaiting orders until further notice via official correspondence." That put us both in a funk for days. My depression increased by worry that Rork blamed me for our predicament, even though he never indicated it. He could be quite moody, however, and for days after Walker's message he was glum.

That lasted about a week. Then he decided I should learn some skill on a harmonica, since he had become rather proficient himself. Alas, his training had no success. I was no good at it, only fit for an accompanying role. Our evening sessions consisted of him playing the real music—an Irish jig or lament—and me sounding a few background tones on the conch shell, or banging the percussion out on a tin pot.

Roosevelt was true to his word and kept in touch. In late May we got a letter from him at his place at Elkhorn Ranch, somewhere out in the Dakota Territory. He'd been out west for months, working his land, and was about to begin a big roundup of five thousand cattle and five hundred horses. He was also close to finishing up his pending book on Thomas Hart Benton. That he bothered to take time to write touched me. The letter brought to mind his infectious personality and energy, and made me smile. I told Rork that he would like Roosevelt. Rork wasn't so sure. He didn't like politicians.

From what he wrote in the letter, Roosevelt obviously knew about our mission's outcome, stating that "a source" had kept him apprised of developments. He continued on with a sober assessment of our situation:

I must unhappily admit, however, that your work, conducted under the most mortal of dangers, will never be recognized for its true significance, for the political powers-that-be have deemed it inconvenient to acknowledge, let alone honor. Thus is the darker shade of glory—when success, which is known by few, benefits the many.

In the meantime, please be assured that there are some who know—in a way that does not compromise the security of your endeavors, or the integrity of your personal reputation—of your sacrifices and successes. Regrettably, they are not in positions to provide reward or recognition. Not yet, at least. But know that they know.

He ended with an intriguing piece of advice.

And so, if I may be so bold, sir, my unasked counsel is to exhibit patience, waiting with the confident serenity of a prophet, for that moment when your time will come again, as I am firmly convinced it shall.

As the long weeks of sweat and bugs evolved into months of enduring the hot, wet summer, I forgot about Roosevelt, and pushed the Cuban assignment from my mind. Then a reminder of our ordeal arrived in the form of the revenue cutter *Dix*.

In early June, I was on the verandah struggling to translate Verne's latest, *Robur the Conqueror,* when I looked up and saw the side-wheel steamer off Pine Island. She had two Cuban fishing smacks in tow, captured by Lacosta Island for smuggling rotgut *aguardiente*. For the next several weeks she diligently poked around the islands, sending her boats ever afar, searching, questioning.

I sailed over to her one day and talked to Captain Fengar, who said that orders had come down from Washington: stop illegal trafficking in rum and guns to and from Cuba. I noticed that Fengar was hesitant to converse with me on that topic, our old comradeship evidently having withered on the vine, so to speak. When I explained that I was on leave awaiting orders, he didn't seem surprised. His attitude made me wish I hadn't visited his ship, and made me wonder what he'd heard about me.

I read a lot when on the island. In mid-August, I finished Twain's newest, a rollicking novel called *The Adventures of Huckleberry Finn*. My next literary escape was the English translation of *An Iceland Fisherman*, a salty fiction by my French navy friend Louis Viaud, who is known to the world by his famous *nom de plume* Pierre Loti. Viaud and I were together at the Battle of Hué in 1883, and he sent me a signed copy. I'd just finished the first page when Whidden arrived, trudging up the hill bearing a cable message from Father Viñes in Havana.

Viñes wished us well, and included a warning to us that a deadly hurricane was approaching southern Florida. Sure enough, one hit Key West three days later, on the eighteenth, causing extensive damage to buildings newly renovated from the fire four months earlier. The eye of the storm passed off to our southwest, so Rork and I were spared the worst of it at Patricio Island.

A positive, and slightly bizarre, item of note was the visit of the Yard Dogs a few days after the hurricane. Former northern soldiers who'd been stationed at Key West during the war, my friends Kip, Brian, and Charlie played folksy tunes in the taverns from Key West to Tampa, seemingly always one step ahead of the law, creditors, scorned women, and irate husbands.

With incongruously straight faces, the boys announced they had big news—Kip was going to stand for election the next year for sheriff of Monroe County. Two years prior, in 1884, Florida had returned to electing sheriffs, so that the office was, according to Kip, "up for grabs, by them with guts." He explained that he had extensive experience for the position, having been in the custody of the Key West sheriff several times, and that he knew the legal and procedural functions of office intimately.

His opponents would be the incumbent, Sheriff Demeritt,

and a black Republican named Charles DuPont. Kip boasted that he already had twenty-two people who promised to vote for him—Charlie informed me as an aside that most of them were former jailmates of Kip's—and he wanted my endorsement.

Puffing up his chest, he added that, "As a naval officer, you've got some class, Peter. And I could use some of that for my campaign." When I replied that, regrettably, I couldn't do that, since I valued my reputation, there was no rancor on his part. Kip just said, "Ah, hell, Peter, then a decent touch of rum will do as your encouragement to me." He got it.

In late August, when the barometer and my disposition were at a low ebb, I received another letter from Roosevelt. It contained an account of the perils and joys of cattle ranching in the Bad Lands of Dakota, none of which sounded appealing to me. Rork said he would prefer sheep—they were easier to handle and slightly smarter than cows. My return correspondence filled Roosevelt in on life among the islands, with descriptions of the strong-willed people and simple events in their lives. I included a description of the local fishing for him, specifically the tarpon. Another letter arrived from Theodore in late September, telling tales of elk hunting in the mountains and including an invitation to visit him in New York City when he returned there in October. It was a kind offer, but I felt it more out of courtesy than true intent. I politely declined.

In mid-October a third letter from Roosevelt arrived, but this one was vastly different. He'd been back in the city for a week, and no longer were there grand references to natural scenes and animals. Now it was politics and his own career. It seemed to me that, for Theodore, cattle ranching out West was merely his vacation—his *vocation* was politics back East. I got the impression that this young man, with the self-assurance of one ten years his senior, was aiming high. Very high. He passed along a revealing anecdote.

A group of us cowboys hopped a freight train for the Fourth of

July celebration at the nearby town of Medora. The whole affair was a grand celebration of our country and I was asked to speak to the subject at hand. I must report that the crowd was appreciative of my oratorical effort. And from therein came an interesting critique.

After my talk, the local editor and I were conversing about politics and I told him I was thinking of taking a government post offered to me, back in New York City. It is a minor position as such things go, commissioner of health, but I feel I would do it justice and, more importantly, that it is incumbent upon a man like me to serve the people in a public and political way. Well, Peter, my newspaper friend astonished me by saying that if such were the case, then he felt certain that someday I would be the president of the United States. Naturally, I was astonished at the notion, but replied that if his prophecy should somehow come true, that I shall do my part to make a good one.

And, needless to say, in such a position, I would also be commander-in-chief of the navy. In that case it would no longer be ignored and you, sir, would be our greatest admiral!

That was followed by another invitation, this one quite insistent, for both Rork and me to visit him in New York City. Included in the envelope were two round-trip train tickets for the journey, a reservation voucher for us to stay at a fancy hotel in the city for seven days, and a cryptic note that there we would receive special invitations to see a tremendous historical event. Roosevelt ended by saying it was his way to say thank you for our mission and our sacrifices. I got the impression he felt somewhat guilty over his role as instigator of the whole affair.

Rork and I talked it over. Sitting there on my verandah, letting the windy wet cool of an afternoon thunderstorm wash over us, it took all of thirty seconds to decide the matter. With our future in limbo, and our present mired in melancholy, and bored to the point of desperation, we agreed that Roosevelt's summons was a gracious gift of *something* to do.

I at once sent a letter to headquarters, providing our address in New York, should the navy department be looking for us. Two days later, boarding the train at its newly constructed terminus at Punta Gorda, we were on our way north.

39

Theodore's Rise

Wednesday, 27 October 1886
The Fifth Avenue Hotel
200 Fifth Avenue
New York City

A gust of cold air stirred the drapes, the precursor of yet another squall line from the rainstorm that had been sweeping through New York. Reluctantly, I closed the tall window in our third-story room, which had provided us quite a view. The autumn-hued trees in the park at Madison Square, social center of the city, watched over lunchtime crowds dashing around under a sea of black umbrellas. In the park, I could see Admiral Farragut's memorial statue glistening from the showers, presenting a far more impressive image than what I remembered of the man himself.

The bellman advised me that until two months earlier, the celebrated torch of Lady Liberty herself had been on display in the center of the park. The great statue from France had just been finished and, with the torch added at its highest point, now stood atop an old abandoned fort on Bedloe's Island in the harbor. New York's newspapers extolled a public celebration that was planned for that week, describing a parade and unveiling ceremony to be held that would be beyond anything seen before. The *Herald* proclaimed that everyone who was anyone would be there. Of course, Rork and I were not of sufficient luminosity to be considered in that stratum, but I thought I might bring back a newspaper or two for family posterity's sake.

To the left out our rain-streaked window stood the famed Delmonico's—just a few doors down from us—where this convoluted odyssey had begun ten very long months earlier. The irony of our present location was not lost on me.

Here I was, back full circle, within the lair of the privileged, in the commercial center of the world, where lying was an art form and consequences were for others to endure. It was about as far, culturally, from Patricio Island as one could get in this country. Indeed, I felt, as I always do in that great city, as if I am in an alien place, one that controls and influences my world, yet is far beyond it.

The Fifth Avenue Hotel, it turned out, was not only the place where the world's elite reposed while in New York City, it was also the headquarters of the state and local Republican Party, and thus of Theodore Roosevelt. He had a suite of his own there, for personal political purposes. A bit much, thought I upon arrival, for the city's health commissioner. But much had changed with my unique friend, as I discovered soon after we had settled in.

Although the trees were beginning their hibernation for winter outside, inside the colossal hotel it seemed that politics—serious politics—was in full bloom, and my young friend Roosevelt was the star attraction. Everyone we met was talking about his nomination to run for mayor, something he'd never even alluded to in his letters. Quite the contrary, in fact—from those letters, I thought Theodore was going to be in charge of metropolitan sewer lines, or something of that sort.

That *was* the initial plan, back in Dakota. But once he returned to the city, his ambition evolved into a three-way race for the top office in the largest city in America, with him emerging as the presumed front-runner. That very morning, I'd read in the New York *Sun,* a Democrat anti-Roosevelt newspaper, an editorial stating that though they thought he wouldn't win the mayoralty, they did admit that Theodore Roosevelt just might soon be a congressman, senator, governor, or someday even president. Heady praise, indeed, from one's adversaries.

I intended to ask about all this when Rork and I met the man for lunch. We waited for some time past the appointed hour, but apparently the swirling tempest of politics had disrupted our modest plans. At one o'clock, accompanied by nervous assistants glaring at their watches, the city's shining political star stopped by our room to profusely apologize in person. Something had come up, Roosevelt explained, and he was unable to have any lunch, but he would definitely see us that evening at an institution called Cooper Union, where he was to deliver a speech. Our places had been reserved. He added in his nasal twang that "we simply *have* to talk" and that he wanted to "hear *everything*" about our Cuban experiences "from the *men* who *made* the *history.*" We would have private time after the speech.

Suddenly he thumped the table, showed his teeth in a huge grin, and said "Ah, *yes*—I nearly forgot!" He pulled out two engraved dignitary invitations to the unveiling of the Statue of Liberty the next day—the special surprise event for us described in his letter. I had heard of people offering large amounts of money to obtain such an invitation, and here Rork and I had them given to us. It was enormously kind of him to arrange, and I thanked him for both of us. Seconds later, flanked by advisors and with the force of a tornado, Roosevelt rushed out the door and headed off to other commitments. I could hear him rattling off orders as he went down the hall. No general was ever as harried or decisive, but

I could see that Theodore loved every second of it.

After the room emptied, Rork gave me his dubious look. "*That* wee bit o' a fella is the big man you've been tellin' me about? No offense, Peter, but he's not a ravin' fanatic, is he?"

It was an exciting scene when we arrived that evening. The red brick of Cooper Union's Great Hall flickered in the reflection of bonfires outside. People milled around, buzzing with talk about the great event about to take place. Rork and I were dressed in civilian attire—when one is on leave, one has the option—but we still stuck out, for our dress wasn't nearly as fine as our fellow guests in the aristocratic section.

The ushers escorted us to our seats up front. Around us were the richest of the rich. Our neighbors' conversation indicated that the Astors, Peabodys, and Rockefellers were one row up. We soon discovered that this was no ordinary event—it was the party ratification of Theodore's nomination as Republican candidate for mayor. Coronation might be a better descriptor.

I only knew of Cooper Union from reading in newspapers about Lincoln's famous speech there in 1860 on the issue of slavery. The room was cavernous, containing an enthusiastic crowd of supporters. The center of attention was a large charcoal or crayon likeness of Roosevelt. Displayed up on an easel in the stage's center, it was draped with American flags and gave the appearance of a religious altar.

The entire event was a bit too theatrical for my taste, but the two thousand attendees loved every part of it. It seemed that all hands present were for Roosevelt, several of the more intoxicated ones in the back shouting, "Make the Dakota Cowboy our city's next mayor!" The melodramatic effect even extended to Theodore's timing—he was late by thirty minutes, and when he did arrive, the crowd roared in excitement.

Theodore beamed to his followers and started right in. It was a brief speech, but in Rooseveltian fashion, it went straight to the jugular. He ridiculed opponents who said his proposed reforms were too radical, saying the time for radical reform had arrived. He attacked dull, feeble, and timid bureaucrats as being too inept for the job. Theodore announced that he was a man who cared not for class, color, or politics, and if he found a man in city government who was dishonest, he would chop his head off no matter what his affiliation or influence.

It was, quite simply, a magnificently rousing speech. Even such jaded old seamen as Rork and me—who distrust the political class mightily—ended up joining the thousands and cheering each of his points. In the end, the bellowing mass of men literally shook the building with their voices.

I marveled at the young man's performance—that night was only his twenty-eighth birthday.

And just then, I sensed someone not looking upward to the man on stage, but across at me. He stood, with reporter's notepad in hand, on the main floor below Roosevelt and off to the side, partially obscured by a great white column. José Martí nodded to me, glanced over at the side door, and headed for it. I quickly informed Rork and asked him to remain while I met with the Cuban.

Outside the hall, he shook my hand and said, "I see you are a supporter of Roosevelt. A good decision. He is going to be a man of power. He has it on his face, in his voice. And he supports independence for Cuba."

I didn't rise to that bait. "No, no, I'm just a friend. I don't get involved in politics, José."

Martí shook his head. "I think you are more involved than you know, my friend. I know by your actions that you support freedom for my people. I am sorry for the tribulations you and your family have endured since we last met. It was not in vain, Peter. The Spanish can slaughter mortal men, but cannot kill an idea."

I ignored the platitudes and switched to something I'd been wanting to tell him in person. "Thank you for your help at Tampa, and in Havana, and Key West. I must say, José, you certainly have friends in a lot of places."

He shrugged. "Journalists have many acquaintances."

The usher who'd escorted me into the hall appeared at the door just then. He waved me back inside, saying that the carriages were leaving for the hotel. It was time to go.

"Look, I want to sit down with you and talk some more, José, but right now I have to rejoin my hosts. I'll be here a few days. Tomorrow I will be busy at the statue ceremony, but how about we meet for lunch two days from now, at the Fifth Avenue Hotel, at noon. I'll buy."

He smiled at the usher's interruption, but seemed perturbed. "That would be pleasant, Peter. And I too have some things to discuss, things that involve you and the Spanish. But they can wait for two days. I will meet you there for lunch on Friday."

We shook hands and I turned to go, but Martí paused, his sad eyes locked on mine. "We will meet again, Peter. Until then, please take care."

I noted that it wasn't some bland farewell courtesy. He'd said it somberly, as a statement of fact. As I headed back in the side door of the hall, I noticed two men on the street watching Martí as he walked away.

Theodore Roosevelt exuded raw energy. How a man so young could have that kind of confidence and drive was a mystery to me. Maybe it was those long months out West. Or perhaps it was his upper-class childhood and education.

Rork and I were in the parlor of his suite. We'd arrived there after the social gathering that followed the speech. All of the self-important followers were gone. The private secretary had departed. Our neckties were loosened, rum was poured for us, tea for Roosevelt, and we were seated about the fireplace. Theodore leaned forward, his smile replaced by concern.

"Peter, I have heard a third-hand version of what transpired with the Cuban affair, but since I was somewhat involved at the outset, I would like to know exactly what happened, directly from you and Mr. Rork."

My narrative was punctuated by his insightful questions. As I went on through the chronology, he seemed more and more humbled to me, as if he were atoning for his responsibility in setting off the train of events. At the end of two hours, he saw the time was after midnight.

"I fear I have kept you up *far* too late," he paused with a shy smile, "for the *second* time this year. So, please let me end this conversation with an *informed* observation: Peter, you are not forgotten in Washington and this, too, shall pass. Your stock is still *highly* valued, sir. Beyond that unfortunately *vague* pronouncement, I have not the liberty to go. Just know that it comes via persons of importance, who appreciate your efforts."

That got my attention. "Thank you. And thank you again for the invitations to the great statue's unveiling tomorrow. Are we meeting there, or ahead?"

Roosevelt's brow furrowed. "Alas, though I would be positively *delighted* in seeing the lovely lady presented to the nation and the world, I will not be able to attend. More pressing matters of even greater import altered my plans. I *will* see you on Friday though, maybe for dinner. Ah, yes, there are some people you should meet. Or rather, they should meet *you*."

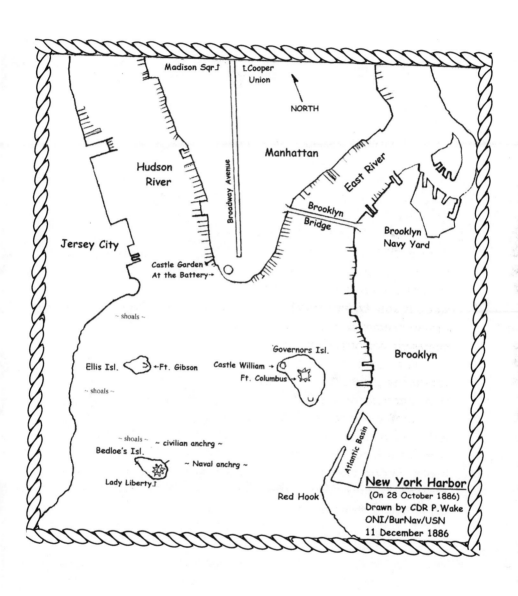

Madison Sqr.

Cooper Union

NORTH

Manhattan

Hudson River

Broadway Avenue

East River

Brooklyn Bridge

Brooklyn Navy Yard

Jersey City

Castle Garden At the Battery →

~ shoals ~

Governors Isl.

Brooklyn

Ellis Isl. ←Ft. Gibson

Castle William →
Ft. Columbus

~ shoals ~

~ shoals ~   ~ civilian anchrg ~

Bedloe's Isl.

~ Naval anchrg ~

Atlantic Basin

Lady Liberty

Red Hook

New York Harbor
(On 28 October 1886)
Drawn by CDR P. Wake
ONI/BurNav/USN
11 December 1886

40

Lady Liberty

Thursday, 28 October 1886
Bedloe's Island
New York harbor

The weather for the event was wet, windy, and cold, and it grew worse as the day progressed. The sun shed weak light, diffused into a vague amber illumination by the misty overcast. The effect on the event's ambience was dismal, more a funeral than a baptism, and not at all what the promoters had promised the tens of thousands who lined miles of harbor front and stood crowded aboard dozens of ships.

At ten in the morning, the marching procession arrived at Madison Square, where the president and senior dignitaries reviewed the participating military, police, and fire units. Once past the grandstand, it sloshed its way down to the Battery. The presidential party, including the foreign diplomats, headed west a few blocks and departed from the Twenty-third Street pier, aboard the naval auxiliary steamer *Despatch*. Lesser mortals, including Rork and myself, boarded private vessels at the south end of Manhattan.

The harbor was bedlam. Two dozen French, British, and U.S. warships sat off the east side of Bedloe's Island where the statue stood. Thousands of flag-bedecked yachts, ferries, cargo vessels, tugs, and small boats clogged the harbor. Every one of them strained to get as close as they could to the scene in the confused chop created by the ships' wakes and the periodic squall lines.

On the tiny island itself, Rork and I were two of twenty-five hundred holders of the exclusive engraved invitations. The elegantly clad line snaked forward under cover of umbrellas from the dock and trooped up the specially constructed stairways to the ramparts of old Fort Wood, upon which the statue was built. As each man and woman ascended, he or she carefully peeked out from an umbrella and observed the proportions of the coppered colossus above us, much of which was still cloaked in canvas, soaring up into the mist.

I must say it *was* impressive, far beyond anything else I've seen, before or since. But the atmospheric conditions weren't conducive to the majesty of the moment, and I wondered how much longer the soaked assembly would be patient, waiting for the main event, when that canvas coat would be dropped, and the lady beneath unveiled.

The organizers, however, obviously betting on a sunny day, had planned on our being entertained *ad nauseum* by orators of domestic and international fame, and so the festivities dragged on. Now that I'd listened to Roosevelt speak, others paled for me and I felt my keenness for the occasion dwindling rapidly. I wasn't alone in that sentiment. Everyone was ill tempered by the time the speeches began.

But I must give the arrangers credit—a more prominent hall of fame could scarcely have been assembled. There, on a platform built above our throng at the base of the statue's pedestal, was the designer, Bartholdi, accompanied by President Cleveland and some of his Washington political apparatus. I saw with surprise that someone had invited white-haired Ferdinand de Lesseps, of Panamanian canal notoriety. His professional star was already descending rapidly by then, but I noted he was granted the first speech.

The French ambassador and his proud entourage basked in their country's glory as the statue's donor, as did their continental neighbors, the ambassadors and ministers of Europe. Senator Evarts, former secretary of state and friend of de Lesseps, was there. Governor Hill of New York was prominently displaying himself, along with the city's current headman, William Russell Grace, who had the distinction of being New York City's first Irish-born Catholic mayor.

Grace was a favorite of Rork's, who'd met him during the navy's famine relief voyage from New York to Ireland in '79. This was before his time in office, when Grace was known as an adventurer-merchant. The man had personally donated fully a quarter of the relief aid that Rork had sailed to Ireland aboard our ancient frigate *Constitution*. To his credit, and Rork's delight, Mayor Grace remembered my friend warmly, and they spent several minutes reminiscing before the speeches commenced.

With Rork otherwise pleasantly occupied, I nosed about the area, nodding to de Lesseps, who clearly didn't remember me from Panama, which was just as well, since I thought him a fraud. I said hello in mangled French to the senior Gallic diplomat. He graciously replied so rapidly that I could not understand anything except that he was smiling as he said it. It was an odd scene all around, with the elite drinking champagne and valiantly trying to ignore the incessant rain that was ruining the day—and their expensive attire. In addition to all of this was the din of periodic naval cannon salutes and incessant steam whistles from the civilian shipping. The whole effect made a setting of perfect chaos. Not exactly what had been hoped for by the organizers.

It was in that scenario that I saw two men I knew in the vast crowd of strangers. The first of the two men brought a smile to my face, for it was Martí, covering the event for his newspapers in South America, as he had the previous evening at Cooper Union.

Standing at the easternmost ramparts of the old fort, we were soon talking about the United States' attitude toward a bloodless Cuban independence. Two weeks earlier, the Spanish had finally emancipated the last of their slaves on their island in an effort to mitigate dissent, but the fervor for independence was hotter than ever. Martí had more hope on the subject than I, and was about to expound on it when he stopped suddenly, his hooded eyes narrowing on something in the distance. I followed his gaze and saw the same two men I'd seen watching him the night before.

"Pinkertons, of the famous detective and guard company. The one that fights the unions," he said beneath his breath. "They have a contract with the Spanish government to guard their diplomatic people, and also to watch the Cubans in the city, especially me. Let them. They will see nothing, for I will do nothing. I am not here to hurt the Spanish ambassador. I am but a writer, and our cause does not make war on diplomats."

His comment inspired me to take a look at the Spanish diplomat. An older man with courtly mien and manners, he was surrounded by not-so-subtle security men scrutinizing the guests around them. Well, really now, their menacing deportment seemed a bit overdone to me, given the situation. After all, we were on a small island, with policemen all around, amidst the social elite of the city. Hardly a hotbed of anarchists.

"The tall, arrogant ones are Pinkertons," said Martí. "The shorter ones are Spaniards. Pinkertons merely do what they are told and follow their rules. Therefore they are predictable. The quiet Spaniards are more dangerous, for they have no rules."

As he said that, I noticed the second man that day that I knew. He was one of the shorter ones, and standing with the security contingent. The man walked over and pointed me out to one of his taller colleagues, evidently a Pinkerton, by Martí's description. Then the short man disappeared behind some of the ambassador's staff. His rolling gait confirmed it for me.

My blood froze. It was Boreau.

I guessed that Martí didn't know him by sight. I also realized that Martí was probably ignorant of anything that had happened to me after the fire in Key West. He'd no doubt heard of Boreau and his actions in Tampa and Key West, of course, but couldn't know of his attack on my home several weeks later.

Seeing me tense up, he asked, "Do you know that man? He is watching you very intensely."

"That's Boreau. The man Ybor deflected away from me. The same man who assaulted your revolutionary friends at the San Carlos Club in Key West, thereby preventing the coordinated Hatuey uprising in Cuba. Your island might have been independent by now, if not for him."

Martí stepped back, the shock visible on his face. "One moment, Peter, please. You know about the Hatuey plan? How did you know? Even your daughter did not have knowledge of the plan."

Knowledge. In Washington, that snake pit of schemers, it is said that, "knowledge is power." Over the years, I have learned a corollary—that knowledge kept secret is extreme power. And I've discovered an even more powerful state of affairs: when others become convinced that you have more knowledge than you really do, especially about their own schemes. This was one of those moments. Better that he not realize the meager extent of my knowledge, and always wonder.

"José, it is my business to know things. It is also my business not to divulge them."

Three Pinkerton men were approaching us. José acknowledged my reply with a nod, then said, "I think they are coming for *you,* my friend, and not me. An unusual situation, to say the least. Perhaps you could join your political leaders—those Pinkertons would not dare molest you there."

Good idea, but my eyes and my mind weren't focused on the Pinkertons. Boreau was my target. My final moments with him at Patricio Island filled my mind. I caught a glimpse of him among his own diplomats, glancing over his shoulder at me. At that point the crowd burst into applause, more cannons thundered, and I realized that President Cleveland was about to speak.

Rork came up to me, immediately understanding that something was amiss.

"What's wrong, sir?"

"Boreau is over there, second row, by the Spanish ambassador. He knows we're here."

Rork's face tightened, but he didn't reply, for we had a more pressing issue. The Pinkerton men arrived, two of them standing back as reinforcements, while the oldest of them faked a smile and said, "Excuse me, sir, but do you have your invitations?"

While showing me his identification card—with the well-known drawing of a watchful eye and the caption "We Never Sleep" under it—he moved around to my right as he talked, making me track around with him, thus losing sight of Boreau and the ceremony. It was a deft move. The Pinkerton man was clever, but I could tell he was used to only dealing with people who could be intimidated. United States naval officers don't fit into that category.

"Certainly, but I'm not in the habit of responding to such requests by men I don't know. I am Commander Peter Wake, United States Navy. This is my aide, Boatswain's Mate Sean Rork of the United States Navy. And now, who exactly are *you?*"

That took him aback a bit. I guessed that Boreau didn't tell him anything other than I was a troublemaker. He told me his name, which I noted was Irish, said he was a private detective on guard duty, and meekly glanced at my invitation. During this dialogue, Martí had backed away unnoticed—the other thugs had their eyes glued to Rork, who was unscrewing his false left hand. He placed it inside his coat pocket and raised an eyebrow at the detectives playfully. From the corner of my eye, I saw Martí heading for the far side of the crowd below the president, where the elite of the elite had gathered.

Even while eyeing the Pinkerton, my mind registered that the ponderous bulk of President Cleveland had ascended to the podium and begun his address. It is strange, I suppose, but almost a decade later, I still remember his words in the background. As my confrontation with the Pinkerton men unfolded, the president began.

"We are not here today to bow before the representative of a fierce and warlike god, filled with wrath and vengeance . . ."

The detective in front of me appeared bewildered as to what to say or do next with an indignant naval officer, so I took over for him. "All right, now that we all know who we are—why did you come all the way over here to ask me that?"

He hesitated and I heard Cleveland's baritone continuing, *"But we joyously contemplate instead our own deity keeping watch and ward before the open gates of America, and greater than all that have been celebrated in ancient song."*

The Pinkerton recovered enough to stammer, "Uh, my boss asked me to, sir. He musta' thought you were somebody else. Sorry, sir. Very sorry. Please enjoy the day, sir."

He made to leave, but I stopped him with a command, "Have Mr. Boreau come over here. I'd like to speak with him. We're old friends, you know."

That little tidbit truly confused him. "Uh, well, he can't do that, sir. He's leaving on the boat right now."

Oh yes, I'd just bet he was—probably when he saw Rork. "I see. Very well, detective, then you're *dismissed.*"

Right at that moment, Cleveland's stentorian tone rose over a sudden increase of rain. *"And instead of grasping in her hand thunderbolts of terror and of death, she holds aloft the light which illumines the way to man's enfranchisement."*

The three Pinkertons walked quickly back to their own group. Rork followed me down the stairway and toward the wharf.

"Orders, sir?"

"We're headed for the dock to get Boreau before he escapes."

Another squall line, this one with dark rolling clouds, was advancing across the harbor from the north. It stretched from the rail yard docks at Jersey City, over to Castle William on Governor's Island. I gauged its velocity over the water. There wasn't much time. It would hit the wharf just as we would.

As we approached, I could see that a small excursion steamer was tied up to the wharf. A puff of steam emerged from her stack, followed by a column of dense black smoke—she was preparing to get under way. On the dock, some sort of commotion was breaking out among some men gathered there. Rork and I started to run the remaining hundred yards.

The squall was faster than I'd estimated. The island just north of Bedloe's was devoured by the dark line. Halyards of the anchored spectator fleet near us began to strum faster on masts. A curtain of wind-driven rain swept across the dock just before we got there, obscuring the steamer, disrupting the men on the dock. They scattered, running for cover, except two. They stood there, facing each other in the downpour.

Martí looked even more emaciated in his soaked condition—certainly no match for a man like Boreau. But he held his ground, arms extended outward, blocking the Spanish agent from getting past him to that steamer, which was casting off.

When we reached the foot of the dock, Boreau slowly turned to us, right hand reaching inside his coat. Neither Rork or I had our pistols—a deficiency I've not repeated since—and I was suddenly at a loss for what to do. The Spaniard glared at Rork, who had that frightening spike in plain sight.

Boreau solved my immediate dilemma by running straight at us, pistol drawn. A double flash erupted from the muzzle just as President Cleveland's speech ended and the harbor exploded in naval gun salutes and steam whistles—so thunderously loud I never heard the revolver, only ten feet from me.

Fortunately, he missed. I felt no searing pain from a bullet, a sensation I am regrettably familiar with, but was temporarily taken aback as Boreau ran by to the west along the seawall, past a startled policeman who had been watching the ceremonies. I instantly realized the Spaniard's intention.

Spectator boats, large steam yachts and schooners, were anchored close to the island. He meant to swim to them. I began running just as he leaped down off the wall, onto the rock riprap surrounding the island's seawall. I called out, "Man overboard! Help him—he's drowning!"

Martí jogged along in the rear, perplexed as to how things were developing, but Rork—God bless him—understood completely and raced alongside me. The policeman's attention was completely engaged by this time, and he too, began running toward our target, albeit with different intentions. Hearing my plea, he evidently thought the Spaniard was attempting suicide.

Boreau waded into the water, then launched himself in the direction of the nearest vessel, a schooner yacht crammed with upper-class swells sitting on deck chairs under a large awning. In my mental extremis, I forwent a gentle entry into the water. Kicking off my shoes, I dove from the wall, over those jagged rocks, and managed to make it, barely surviving my foolishness. The water was cold, stunning me temporarily, but my anger— Useppa's anguished face flashed in my mind—provided the energy required and I quickly got up to speed, gaining on him rapidly. The ebb tide was running strong and we both were being swiftly taken out into deeper water, toward the spectator fleet.

A splash behind signaled that Rork was still with me. I heard the policeman yelling over to the yacht to try to "save that drowning man!" People along the wharf joined in the chorus. Several people aboard the schooner were now pointing to Boreau, who was flailing away toward them. The Spaniard needed only another seventy-five feet and he'd be at the yacht.

That is when I caught him.

"*Stop—I'll save you!*" I yelled for all it was worth to the audience afloat and ashore—then I grabbed him by the arms, took a gulp of air, and let my weight sink, pulling him down. As we submerged deeper into the black water, I pinioned his biceps.

I heard a muffled explosion, then another, and realized he was firing his pistol. I was able to wrap my legs around his torso, and we sank even faster. We dropped further into the darkness, my lungs now searing, like that night they were burned in the fire. Boreau struggled, kicking and twisting, but my thighs kept tightening and he couldn't even move his hands now. I could hear him screaming as my left hand clawed his throat and my right penetrated his eye sockets. We would both die. I didn't care.

His body went limp but I kept squeezing him, fearing a ruse. My ears were pounding as we hit the muddy bottom thirty feet down. Boreau's body didn't react to the impact, folding into a lump in the ooze around us. I remember at that moment the logic of my mind began to take over from the rage. I realized that it was done. He was dead.

I let go and pushed off, suddenly desperate to live, flailing to get up to the surface again. I forced myself to exhale, to let go of that precious air in my lungs, hoping I could survive the ascent long enough to breathe again.

It was a close-run thing. I ran out of air and water rushed in, choking me as I hit the top. Rork was there, treading water and holding my head up above the waves, allowing me to expel the seawater and get some sweet fresh air inside me.

Someone at the yacht shouted in admiration. I saw a small boat pulling for us. Then I lost awareness and collapsed, surrendering to Rork's strength as he towed me to safety.

We were hoisted over the launch's gunwales, then gently helped up onto the deck of the yacht, many of the guests recoiling in horror upon seeing Rork's spike. The professional captain soon understood that we were seamen, though, and ordered us to his cabin, where the stewards warmed us with brandy, blankets, and dry clothes.

An hour later, attired in the captain's spare clothes, we emerged into the salon to an ovation. Lady Liberty's ceremonies had concluded and the schooner was bound for her dock in Brooklyn. It was still dismal out and all guests were packed down below, thoroughly thrilled with what they regarded as a heroic attempt to save a man's life, right in front of them.

Rork, who by then had reattached his rubber hand, let me handle the questions. No, I didn't know the man, or why he jumped into water. Yes, Rork and I were in the navy and had special invitations, courtesy of Theodore Roosevelt, to attend the event on the island. Yes, I supported Roosevelt and thought he would make a fine mayor of the great city of New York.

The last question I answered firmly: No, I didn't want any newspaper publicity for my deed. After all, I'd failed to save the man, and felt bad about that. There was an audible gasp of sympathetic admiration.

Rork looked me in the eye and said not a word.

41

Honor's Call

Wednesday, 3 November 1886
The Fifth Avenue Hotel
200 Fifth Avenue
New York City

Rork and I had lunch with Martí the next day, Friday, as previously planned. We talked about the situations in Cuba, Key West, and Ybor City, but Martí did not reveal any new information to me. He shyly said he was only a writer and philosopher, and would occasionally "hear things."

Exasperated, I finally asked, "How did you know Roosevelt would be on that train to give him the riddle message?"

He looked me in the eye and answered with his own question. "What message was that, Peter?"

We ended up regarding each other with sly smiles and mutually let the topic go.

He did, however, enlighten us about the commotion on

the dock at Bedloe's Island. He'd been trying to delay Boreau's departure on the steamer by instigating a conflict, hoping that either we, the police, or someone could do something about the Spanish murderer. Boreau was about to shoot Martí when our arrival diverted his attention and his target shifted to me.

The newspaperman in him was full of questions about what had happened with Boreau and me in the water. From Martí's vantage point on the seawall next to the policeman, he couldn't see the details, which I thought just as well. Well into the lie by then, I told him I had tried to save Boreau in order to bring him to trial for murder in Florida for the deaths at the Key West fire. Then I told him there probably wouldn't have been enough evidence to convict anyway, so I suggested that he *not* write about any of it. I maintained my silence about the episode at Patricio Island.

The Cuban looked at Rork, then at me. I could tell Martí didn't believe my story. He sighed, his hooded eyes betraying nothing as he said, "Then there is nothing to write about."

We moved on to national and international affairs, and I listened to his opinion on them with great interest. He was unusually well informed. His parting comment stayed with me, however, for it proved prophetic: "You, my friend, fully understand how very high the price of honor can be. Until we meet again— and I am certain that we will—I wish you good fortune, Peter."

On Wednesday, November third, Rork and I were still at the Fifth Avenue Hotel, due to leave the next day. It was the morning after the city's great political contest, and a pall had settled over the hotel. Newspaper headlines showed Roosevelt's earlier prediction that the election would be close but in his favor was grossly false. It wasn't anywhere near close—he had lost overwhelmingly, finishing a distant third place with only sixty thousand votes, out of 219,000 cast in the city.

Rork and I wandered through the hotel to his campaign offices late that morning and found him alone at his desk in the deserted suite. Posters, newspapers, invitations, and assorted other detritus littered the floor and tables, like debris I've seen scattered on battlefields. A funereal silence palpably completed the resemblance. Two charwomen were busy cleaning up the place for the next tenants, studiously ignoring the solitary man sitting there, who only days before had been the talk of the nation.

Theodore was philosophical when I inquired as to his state of being. "Well, not *all* is lost, Peter. My dear friend Henry Lodge won his race in Massachusetts, and is heading for Congress. You remember him, I believe."

He exhaled for several long seconds. Then his tone changed from reflective to energetic—the old Theodore was back. "And I will be just *fine*. Now I have time for more *important* things in my personal life."

"Really? What do you have in mind?"

He produced that infectious grin, wonderful to see again.

"You know *what*, Peter?" He lowered his voice. "I'll let you both in on a little confidence that isn't public yet. I'm headed off to England, to marry my fiancée."

"What? You've never said anything about getting married. When did you become engaged?"

His mood rose as he explained. "Late last year, gentlemen, to a lovely and absolutely *charming* lady named Edith. Known her *forever!* Why, we've been the very *best* of friends since childhood.

"And this very Saturday, we're taking that new Cunard liner, *Etruria*, across to Liverpool. What a fascinating ship she is. Did you know—that at almost eight *thousand* tons—she can do nineteen knots? That's bigger and faster than *Chicago*, our newest and best warship. Amazing! Why can't our *naval* ships do that, I ask? A simply *deplorable* state of affairs, that. How can we be a great nation when merchant ships are faster than our warships? Something needs to be done. And, by gad, if I ever have a *real* say in the matter, it shall be."

Knowing that once he got going on our navy he'd never stop, I changed the subject back to *him.* "Theodore, why in the world did you keep the engagement secret?"

"Out of affection for my dear Edith. *Protection* from reporters, you see. And we must continue to do so. Of necessity, we'll be incognito on the ship, of course. The press is positively *predatory* these days. Once over there in England, we'll be married in a few weeks and then begin some traveling for a while. I suppose the press should be told at that point."

Then, out of the blue, Roosevelt snapped his fingers, blurted "Oh!" and began digging around in his coat pocket. He pulled out a telegram message form and waved it in front of us. His right eyebrow rose up in excitement as those famed teeth burst into sight, the whole effect looking like a bespectacled pirate about to do something wicked.

"Oh, by *Jove,* I nearly forgot! You too, my friends, have some *good* news. *Very* good news. Please forgive my rude *tardiness,* but the swirl of yesterday's electoral events has fogged my mind until now. Here, Peter, take this. It was handed to me by my staff yesterday evening, amidst all the wailing and gnashing of teeth and finger-pointing. It would appear you both are *personae gratae* once again."

As I read the telegram quickly, my cheeks flushed, and I couldn't help matching Roosevelt's smile. Rork looked on, his face cautiously expectant.

When I recovered my wits, I asked, "Good Lord, what was it that you wrote him, Theodore?"

"Why, merely *common* sense, Peter, nothing more. I suppose *now* I'll have to send him a critique of *his* last book too—he just finished his personal history of the naval Civil War. And it will have to be a *complimentary* critique, of course." He paused to wink at me. "Authors can be *so* sensitive about such things, you know."

Rork took the message out of my hand and read it aloud to himself.

2 NOVEMBER 1886
FROM: DD PORTER/NAVAL HQS/NAVY
DEPT/WASHINGTON DC
TO: T.ROOSEVELT/FIFTH AVE HOTEL/
NEW YORK CITY
XX—GOT YOUR LAST & AGREE—X—
TELL THOSE TWO LOLLYGAGGING
SCOUNDREL FEATHER MERCHANTS
WAKE & RORK TO GET BACK HERE—
X—REPORT IN AT ONI—X—THEIR
UNDESERVED VACATION IS OVER—X—I
HAVE WORK FOR THEM—X—GOOD
LUCK ON MAYOR CONTEST—X—STILL
WAITING FOR YOUR OPINION OF MY
LAST BOOK—XX

"Well, I'll be . . . we're off the beach," he muttered. "An' back in me Uncle Sam's navy."

His good deed done, Roosevelt stood to go and grasped my hand in his usual death grip.

"It appears that *all* of us have had a quiet victory, my friends. I will soon be bathed in certain *love,* and now that you've enriched the federal government's intelligence on Cuba and Spain, they'll probably have you two immersed in some *adventure* somewhere inside of a week. Hmm . . . *action.* Actually, in some ways, I *envy* you."

It was a pure, unabashedly romanticized, Theodore Roosevelt sentiment. Walking through the empty campaign room, he lingered for a moment by the door. He waved a hand over the scenery of political defeat and said, "Let us not waste further time here, men, in this place of battle lost. No, sirs, you both must *hasten forward!* For I hear the stirring trumpets of *duty* and *honor* calling you yet again, my friends."

In the nine years since that morning, I've never learned what Roosevelt had written to Admiral Porter to elicit such a telegram. Porter has been dead four years now, and Theodore isn't talking. It is a secret kept between them.

Roosevelt is good at keeping secrets. So was Martí, who never did tell me the extent of his involvement in that original riddle message to Roosevelt. The two of them became regular correspondents of mine, symbiotically exchanging information and opinions, and using me as a conduit for years.

And what of my family? My son, Sean, continued his years of naval education at Annapolis, though my own career's acceleration reduced the opportunity to see him.

Useppa stayed in the Washington area for the next school year, but she missed Key West and her friends there terribly, eventually returning. The island city rebuilt after the fire and hurricane. People who had fled the disasters returned. The place has become an even more successful enterprise than before, with a new wave of newcomers—fishing tourists and yachtsmen.

The intrigues of revolutionaries and Spaniards continued for a while, but the horror of the Great Fire of '86 did much to concentrate the inhabitants on resurrection, rather than insurrection, over the next few years. By the mid-nineties, however, the revolutionists' efforts had been rekindled—as hot and heavy as ever.

It may be legitimately asked whether I have ever regretted my actions at Bedloe's Island on 28 October 1886. My answer is succinct: no. But I realize that appears a scornful reply, so allow me to further explain.

I have always tried to steer my life along the guidelines of honor. But age—and painful experience—has demanded that I see honor as a concept with many shades, some of which are darker, more difficult to justify to those who are fortunate enough to not know the baser behavior of men.

And thus, during my career around the world, when

confronted by that dead-hearted evil that resides in some mortals, I have done things that may be considered by various people outside the bounds of honorable conduct. That is their luxury, as members of a gently sophisticated society, in this ninth decade of the nineteenth century.

I, however, believe my actions were within the darker shades of that noble precept by which I attempt to live. The events at Bedloe's Island were, unquestionably, the very darkest shade of personal honor, but absolutely and irrevocably necessary.

Curiously, seven years after that wet October in New York, Martí, Roosevelt, and I were somewhat reunited in another little-known matter. Within the space of a few months in 1893, the Spanish tried to poison José to death in Ybor City, I was nearly shot to death in eastern Cuba, Theodore came exceedingly close to political demise in Washington, and America grew near to war with Spain.

But that is a story for another time. The events of 1886 have exhausted me, even all these years hence, so I will end this narrative now. Besides, the sun has descended into its pastel altitudes, casting shadows across the island. I hear the cry of the osprey and squawk of the herons as they wing homeward in the dimming light. And yes, there is Rork, clumping about on the windward side of the bungalow, settling into a rocker. Surely by now the reader knows what these signs mean.

I am expected on the verandah for drinks, where we will reflect on the day's accomplishments, and gratefully toast God for granting us another glorious sunset at Patricio Island.

Peter Wake
Commander, United States Navy
Special Assignments Section
Office of Naval Intelligence

Chapter Endnotes

Here is some background information, organized by chapter, to help the reader better understand the places, people, and events Peter Wake experiences in this novel.

Chapter One—Lobster *à la* Newberg

That storm broke records around the country, including Florida, where freezing conditions were seen in many places for the first time.

The crowd Wake met that night at Delmonico's formalized their association in May of 1887 into the Federal Club, an organization that exists to this day. Henry Cabot Lodge did indeed go to Congress and became one of the most powerful political influences in American history.

David Dixon Porter, son of a famous naval father, left the navy in 1891 after sixty-five years of naval service. He died shortly after retirement, at age 78. He wrote three novels and five nonfiction books.

Roosevelt's story of lobster Newberg was true. Like Charles Delmonico's cut of steak, it soon became an internationally known dish and synonymous with the Delmonico restaurants.

For more on how Peter Wake attained those politically discomforting medals, read *A Different Kind of Honor,* about his assignment to South America in 1879–1881; and *The Honored Dead,* about his mission to Indo-China in 1883.

In 1898, Bowman McCalla commanded a naval landing force at Guantanamo Bay, Cuba, where he established the naval base that remains to this day. He was later famous for his leading the landing force of U.S. sailors and Marines that joined other countries' military forces in rescuing the international community at Peking in 1900. During the operation he was wounded three times. He eventually made flag rank and was widely respected in the navy as a "real fighting admiral."

Roosevelt at this point was still grieving. He never mentioned his dead wife and mother in public again. Daughter Alice later became known as a precocious teen in the White House, the darling of her daddy's eye. When asked about her antics, President Roosevelt said, "I can either control Alice, or I can be president—I cannot do both."

Boxing was illegal in New York in the 1880s, so they put on

"exhibition matches" at Gilmore's Garden. John L. Sullivan was charged with "fighting without weapons" there in 1884. Owned by the Vanderbilt family, the place later became known as Madison Square Garden.

Chapter Two—A Plea from Babylon

Roosevelt did not live in New York City much at this point. The family townhouse at 422 Madison Avenue was run by his unmarried sister Bamie, who cared for baby Alice.

The 137th Psalm was not widely known by the Catholic and Protestant laity at that time, and many times the last three verses were omitted as being offensive or confusing. In Cuba, however, as in Italy, it was seen by many as a Biblical analogy to the suffering by people under foreign occupation. In the 1970s it was used in the musical *Godspell.*

Chapter Three—The Scribe

Martí lived and worked in Manhattan. He was not a well-known revolutionary yet, being thought of by the Cuban ex-patriot community as an intellectual, as opposed to an actual fighter. In the late 1880s and early 1890s, Martí did become famous as the most articulate of the revolutionaries, and one of his published poems—*Versos Sencillas* (*Simple Verses*)—was influenced by the 137th Psalm. *Versos Sencillas* was originally contained in a letter to a friend in Mexico that was published in 1891. He appreciated the United States, but was concerned about it dominating Cuba after independence. Martí eventually went to war, leading the Cuban patriots in the field, until his death in 1895.

Chapter Four—Politics on the Potomac

Whitney had no naval experience, but he was a reformer. He supported the modernization of the navy and is remembered as an effective secretary.

Commodore John Grimes Walker graduated first in the USNA class of 1858 and was already a legend by 1886. He commanded the Bureau of Navigation (the senior bureau of the nineteenth-century navy) from 1881 to 1889, under which ONI had existed since 1882. Walker, a widely respected naval officer, was a vigorous proponent and protector of ONI's early years. He died at age 72 in 1907, after serving his country for 57 years.

The South China Sea island Wake is referring to is Condore, part of Vietnam then and called Con Son now. For details, read *The Honored Dead.*

Chapter Five—The Refuge of Bachelors
Patricio Island still exists and is part of the Pine Island Sound National Wildlife Refuge. Useppa Island is now an exclusive private community.

For details of Wake's wartime service in the islands around Patricio, read *At the Edge of Honor, Point of Honor,* and *Honorable Mention.*

Rork's wounding at the imperial city of Hue is recounted in detail in *The Honored Dead.* The amputation was due to a post-wound infection, and the subsequent "appliance" was manufactured for him by the French Navy in Vietnam.

For more on Wake's encounter with de Lesseps in Panama, read *A Different Kind of Honor.*

You can find Lt. Kimball's 1885 report about Panama at the national archives in Record Group 38.4.

Chapter Six—Key West
In researching this book I found references to Bautista and Artell in Key West, but none about Leon. Did Wake give the man an alias? If so, who was he really? We'll never know.

The wedding, an emotional event so important in Wake's life, is described in detail in *Point of Honor.* The African cemetery where it took place has recently been located on the island's south beach, near the West Martello Tower at Higgs Beach.

Chapter Seven—A Methodist Friend
Lefavre is an alias. Wake used them in his narratives to conceal the names of his operatives and his enemies. A Pastor Deuflofleu is documented in history as the leader of the Methodist minority in Havana, with many contacts in Key West, but it is doubted he was the same person Wake met.

Wake, a Methodist, had a long and successful relationship with the Jesuits, as described in *An Affair of Honor, A Different Kind of Honor,* and *The Honored Dead.*

Chapter Eight—Midnight, with the Light of Day
Marrón is another example of Wake using a false name for intelligence purposes. Historical information shows that the head of counter-revolutionary intelligence operations in Havana and Key West was actually a Colonel Martinez, with the deceptively benign title of Commander of the Office of Public Affairs.

The dungeon of the Audencia, next to the prison, was a place of terror in colonial Havana for centuries. It no longer exists.

Unfortunately for Wake, the bishop of Havana at the time, Ramón Fernández Piérola, was not a Jesuit. He served in Havana until 1887, when he became the bishop at Avila, Spain.

Chapter Nine—Robin Hood
Gallo Sosa was the most well-known and feared bandit in the Havana district. He occasionally worked with the revolutionaries, when it suited his ends.

The unusual celestial alignment to which Wake refers, actually happened in the skies over Havana that evening in 1886.

Chapter Ten—The Hurricane Man
Father Benito Viñes, director of the Royal College of Belém since 1870, became famous in the scientific world as the "Father of Hurricane Meteorology." His accurate predictions of hurricane landfalls saved many lives in that storm-ravaged part of the world. Forty-nine years old when he met Wake, Father Viñes continued in his hurricane work for another seven years, until he died on 23 July 1893.

The Jesuits first met Wake in 1874, where they saved his life in Spain and his career in Italy, all of which is described in *An Affair of Honor*. He put his career and life on the line to help them at Peru in 1880 in *A Different Kind of Honor*, and they assisted each other in Cambodia and Vietnam in 1883 in *The Honored Dead*.

The Jesuits endured a difficult period in the mid-nineteenth century. They had been evicted from Spain, France, Germany, and even Rome in 1873, when Father General Beckx shifted their headquarters to Florence, where it remained until 1895. However, Pope Leo XIII, a reformer elected to the papacy in 1878, continued his friendship with the order during that turbulent time.

Chapter Eleven—That Impertinent Fool
Powhatan, in the navy for 30 years, had a very bad reputation as a ship constantly in need of repair. She was decommissioned and sold in June 1886.

Gustavius Gaston was not the captain's name. Wake had an ongoing feud with the man for the rest of his career and sensibly used a fictitious moniker in this story. I have continued that decision.

Chapter Twelve—The Tangled Web
The navy's earliest codes were laughably simple, when viewed with our

twenty-first-century hindsight. However, at the time they were better than the plain language communications used until 1885. The Navy Secret Code, Commodore Walker's brainchild, changed all of that in 1888. Wake's reference to the man named Hawke is borne out in historical documents, but his speculation as to the man's motives has no proof in the records.

The Trans-Oceanic Cable Company's telegraph cable went from Havana to Key West, from there up through the Gulf of Mexico to Punta Rassa (via Sanibel Island), and hence up the peninsula to the rest of the United States. At each point along the way, a station operator could read the message traffic.

Boreau is an alias Wake assigned to that Spanish agent. The records show that a lieutenant worked for Colonel Martinez in Havana and may have been in Key West.

Instituto San Carlos was originally on Anne Street, but moved to the Fleming Street location in 1884. Destroyed by the fire of 1886, it moved to its current impressive location on Duval Street in 1890, where, on 3 January 1892, it was the venue for José Martí's famous announcement of the unification of all the revolutionary fronts in the fight against the Spanish.

Chapter Fourteen—Orders

The Posse Comitatus Act of 1878 originally referred only to the U.S. Army. The Navy and Marine Corps were added under the color of that law by Department of Defense regulation in the early 1950s. The Air Force was added in 1956. The Department of the Treasury's Revenue Service evolved into the Coast Guard in the twentieth century. The Coast Guard is normally not included in the Posse Comitatus prohibition, unless it has been transferred to the Navy in time of war. Those Coast Guard units would then lose their law enforcement status. Posse Comitatus is Latin, meaning "Power of the Country," as in *to raise the local forces of a community*.

Chapter Sixteen—No Name Key

Alex Malinovsky is an alias, which I presume Wake got from the name of a prominent early nineteenth-century historian. The eastern end of Watson Boulevard on No Name Key is the general area of the Russian's plantation, of which nothing remains. However, there is a great watering hole on the island—the No Name Pub. Visit www.nonamepub.com to learn about its colorful history. They have great pizza and cheeseburgers.

Chapter Seventeen—Revelations in the Dark

Pye's Harbor Key is now called simply Pye's Key. Loggerhead is now called Key Lois. For centuries it was a well-known sea turtle nesting place. In the 1990s it held a commercially operated breeding colony of Rhesus monkeys.

Traveling to the southern end of modern-day Spanish Main Drive on Cudjoe Key, you can see Gopher Key to the south, and Sugarloaf off to the west.

You can visit the area where Wake and Rork came ashore on Sugarloaf, but it won't be easy. Drive south down State Road 939B from Mile Marker 20 on US 1, across from Mangrove Mama's (www.mangrovemamasrestaurant.com), which has excellent conch fritters. 939B is a rough road, more of a path, but about a mile in you'll see the mangrove jungle described in Wake's account and understand why it was a perfect place for smugglers.

Chapter Eighteen—A Long-lost Friend

Waddell's Plantation at Cape Sable consisted of tens of thousands of coconut palms, which were harvested for the copra oil, squeezed from the meat of the nut. The plantation went out of business in the early twentieth century, but the palm groves stood until the great hurricane of 1935, when the area was obliterated. Old time sailor and fisherman Charlie Green told me thirty years ago that he remembered the original plantation site. It was thought to be haunted when he was young in the 1920s, due to the many sinister things that happened there over the years. It is still an eerie and beautiful place.

Bain is an alias, as is usual with Wake's informants.

The area of old Fort Brooke now has skyscrapers and convention centers on it. But the streets in the modern city just north of there are the same that Wake walked in 1886.

Chapter Nineteen—Little Havana

Ybor City became a very prosperous center of Latin culture and business from 1886 until the middle of the twentieth century. It fell on hard times in the 1960s but has seen a renaissance since the 1990s. Museums, restaurants, clubs, and stores now abound, making it a great place to spend your money and time.

Don Vicente Martínez Ybor (1818–1896) was one of the premier

Hispanic businessmen of America. His company town sold homes to his workers at cost, encouraged free enterprise and education, and provided a model for other manufacturers of how to attract and retain valued employees. He is remembered fondly in Tampa and Key West. Manrara was his partner for many years.

Chapter Twenty-One—The Bluff

To this day, U.S. Customs agents, the professional descendants of nineteenth-century treasury agents, have the widest authority and jurisdiction of any law enforcement officers in the country. However, technically, Wake would not have outranked Captain Fengar, a man who the records show was quite effective.

Florida records show that the Sarasota Assassination Society was a very deadly, feared group. By the late 1880s their terror had dwindled, broken by the courageous prosecutions of 1885.

Chapter Twenty-Three—The Ambush

Horse Shoe Shoal is now called Jug Creek Shoal. The swash channel is now even shallower.

Chapter Twenty-Four—Tree Shaking Time

The name Dort was possibly another example of Wake using a cover moniker. Records show a treasury agent was in Key West during this period, investigating Harris after numerous Spanish government complaints about Harris' bias had reached Washington. There was never a prosecution of Harris.

Newspaper accounts support Wake's description of Gould's visit to Key West and the naval boat race in the harbor. And yes, Roosevelt despised Gould—a sentiment that was mutual.

Joaquin Torroja was the Spanish consul in Key West from 1884 to 1889, and a prodigious reporter of events there.

Chapter Twenty-Nine—Tears through the Ash

The Great Fire of April 1, 1886, destroyed quite a lot of Key West, and is the most catastrophic event in the island's long history.

To this day, there are many rumors concerning the cause of the fire, most centering around Spanish agents deliberately setting it to thwart the revolutionaries' efforts. However, there are also theories that back up Wake's assertion that the fire was an accidental result of the raid by Spanish agents on a Cuban committee meeting. Interestingly, the 3 April 1886 issue of the *Tobacco Leaf*, a cigar worker newspaper, states that a rumor was going about that a naval officer observed a man starting a conflagration on that night and had fired two shots at him, but he got away. No name for the naval officer was given. The Jacksonville *Times-Union* reported on April 5, 1886, that a body was found in a cistern, but it was not confirmed by authorities.

In a 3 April 1886 report to his superiors, Spanish Consul Torroja blamed Cuban revolutionaries for the fire. He said that while they were playing cards late that night at the café, an argument ensued and one of them shot a pistol, then knocked over an oil lamp while trying to flee, which started the fire.

After the fire, tensions between Spaniards and Cubans in Key West rose drastically. Consul Torroja blamed Reverend Juan Bautista, of St. John's Episcopal Church, for spreading rumors that Spanish agents had started the fire. He reported that other Cubans had called for the consul to be "dragged down the main street."

In this fire, Vicente Martínez Ybor lost his main cigar factory, which resulted in his speeding completion of his new Ybor operations. He moved to his newly built home in Ybor City, *La Quinta*, at 12th Avenue and 17th Street, after the fire in Key West. His huge Ybor City cigar factory, which still stands at 9th Avenue and Avenida Republica de Cuba, was stoutly built of fire-resistant brick because of what he went through in Key West.

Sadly, the famous Russell House Hotel burned down in the fire.

There is no record or factual support of a *Grito de Hatuey*.

Most of the places in Wake's account were destroyed in the fire, the locations since rebuilt into something else. Curry's Saloon is a condo. Russell House's location is a trinket shop and the parking lot for the Hog's Breath Saloon. Schuerer's Grocery & Bakery is now a scooter rental, across from the famous Green Parrot Bar. The county courthouse was rebuilt in 1890 and still stands at the original spot. The old federal courthouse's location is now the post office—the U.S. courthouse moved to Simonton Street. Pinder's Grocery & Provisions is now the parking area for the legendary Schooner Wharf, which occupies land filled in decades after Wake's visit. Built in 1852, Building One at the Naval Depot is still standing by Clinton Square, across from Mel Fisher's museum. Wake would've known Building One well, from his earliest days during the Civil War.

The San Carlos Institute's location in 1884–1886 is the subject of some debate among historians, but most agree it was on Fleming Street near Duval Street, on or near the southwest corner. The current alley paralleling Duval Street behind Margaritaville, that runs south off Fleming Street, across from La Concha Hotel, corresponds to the alley the Cuban Key Westers called San Carlos Street in the 1880s. After the fire destroyed the San Carlos Institute, it was rebuilt in its present magnificent form on Duval Street, close to Margaritaville. In fact, the location of the Cuban café, where the 1886 fire is thought to have originated, appears to be in the area of Margaritaville, but it is impossible to be certain.

Chapter Thirty-One—The Electric Man

Built to prevent shipwrecks, Sanibel Island's lighthouse was completed in August of 1884. Ironically, during the construction, part of the equipment for the light itself was involved in a shipwreck on those very shoals. The equipment was salvaged and installed. Richardson and Johnson were the first lightkeepers assigned there.

The Fort Myers Press seems to corroborate Wake's account, reporting 3 April 1886, that on the night of March 31, the Edison boating party took refuge at Punta Rassa during the worst of a storm. The next day they headed north to the Peace River to pick up Mina's parents.

Edison did indeed have a considerable disagreement with Gilliland over the next few years, resulting in the Edisons' not visiting Seminole Lodge from the late 1880s until the late 1890s. After that point, however, they were beloved annual residents of Fort Myers until Edison's death in 1931 and Mina's death in 1947. Their fascinating home is open to the public.

Edison's interest in naval technology grew over the next thirty years. In 1915, he became the chairman of the Naval Consulting Board, a group of the top scientists in the U.S. committed to developing new weapons and systems for the navy. One of their successes was dazzle camouflage for warships.

Chapter Thirty-Three—Reporting In

Fort Myers was frequently referred to as Myers during this period, but Wake always called it by its original military name. Several of the homes built from the original fort's lumber still exist downtown.

Harrsenville was just a few fisherman's huts until the turn of the century. In 1927, Lee County Commissioner Harry Stringfellow (a Pine

Islander) got a road built out to Pine Island from the mainland. The road was built across several islands (Porpoise Point, Matlacha, West, and Little Pine) in Matlacha Pass. In the 1930s, a commercial fishing village of squatters' shacks, which subsequently became known as Matlacha (pronounced matt-la-SHAY), sprang up along Pine Island Road. It is a quirky Old Florida place to this day. I have lived there for several years.

I can find no record of land owned by Harris near Burnt Store.

Chapter Thirty-Five—*Venganza*

Wake's 1882 Spencer shotgun was indeed an efficient weapon, designed for rapid ejection and reloading through a port at the top of the receiver. It was the first practical pump shotgun.

The Merwin-Hulbert pistol had hard rubber grips over an extended frame butt, which was shaped into an eagle-like beak for pistol whipping and crushing in an opponent's skull—hence the brutal name.

Chapter Thirty-Seven—Executive Decision

Theodore Roosevelt's mention of boat pirates in the telegram to Wake referred to his hundred-mile, two-week-long chase in a blizzard after three armed thieves who had stolen his boat on the Little Missouri River in Dakota Territory. Roosevelt, a deputy sheriff, eventually got the desperadoes, who were led by the notorious "Redhead" Finnegan, and escorted them another sixty miles to the nearest town, Dickinson. Afterward, he famously understated, "There is very little amusement in combining the functions of a sheriff with those of an Arctic explorer."

Chapter Thirty-Eight—Uncertainty

The *Key West Democrat* reported that Captain Fengar and the *Dix* captured the Cuban sloops *Paco* and *Isabel* at Charlotte Harbor on 6 June 1886, and charged the captains and crews with violating federal customs laws.

On 24 January 1902, the *Punta Gorda Herald* reported that the Padillas were convicted by federal court in Tampa for their 1901 arrest on smuggling rum, cigars, and tobacco from Cuba. The sentence was three months in the Lee County Jail at Fort Myers. On 12 June 1902, the U.S. Revenue Cutter *McLane* took ten armed soldiers from the Key West barracks, under the command of 2nd Lt. William Peck, to Lacosta Island to search for smugglers on the island. They found nothing. Padilla's family had departed the island four days earlier for Belle Aire, farther up the coast. The Padillas later returned to Lacosta, and their descendents still live in these islands. They are considered valued citizens and friends.

Roosevelt did, indeed, speak at Medora, Dakota, on 4 July 1886. The editor in question was Arthur Packard. This story has been retold in several biographies of Roosevelt.

The hurricane to which Wake refers was a massive storm that hit Key West on 18 August 1886, with Category 4 winds. Two days later it smashed into Texas as a Category 5.

For details of Wake's friendship with French naval officer Louis Viaud, alias Pierre Loti, read *The Honored Dead.*

Chapter Forty—Lady Liberty

The Pinkerton National Detective Agency was started in the 1850s by Allan Pinkerton. By 1861, Pinkerton was a well-known and successful detective who guarded Lincoln en route to his inauguration, foiling an assassination attempt. During the Civil War, his detectives gathered intelligence for the Union army. After the war, Pinkerton's agency did protection work and investigated crimes and labor conflicts. As Wake relates, the Pinkerton company did indeed work under contract for the Spanish government, regarding the revolution in Cuba. Eighteen novels and nonfiction books are attributed to Pinkerton, who died in 1884 of accidental causes. As a sign of his success, for many years "Pinkerton" was a commonly used slang term for detective. Pinkerton is still widely respected in the security profession, and is now a subsidiary of Securitas, Inc.

Acknowledgments

When I started this project in 2006, I had no idea just how immersed I would become in the sordid world of revolutionary intrigue in 1886 Havana, Key West, and Tampa. The more I discovered, the more questions were raised in my mind. It was a fascinating journey, and along the way I was blessed to receive wonderful input from some outstanding authors, together with information from my rather diverse worldwide crew of source experts. Here are the more important sources.

I was pointed in fruitful directions by acquaintances at the Office of Naval Intelligence (ONI) and assisted by the Naval Historical Center. Cornell University Library's *Making of America* section (both book and media collections) was of great help with period accounts. Peter Karsten's first-rate *The Naval Aristocracy,* Donald Canney's *The Old Steam Navy,* and CDR John Alden's *The American Steel Navy* were once again my guide for understanding the Washington naval culture of the 1880s. The Library of Congress's map collection staff was pleasantly efficient with my quest for the detailed 1884 Key West map.

In the Florida Keys, Mike and Renee Maurer allowed me the use of their wonderful home during my research trips. Key West's extraordinary historian and archivist, Tom Hambright, of the Monroe County Library, was a trove of nuance and lore regarding the personalities and politics of that island during the scheming of the 1880s. In addition, he allowed me to peruse records from *The New York Times,* the *Florida Times-Union, The Tobacco Leaf,* and other material from deep within the Key West Library's vault. The *Island Gazetteer* database, compiled by Jim Clupper of the Monroe County Public Library at Islamorada, was another big help in historical geographic information.

Among the many books providing information for this project was David McCullough's *Pathway Between the Seas,* still the defining tome of the Panama Canal, one of my favorite places in the world. Jeffery Dorwart's excellent history, *The Office of Naval Intelligence: The Birth of America's First Intelligence Agency, 1865–1918,* yielded considerable insight into the early years at ONI. Edmund Morris's *The Rise of Theodore Roosevelt* is the seminal volume on that most remarkable of our presidents. Louis A. Pérez's *Cuba Between Empires 1878–1902* gave me awareness of the turbulent situation in Cuba in the mid-1880s.

For the Cuba–Key West connection, I turned to Consuelo Stebbin's great new book, *City of Intrigue, Nest of Revolution*, Ada Ferrer's *Insurgent Cuba*, Dr. Loy Glenn Westfall's *Key West: Cigar City, USA*, Jefferson B. Browne's 1912 book *Key West, The Old and The New*, Walter C. Maloney's 1876 book *A Sketch of the History of Key West*, and John Viele's *The Florida Keys: A History of the Pioneers*. Chaz Mena, the well-known New York actor, is a student and portrayer of José Martí, and shared with me many subtle shades of the man's character. Geographical-cultural assistance about Havana came from George Alcober, Kiko Villalon, Jesus Barreiro, Juan Ramon de la Paz, and Miguel Rodriguez. Roberto Giraudy and Ela Ugarte, foremost Cuban historians, were my wonderful hosts in Havana, and made my research there so much more productive.

Information about Tampa and Ybor City came from Frank Lastra's matchless book *Ybor City: The Making of a Landmark Town*, Dr. Loy Glenn Westfall's doctoral dissertation *Don Vicente Martinez Ybor: The Man and his Empire*, Canter Brown's *Tampa in Civil War and Reconstruction*, and Jose Muniz's *The Ybor City Story 1885–1954*. Eminent Ybor historian E. J. Salcines and the Ybor City State Museum's Nancy Garrson assisted with background.

In southwest Florida, Randy Briggs' great team of biblio-sleuths at the Pine Island Library found rare books that I needed, while the historical reference staff at the main Lee County Library facilitated my searching the 1886 records of the *Fort Myers Press* and *The New York Times*.

There are several books on southwest Florida's history that proved vital to me. *The Edisons of Fort Myers*, recently published by Tom Smoot, is an excellent description of not only the great inventor, but the area as well. Canter Brown's *Florida's Peace River Frontier* is a masterwork of regional history, as is Lindsey Williams and U. S. Cleveland's *Our Fascinating Past*. Betsy Anholt's *Sanibel's Story*, Dana Gibson's *Boca Grande*, Elaine Jordan's *Pine Island, the Forgotten Island* and *Tales of Pine Island*, and Mary Kaye Stevens' *Images of America: Pine Island* imparted facts and flavor as well. Janet Snyder Matthews' *Edge of Wilderness* supplied background on that infamous scourge, the Sarasota Assassination Society.

Religious understanding came from Catholic Father Cas Obie, Episcopal Vicar Ann McLemore, and Methodist pastors Jim Reeher and Edward Kellum. Well-known to my readers by now is Nancy Glickman, the lovely amateur astronomer who researched the celestial events of 1886 portrayed in this book, and did some very good critical reading as well.

My "eyeball recon" in Havana was productive and pleasant because of dear friends there. I urge everyone to try to get to Havana—a vibrant city well worth the effort.

The scribes of the Parrot Hillian Writers' Circle are still my sounding boards—Kaydian Wherle and Roothee Gabay have been aboard this literary voyage since we weighed anchor. And old pal Randy Wayne White, famous novelist, islander, and waterman, has always supplied me with good professional advice and excellent rum.

But most of all, it's been my intrepid band of readers around the world who have given me the strength and élan to keep fighting the good fight, no matter what.

Thank you all so much.

Onward and upward!
Bob Macomber
Serenity Bungalow
Matlacha Island
Florida

A final word
from the author

Even more than my others, this novel captivated me. Of course, 1886 was an amazing year, the nexus of so many political, natural, and cultural forces in Florida and Cuba. But there was more than that enticement for me in this project. On this one, my personal connection was always hovering in the background. You see, like a beautiful but dangerous woman, Cuba has entranced and scared me all my life.

My bond is long and heartfelt. Conceived in Cuba, I was born in the United States on the anniversary of the Cuban Declaration of Independence (*El Grito de Yara*); a century, to the year, after José Martí's birth. Growing up in America with Cuban "aunts" and "uncles," I became immersed in their stories, and our own as well.

There are lots of smiles that go with my Cuban memories over the years—the wonderful food, the smooth tropical drinks, the seductive music, the vibrant art, the dry humor, the brilliant intellects, the compassion for human frailties. It is impossible to resist that island transforming your soul, even far away from her languid shores.

Cuba . . .

Tears and joy.

May she know liberty, justice, and peace for her people—*por fin, y para siempre, una Cuba libre.*

> *Robert N. Macomber*
> Serenity Bungalow
> Matlacha Island
> Florida

Other Books in the Honor Series

At the Edge of Honor by Robert N. Macomber. This nationally acclaimed naval Civil War novel, the first in the Honor series of naval fiction, takes the reader into the steamy world of Key West and the Caribbean in 1863 and introduces Peter Wake, the reluctant New England volunteer officer who finds himself battling the enemy on the coasts of Florida, sinister intrigue in Spanish Havana and the British Bahamas, and social taboos in Key West when he falls in love with the daughter of a Confederate zealot. (hb, pb)

Point of Honor by Robert N. Macomber. Winner of the Florida Historical Society's 2003 Patrick Smith Award for Best Florida Fiction. In this second book in the Honor series, it is 1864 and Lt. Peter Wake, United States Navy, assisted by his indomitable Irish bosun, Sean Rork, commands the naval schooner *St. James.* He searches for army deserters in the Dry Tortugas, finds an old nemesis during a standoff with the French Navy on the coast of Mexico, starts a drunken tavern riot in Key West, and confronts incompetent Federal army officers during an invasion of upper Florida. (hb, pb)

Honorable Mention by Robert N. Macomber. This third book in the Honor series of naval fiction covers the tumultuous end of the Civil War in Florida and the Caribbean. Lt. Peter Wake is now in command of the steamer USS *Hunt,* and quickly plunges into action, chasing a strange vessel during a tropical storm off Cuba, confronting death to liberate an escaping slave ship, and coming face to face with the enemy's most powerful ocean warship in Havana's harbor. Finally, when he tracks down a colony of former Confederates in Puerto Rico, Wake becomes involved in a deadly twist of irony. (hb)

A Dishonorable Few by Robert N. Macomber. Fourth in the Honor series of naval fiction. It is 1869 and the United States is painfully recovering from the Civil War. Lt. Peter Wake heads to turbulent Central America to deal with a former American naval officer turned renegade mercenary. As the action unfolds in Colombia and Panama, Wake realizes that his most dangerous adversary may be a man on his own ship, forcing Wake to make a decision that will lead to his court-martial in Washington when the mission has finally ended. (hb)

An Affair of Honor by Robert N. Macomber. The fifth novel in the Honor series. It's December 1873 and Lt. Peter Wake is the executive officer of the USS *Omaha* on patrol in the West Indies, eager to return home. Fate, however, has other plans. He runs afoul of the Royal Navy in Antigua and then is sent off to Europe, where he finds himself embroiled in a Spanish civil war. But his real test comes when he and Sean Rork are sent on a mission in northern Africa. (hb)

A Different Kind of Honor by Robert N. Macomber. In this sixth novel in the Honor series, it's 1879 and Lt. Cmdr. Peter Wake, U.S.N., is on assignment as the American naval observer to the War of the Pacific along the west coast of South America. During this mission Wake will witness history's first battle between ocean-going ironclads, ride the world's first deep-diving submarine, face his first machine guns in combat, and run for his life in the Catacombs of the Dead in Lima. (hb)

The Honored Dead by Robert N. Macomber. Seventh in the award-winning Honor series. On what at first appears to be a simple mission for the U.S. president in French Indochina in 1883, naval intelligence officer Lt. Cmdr. Peter Wake encounters opium warlords, Chinese-Malay pirates, and French gangsters. (hb)

Other Fiction from Pineapple Press:

Seven Mile Bridge by Michael Biehl. Florida Keys dive-shop owner Jonathan Bruckner returns home to Wisconsin after his mother's death. What he finds leads him to an understanding of the mystery that surrounded his father's death years before. (hb)

A Land Remembered by Patrick D. Smith. This well-loved, best-selling novel tells the story of three generations of MacIveys, a Florida family battling the hardships of the frontier, and how they rise from a dirt-poor Cracker life to the wealth and standing of real estate tycoons. (hb, pb)

Alligator Gold by Janet Post. On his way home at the end of the Civil War, Caleb Hawkins is focused on getting back to his Florida cattle ranch. But along the way, Hawk encounters a very pregnant Madelaine Wilkes and learns that his only son has gone missing and that his old nemesis, Snake Barber, has taken over his ranch. (hb, pb)

Confederate Money by Paul Varnes. Two young men from Florida set out on an adventure during the Civil War to exchange $25,000 in Confederate dollars for silver that will hold its value if the Union wins. They get mixed up in some of the war's bloodiest battles, including Olustee. Along the way, they meet historical characters like Generals Grant and Lee, tangle with criminals, become heroes, and fall in love. (hb)

Black Creek: The Taking of Florida by Paul Varnes. This novel is set in the midst of the historical upheaval caused by the Seminole Wars. White settlers Isaac and his son, Isaac Jr., serve as scouts in the Second Seminole War. Isaac Jr. is torn between his loyalty to his family and white neighbors, on the one hand, and his unique understanding and appreciation of the Indian way of life, on the other. (hb)

Nobody's Hero by Frank Laumer. In December of 1835, eight officers and one hundred men of the U.S. Army under the command of Brevet Major Francis Langhorne Dade set out from Fort Brooke at Tampa Bay, Florida, to march north a hundred miles to reinforce Fort King (present-day Ocala). Halfway to their destination, they were attacked by Seminole Indians. Only three wounded soldiers survived what came to be known as Dade's Massacre. This is the story of one of the them, Pvt. Ransom Clark. (hb)

For God, Gold and Glory: De Soto's Journey to the Heart of La Florida by E.H. Haines. Between 1539 and 1543 Hernando de Soto led an army of six hundred armored men on a desperate journey of almost four thousand miles through the wilds of *La Florida*, facing the problem of hostile natives, inadequate supplies, and the harsh elements, as they left a path of destruction in their search for gold and glory in the name of God. Told from the point of view of de Soto's private secretary, this is a riveting account of the tragic expedition. (hb)

For a complete catalog, visit our website at www.pineapplepress.com. Or write to Pineapple Press, P.O. Box 3889, Sarasota, Florida 34230-3889, or call (800) 746-3275.